2/2014

y

DISARM

DISARM

THE COMPLETE NOVEL

JUNE GRAY

BERKLEY BOOKS, NEW YORK

THE BERKLEY PUBLISHING GROUP
Published by the Penguin Group
Penguin Group (USA) LLC
375 Hudson Street, New York, New York 10014

USA • Canada • UK • Ireland • Australia • New Zealand • India • South Africa • China

penguin.com

A Penguin Random House Company

Library of Congress Cataloging-in-Publication Data

Gray, June, 1979–
Disarm: the complete novel / June Gray.—Berkley trade paperback edition.
pages cm
ISBN 978-0-425-27212-1 (alk. paper)
1. Secrets—Fiction.   2. Love stories.   3. Erotic fiction.   I. Title.
PS3607.R39515D57 2013
813'.6—dc23   2013023863

PUBLISHING HISTORY
Berkley trade paperback edition / February 2014

PRINTED IN THE UNITED STATES OF AMERICA

10   9   8   7   6   5   4   3   2   1

Cover photo of couple by Claudio Marinesco; planes by Thinkstock.
Cover design by Lesley Worrell.
Interior text design by Tiffany Estreicher.

To the men and women married to the military:
You are the strongest, kindest, most courageous people I've ever had
the pleasure of knowing and I am proud to be in your company.
Military life is tough, but we are tougher.

ACKNOWLEDGMENTS

Military life is not easy. When marrying a service member, you never really know what you're signing up for: deployments, PCSs, TDYs, and every other acronym under the sun. You are often separated from your loved ones and you have to learn how to deal, how to become both the mother and father of your family. This story is personal for me because it draws from my own experience of being a military wife, and I am both afraid and excited to share it with the world.

I must first thank my husband, who swept me off my feet in Oklahoma over ten years ago. Thank you for answering my endless questions about the military, and of course, for your sweet spreadsheeting skills. I love you and this little family we've created together.

Salamat to my amazing family, who supported me every step of the way.

To my beta readers: Beth, Lara, Alicia, Kerry, and Shannon. Thank you for your time and your willingness to help. I cannot express how much your friendship means to me.

To my original editor MJ Heiser at Clean Leaf Editing: Thank you for whipping my writing into shape and helping me create a manuscript worth publishing.

Thank you to Kim Whalen for giving me the opportunity to stretch out and reach for things I'd never dared to before, and to Cindy Hwang for believing in this story of mine.

Thanks to Todd, Rina, and the team at the Cherry Bean Cafe. You guys always made me feel welcome, even if sometimes I overstayed.

A big shout-out to Mimi Strong for convincing me to finally put on my big-girl panties and write something steamy.

Finally, to the readers: thank you for giving Henry and Elsie a chance.

Visit my blog at authorjunegray.blogspot.com for more information on upcoming projects, news, and short stories.

PART ONE

DISARM

1

ASSESSING THE SITUATION

It wasn't my fault—at least, not entirely. Henry Logan, my room-mate and a captain in the Air Force, was technically to blame. The guy had been acting so unusually moody for the past five weeks that I was getting desperate to see a smile on his face. So that Saturday night, I suggested we head to our favorite bar at Bricktown and just drink the night away, confident that Henry, even in his grumpy-bear state, could never turn down beer.

After parking his convertible Mustang, we walked down the street to Tapwerks in silence. I waited for him to open up, to tell me what had been bothering him, but no dice.

"What is with you lately?" I asked.

Henry stuck his hands in his jacket pockets and shrugged. "Nothing, why?"

I raised an eyebrow at him. He could successfully pull off the nonchalant attitude on anyone but me. I'd known him for thirteen years and had lived with him for two. I could decipher his every expression, sometimes to the point of reading his mind. "Come on. Are you on your period or something?" I asked with a teasing jab of the elbow. "Do you need to borrow a tampon?"

That finally got a small laugh out of him. "Elsie, you are such a brat," he said. He reached over to ruffle my curly brown hair, but I anticipated the move and did a little ninja-ballerina maneuver to avoid him.

"Hey," I said, "leave the hair alone." I slipped my arm through his as we stood in line outside the bar—Tapwerks was *the* place to be on weekends—and tried to pilfer some of his warmth. He was six-two and built like a brick wall; he had plenty of everything to spare.

As I craned my head to study the people in line, dressed up in their casual best, I suddenly caught a glimpse of Henry, his face partially lit by the soft glow from the bar's windows. It struck me then that he was really no longer that awkward kid I grew up with but a *man*, and a gorgeous one at that. I'd always known he was good-looking—hell I'd had a crush on him since my brother started hanging out with him in their sophomore year of high school—but the way the shadows played on his face rendered planes I never knew existed. His short dark hair and the scruff on his strong jaw lent a nice contrast to his olive skin, and he had a proud nose with a little cleft at the end that matched the cleft on his chin. But it was his eyes that drew my gaze, those icy blues that seemed as if they could see into my every thought.

I stared at him for a long moment, feeling a strange tickle in my chest, when I came to the realization that he was staring back.

"You okay, Elsie?" he asked in that husky, gravelly voice of his. Had he always sounded so sexy?

I gave him my best sunny smile, shaking off the confusing feelings that had snuck up on me. "Just wondering why you don't have a girlfriend."

His lips quirked up a little and I felt an elbow nudge me in the side, but he didn't bother answering the question.

———

Inside, the two floors were at full capacity and there were no available tables or chairs, so we stood at the bar, trying our hardest to get the bartender's attention. I was only five-six, so Henry theoretically had a better chance at visibility, but somehow, the male bartender's eyes just kept flitting right over him as if he were invisible.

"Let me try." I stepped up on the brass rail that ran along the bottom of the bar and squeezed my arms together, causing instant cleavage over the low neck of my loose top.

The bartender noticed. He finished up his orders and came right to me with an appreciative smile. "What'll it be?"

"Woodchuck Cider, Sam Adams, and two tequila shots," I said, and straightened up.

Henry was doing the big-brother scowl when I joined him back down on the floor.

"What?" I asked, preparing for the lecture. "When you've got 'em, use 'em."

He glowered down at me with a disapproving purse to his lips but said nothing. God, was nothing going to get him to talk?

After downing our shots, Henry and I stood around with cold bottles in our hands. He continued to scowl at me and I pretended not to notice by looking elsewhere. Thankfully, I saw a few of his Air Force buddies across the room and they waved us over to their table. Henry grabbed my hand as he led the way through the sea of bodies, his large frame parting the crowds so that I wouldn't get swallowed up.

"Hey!" Sam, another captain, raised his beer bottle in greeting.

I clinked his bottle with my cider. Henry gave a cool little jerk of the head and said, "Hey, man." The two men exchanged a silent look before Henry gave the slightest shake of the head.

Sam's girlfriend, Beth, gave me a hug before I could figure out what the guys were communicating. "How are you?" she asked. "Haven't seen you in a while."

"I've been good. Busy," I said, keeping an eye on Henry. "You?"

Beth started to say something, but the band began to play and cut her off. For a while, we all stood there and bobbed our heads to the rhythm of the rock group, all except for the stiff corpse beside me. Sometimes Henry knew how to really kill a good time, but as his friend, it was my duty to pull him out of this funk he was in.

I stood on my tiptoes and pulled him down so I could yell in his ear. "You wanna dance?"

He looked at me, then at the near-empty dance floor, then back at me again. "Hell no."

I pretended not to hear. I grasped his hand with a cheeky smile and pulled him through the crowd and onto the dance floor.

"I said no," he said and turned to leave.

But I still had ahold of his hand, so I jumped in front of him and danced to block his way. I pulled his arm around my waist and gave him my most seductive smile as I began to sway my hips to the music.

He rolled his eyes but I kept on dancing, sure that sooner or later he would relent. He knew how to have a good time; he just had to be pulled out of that scowly shell of his.

The crowd on the dance floor swelled and I was unexpectedly pinned to Henry, my hips grinding into his before my brain could tell it to stop.

The effect was instantaneous and twofold. Henry's expression changed at the same moment I felt something stir in his jeans. My face went up in flames, but when I tried to pull away, his arms tightened around me and pulled me closer.

"Where are you going?" he asked in my ear, his warm breath tickling my neck. "I thought you wanted to dance?"

My heart was pounding a million miles a minute through my chest, but I had teased the beast out of hiding and I now had to face him. I looked up at him, acting as if having an erection against my stomach was not a big deal, and tried to take advantage of our close proximity. "Why won't you talk to me?"

"I don't want to talk tonight," he replied, his eyes focused solely on my mouth. The breath hitched in my throat when he ran his tongue along his lower lip. "I'd rather do other things."

That was about the time I lost my cool. This was Henry, my closest friend, my roommate, my surrogate big brother. He was a great many things to me, but he was definitely not someone I made out with. I'd stopped hoping for that a long time ago, when he'd made it clear that he saw me as nothing more than a little sister.

Now here he was, bowing his head with a dark look on his face, his arm tight around my back. The fifteen-year-old me was squealing with glee, but the twenty-six-year-old was, admittedly, a little flustered.

I twisted out of his embrace and took a step back. My face was overheating, my heart was trying its hardest to hammer its way through my chest, and my body was tingling with that special kind of sexual exhilaration.

Henry's face broke into an impudent smile. "Are we done playing this game?" he called out to me over the music.

I nodded. Yes, we were definitely done. For now.

———————

Here's something you should know about Henry and me: We never meant to live together. He and my brother, Jason, met in high school and attended college together. For as long as I could remember, Jason had always intended to join the Air Force—it was kind of a given since my father and grandfather were both retired pilots. My guess was that Henry hung out with Jason enough that he too became convinced the military life was for him. So they had gone through ROTC together and eventually were sworn in to the Air Force, Jason as an Intelligence officer and Henry as a Security Forces officer. Not surprisingly, they were both sent to Tinker Air Force Base in Oklahoma and, of course, lived together in an apartment on the south side of the city.

I was always the outsider, the third wheel. I was two years younger and a bit of a pest, always asking to join them in their adventures. Besides that, I was a *girl* and had cooties, so I was almost always left behind, rejected and heartbroken. Very early on, even before his braces came off, I was convinced that Henry and I would get married. During my early teenage years, when I was barely past the Disney stage, I pictured him as my Prince Charming. Then, during my rebellious years, he was my imagined bad boy who would whisk me off on his motorcycle. But these fantasies were nothing but the daydreams of a girl who then grew up to realize that the boy of her dreams was far from perfect. The sobering reality was that Henry was a flawed guy who oftentimes tiptoed into jerk territory, as all men are wont to do.

After graduating from college, I accepted a web design job in Oklahoma and crashed on their couch for a few months while I saved up enough money for an apartment. Henry was not keen on the idea and, in fact, tried his hardest to find me another place to live. I still remembered coming to the table one Sunday morning and finding the newspaper opened to the classifieds with some listings already highlighted, his not-so-subtle way of telling me to stop cramping his style.

Henry inspired me to find a place faster, but then Jason was deployed to Afghanistan and asked me stay in his room for the six months that he'd be gone. To save money, I jumped at the offer.

Little did I know that my brother would never come back.

He was gathering intel, walking around a Kabul neighborhood talking to the nationals, when someone started shooting out of nowhere. Jason never even had a chance. Even now, his death makes no sense to me, and I still hold on to the hope that one day they'll find him somewhere in the Afghan mountains, roughed up but still alive, that the person we'd buried was actually someone else.

It's a long shot, but the ability to fool myself is one of my best talents.

So it was with a smile that I walked out of my room the next morning, pretending that nothing happened at Tapwerks the night before. I shuffled to the kitchen in my flannel pajamas and turned on the coffeemaker. Henry came out of his room, still committed to that sullen persona, and reached for the coffee mugs. I started frying some eggs and he put the bread in the toaster. When the coffee was done, he poured and fixed mine the way I like it and took our mugs to the table. I slid the eggs onto two plates, placed a piece of buttered toast on each one, and joined him at the table.

We ate quietly, hiding in our own thoughts to avoid talking about last night. I wasn't sure if it was even worth talking about; maybe he had just been playing around to teach my nosy ass a lesson. But my, what a long, hard lesson it was.

I had to gulp down coffee when the toast stuck in my throat, chalking up my impure thoughts of Henry to sex deprivation. I just needed a good lay, that was all.

The last time I'd had sex was more than a year ago, when my relationship with a guy from work fell apart a few months after Jason's death. I hadn't been able to cope with the grief and Brian had been inept at offering comfort, so the relationship ended. Still, even though Brian hadn't been the best lover, he'd been a step up from the Rabbit.

That was around the time my friendship with Henry was tested and cemented, when we fought and made up in cycles due to our grief. But at the end of it, Henry and I emerged with an unshakable bond forged out of loss. He and I became family.

"What are you up to today?" he asked, scratching at the dark hair on his chest.

"Just going to run at Earlywine," I said, finishing my eggs. "Why, did you want to do something?"

"Nah," he said, holding his head in his hands. "I'm just going back to bed. Sleep off this hangover."

"You're hungover?" I asked. We had left Tapwerks soon after that charged moment on the dance floor. He had only had the shot and one beer.

He gathered the empty dishes and placed them in the sink. "I had a few more beers after you went to bed last night."

I raised my eyebrows. This was the third time in so many weeks he'd been drinking alone. Something was definitely bothering him. "Henry," I began, leaning against the sink. "Do you want to talk?"

He scratched the scruff on his face, considering me for a moment. "Maybe some other time," he said and walked back to his bedroom.

———————

I threw some laundry in the washer and tidied my room, giving Henry plenty of time to come find me and spill his guts. At around three o'clock, I finally admitted that he was really not going to talk, so I put on my workout clothes and drove to the park to run my worries away.

Earlywine is a large grassy area that spans three blocks with a waterpark in the center as well as a YMCA building. A two-lane running track borders the park and, as usual, was busy on a warm Sunday afternoon. Everywhere I looked, families were grilling, kids were playing soccer, and people were running or power walking. As I watched the activity, I was struck with a sudden bout of homesickness. I hadn't made it back home to California since Christmas and I was starting to miss my parents, but going back home meant going back to the place I knew Jason best, and it still hurt, even after all this time.

I eyed the cute guys as I ran to take my mind off things, and God help me, I couldn't help but imagine each good-looking guy running naked. It was all Henry's fault, rousing my sex drive with that little stunt he pulled last night. I'd suppressed my appetite for so long that I'd become comfortable with it, but it had awakened and boy, was I ravenous.

A guy ran past me, wearing shoes, shorts, and little else. As he zipped by, I was able to give his backside a nice inspection. He had nice, sweaty muscles on his back, and his calves were well defined as he ran. He must have sensed my ogling because he looked over his shoulder and flashed a toothy grin, urging me to catch up.

I geared up to run faster when I heard someone calling my name. I stopped when I saw Danielle, the girlfriend of one of Henry's buddies, coming my way.

"Hey!" I greeted, casting one last glance at the guy, hoping he'd do another lap of the park. I turned my attention back to Danielle, noting her running outfit. "You look great."

She smiled widely. "Thanks. I reached my goal weight last week, so I bought a new outfit to celebrate."

I gave her a thumbs-up. Danielle had been overweight when we met at a party several months ago, but now she was wearing capri pants and a tank top and looking healthier than ever. I suddenly felt frumpy in my running shorts that bunched in the middle and old UCLA T-shirt with a hole in one of the armpits.

"So, are you ready for the deployment?" Danielle asked as she began her leg stretches.

I froze. "What deployment?"

"Didn't Henry tell you?" she asked, a look of trepidation crossing her face. "The squadron is leaving in two weeks."

"What?" My heart, which was already trying to recover from running too fast, was now thundering again. "How long have they known?"

"Mike knew two months ago," she said with an apologetic shrug.

I tried to rack my brain for reasons why Henry wouldn't tell me about the deployment and only one thing came to mind. "They're headed to Afghanistan, aren't they?" I asked through the lump in my throat.

Danielle's shoulders slumped. "Why wouldn't he tell you? Aren't you roommates?"

My nose was flaring unattractively, I was so mad. "Yes, we are."

"I'm sorry. I didn't mean to stir up trouble."

I gave her the feeblest smile I could manage under the circumstances. "It's not your fault." I said my good-byes and headed to my car. Henry wasn't going to have the chance to die in Afghanistan like my brother because I was going to kill him first.

2

LOCK AND LOAD

I wasn't overreacting to the news of the deployment. At least, *I* didn't think so. It's just that, when it comes to secrets, Henry and I haven't had the best track record. First there was the Bobby Santos incident in high school. Bobby was a sweet—if a little too shy—guy who had solicited Henry's help to ask me to the senior prom, knowing that Jason would have likely said no. Somehow, Henry had managed to forget to tell me, and I'd only found out about it after the event, when Bobby's cousin confronted me in the hallway for standing him up. Henry had apologized, saying he simply forgot, that he had other things on his mind. Forgot, my ass.

Then there was the secret to end all secrets, the one that almost prompted me to move out. Henry had known about Jason's death pretty much the same day it happened, but he didn't tell me until much later, when the official word came out and family and friends were notified. He told me he was trying to protect me, that he wanted to delay the moment when my life changed. Now I'm able see it for the thoughtful gesture it was, but back then, I had been so livid I had left without a word and hadn't come back from California for an entire week. Jason's funeral wasn't held until a month later, when his body was finally returned, but at the time, I'd just needed to get away.

To this day, I still wondered how he managed to act normally and not give away the secret that his best friend had been killed in action. Henry, it appeared, was a very convincing actor.

So really, I wasn't overreacting when, on the way home from the park, I ran a red light, nearly rammed into the slow-moving apartment-complex gate, and parked my Prius like a drunk driver. I tore up the concrete stairs of the building and entered our apartment, slamming the door behind me. "Henry!" I shouted, stalking over to his bedroom and pounding my fist on his door, relishing the idea of aggravating his hangover. "Henry Mason Logan, you get your ass out here right now!"

His door opened a crack and he peered out, his face a scruffy, rumpled mess. "What the hell?" he croaked.

"Are you deploying to Afghanistan in two weeks?"

The sleep slid off his face immediately. "Yeah."

"Were you planning on ever telling me?"

"Yeah. Eventually."

"When? On your way onto the plane?" I willed the tears back. "Why didn't you tell me? I thought we were friends!"

He threw open the door, looking weary. "I didn't know how to tell you." He took a step closer, but I stepped back.

"I think a 'Hey, I'm going to the place where your brother died' would have sufficed."

"That's exactly why I didn't tell you. I knew you'd freak out." He ran a hand through his short, dark hair.

"How can I not freak out? Jason went there and never came back!" My entire body was shaking from the effort of trying not to cry. Henry had seen me cry plenty of times before, but somehow it seemed important that I kept my cool now.

"What happened to Jason won't happen to me." He approached me with outstretched arms. "Elsie . . ."

"I don't care," I said, evading his touch. I was being unfair; I knew this, and yet I couldn't stop the hysteria from taking over. My control evaporated and the tears rushed down my cheeks in rivulets. Jason's death was a mark on my heart that would stay with me forever. I couldn't even begin to imagine what losing Henry would do to me too. "Is there any way you can get out of it?" I whispered. "Please?"

I felt like a selfish moron for asking, but I couldn't help it; I was nearing desperation. If Henry went to Afghanistan, he would never come back—I felt the certainty lodged deep in my gut.

Henry's dark eyebrows drew together as he shook his head. His jaw was stiff when he said in an irritated tone, "You know I can't."

"But—"

He took hold of my arms. "Listen to me, Elsie. I *can't*. It's not possible," he said firmly, then added in a softer tone, "but I would if I could."

I couldn't say anything, didn't even know what I'd say if my vocal cords weren't tied up in knots, so I walked away and hid from the truth in my bedroom.

———

I didn't talk to Henry for the next twenty-three hours. I needed a little time to cool down, to think through my anger to keep from saying things I would really regret.

I couldn't decide which hurt more: the fact that he was headed to the place that claimed my brother or the fact that he didn't tell me.

Anger and fear—mostly fear, if I was being completely honest—roiled inside me in waves. If I saw Henry, I didn't know if I'd want to plant a fist in his stomach or if I'd want to grab hold of him and never let go.

He was up before me the next morning, waiting in the kitchen with an olive branch in the form of a perfectly made cup of coffee. But I brushed past him and made my own in a to-go cup, not bothering to say good-bye before I walked out the front door.

I stayed at work until seven thirty and ate dinner with a coworker before I finally decided to go home. Henry had fallen asleep on the couch, a book lying open on his stomach.

I crept closer out of curiosity and saw the book's title: *The Art of War* by Sun Tzu. How apt, since we were in the middle of a battle of our own.

I meant to leave but something about the way he slept compelled me to stay, how his eyebrows were drawn together even in sleep, his mouth pursed in a thin line. For a minute, I set aside my anger and remembered the very first time we met. We had just moved to Monterey after Dad retired from the Air Force, so Jason was the new kid at the high school. Henry had introduced himself at the lunch line and invited Jason to sit with his friends. Not too long after that, Henry came over for dinner.

I was still in junior high then, all sass and gangly limbs, with curls that always frizzed by the end of the school day, so I was not prepared at all when the boy of my dreams walked through the front door after my brother. Henry sported dark, unruly long hair and a quiet intensity to match. He didn't smile much because of his braces, which gave him a sullen mien, but he was good-looking even then. To my teenage eyes, he was hotter than anything *Tiger Beat* had to offer, hotter even than Jonathan Taylor Thomas.

"Your hair is out of control," he told me as we shook hands.

"Yours is worse," I said without hesitation.

He smiled then, all braces and crinkly eyes, completely transforming his entire face. Just like that, I was a goner.

His long hair and best friend were both gone now, and whatever Henry and I had left in common was fast dwindling. And the one thing we had for sure—the trust—was being put to the test.

I wasn't a complete unreasonable dumbass though. I knew that families said good-bye to their loved ones every day, that I wasn't the only person in the world in this situation. Plenty of service members were gone for a year at a time—missing birthdays, anniversaries, even the birth of a child—and I certainly wasn't the only person in the world to lose a loved one to the war.

I *knew* this, and yet my heart would not stop aching anyway. Henry was leaving in two weeks. I'd be alone in this apartment with only my fears and bad dreams to keep me company.

Henry made a little sound in the back of his throat, a cross between a moan and a growl, but he remained asleep. I felt the last of my anger melt away when the crotch of his jeans started to stir, but before I could even see where *that* would lead I nudged him awake. "Henry."

He opened his eyes and his sleepy smile just about melted my panties. Did he look like that right after sex? Why was I suddenly so intent on finding out?

"Hey," he said huskily. His hand shot out and grabbed mine to keep me from leaving again. "Talk to me, Els."

I searched his face and found regret. "I wish you'd told me."

His eyes held mine. "Believe me, so do I," he said. "I hated having to keep it from you, but I really couldn't find the right way to tell you."

I gave a short nod. "I know. But I need to know I can trust you—"

"Of course you can trust me."

"—to treat me like an adult."

He sighed, his wide chest rising and falling. "I can't help it. I've always felt protective of you." I felt him squeeze my hand. "And I know you're an adult. You've grown up into a beautiful, wonderful woman."

Even though my face felt warm, I said, "Flattery will get you nowhere."

"Sometimes it gets me out of trouble," he said with a grin. "So we have this weekend to do something fun. What should we do?"

I raised my eyebrow. "You want to spend your last weekend with me? You're not going to go see your parents?"

"No." He said nothing else about the complicated relationship with his parents. He never did. "And most of my predeployment ducks are in a row. So I'm all yours this weekend."

I thought of something we hadn't done in a while, something we'd loved doing when Jason was still around. "How about we go hiking and camping at Red Rock Canyon?"

"And some rappelling?" he asked, his eyes bright with excitement.

"Definitely."

He sat up and threw the book aside. He squeezed my hand, a silent promise that he would never do me wrong again. "This will be fun."

3

CLASSIFIED INFORMATION

Sometime after Jason's death, I started having nightmares. They were violent at first, causing me to thrash and scream, but Henry had been there to wake me from them each time, to hold my head as I cried. Sometimes I climbed into bed with him in the middle of the night, a preemptive strike against the night terrors. Just the act of sleeping beside him, without even touching, gave me the comfort I needed to stay asleep.

I hadn't had any nightmares in a while. Until tonight.

I dreamt that Jason was walking around a run-down, deserted neighborhood of cement buildings without his weapons or any form of communication. He passed a mangy dog and stopped to pet it, and in that small moment of distraction, a sniper on the rooftop was able to take him out. This dream was different, however, because Henry ran out into the street without body armor and crouched beside my fallen brother. He was shot in the back of the head.

I woke up, shaking and covered in sweat, suddenly filled with an overwhelming need to see Henry and make sure he was okay. So even though it was after midnight, I tiptoed past the living room and peered into his room.

I was relieved to find him very much alive, lying on the bed in nothing but a pair of sweat pants, watching TV with his hands folded behind his head. "Hey," he said. "You okay?"

"I . . ."

He sat up. "Bad dreams?"

"You were in it this time."

He patted the space beside him. "Wanna bunk?"

I stopped at the foot of his bed, suddenly unsure of myself. We'd spent many hours here, talking and crying and cementing our friendship. He'd never tried anything, had never expressed any sort of sexuality with me until the other night. So why was I so nervous all of a sudden?

"Would you just come here already?" he asked, breaking through my uncertainty.

Without another word, I climbed on the bed and lay beside him, staring up at the ceiling.

"You want to talk about it?"

I shook my head and we remained unspeaking for a long time.

He finally broke the silence. "I really am sorry I didn't tell you sooner, Elsie."

I looked at him. "I'm sorry for reacting exactly as you thought."

"I just couldn't find the right time or place to tell you. Believe me, I thought about it day and night."

"You don't always have to protect me, you know. I can handle it. I'm not a little girl anymore, in case you haven't noticed."

His blue eyes blazed on my face with a look that made my ears burn. "I have."

I was sure he could hear my heart pounding through my shirt. "So no more personal secrets, okay? You'll always have your classified information, I know that, but you hiding something like this from me . . . well, it hurts."

He held out his pinky and we sealed the deal. "Promise."

We looked at each other for a long time, not saying anything.

"So what now?" I finally asked.

"We deal with it, I guess. Not much else we can do." He let out a slow breath through his nose. "The chance of that happening to me is pretty slim, you know. My job is to guard the base, not mingle with the natives."

"Can I get that in writing?" I asked with a smile. "I want a written guarantee, notarized even, that you will be okay."

He gave a short chuckle. "I can't do that. But I can make you a promise that I will try my hardest to come back home in one piece."

Tears sprang to my eyes unexpectedly. "I honestly don't know what I'd do without you," I said with a quivering voice.

"Hey," he said, gathering me into his side. "Don't cry."

I laid my cheek on his bare skin, tears falling from my face and soaking into the short, dark hair of his chest. "You smell nice," I said between sobs.

"Sometimes I do this thing called *shower*," he said to try to lighten the mood. "Try it sometime."

I gave him a playful jab on the stomach, glad to have the old Henry back. "Smart-ass."

He grabbed my hand and smacked me with it, his favorite way of tormenting me since our teens. "Stop hitting yourself, Elsie," he said with a laugh. "Hurting yourself won't do you any good."

I struggled against his strong arms, laughing despite the moisture on my face. I twisted around and somehow found myself on top of him.

Henry bit his lower lip. "Are you trying to seduce me?" he asked with a cheeky grin.

I pinched his nose and slid off him, feeling a surprising jolt as my nipples rubbed against his chest. Ignoring the confusing feeling,

I resumed our snuggling position, resting my hand on his stomach. He placed his hand on mine and gave a contented little sigh that I felt in my bones. I melted into his side, finding myself suddenly sleepy.

"I don't know what I'd do without you either" was the last thing I heard him say before the weight of the deployment proved too heavy for my eyelids.

———

I was having a surprisingly erotic dream where Henry and I were naked together, his large hands caressing my body as we kissed like we would never see each other again. I could feel his erection pressing into me, his desire so palpable I could almost smell it. He reached down between us and his hand cupped my mound, making me moan when his fingers slipped inside. To return the pleasure, I gripped his thick erection and began a gentle tugging motion.

"Uh, Elsie," he said.

"Henry," I moaned against him, pumping faster.

"Elsie, wake up."

My eyes opened with a start, surprised that it had all been a dream. It had felt so real.

"Umm . . ."

My eyes flew down in horror when I realized that my hand was, indeed, inside Henry's pants, my fingers still wrapped around his erect penis.

"What the hell!" I cried, scrambling away in horror. "What was my hand doing in there?"

Henry stifled a smile as he fixed his waistband. "I think you know what you were doing."

"I mean, why was it in there, in your pants? Did you do that?"

He laughed now, hearty and thick. "Hell no. That was all you. I woke up with you manhandling me."

I covered my mouth with my hand—the *other* hand—feeling my face go up in flames. "Was I moaning too?"

"Maybe a little."

"Oh my God! I thought I was dreaming." I covered my face with my hands, dying of embarrassment.

He bit down on his lip but was not successful in hiding his amusement. "You dream about jerking me off?" he asked.

"No!" I cried. "I'm sorry for molesting you," I said and fled the room as quickly as my feet could go, with Henry's laughs trailing behind me like toilet paper stuck to my shoe.

———————

I went to work thirty minutes early the next morning out of sheer embarrassment. I didn't want to have to see Henry's smirk, didn't want to have to explain why my unconscious hand was touching him in his private places.

Several people came by my cubicle at work, asking if I was running a fever because my face was still so red. *Oh, it's just because I accidentally jerked off my roommate this morning*, I thought about saying, then died a little more inside.

I found it hard to concentrate on work. Every time I typed something or reached for my mouse, I'd inadvertently glance down at my hand and remember how Henry had felt in my grip, that soft, velvety skin that gave way to the solid muscle underneath. I imagined guiding him inside me, filling me up completely with that dark look on his face. . . .

I stood up, my entire body overheating, and ran to the bathroom as fast as my boots would allow. I meant to only splash cold water on my face, but as soon as I was in the privacy of the bathroom, I knew there was really only one way I could get through the day, so I locked myself in a stall, lifted the hem of my skirt, and slipped my hand inside my panties.

My body relaxed somewhat for the rest of the day, but the moment I pulled into the apartment parking lot the desire came rushing back. When I slid the key inside the lock, I almost decided to forgo thinking and just fuck Henry senseless.

Yes, the F-word, because he wasn't getting anything less. I was so aroused, I even entertained the idea of fucking him twice.

My hot fantasy was doused when I walked inside and found Henry and another guy in the living room, each lounging on a different couch with a beer in hand. They had been talking about work but stopped when I walked into view.

"Hey," Henry greeted, his face carefully devoid of expression. I was almost in the clear when his blue eyes slowly slid down my body, inflaming me to the core. My knees just about buckled.

I didn't know when he'd acquired that special power over me, but I wanted it gone. I couldn't afford to burst into flames every time he looked my way.

"Elsie?" he asked, frowning.

I blinked, realizing I'd spaced out for a second. "Huh?"

A shadow of a smirk crossed over his mouth before he said, "Elsie, meet Lieutenant Jack Coulson. He's moving to an apartment across the courtyard."

I shot Jack a smile, noting the youth and inexperience in his face. He couldn't have been more than twenty-two. "Nice to meet you."

Jack stood up and shook my hand. "Pleasure," he said.

"Do you work together?"

Jack remained standing. "Yes, ma'am. I just moved to the Seventy-Second Security Forces Squadron. Captain Logan is my boss."

I looked over at Henry with a raised eyebrow. My first impulse was to say something funny but remembered to keep my snarky mouth in check. Henry was this guy's boss and needed to maintain a sense of authority. "That's great," I said instead.

Henry cast that blue gaze at me, his eyes once again doing the sexy slide down my body that felt very much like a caress.

I turned away, sick of my body's disloyal reaction to those looks. It wasn't as if I was really attracted to Henry; I just needed a good lay and he happened to be the nearest available guy. That's all it was. Surely there were other guys who might be interested.

I excused myself, deciding a long run at the park was just what my body needed.

———

Nearly an hour later, I was back at the apartment, sweaty and still frustrated. I'd run four miles, yet my mystery runner never showed up. I hopped in the shower, hoping to cool down—which worked for the most part, until afterward, when I came out to the living room completely dressed to find Henry definitively *not*. His shirt was off (did the guy even own one?) and he was sweaty from helping Jack move his stuff up the three flights of stairs.

He had his back to me so I was able to leisurely look over his muscular back, from his wide shoulders that tapered down to a lower back that sported two dimples dipping below the waistband of his jeans.

He turned around, wiping his chest with a balled-up shirt. "Hey, what do you want to do tonight?"

Hmm, what *did* I want to do tonight, apart from the obvious? "I was just going to eat a peanut butter sandwich and read a book," I said as casually as I could.

He raised his eyebrows. "You sure? I was going to order a pizza."

My eyes flicked down to his torso—he had the nicest six-pack abs of anyone I knew in real life—before I looked away. "I'm sure."

He cocked his head. "Come on. I'm leaving next Friday. Spend some time with me."

Well crap, why did he have to put it that way? Still, his words helped because the impending deployment was the sexual damper that I really needed. The fact was, he was leaving and I should be spending time with him. "Okay, fine," I said with an exaggerated sigh. "But please put a shirt on."

He grinned and lobbed me the phone. "Call the pizza place, will you? I'm just going to jump in the shower."

———

Henry and I ate sitting on the carpet, leaning against the suede couch. The couch had been Jason's first major purchase and he had ordered a five-foot no-food radius around it when it was still brand-new. After his death, it became a ritual we observed to preserve Jason's memory.

I put on a movie about superheroes as we ate, glad to have some distraction for a while.

"If you had any superpower," I asked. "What would it be?"

"What would I choose, or what would I be born with?" he asked, balancing a beer bottle between his legs. "Because if I was born with a superpower, I'd say it's being really, really ridiculously good-looking."

I threw a crumpled napkin at him. "No, I meant what would you choose?"

He took a large bite of his third slice of pizza and chewed a moment before saying, "I would choose the ability to fly."

"Huh, I would have chosen invincibility for you." *So you could come out of the war unscathed*, I wanted to add, but didn't want to ruin the mood.

"So I can sneak into your shower and see you naked?"

I smacked his arm. "No, *invincibility*."

"Oh, *that* invincibility," he said with a laugh, looking happier than I had seen him in months. He took a swig of beer, then said, "So, hey, are we going to talk about what happened this morning?"

The question caught me by surprise and my brain struggled to come up with an elegant response. "I, uh . . ."

"Because I think the elephant in the room needs to be addressed," he said. "And I'm not referring to my colossal size."

I burst out laughing, finally finding my voice. "You're not that large, my friend."

"How large would you say then?" He held his hands two feet apart. "So about this big, right?"

"Riiight." I chuckled, feeling the embarrassment melting away. "I'm sorry. I don't know what that was about."

"I think that was about your hand on my dick." He laughed at my shocked reaction and continued, "Would you rather I call it my phallus? My hammerjack? How about my *porksword*?"

I spit out my drink, having never heard the last one before.

Henry's eyes glinted with mischief. "For the record, you are more than welcome to churn my butter any time. Seriously, morning, noon, night, whenever."

My laugh caught in my throat as his words painted a very vivid picture in my overactive imagination. I took a large drink from my glass of water, torn between changing the subject and pressing him for more details about what I could do with his penis.

I started when he pressed the cold bottle of beer to my cheek. "You're all red," he said, his face suddenly closer than I remembered. He touched his thumb to my cheek and traced along my jawline. "Have I ever told you that I love your complexion? It's like milk, so creamy but always quick to take on color."

I couldn't breathe. I didn't know what the hell had happened to me, but somewhere between finding out his secret and waking up with my hand in his pants, I had devolved into someone who could barely form a coherent sentence. I didn't want to be that girl who got all googly-eyed when an attractive guy paid attention to me, but I couldn't react to his nearness any other way. Henry had me stupefied.

When his thumb traced my lower lip, I lost it. Or rather, I let that thin wire of control snap. I spanned the space between us and kissed him, and he, thankfully, didn't pull away. Instead he grasped the back of my head and deepened the kiss, our tongues a slippery, tangled mess. He gently bit down on my lower lip, then pulled away, giving me that dark, heated look I'd fantasized about. "Elsie, I . . ."

I waited for the rest of the words, but he said nothing else. He just ran a hand through his hair, then rubbed his forehead.

"What is it?" I asked, ready for him to get it out so we could get back to kissing already.

"This can get complicated," he finally said.

"It doesn't have to."

He looked at my lips for a long time, then, with a sigh, finally met my eyes. "We'd better not," he said, leaning his head against the couch and closing his eyes. "I'm sorry."

4

DETONATION

I couldn't sleep that night, my brain in overdrive from the pork-sword fondling and the kiss and what Henry said about complications. He was leaving in eleven days and would not be back for half a year; it wouldn't do us any good to start anything now, especially something as tricky as sleeping together.

But a small part of me wanted it anyway, wanted to push through the barrier that had held us back all these years and find out what the hell was on the other side. All these years I'd held my crush at bay, thinking that nothing could ever happen between us, that we were forever banished to the friendship wasteland.

What if there was somewhere else, a terminal in between where we could be together in body and keep our hearts separate so as to not endanger the friendship? Did such a place even exist?

I finally fell asleep when I came to the only logical conclusion, the possibilities filling me with a sense of hope.

The next day I came home from work with a plan and a bag of take-out from Chili's. I pulled out plates and started setting the table when Henry came walking out of my bedroom wearing camo pants and a tan undershirt that hugged his muscles.

"What were you doing in my room?" I asked with a raised eyebrow.

He held up a pistol leg-holster that I'd used last Halloween when I'd dressed up as Lara Croft. "I was getting my stuff together and couldn't find my other holster. And lo and behold, it was in your room."

"Sorry," I said. "I guess I forgot to return it."

"Ah, yes," he said with that sexy, sliding look again. "You can have this one if you would just wear that costume every day."

I was thinking of a suitable retort when the food caught his attention. "What's all this?" he asked, standing in front of the counter.

"Just wanted to remind you of what you'll miss out on while you're gone."

He dipped his finger in the barbecue sauce and sucked it into his mouth. "You are not playing fair."

I leaned over the counter and pressed my arms together, just like I'd done at the bar, the V-neck of my wraparound dress the perfect frame for my assets. "Hey, when you've got 'em, use 'em."

Henry's eyes tried their damnedest to stay off my cleavage, but in the end, the gravitational pull was too much. He swallowed, frowned, then tore his eyes away from my chest. "What are you doing?"

I held his eyes, trying to convey my message. "Reminding you of what you'll miss out on." My heart pounded wildly as he studied me, his expression changing from doubt to desire.

After what seemed like forever, he pushed away from the counter and stalked over to my side, placing his hands on either side of me, trapping me in place. With his face mere inches from mine, he asked in a pained voice, "Do you have any clue what you do to me?"

I shook my head, but I really did.

He took a half step closer, pressing his erection into my stomach. "You drive me insane," he said in that gravelly voice. He lowered his head and I felt his breath on my neck, on my ear. "You make me want something I can never have."

My breath came out in ragged gasps when I said, "I'm all yours, Henry."

His hands grasped at the skirt of my dress, balling them up in his fists. "I've wanted you for the longest time, Elsie," he said. "If you're unsure about this, tell me now and I'll step away and we can go back to pretending that everything's the same."

The hem of my dress rose a few more inches up my thigh as he gathered more fabric in his hands. I was transfixed by the curve in his upper lip, the way it offset his thick lower lip.

"Elsie, tell me," he ground out.

I pulled on his dog tags and brought his face to mine. "I want you just as much as you want me," I whispered against his lips.

His hands gripped my butt and lifted me up on the counter at the same time his head dipped down for a kiss. He slid my dress up my thighs, his palms warm on my skin, and suddenly, his hands were inside my lace panties. I gasped when his fingers found my entrance. He pushed one long finger inside, and I squeezed him as I moaned.

"You really want this?" he asked, uncertainty still evident in his voice. Or maybe he just liked hearing me beg. He pushed another finger inside and started a slow and slippery stroke. "Or this?"

"What do you think?" I asked, knowing I was soaked.

"I think," he began, flicking his fingers upward in an exquisite way that made me gasp, hitting just the right spot.

"That—" Another flick.

"You—" I gasped.

"Are—" I squeezed him hard, intensifying the sensations.

"Sexy—" *So close.*

"As fuck." With that, he began to move his fingers rapidly, and after only several seconds, I threw my head back and came around him, my legs and my insides trembling as he kept up the assault.

I grabbed his head and kissed him, moaning into his mouth. "I want to feel you inside me."

He hesitated, glancing at his bedroom, when I grabbed his head and kissed him again. "I'm on the pill," I said. "And I'm clean. Are you?"

"Oh yeah," he said and swept me up in more kisses. I unbuttoned his pants and slipped a hand into his boxer shorts, wrapping my fingers around his hard shaft. He gripped my wrist, preventing me from stroking him.

"No. I want something else." He pulled down his pants and boxer shorts, his large cock flying free.

I looked down at it properly for the first time, impressed not only with its length but its girth. Henry was a big boy with a big toy to match.

"You ready?"

When I nodded, he pressed the head to the entrance and then slid inside in one clean stroke. I gasped, feeling so full I could burst. I squeezed him as he pulled almost all the way out, then slid back in, inch by delicious inch.

I pressed my mouth to his neck to keep from screaming out loud, my body a jittery bundle of raw nerves.

"Elsie," he said between his teeth, his hands on my butt as he began to increase the pace. I wrapped my legs around his waist and he sank in even deeper. "You feel so fucking good," he groaned against my hair.

I came again, the orgasm bursting through my body like a white-hot tidal wave. Henry gave a little grunt and pumped faster, gripping me so tight against him he was very nearly lifting me off the counter. With one final thrust his body went rigid and he pressed his face into my neck, trying to catch his breath. I grasped the back of his head and held him tight, never wanting to let him go, wanting to keep him inside me forever.

After a moment, he looked up, his eyes an ocean of emotions. He looked grave when he said, "There's something else I haven't told you."

My heart stopped. It couldn't possibly take more bad news, not now.

"I'm in love with you, Els," he whispered, as if afraid of being heard. "I've loved you since that day you first cut my hair."

Instead of dealing with the startling confession, I jumped right into the memory. I was just fifteen and Jason and Henry were about to head off to college. Henry had always sported a longer style that brushed his shoulders, but he needed to have short hair for ROTC. Since our mother wasn't home, I was the only one qualified to use the shears, so I had performed the difficult and heartbreaking task of buzzing off all that beautiful dark, wavy hair. I had felt his eyes on me through the mirror but kept my focus, careful not to send Henry off to college with a wonky buzz cut. Sabotage did occur to me in a moment of pure selfishness—thinking that the college hussies might leave him alone if he had a bald spot on the side of his head—but ultimately I could not do it. I was already defacing something beautiful, cutting off the thing that bound us together, and couldn't possibly mar him even more.

When I was done, I looked at him in the mirror. Gone was the boy that I had once known. In his place was a clean-cut young man, ready to take on academia and the world, and it finally sank in that he was leaving me. He would never again live only two houses away, never again come over to hang out and play video games.

My heart had broken ten times over that day.

But now that same boy was in my arms, telling me that he was in love with me, which left me confused as hell. I used to think I could read his every thought, but his confession blindsided me, made me wonder if I knew him at all.

"I didn't know . . ." I began. "I thought this was just sex."

He jerked back as if I'd pressed a hot poker to his chest. "In all the time that you've lived here, how many times have you seen me *just have sex* with a woman?"

I shrugged, thinking back to all the women that had accompanied Henry to our home. He had had two girlfriends since I'd lived here, and both of them lasted at least a few months—definitely longer than a one-night stand. "None," I said in a tiny voice.

I felt hollow when he pulled out of me and pulled up his camo pants, as if he could somehow take back all of the pleasure he'd given me only a few minutes earlier. I shook my head, wondering how the hell things had gotten derailed so quickly. "This isn't how it's supposed to go."

He gave me a disquieted look that told me he hadn't expected this ending either, but like a gentleman, he helped me down from the counter and straightened my clothes. "Well," he began, trying for a lighter tone, "thanks for the good sex. I'll eat the ribs later."

If he was trying to wound me, he had succeeded. With an aching chest, I watched him grab his keys from the hook and leave.

5

UNDER RUBBLE

During my senior year in high school, Henry came home for the Christmas holidays a few days earlier than Jason. The last time I'd seen Henry had been nearly a year before, and if I thought I looked grown up, Henry had me beat. I had driven home from school when I saw this person standing on my porch with his hands in his jacket pockets, looking awfully familiar but too grown-up to be the boy I knew.

I parked in the driveway and ran up to him, forgetting myself for a moment as I launched myself into his arms. "Henry!" I cried, wrapping my arms around his neck. "When did you get here?"

He laughed and set me down. "Just an hour ago." He held me at arm's length, a small smile playing at the edge of his lips. He touched my hair, which I wore shorter now that the curls had relaxed a little. "You look so different."

"Well you . . ." I looked up at him, searching for the words. He was already tall, but over the past year, he'd filled out a little and had actual beard stubble. I rubbed his jaw and laughed, tickled by the sensation and the guy before me.

"Elsie . . ."

We both turned at the voice, and I remembered with a start that

I had a passenger in my car that day. I pulled away from Henry as if I'd been caught doing something indecent and turned to Zach, my new boyfriend.

"Hey, Zach," I said in my most casual tone. "This is Henry, my brother's best friend."

I turned back to Henry and was taken aback by the look on his face, a confounding mixture of betrayal and disappointment. The expression dissolved into a cordial smile a moment later, and I never saw that look again. Until today.

———————

Henry hadn't made it home by the time I went to bed. I checked my cell phone several times, sure that he would have texted me by now, even if to just berate me. He and I fought like brother and sister on a regular basis, but never before had it actually hurt. Never before had we made each other feel one inch small.

He loved me.

That was a bombshell of a confession that had come when I was least expecting it. Now all of his actions, all of those long, silent looks he'd been giving me came into question. What had been going through his mind all this time?

I guess no matter how much you think you know someone, the harsh reality is that you never really know anyone at all.

———————

I woke up sometime in the night when the hinges of my door squeaked open and Henry's soft footsteps crossed the room. The bed gave way under his weight as he climbed in and curled around my back. "I love you, Elsie," Henry said, burying his face in my hair. "I just wanted you to know before I left."

My heart skipped a beat at the tenderness in his voice. "Thank you for telling me," I said. "Why didn't you say anything before?"

He shifted around and rested his cheek on the side of my head. "I don't know. You used to be just a little girl, but somewhere along the way, you went from Jason's bratty sister to this beautiful woman with a glow about you."

I grasped his wrists and pulled his arms around me, his words warming me from the inside.

"After Jason died, I felt like I needed to take his place and be your big brother. I wasn't supposed to have romantic feelings for you," he said. "But God help me, I couldn't fight it. Not when we live in the same apartment, spending too much time together.

"Look, I don't need you to tell me you love me too if you don't actually feel that way. I just wanted you to know that tonight, being with you, meant something."

I twisted in his arms and faced him. "It wasn't just sex for me either. And I do love you, Henry, but I don't know yet if I'm in love with you."

He nodded, pressing his forehead to mine. "I can deal with that."

"But I do need you."

"Yeah?" he asked with a saucy grin.

"I need you to stay if this thing between us ends. You can't just move out and cut me out of your life."

He nodded solemnly.

"And I need you to come back safe and sound." My chest felt tight with that certain knowledge that he would never come back, but I pretended not to feel it. After all, what did I know? I was no psychic.

"I'll try my best." His hands stole inside my shirt and ran up and down my back. "I need you to do something for me."

"Anything," I breathed, the sensation of his rough palms sending tingles up to my scalp.

"I need you to be here when I get back."

I kissed the tip of his nose. "I'll be here. I'm not going anywhere."

And then we were on each other, our hands rubbing, grabbing, fondling with complete abandon. We shucked our clothes with a speed born of need. I moaned when his bare skin touched mine, my breasts crushed against his chest as we kissed. He bent down and took one nipple in his mouth, sucking hard, and I arched my back and rubbed my fingers along his scalp, urging him on. He moved to the other breast, laving it with the same attention as the one before. I squeaked when he bit down on my nipple, causing an instant rush of moisture in my crotch.

He licked the valley between my breasts then moved lower, pressing kisses on my stomach, my belly button, and the insides of my thighs. A grin flashed across his face a moment before he disappeared between my legs.

I'd received oral from a man before, knew what a tongue felt like down there, but Henry was in a whole other league. I didn't even want to know where he'd learned the moves, but his tongue was masterful as it licked and glided through my folds in a languid but firm manner. I sucked in a breath when he pushed his tongue inside me and his entire mouth covered my mound, forming a pressurized vacuum of pleasure.

"Oh God," I breathed, grabbing his head as my insides clutched at his tongue, wanting more. There was not nearly enough of him inside me. My back arched up off the bed and, just as I was about to explode, the wretched man pulled away. "What? Why did you stop?" I shrieked.

He positioned himself above me. "Because," was all he said before he slammed into me and the orgasm raced through my body. He pulled out and slammed back to the hilt, giving me another wave to crest. I screamed the third time he pounded into me, the orgasm going on and on.

He stilled then, his eyes closed and eyebrows drawn together, enjoying the sensation of my vaginal walls convulsing around him.

"Elsie," he said with a trembling voice. He withdrew slowly and entered even slower still, continuing the relentless torture at a pace that had me clutching at his butt, urging him to go faster, but he kept the unhurried pace, his arms on either side of my head as he kissed me tenderly.

Henry was making love to me.

The realization hit me like an avalanche and I was buried under the rubble. Tears pooled at the corners of my eyes as I gazed up at him, unable to believe that this man, who was once just a boy, was mine. At least for the moment.

I wrapped my legs around his back and urged him deeper into me. He never picked up speed, never wavered in his steady thrusting, and I felt another orgasm building. With each drawn-out stroke, my muscles wound tighter and tighter, my body coiling into him until the final stroke that snapped me, made me scream his name as he shuddered his release.

Afterward, he did the atypical and stayed in my room, sleeping on the bed that he'd deemed "too soft and girly smelling" forever ago, wrapped around me like my very own man-blanket. For the first time in a long time, since Jason's death really, I fell into a deep and contented slumber.

———————

You know that saying about taking a step back to get a fresh perspective? Well, I didn't really need to step back to clear my mind; all I needed was six hours of sleep. When I woke the next morning to the sight of Henry's calm face beside me, my heart just about burst with a feeling so acute, so fierce, that only a fool could have mistaken it for anything else.

I had been deluding myself all of these years, thinking I could live my entire life as nothing but his roommate. I thought I'd successfully extinguished the torch that I carried for him, but in the space of a few days, the embers had been rekindled and the whole damn thing caught fire.

I was madly in love with Henry: always had been, probably always would be.

Admitting it exhilarated and scared the hell out of me. It was akin to leaning all the way back on a swing, feeling the rush and seeing the world at a new angle yet knowing there was a very real chance of crashing to the concrete below.

Still, I knew, as I traced my finger gently down his forehead, along the bridge of his nose, that this was one risk I was willing to take. When I reached his lips, he opened his mouth and bit my finger.

"Good morning," he said with a sleepy smile. He touched my shoulder and ran a palm along the contours of my waist and hip. "I'm a little sad to wake up to you touching my nose instead of . . . other things."

I reached down to straighten out the situation when I spied the clock on my bedside table. I sat up with a heavy sigh. "I have to get ready for work."

He buried his face in the pillow and grumbled. "No, no, no." He then waved a hand across my face and said, "You will take a sick day today."

"If only I could, Henry-Wan Kenobi, but I have important clients coming in," I said, giving him one last, lingering kiss. "To be continued."

———————

Work was excruciating. My meeting with *The Oklahoman* about their website redesign took a long time as we hammered out the concept. To be honest, it probably took longer because my mind was not in that conference room but far off at Tinker Air Force Base, where Henry was trying to complete his predeployment checklist.

We only had a week left together; it seemed such a shame to waste it apart—but what could we do? We were adults with responsibilities, even if we were acting like lovesick teenagers.

Right before lunch, a client's website crashed and, since it was my project, I was forced to ditch my idea of taking a long lunch to visit Henry and fix the problem instead. So I put my head down and got to work, hoping to be able to skip out of work early at least.

Around twelve thirty, there was some commotion outside my cubicle, but I wanted nothing to do with it. Gideon, my gay hipster cubicle neighbor, popped up over the wall and gave me a rare smile. "You have a visitor," he said and jabbed a thumb toward the reception desk.

I looked up to find a handsome captain in his ABUs—short for airman battle uniform—walking toward me, a beret and a single red rose in his hand. My heart did a happy little jig at the sight of him, looking so dashing in the uniform I'd seen him wear a hundred times before. He slipped his beret in a leg pocket and held out the rose.

My coworkers' heads popped up from their cubicles one by one, like little prairie dogs, flashing knowing smiles and popping back down again. I pulled Henry inside my cubicle and forced him down onto my chair, hoping a member of management wouldn't decide to walk by at that moment.

"Well hello," he said and pulled me onto his lap.

I wrapped my arms around his neck and took his gorgeous face in hungrily. "Do you want to go to the conference room upstairs?" I whispered in his ear. "It should be empty at this time of day."

Henry looked extremely tempted, but he shook his head. "I really want to, but I have to head back to work. I just came here to deliver this," he said, tipping me back, and planting a searing kiss on my lips.

We surfaced a few minutes later, utterly turned on without any way to deal with it. With a sigh, I pulled him up and we emerged from our own little world.

He gave me a courteous nod. "Ma'am," he said formally, then leaned down and blew in my ear. "To be continued."

After he left, a few people walked by my cubicle to ask about the rose and the handsome airman who'd brought it. The inevitable question "So is he your boyfriend?" was asked, but for once, when it came to my relationship with Henry, I didn't know what to say.

———————

On my way home I got stuck behind every slow car or truck in Oklahoma. It was a conspiracy; that's the only way I could explain why everyone seemed to be in on some big plan to keep me from getting home. But as soon as I opened that front door, I ran to my man—yes, in my mind I'd claimed him already—and leapt into his arms. To say I devoured his face was kind of an understatement.

Henry backed up into the couch and sat down, taking me with him. He grumbled something about putting steaks on the grill, but a tornado could have been whizzing past our window right then and you couldn't have peeled me from that couch. Instead, I unzipped his pants, drew aside my thong panties and pulled him deep inside me.

Later, after we finally got around to cooking and eating dinner, we lay on his bed sated and drowsy. He was lying on his back and I was sideways across the bed, my head resting on his stomach, as we talked about the past, too afraid to talk about the future in case we didn't have one.

"How about that guy in your senior year?" Henry asked. "Did you guys date long?"

I smiled against his stomach. "You jealous?"

"I was."

I ran my fingers over the soft skin covering his ribs. "We only went out until after New Year's," I said. "I'd have broken up with him sooner if you'd told me how you felt."

"I almost did a few times." He twisted his finger around a lock of my curly hair. "I came home early that Christmas to spend some time with you without Jason around."

"Would you have told me then?"

He shrugged. "Maybe. If all the stars aligned. But I guess they didn't." His blue eyes took me in for a long time until I became uncomfortable.

"What?" I asked, covering my face with my hand. I peeked through my fingers and grinned.

He pulled my hand away. "I was just wondering what Jason would think."

"He'd probably tackle you to the ground, maybe give you a black eye or bloody lip," I said. Jason would have grumbled but, deep down, I liked to think he would have been happy for us.

"Sounds like Jason," Henry replied with a rueful smile. He pressed his palm to my cheek. "I think he knew. I was always asking about you, trying to sneak your name into conversations. Every time we talked about coming back home, he'd ask me if I was looking forward to seeing you, but I'd just ignore him."

I beamed so hard my cheeks hurt. "You wanted to *huuuug* me, you wanted to *kiiiss* me," I said in a singsong voice.

He sat up and tickled me and we wriggled around on the bed like children until his cell phone vibrated on the nightstand. He looked at the caller ID and said, "I need to take this."

I went to use the bathroom to give him some privacy. On my way back out, I caught a glimpse in the mirror that gave me pause. My hair was tangled and any trace of makeup had been wiped off my face, and yet I looked positively delirious with happiness. I finally saw the glow Henry had been talking about.

He was wearing pants and a grave expression when I rejoined him on the bed.

"What's up?" I asked. "Everything okay?"

"That was the commander," he said in a voice that made the hairs on my arms rise.

I didn't want to hear whatever bad news was coming, but I had asked for honesty and it was too late to take it back. "What is it?"

"The deployment date has been changed."

A hopeful little thought bubbled up from my chest. "It's been pushed back?"

"It's been moved up."

I spoke around the thought that had lodged painfully in my throat. "When?"

A gloom settled over Henry's handsome features. "To this Saturday. As in two days from now."

That was about the time I fell off the swing and fell face-first onto the ground.

6

OVER AND OUT

We held each other that night, never once losing contact as we slept. I clutched him to my chest, afraid of losing his warmth, and in turn he nestled me in his arms with his lips pressed to my head.

I woke with a start around two a.m., nearly hyperventilating from the thought that I hadn't even told him how I felt. "Wake up," I whispered against his chest, pulling away.

He was hard to rouse after the night we'd had, but I needed to tell him. We were fast running out of time. "Henry, wake up."

"Yes?" he rasped, keeping his eyes closed. He pulled me back against his chest.

"I have to tell you something."

"Can you tell me tomorrow? I was having a nice dream."

I pushed against him. "No, you need to know now."

His eyes remained shut. "So . . . ?"

"I love you," I whispered.

Henry was so still that if it weren't for his rapid heartbeat, I might have thought he had fallen back asleep.

I pushed up to one elbow. "I said I'm in love with you."

One corner of his mouth curled up. "I already know."

"What? For how long?"

He finally opened his eyes and fixed them on me. "You've always been in love with me. You just needed time to remember."

"But . . ."

He laughed at my dumbfounded expression and pulled me back down into his arms. "I love you too, Els. Now go back to sleep."

————

I wanted to call in sick the next day, but Henry had a lot of last-minute things to take care of, like making sure his training and medical papers were up to date. "I also have to update my will," he said as we sipped our morning coffee with me sitting on his lap.

His will.

My spine stiffened, that one word bursting my happy little bubble. All of a sudden my fears came racing back, crushing my lungs.

Henry felt the sudden change of mood. He squeezed my side and said, "I will be okay. Updating my will is just customary."

I stood up and faced him, intent on swallowing my fears. "Of course it is," I said, giving him one last kiss. "Well, I should get going."

His hands rested on the back of my legs and slid up my skirt. "Have a good day," he said huskily, his fingers playing with the edge of my panties.

I kissed him and pulled away. "Bye."

————

I ate my lunch at my desk, turning my head every time someone walked by, hoping that Henry had found a sliver of time to come see me again, but he didn't come. I stared at that red rose sitting inside an empty glass water bottle and ate my food like a zombie. I couldn't even tell you what I put in my mouth, I was so out of it.

After work I rushed home, jittery with the knowledge that the seconds were ticking by. As I drove I convinced myself to live for the moment, to pretend that tomorrow didn't exist—and almost succeeded until I walked in the living room and found a pile of his stuff on the floor. Two dark green duffel bags with his name embroidered on the side, folded ABUs, tan boots, gloves, a helmet. My heart stopped when my eyes rested on a body armor vest. I picked it up, wondering how it could possibly protect Henry when it hadn't been enough to save my brother.

This was really happening. Henry was really going to leave tomorrow.

I dropped the vest, suddenly too exhausted to even hold myself up. I sank to the floor and stared at the deployment pile, trying to convince my lungs to simply keep breathing.

"I didn't know you were ho—" Henry stopped when he saw me. I must have looked like a hot mess, but he didn't mention it. "I have something to show you." He held out his hand and pulled me up off the floor. We walked through the living room and he opened the sliding door that led to the balcony.

"I wanted you to have your camping trip," he said, stepping aside so I could see. He had placed one of our kitchen rugs on the cement balcony and erected a tent on it. Beside it stood a camping stove and two metal skewers.

I peered into the tent and found our sleeping bags zipped together to make one oversized one. "Nice."

"But there's more," he said and produced a box of graham crackers, a bar of Hershey's chocolate, and a bag of marshmallows.

"You've thought of everything, Captain Logan," I said with the best smile I could manage. I gave him a kiss, pushing the sad thoughts to the back of my head, pretending for at least tonight that the pile of stuff in the living room didn't exist.

Having sex in a tent is not that hard, but when you're suspended three floors up with a six-foot-two man on top of you, it can get downright tricky. So we switched positions and I rode him, hoping that the tent's walls were not in any way transparent. My head kept hitting the metal rods, so I had to bend down, which provided Henry ample access to my breasts. He grasped them in his hands, devouring each one in turn, while I rocked back and forth carefully. I tried to memorize the way he filled me up, the sexy growl he made when I squeezed him extra hard. He was in so deep, he was pressing against my core.

I covered his mouth with my own when I came, afraid to make too much noise should the neighbors overhear, but what I really wanted to do was shout, to rant and rave that it wasn't fair. I had finally found the love of my life but now he had to leave. I pressed all of the emotion into a kiss, knowing that Henry shared it with me, felt it with me. We were nothing if not two parts of a greater whole.

Later, we unzipped the roof canopy and looked up at the stars as we lay wrapped up in each other. The evening air was cool but Henry was warm and chased away the chills brought on by the fear.

"Are you scared?" I asked, playing with his dog tags, trying not to think of what they represented.

"No. This is what I've been training for," he said. "A lot of people will be relying on me to keep them safe."

Then whose job was it to keep Henry safe?

"I'm sure you'll be fine," I said, pushing the thought away. Maybe it would come true if I said it enough.

"Els," he began tentatively. "What do you want this, *us*, to be?"

I twisted my head to look up at him. "What do you want?"

"I want you to be mine only," he said and added with a grin, "and wearing that Lara Croft costume at all times, but for my eyes only."

"Greedy."

He fixed that intense blue gaze on me. "I've waited a hell of a long time for you. I'm not about to share with anyone else."

"I want you all to myself too," I said. "And if anyone tries to steal you from me, I will shank a bitch."

I felt the vibrations through his chest as he chuckled. "So it's settled. You're my girlfriend."

"It's settled," I said with a happy little nod. "What would you have done if I'd said I wanted to see other people?"

He shrugged, his confidence so disarming. "Never even occurred to me."

———————

Henry gently shook me awake from a nightmare, pulling me away from the gunshots and blood. "You were having a bad dream again," he said, rubbing my arm.

"I wasn't screaming, was I?"

"No. You were breathing weird, almost like you were sobbing."

It was early yet and I was still sleepy, but I fought to keep my eyes open if only to keep the gory images away. I couldn't even think about who would comfort me from the bad dreams once Henry left. I guess it would have to be me for a while.

He reached for the watch he'd hung on the tent rod. "Go back to sleep. It's only five."

"Henry," I whispered, pressing a hand to his chest. "Make love to me."

His heart began to race under my palm and I knew what he was thinking, what we were both refusing to acknowledge: that this was the final time we would be making love before he boarded that plane.

His voice broke when he said, "I love you, Elsie." He kissed me as he lifted my leg. I gasped when he pushed his way in, my raw nerves singing as he filled me once more. We made love on our sides, he grasping my hip for leverage as he drove into me. His movements were less gentle, more urgent, and I matched him, trying to prolong the end that would inevitably come. But all too soon, I came shuddering around him, which triggered his own release. He clutched at my hip, gripping me to him as he gasped against my ear.

"I love you so much," I choked out, hugging him so tightly I could barely breathe. "Come back to me."

———————

All too soon, the time came to say good-bye. We stood in the parking lot on base, a motley crew of airmen and their families. Henry held my hand as we stood on the outer edges of the crowd watching people say their good-byes even before the bus arrived to take them to the hangar.

I was keeping my cool relatively well under the circumstances. Every time a sob bubbled up from my chest, I held my breath and counted to five. It was working until I saw a family—mother, father, and their daughter of about four. The woman was the one in uniform and her eyes were already red with tears. She took a deep breath, bent down to her daughter's eye level and told her to be strong for Daddy. That she loved her and would miss her. The child nodded bravely even as her lips trembled. When the woman tried to stand, her daughter grabbed her sleeve. "Mom, don't go," she said in her tiny voice and broke her mother's tear ducts wide open.

I completely lost it.

I turned away from Henry so that he wouldn't have to see my face crumpling, but he knew; he squeezed my hand and pulled me into his side, holding my head against his chest as he protected me one last time. I sobbed into him, trying to breathe in his scent through the thick material of his ABUs. Finally, when the signal to load the bus came, I took a deep breath and gathered myself.

Henry lifted my chin and kissed me tenderly. "I'll be back soon, don't worry," he said with a cocky grin that didn't quite meet his eyes. "Six months will fly by."

"I'll be waiting." I watched him pick up his bags and walk off, craning my neck when he was swallowed into the crowd, trying to catch one last glimpse of the man who had captured my heart and was now taking it to Afghanistan. I didn't see him again until after the bus began to pull away and I saw him waving through the dark window a moment before the bus turned the corner.

And then Henry was gone.

PART TWO

BESIEGE

1

TENDING THE HOME FIRES

Henry Logan was gone. Just like that, the bus turned the corner and he was gone from my sight.

Not going to lie, that was one of the hardest things I've endured.

I drove his Mustang home from base with tears streaming down my face. I didn't care; I'd just said good-bye to my best friend, my roommate, and the love of my life. If that doesn't make me deserving of a moment of blubbering weakness then I don't know what does.

Even the cop who pulled me over for speeding on I-45 took one look at the hot mess that I was and knew. "Coming from base?" he asked.

I nodded, wiping at my face, not wanting him to think that I was turning on the waterworks to get out of a ticket. "Yeah."

"Deployment?"

I nodded again. I was going to get my very first speeding ticket— my first ticket period—on the same day I lost the first love of my life. And thus, I brought balance back to the Force.

"My stepson left today as well," the cop said.

"Sucks, doesn't it?" I asked, sniffling.

He laughed. "Not for me." He looked at my license and Henry's insurance card and handed them back. "I'll let you go with just a warning."

Really? "Really?"

"Deployments are tough," he said. "Just keep it under sixty-five, all right?"

I gave him a smile, his mercy the bright spot in my otherwise bleary day. "Thank you, officer. I will."

———

I dreaded walking into our apartment, and for good reason it turned out, because as soon as I walked inside, the loneliness almost suffocated me, as if Henry's absence sucked out all the oxygen from the building.

"I can do this," I said out loud.

Saturday had barely begun; the whole weekend stretched out for miles in front of me, with wallowing and crying as my unwanted passengers.

Determined not to go down that road, I changed into my running gear and went to Earlywine Park, hoping the running endorphins would do something to lift my mood.

After an hour of running, I didn't feel the high that usually comes after a great workout. Instead I'd successfully exhausted my body so that I could barely stand straight as I took a shower, which only added to the general feeling of gloom that I wore like a second skin. That night, I crawled into Henry's bed, afraid of waking up alone from a nightmare.

I slept on the center of the mattress, hugging his pillow to my chest and inhaling his scent. With my eyes closed, I could almost convince myself that he was sleeping beside me but almost, in this case, just wasn't good enough.

The next six months were going to be hell.

Beth Belnap invited me out to dinner the next night. Her boyfriend, Sam, had also deployed so we were in the same shitty boat with a six-month-long horizon ahead of us. This was the second deployment Beth had endured and had all sorts of nuggets of wisdom to impart.

"It'll get easier, I promise," she said as we sipped our drinks and waited for our dinner.

I nodded, glad to know that someone had been through it before and come out sane. "I hope sooner than later. I'm tired of crying."

She gave me a sympathetic look. "The first time is always the worst."

"Does it get easier at night? Do you miss having him in bed with you?"

Beth raised her eyebrows. "I thought you and Henry were roommates?"

"Oh. I guess you might not know yet," I said, putting down my margarita glass. "But a few days after that night at Tapwerks, Henry told me he loved me and things . . . just kind of happened."

Beth laughed. "Oh my God, I totally called it. When you guys were on the dance floor, I told Sam that there was definitely something going on there. You two were looking at each other with all this sexual tension. It looked like Henry was about to maul you right then and there."

I blushed, remembering the first time I'd ever seen Henry as more than just a brother figure, when he'd pressed himself into me on the dance floor and had uttered innuendo in my ear. Only seven days had elapsed since that night yet it felt like forever ago. "This past week has been . . . intense," I said.

Beth's smile faded. "Then this is extra hard for you. Being so new to the relationship and all," she said. "I went through that with

Sam's first deployment. We'd only been dating a month before he left. It was hell." She patted my hand on the table.

"This past week has been a roller coaster," I said, trying to keep the tears in check. I took a steadying breath and tried a grin. "So, when do you stop crying at the drop of a hat?"

"The first time took about a month, for me at least."

I blew out a breath. "Okay. That seems like a long time," I said. "But at least I'll eventually stop missing him so much, right?"

She shook her head. "I think it's more like you just get mentally tougher, so you learn to avoid dwelling on the fact that he's gone."

"How do I do that?"

"I'm not sure. You just do it. When you start thinking about how much you miss him, just distract yourself. Put on a movie, read a book, do anything. Just don't give any thought to how much you miss him."

"Does that actually work?"

She shrugged. "Sometimes."

———

I didn't hear from Henry until the Tuesday after he left. I tried to take Beth's advice and keep myself occupied but it was impossible to concentrate without knowing Henry had made it to Bagram Air Base safely. I was beginning to think I wouldn't be able to focus on anything for the next six months.

Then on Tuesday morning, at some godawful time, my cell phone began to ring. I was instantly alert and cried into the phone, "Henry?"

"Hey, Els!" Hearing his voice felt like heaven; it caressed down my back and loosened the knot of worry around my heart. "We made it. We're here."

I sat up, glad to finally have some time to talk. "I'm happy to hear that. It's so good to hear your voice."

"You too. How are you?" he asked.

"Absolutely miserable," I said.

"Listen, I have to get going. Other guys have to call home," he said. "I love you, Elsie. I miss you so much already."

"I love you too," I responded, and much too quickly, the call ended. I hugged his pillow to my chest and for the first time in so many days, I finally breathed a tiny sigh of relief. Henry was okay.

Three days down, a bajillion more to go.

———

The first week of deployment was definitely the toughest. The imbalance to my routine was terrifying, and I often fumbled around like I'd forgotten a step. At night I sat in the apartment, feeling so lonely I thought I'd go out of my mind, and watching those sappy romcoms that Henry refused to sit through certainly didn't help—in fact, it had the opposite effect.

My body also physically ached from missing him, a feeling that was wholly new to me. After Jason died I missed him intensely but I never felt an ache in my bones, as if I were walking around with a missing limb, like I was currently experiencing with Henry.

Then it started to get better. Thankfully.

After that initial month, I finally started to sleep in my own bed again. Partly because I missed my pillowtop mattress, but also because I knew I couldn't sleep in Henry's bed forever. It was high time I put on my big-girl panties and sleep in my big-girl bed.

Henry called as often as he could, which amounted to a five-minute call every four or five days, but he emailed almost every day. He mostly talked about the base and his job, but sometimes he'd write out long, graphic emails detailing what he wanted to do to me. Those emails would get me so aroused, I eventually had to go into the back of my closet and break out my stash of battery-operated buddies.

The best part of Henry's emails was always at the end, when he'd write that he loved and missed me, that he couldn't wait to come home to me. I didn't think I'd ever tire of seeing those words.

———

In the third month, the emails stopped. So, too, did the phone calls. I called Beth in a mild state of panic, and she confirmed that she hadn't heard from Sam either.

"But they're probably just on a base comm lockdown or something," she said. "They do that from time to time."

She promised she would call if she heard anything, so I sat on my hands, trying to remain cool. I waited with a sick feeling in the pit of my stomach, that little ball of dread growing with each passing moment.

One night, while I was trying to distract myself with a *Firefly* marathon, my cell phone rang with a call from an unknown Oklahoma number. The caller turned out to be David Novak, Henry's buddy from another squadron on Tinker.

"Hey, Elsie," he said. "How are you doing?"

"I'm okay. Trying to keep busy. You?"

"Doing good. Just got back from a TDY in Vegas."

TDY stood for Temporary Duty, a trip that sometimes lasted a few days, sometimes weeks. "Sounds rough."

"Oh, it was. All that sun, booze, gambling, women. I'm exhausted." He laughed. "Anyway, Logan asked me to check up on you before he left. So this is me checking up on you."

My heart warmed at the thought. "That's sweet. Thanks, I'm fine." I bit my lip, wondering if I was crossing any boundaries, but ultimately decided the question needed to be asked. "Although, I did want to ask if you'd heard anything from Bagram."

Dave was quiet for a long time. Too long.

My heart began to beat at double speed. "Is Henry okay?"

He cleared his throat. "Well, it hasn't been released to the media yet. So I can't tell you."

"It?"

"There was an incident."

The hair rose on my arms. "But is Henry . . . Is he okay?"

Dave sighed. He was in the same squadron that my brother was in, knew that Jason's death hit me hard. "Yeah. He's fine."

I breathed a sigh of relief all the way down to my toes. "Thanks, Dave."

"Just keep an eye out. I'll be able to tell you more about it once the media starts squawking."

"I will. Thanks."

"So, hey, a bunch of us are going out this Friday. Do you want to come?"

"Sure, why not." That's one Friday that I wouldn't have to spend alone.

"The other guys are bringing their girlfriends, so you won't be the only girl," he said.

I smiled, the first real one in so many weeks. "Sounds like fun."

Dave insisted on picking me up on Friday night and I accepted, not really eager to walk around Bricktown in the dark by myself. Everyone was already there when we arrived, and they greeted us with drunken shouts and cheers. I played fast and loose with the alcohol, glad that for once my thoughts were not being monopolized by a certain tall, dark, and sexy man.

"Hey, did you see on the news today?" Kelsie, the wife of one of the captains, asked as we sat around the booth. "The base was attacked."

Dave nudged me with his elbow, letting me know that this was what he had been referring to.

"What happened?" I asked. "I haven't had a chance to watch the news." Honestly, I'd actually been avoiding any coverage on Operation Enduring Freedom for fear of picking up more unfounded fears. Remaining ignorant about the goings-on in Afghanistan meant less ammo for my nightmares.

"A suicide bomber drove a passenger van with a VBIED to the gate and shot the poor guy on duty," Kelsie said.

"VBIED?" I asked.

"Vehicle Borne Improvised Explosive Device," Dave said. "The fucker was killed before he could get on base, but he managed to detonate the bomb and take out the gate and a large portion of the fence. A few of the buildings nearby also sustained damage."

My heart was pounding wildly even as I told myself that Henry was fine. Still, at least one person had been hurt in the attack "Were there any casualties?"

I looked up at Dave, who was nodding solemnly. "One airman was shot and killed, while another lost his leg to flying debris."

I covered my mouth and realized that my hand was trembling. It could have just as easily been Henry at the gate that day.

Dave noticed my immediate change in mood and began to rub my back. "Do you want to get some air?" he whispered.

I nodded and tried a polite smile for the rest of the table. "Sorry, guys. I just need a few moments."

"You okay?" Kelsie asked.

I swallowed hard, feeling the familiar tightness in my chest. "My brother was killed in Afghanistan," I said and excused myself before they could ask questions.

Dave accompanied me outside, standing awkwardly by with his hands in his pockets as I paced the sidewalk.

"You should go inside," I told him, taking deep breaths to calm my nerves. "It's cold out here."

He smiled crookedly. "I'm not about to let you stand out here by yourself." He kicked at a discarded bottle cap on the ground. "I'm sorry about your brother. Jason was a really good guy."

I nodded. "Yeah, he was."

"He was so proud of you, you know."

I looked away, wanting to hide the tears that were threatening to fall. "He talked about me?"

"Yeah, all the time," Dave said. "Logan too. He's always talking about you."

That brought an unexpected smile to my face.

Dave came closer and rubbed my shoulders, a touch that seemed comforting at first, until it went on a little too long. I frowned up at him and opened my mouth to ask what he was doing when he bent down and touched his lips to mine.

I pulled away as if electrocuted. "What—"

Dave held his hands up and took a step back. "I'm sorry."

"What were you doing?"

"I think I was trying to kiss you."

"I know that," I said. "But why?"

"Because I like you?" he said, the end of the sentence lilting up as if he was asking a question.

I paused, wondering if Dave was a slimy jerk or if he was just not aware of the situation. "You do know that Henry and I are together, right?"

His eyes widened, giving me the answer. "Shit. I didn't know." He stuck his hands back in his pockets. "Fuck. Sorry. That jackass should have told me."

I couldn't have agreed more. "Don't worry about it," I said. "Honest mistake. It's his fault for not telling anyone."

"My mistake, really," Dave said with a wry grin. "I should have asked you out sooner."

2

HOMECOMING

The emails resumed, but they didn't sound the same. Gone was the intimacy of his words, replaced by nonchalant, almost robotic descriptions of his life there. I asked about the attack during one phone call but he just evaded the question and suddenly had to go. Since I didn't want any more abrupt ends to the calls, I never brought it up again.

The third, fourth, and fifth months all blurred together. Keeping busy was not the problem; it was trying to keep my mind from straying back to Afghanistan that was tough. Beth's tactic of self-distraction was hard to apply when everything around me reminded me of Henry, from his car keys that hung on the hook to his established seat at the dining table.

I read a ton of books, caught up with friends, ran a lot, and probably wasted too much time on the Internet. I spent many hours at the office, trying to lose myself in work to while away the lonely hours of the night.

Then the final month came and, I swear, time slowed. I felt like I was moving in slow motion, that no matter how I distracted myself, I'd look at the clock and find that only a few minutes had elapsed. It was so much worse than the first month.

The anticipation was killing me. He was so close to coming home, yet still thousands of miles away. In preparation, I tidied up his room, vacuumed every nook and cranny of the apartment, and dusted every surface. I filled the fridge with his favorite food and beer, going so far as buying the bottled olives that he loved so much.

Finally, the most special Wednesday of the entire year arrived. I jumped out of bed with extra spring and took an extra long shower, humming to myself about my boyfriend being back, hey la, hey la. I dressed carefully, then drove to base a whole hour before they were scheduled to arrive. They checked my license at the visitor center, handed me a pink slip, and let me drive through the gate with a knowing smile.

I stood at the designated waiting area with the others. Our excitement was a living, breathing thing, so palpable you could almost reach out and touch it. We looked at one another—wives, girlfriends, family, and friends—with unconcealed excitement bursting all over our faces. Some people had created welcome signs; others held balloons and flowers in their hands. I had only the hopeful heart pinned prominently on my sleeve.

Everybody cheered when the bus appeared from around the corner. We cheered when it drove into the parking lot, and we cheered when it pulled up in front of us, but we were deathly silent when the bus hissed to a stop, as if shushing us.

We all held our collective breaths when the door opened, and I swear, it must have taken five minutes for the first person to step down off that bus, but when he did, a woman squealed from somewhere within the crowd. My eyes remained glued to the bus door as airman after airman stepped down. My heart lurched in my chest every time those tan boots came into view; I thought I'd pass out after about the tenth guy who wasn't Henry.

Then he appeared and, for a few moments, I forgot how to breathe. Henry stepped from the bus and cast his gaze around. From across the sea of people, our eyes met and his sullen face broke out into a smile that lit up his entire face. I honestly don't know how I managed to walk toward him when all of my brain cells were currently fried, but I suddenly found myself standing in front of him. He was within touching distance but I suddenly couldn't figure out what to do with myself.

"Oh, Els." He bent down and buried his face in my neck, holding me tight for a long, wordless while.

I couldn't stop the tears if I tried. Feeling him in my arms again felt like surfacing from a deep ocean and finally taking a breath. I pulled away and held his face in my hands, enjoying the sight of him. He was thinner, the skin under his eyes a little darker, but his blue eyes carried the same intensity as before.

"Will you just come here?" he said with a grin and pulled me to him, our lips mashing together in six months worth of pent-up frustration. When we finally pulled away to breathe, he pressed his forehead to mine and said in that husky, gravelly voice, "God, I've missed you." His thumbs wiped away the tears on my cheeks and he kissed me again.

"I missed you too," I said and hugged him to me.

We walked back to my car hand in hand. He walked around to throw his stuff in the trunk but when I went to open the driver's door, he was suddenly behind me, boxing me in with his arms. He pressed his erection into my back and whispered against my ear, "I can't wait to be inside you again."

I was instantly wet, ready to jump on him then and there, but he was in uniform and we were surrounded by people.

"Get a room," one airman called as he walked by.

"Shut up, Jackson." Henry said with a tight smile.

My face flushed as I dodged out from under his arms. "To be continued," I told him and got into the driver's seat before I did something I would later regret.

Henry, however, was incorrigible. As soon as we drove off base, his hand landed on my thigh, then slid upward, warming the skin in its wake.

"We're going to crash, Henry," I warned.

"That's okay," he said, his fingers inching under my skirt, sliding upward ever so slowly. He gasped. "Oh my God, you're not wearing underwear."

I chuckled and flushed and throbbed all at the same time. "Surprise."

"Pull over," he ordered.

"Where?"

"I don't care, just take the next exit," he said, nudging my legs apart. His fingers slipped along my folds before sliding inside me.

I let out a hiss between my teeth when he found that most sensitive spot and began to rub it. The car might have swerved a little.

"Henry," I said, gripping the steering wheel so tight my knuckles were turning white. "Not right now."

"Yes now."

"Wait till we get home."

"I've waited long enough. Pull over."

I squeezed my legs together to keep his hands from moving but those damned, delicious fingers kept flicking higher. I tried to remain relaxed to fight off the impending orgasm, but months of deprivation had made me so desperate that my muscles clenched around his fingers of their own accord.

"Do you really want your first time back in a tiny car, on a dirt road?" I asked, finding it hard to catch my breath. It's a wonder I even managed to keep my foot on the pedal at all. This was dangerous.

"I don't care. I just want to bury myself inside you."

I groaned at his words. I was so close.

An exit came into view and I swerved onto it, the last of my resolve completely gone. Half a mile off the highway, I parked in the lot of an abandoned gas station in a heavily wooded area.

As soon as I set the gear into park, Henry grabbed my hips and pulled me up and over the center console. I performed a minor miracle by straddling his large body in the passenger seat of my narrow Prius. His hands roamed everywhere, digging his fingers into my ass cheeks as he ravaged me with kisses. My fingers made swift work of undoing his pants and I gripped his shaft, guiding the tip to my entrance. His hands squeezed my hips, urging me to take him all at once, but I took my time sliding down, relishing the feel of him stretching me once again.

"Elsie," he whispered against my neck. He groaned when he was all the way in. Henry was home.

He lifted my shirt up and unclasped my bra, burying his face in my breasts. "I love you," he said through a mouthful of nipple.

I grasped the back of his head and kissed him roughly as I slid up and down on his engorged member. I ground my hips into his and experienced a brand-new sensation that quickly sent me reeling toward the edge. Henry clutched my hips once more and took control, slamming me onto his lap over and over.

I threw my head back and came with a force that took my breath away, waves of pleasure streaking through the very center of me.

A few strokes later, Henry gave a shout, his rear lifting up off the seat as he climaxed.

We sat there panting, his face still pressed against my chest. "I can't believe I lived without that for so long," he said against my pounding heart.

All I could do was nod in agreement. We'd survived.

———

Beth said that when Sam came home from his first deployment it was as if nothing had changed, but from the moment Henry walked into our apartment, he looked out of place. He dropped his bags by the front door and ventured into the living room with a bewildered look on his face.

"Something's changed," he said with a frown.

"What? I haven't moved anything." I'd purposefully kept things as they were, partly because I wanted to preserve his memory and partly because I didn't want him to feel like a stranger in his own home.

He walked over to the mantel and picked up a new picture frame, the only thing that had changed in the entire place. "This is new," he said, gazing at the picture of him, Jason, and me when we'd gone skiing in Colorado a few years ago.

"I've always loved that one," I said, walking over and hugging him from behind. "I figured we needed some pictures around here."

He put down the frame and held my hands closer to his chest as he took a deep breath. "It's so weird to be back here."

I pressed my cheek against his back, taking in his scent. "It feels good from this angle."

He turned in my arms with a wicked smile. "Let's see if my bed feels the same," he said and lifted me up off my feet. I felt light-headed as he carried me into his room and laid me on his bed. His eyes roamed all over me, taking me in like a blind man who can see again. He began to unbutton his gray ABU coat, his eyes never leaving my face.

I found it hard to breathe as I watched him pull his tan shirt over his head and step out of his pants. He stood before me, completely at ease with his masculine nakedness.

My eyes flew all over his body, not knowing where to land. His chest and abdominals were more defined and his arms were definitely larger, among other things that also seemed to have increased in size.

I crawled over the bed and made my way to him, and with a saucy smile, I took hold of his penis and licked its tip.

He drew in a breath and tangled his fingers in my hair.

I took him into my mouth slowly, driving him crazy with anticipation. When his tip nudged my throat, I wound my fingers around the rest of him and began a gentle sucking and tugging motion.

He looked at me, his blue eyes blazing with fierce desire and something else, something that looked like possessiveness. His fingers pushed at the back of my head, urging me to go deeper, faster. I was only too happy to oblige, enjoying the salty taste of him, the feel of his velvety skin against my tongue. I had dreamed of doing this very thing to him for months, but the reality was so much better.

He tensed and pulled away abruptly, grabbing me by the shoulders and pulling me up and off the bed. He kissed me as he peeled the clothes away from my body with ferocity.

Then he spun me around and bent me over the bed, and I felt his member nudging at me a second before he slammed into me.

I gave a shout at the exquisite invasion, at his forceful gesture. This was not a man who wanted gentleness. Henry was a man deprived; he wanted everything all at once and he wasn't going to be polite about it.

The thought sent a bolt of excitement through me, the implicit understanding of safety mixed with the promise of danger.

His fingers wound in my hair and pulled back, twisting my head around so he could kiss me. That simple gesture was so unlike him that it drove me wilder, made me buck against him in an effort to get more of this hungry male.

In all our years knowing each other, I never would have thought Henry had this in him, this aggressiveness, and, admittedly, it was really turning me on.

He curled over me and positioned one hand between my legs, his fingers massaging my clit rapidly as he pounded into me from behind. It didn't take long before I was coming, screaming into the quilt as wave after wave of pleasure crashed over me, his fingers still moving, wresting every ounce of pleasure out of me. Henry clutched me against his chest and hammered into me one last time before he went rigid, groaning his release against the back of my neck.

We collapsed on the bed, his mass a pleasant weight on me, like an anchor keeping me in place. But all too soon, he pushed up with his arms and planted kisses on my back as he slowly pulled out.

When I came back from the bathroom, he was lying on his back with his arms folded behind his head and a satisfied look on his face. He gathered me into his side and let out a long sigh as I wrapped an arm around his waist.

"It's good to have you home," I whispered, my breath ruffling the dark hairs on his chest.

"It's good to be home," he said, kissing my head. "You have no idea how many times I dreamed of doing that to you, pounding you on the bed like that."

My face flushed at how uninhibited I had been and how much I had liked it. "What else did you dream about?"

"That was it," he said evasively, then jumped out of bed. "Hey, I have gifts for you." He came back with one duffel bag and started rummaging inside. He laid a few things on the bed and sat down beside it. "Here's one," he said, handing me a dark blue rock. "The stone is lapis lazuli and came from a mine in the Badakhshan province of Afghanistan."

I flipped the smooth stone over in my palm. "Thank you."

"It's to replace that pebble you gave me before I went off to college," he said.

"I remember that beach pebble," I said. "Whatever happened to it?"

"I lost it," he said, looking abashed. "Or rather, my roommate in college threw it out."

I made an indignant noise as he handed me a piece of pink fabric, folded up into a small square. I unfolded what turned out to be a scarf, admiring the intricate gold thread designs, and was surprised to find a small pouch nestled inside. I pulled out a pair of violet-blue earrings and a matching necklace. "Out of the same kind of stone?" I asked, slipping on the teardrop-shaped earrings.

"Yes. The vendor told me that Cleopatra's eye shadow was made out of ground lapis lazuli." He slipped the necklace around my neck, which was a thick chain with a three-teardrop design. His eyes took me in for a long while before he finally said, "Blue is your color."

I smiled. "Like the color of your eyes." I held his gaze, wishing I knew what the hell was going through his mind.

He swallowed, then said, "You're different."

Out of everything, I was definitely not expecting that. "I am? How?"

"I don't know. You always just seemed so restless before, and now . . ." He ran a finger along my jaw. "It's like a stillness has descended over you."

I must have looked heartbroken because he quickly added, "I mean that in a good way."

I lay back into the pillows and chewed on his words. The past six months had forced me to become independent. I had always had Jason or Henry to depend on, but without either of them, I'd been forced to rely on me. It had been a sobering, empowering, lonely experience. "I guess I've changed," I finally said.

I looked up at him and studied the dark circles under his eyes. I wanted to point out that he was different as well, as if a shadow was blanketing him, but didn't think it would be received well. So I just put away the gifts and pulled him back onto the bed, hoping that the morning light would bring us back to ourselves.

———

I woke up shivering some time later. I burrowed under the blanket, trying to locate Henry's warmth but he was nowhere to be found.

When I opened my eyes, I found myself alone in a dark room and for one terrifying moment, I thought I was in a new nightmare. Then I heard the front door slam shut and the jingle of keys as they landed on the countertop. The bedroom door squeaked open and Henry peered in.

I sat up, pushing unruly hair out of my face, and turned on a lamp. "Hey, where did you go?"

He came inside and sat on the bed. He was wearing a black moisture-wicking sweatshirt, shorts, and tennis shoes. "I couldn't sleep so I went running."

"What time is it?"

He looked at his watch. "Nearly midnight."

"And you're not sleepy?"

He shrugged as he pulled off his clothes and walked to the bathroom. "I'm just jet-lagged."

"Henry?"

He looked over his shoulder, the bathroom light illuminating the lines on his face. "Yeah?"

"Everything okay?" I asked. He still hadn't told me about the attack on the base; I was beginning to wonder if he would talk about it at all. I'd read about PTSD and its symptoms, hoping to be ready should Henry be affected by the attack, but so far, I still wasn't sure. I wished there was some sort of litmus test I could give him, to get a definitive answer so I could formulate a plan of attack, but all I had was the man himself and he wasn't in the mood to disclose that information.

"I'm good," he said and closed the bathroom door.

3

PROBLEMS IN LOGISTICS

The next day, after getting ready for work, I went to the kitchen to prepare breakfast. Henry came out of his bedroom a few minutes later already in his ABU pants and a tan undershirt. He placed his jacket on the back of the chair and headed to the coffeepot.

"I've already poured some out," I said, cracking eggs into the pan. I turned to grab the salt and pepper and ran into his back. He dodged out of the way, but accidentally hit me with the drawer as he pulled out some forks.

"Sorry," he said, massaging my hip.

I doubled over as his fingers brushed against a ticklish spot and the spatula in my hand smacked him in the chest. "Sorry," I said, reaching for some paper towels to dab at the mess.

He looked down at his shirt, at the oil stain that was already blooming on the cotton fabric, with an unreadable expression. He stepped out of the kitchen and pulled the shirt off, shaking his head. "Damn, that was my last clean undershirt," he said and strode off to his bathroom.

I looked around the kitchen, unable to figure out why I suddenly felt relieved to be alone. Taking advantage of Henry's absence, I quickly cooked the omelets, made toast, and set everything out on the table. By the time Henry emerged from the bathroom, everything was ready. After putting his shirt in the dryer, he stood at the table with his hands on his hips.

"You all right?" I asked, sipping my coffee.

He frowned. "You did it all without me."

A pang of regret shot through me. Henry and I had always made this breakfast together before he left for Afghanistan but today it seemed easier to just do it all myself. "I guess I got used to doing everything alone."

"Next time, I can help." He sat down and took a sip of coffee. "But this looks good," he added and we ate.

———————

By the next morning, I'd figured out that I needed to relinquish some control in the kitchen. I left the coffee untouched, hoping that he would figure it out, but he stood at the other side of the counter and watched me with wary eyes.

I guess he needed an embossed invitation or something. "Can you do the coffee, please?"

He grinned and entered the fray, grabbing the can of coffee beans and preparing the coffeemaker. It took some time and a few bumps, but we finally learned how to move around each other again, as if retracing the steps to our little daily dance routine. When we sat down to eat, we raised our steaming mugs of coffee, celebrating our little victory with knowing smiles.

———————

While our breakfast routine was back on track, Henry's sleep schedule was still off-kilter. He continued to toss and turn at night, and soon my own sleep also began to suffer. The only time I fell into a deep sleep was when he'd climb out of bed at four a.m. to go running, when the bed would finally be still and I could relax.

One night, I decided to try something different to see if it would help. I kissed him good night in the living room then headed to my room.

Henry was right at my heels.

"Why the hell are you in here?" he asked, watching from the door as I crawled under my duvet.

"If I remember correctly, this is *my* bed."

He rolled his eyes. "I mean, why aren't you sleeping in my room?"

"To let you get some sleep," I stated simply. I fluffed my pillow and lay down.

"It's just jet lag," he said, walking across the room and standing over me with arms crossed over his chest.

I gave him a skeptical look. "Jet lag doesn't last this long." I sighed. "Look, I just want to see if my presence, or lack thereof, will help you sleep better."

He raised one eyebrow. "If you think that sleeping by myself will do me good," he said, throwing aside my covers, "then you don't know me very well at all." And with one swift movement, he lifted me up in his arms and stole me out of my room.

In his room, he deposited me on his bed and fell in beside me. "You're not the reason why I can't sleep, okay?" he said.

"Then what's bothering you?" I asked. When he said nothing, I whispered, "Hey, let's talk."

"About what?"

"Whatever. Anything you want."

He shifted so that he was looking at the ceiling and no longer at me. He said nothing, only turned off the bedside lamp.

"Maybe about what happened over there," I said, hoping the cloak of darkness would give him the courage to speak.

The pillow rustled when he shook his head. "Just give me some time, Els. I just need to process."

I wasn't exactly sure what processing entailed, but I gave him the benefit of the doubt, as I always did, and hoped that it wouldn't be long before he was back to normal.

Sometime in the early hours, the buzzing of his phone pulled me from sleep. "Your phone," I croaked, touching Henry's arm.

All of a sudden, Henry wrenched his arm away, forming a fist as it flew up to protect his face. He sat up with a start, breathing heavily, his muscles coiled for attack.

I lay beside him, frozen in place, my brain still trying to process what the hell had just taken place.

His head jerked to the buzzing on the nightstand. He finally relaxed when he reached over to turn the phone off.

"Are you okay?" I whispered, wanting to touch him yet too afraid to move.

He turned to me as his hands searched in the dark for my face. "I didn't hurt you, did I?"

I shook my head, my heart still thudding wildly.

"I'm sorry if I scared you," he said gently. He pressed a kiss to my cheek, then climbed out of bed, pulling on his clothes for another long morning run, not bothering to explain what had him on edge.

———

Thus began our new normal. Henry was always up early, if he slept at all, and ran laps at the park. He was always back by the time I climbed out of bed to get ready for work. We'd eat breakfast together and kiss good-bye at the parking lot.

In the afternoons, after coming home from work, he'd give me a kiss before heading off to the gym for a few hours, making me feel like I was living alone again. Some nights he didn't return until I was climbing into bed—my own—and he would pull the caveman stunt by throwing me over his shoulder and taking me to his room. The fun of it wore off after a while.

Even though we had plenty of sex, I felt detached from him in a way I've never felt before. I'd always taken pride in being able to read his moods, but now I was mystified by the sudden veil that would lay across his features, often at the most random times. I felt like I was standing on a dock, reaching out as far as I could, and Henry was in a boat that was drifting away with the morning tide.

So I did the only thing I could to still feel connected to him—I would wrap my arms around him, press my cheek to his back, and just thank God that Henry was alive, that he was safe, and that Afghanistan didn't take him from me too.

One day, I received an envelope with Henry's handwriting on it mixed in with the junk mail. It was addressed to me and post-marked in March, at the beginning of the deployment. I couldn't decide which was more surprising: the fact that it was delivered so late or that it arrived here at all.

I didn't know why my fingers were shaking as I gently tore open the envelope, but I felt jittery, unsure of what I was in for.

Dear Elsie,

So here it is, your very first romantic war letter! I still can't believe I'm writing you like this, in such an intimate way. I've always wanted to write you a love letter but now it's legit, now I can actually send it off with due reason.

We arrived a week ago after a hellacious series of plane rides. It sucked. We got halfway here but somewhere over the Atlantic, there was a problem with the plane and we had to go back to Bal-timore. So we had the distinct pleasure of sitting in a People Mover on a runway for six hours, not able to go into the terminal because we hadn't gone through security. Then we stopped in Ire-land at four a.m., where they opened the bar for us for twenty minutes while we refueled (yay Guinness!). Then we flew to Cyprus where we stayed in the plane for six hours, and from there we flew to Kuwait City, then finally, we caught a convoy to Bagram Air Base. All in all, the trip took forty-six horrendous hours.

I would much rather have spent those forty-six hours in bed with you.

So life at Bagram Air Base is not so bad. It was information overload the first few days, but now my team and I have the hang of it. I oversee the airmen who guard the base, while I myself go to a lot of meetings and briefings. The food in the chow hall isn't half bad (it's not half good either) but beer here is plentiful. The only problem is that it's nonalcoholic beer. It's pure torture but we drink it anyway. I will be such a lightweight by the time I come home.

I've found that we have a lot of free time here. Most guys watch movies, read, hang out. One of my guys, Hanson, is learning how to play the guitar. I run a lot and go to the gym. I'm hoping to be ripped by the time I get back to you. I know how much you like to touch my muscles, one in particular. ;)

I miss you. I didn't think it was possible to miss someone this much. I think that look on your face as the bus drove away will forever be embedded in my brain. I hate that I'm putting you through all of this unnecessary worry and pain. I know that my telling you my feelings right before I left was selfish, but I just couldn't leave without saying anything. I couldn't bear it if I were stuck here day after day, while you were back there not knowing that someone loves you with all of their being.

I love you, Elsie. I've been crazy about you for as long as I can remember. Every douchey thing I've done to you in the past, everything I did to keep you from other guys, that was just me trying to save you for myself. But something always held me back, whether it was Jason, or that scary look your dad gets, or maybe it was just the thought that if we're together too soon, we would end up ruining what could be in the future. So I waited for the perfect time, and waited and waited. Obviously, I couldn't wait anymore. I wouldn't say a week before a deployment was the perfect time, but sometimes the truth has a way of coming out whether you want it to or not.

Do you remember the first time I came back from college? You told me I'd gained the freshman fifteen and I told you you'd gained the junior-junk-in-the-trunk. The look on your face was hysterical, but you really got me back when you just wiggled that ass at me as you walked away. You thought I was mad at you because I rushed home. I was actually just trying to hide my hard-on!

I'm laughing right now as I think about that. I think that's why I was so drawn to you from the beginning—you were the goodness and light when my life was so full of darkness. And you really know how to tickle my funny bone (insert other bone joke here).

You are the sweetest, kindest person I know, and even if we weren't together, I'd still think that. I still can't believe the past week before my deployment really happened. My biggest teen fantasy has been fulfilled.

You have no idea how hard it's been, watching you parade around our apartment in only a towel or when you wear shirts without a bra. You thought I didn't notice, but trust me, guys have a sixth sense when it comes to breasts and the amount of fabric covering them. But I didn't want to make you feel uncomfortable, so I tried to ignore you and your innocent seductions, until you sexy-danced with me at the bar. That night I knew I couldn't hide my feelings anymore, couldn't pretend that you're just my figurative little sister. Basically, I couldn't keep my hands off you any longer. That was a dangerous game you played, but I guess, in the end it paid off.

I'm in pain here. I'm in a constant state of arousal because you are always in the back of my mind, teasing me in that way that you do. I love being inside you, feeling you tighten around me. Somebody needs to bottle that feeling and sell it because it's fucking fantastic and I'm not sharing you with anyone, so.

These six months are going to be hell. I'm going to ravage you a hundred different ways when I get home. Count on that.

I love you, Elsie. I can't say it enough. I'm a very lucky guy to be coming home to you.

Henry

My tears landed on the lined paper as I folded it up, feeling like I'd had a glimpse of the past, to what Henry used to be. It made me physically ache to see the stark differences between the two men, to know that the man in this letter wasn't the same one that came back.

I hugged the paper to my chest, hope renewing me. Here was proof, a map to the man I had fallen in love with, and I would find a way back to him no matter what.

————

One Friday night, after a particularly trying week, we went to Tapwerks to belatedly celebrate his homecoming. I invited everyone I could think of, including Beth, Sam, and Dave. In the end, there were about nine of us, all standing around a table and talking over the loud music.

I kept glancing up at Henry, too occupied with his enjoyment to really enjoy the atmosphere myself. But he seemed content, laughing and joking around with his buddies, so for a moment, I allowed myself to hope that maybe all he needed was a night out with friends to restore him back to himself.

I could really be naïve sometimes.

I'd almost forgotten the Dave incident, being too consumed by Henry, but Dave apparently hadn't. He stood as far away from me as possible and refused to look at me, probably under the impression that if he didn't acknowledge my presence, then that kiss never happened.

When Henry went to the bathroom, Dave pulled me away from the table and asked if I was going to tell Henry what had happened.

"It's up to you," I told him, filled with the happy buzz that came with good friends and good drinks. "Either way, I think he'll be fine."

"But you're his girlfriend," he said with a frown.

"It wasn't a big deal," I insisted, waving the issue away. "Really."

"What's not a big deal?"

We both turned to find Henry standing beside us, his eyes flicking back and forth between Dave and me.

Dave shrugged. "Nothing, man. I was just asking Elsie if she wanted another drink," he said and walked off toward the bar.

I couldn't bear to feel the weight of Henry's stare, so I excused myself and headed to the bathroom, mentally kicking myself. I should have just told him right then instead of avoiding the question like a guilty idiot.

I emerged from the ladies bathroom a few minutes later, resolved to tell Henry everything, when a pair of hands grabbed me from behind and pulled me into a dark alcove. Hands flattened over my mouth and I was pressed against the wall, my heart thumping right through my chest to the painted concrete. I struggled, tried to push away from the wall, but I was pinned into submission by a large body.

I opened my mouth to scream when a voice whispered against my ear, "It's me."

My body relaxed at the same time Henry loosened his hold. I twisted my head to look at him. "What the hell are you doing?"

"Interrogation," he said with a chuckle. His hand slid from my stomach down into the waistband of my jeans. Before I could ask him what he meant, he rubbed his hand over my panties, making the fabric damp with my arousal. "Does this feel good?" he asked huskily.

I melted onto his hand, enjoying the sensation but not getting nearly enough. "Yes, more."

He flipped me around to face him. I wrapped one leg around his waist just as he began to grind his hard length into me, the pleasure muted through too many layers of clothing. I tried to kiss him, to get more of him, but he dipped his head and kissed my neck the way I liked. "What were you and Dave talking about?" he said with his teeth on my earlobes.

I closed my eyes, unable to think past the haze of desire he had me under. It seemed like such an innocuous question that the red flags didn't go up immediately. "It's nothing. Just what happened a few months ago."

Henry kept nuzzling me as he asked, "What happened a few months ago?"

I moaned when his erection hit me in a particularly tender spot. "It was nothing."

Henry pulled away, his face completely still except for the storm in his eyes. "What happened?" he asked again, his jaw tightening.

I grasped the back of his head and tried to pull him in for a kiss but he resisted.

"Damn it, Elsie, tell me."

I sighed. "He kissed me."

"What?" Henry set my leg down and took a step back, looking at me as if I were a stranger. "Dave kissed you?"

"He didn't know we were dating," I said quickly.

"That peckerhead kissed you?"

"Yes, but it was nothing. Just lack of information."

Henry turned on a heel and took off, leaving me suddenly cold and bewildered.

I ran after him and rounded the corner just in time to see Henry pull Dave away from the bar by the collar and punch him in the face. I dove in between them, somehow still hoping to salvage the night.

Sometimes optimism can be my biggest weakness.

Henry pulled me behind him as Dave regained his footing.

Dave touched the blood on his lips and wiped it with a shirt-sleeve. "I take it Elsie told you."

"Yeah, she told me," Henry said, huffing.

Dave seemed relaxed under the circumstances. He just shook his head and said, "I'm sorry, man. It was a mistake."

"A mistake is asking you to watch over my girlfriend."

"You always said she was like your little sister," Dave said, motioning to me. "I didn't know."

"Well, now you know," Henry said, his hands fisting at his sides. "You gonna fucking kiss her again?"

Dave held his hands up. "Look, man, you got your dig in. I deserve it. Let's leave it at that."

"Come on, let it go," I said, holding tightly on to Henry's arm.

He turned to me with a chilly look that froze me in place, then turned back to Dave. "Stay away from her, Novak," he spat out before wrapping a possessive arm around my shoulders and leading me away. I twisted away and mouthed an "I'm sorry" to Dave and, with a heavy sigh, followed Henry out the door.

4

SHOCK AND AWE

Throughout our teenage years, Henry was always there, like a shadow looming over everything I did. For the most part his presence wasn't an intrusion, more like a comforting blanket. I knew I was safe with an older brother and his best friend always watching out for me.

Sometimes, though, he could be such an overbearing jackass, even more than Jason. One night in particular, Henry crossed the line and caused a rift in our friendship that spanned two weeks. It was during the homecoming dance of my sophomore year, when I'd gone with a senior named John. Henry, Jason, and the rest of the football players were also in attendance with their own dates.

John was the second-string quarterback and was good-looking. He wasn't as popular as the other first-stringers, obviously, but he knew how to charm the pants off a girl, or so I'd heard.

I was actually kind of nervous that night, worried that he thought I would put out after the dance. I wouldn't say I was a prude, but well, I was still holding on to my V-card, still waiting for the perfect guy to come along and sweep me off my feet. John, as nice as he was, just wasn't that guy.

Still, try he did. We were on the dance floor, swaying to a song by the group 98 Degrees, my arms around his neck while his hands were on my waist and sliding slowly down.

I gulped when they reached their intended destination. "John," I said in warning, tugging his arms up higher.

"You just feel so good, babe," he said against my ear, and in that moment I could see why most girls went gaga over him. John had a way of making you feel like the sexiest girl in the world. "You have such a nice ass."

Well yes, I did have a nice rear. "But people can see."

He dipped his head and touched his lips to my jaw and my knees just about buckled. His kisses felt so good as they traveled down to my neck and his hands returned to my butt, and even though I didn't really want to go all the way, I at least wanted to get partly there. So I let him grope me, right in the middle of the dance floor of our high school gym.

My eyes were closed and I was enjoying the sensations of John, when all of a sudden he was ripped away from me. I opened my eyes to find John stumbling backward, Henry standing off to the side with a murderous look on his face.

"What the hell, Logan?" John shouted when he regained his balance.

Henry ignored him and turned to me, his entire face flushed, but before he could say anything, John grabbed him by the arm. Henry pushed him away and John pushed back, neither boy wanting to throw the first punch since two students had been expelled for fighting just the week before.

A crowd gathered around us, and I swear, I must have blushed ten shades of red.

"You were practically molesting her in front of the whole school," Henry shouted.

"It's not molesting if she wanted it!" John yelled back.

Jason pushed his way into the center and that was about the time

I decided I'd had enough. I turned away and dove into the crush of people behind me, hoping enough egos were being flung around that nobody would notice I was gone. I made it as far as the hallway before Henry and Jason caught up with me.

"What the hell was that about?" Jason asked. He touched my arm and looked me over. "Was he hurting you?"

"No!" I cried. "We were just dancing when Henry came and ruined the night."

Henry shot me an incredulous look. "What? He was fucking manhandling you out there."

I stomped my foot. "He was not!"

Henry's nostrils flared and his jaw muscles worked as we stared each other down.

"So let me get this straight," Jason said, looking at the both of us. "You and John were dancing like horny toads, and Henry put a stop to it. Is that right?"

Henry gave a curt nod.

Jason snorted. "You two are ridiculous. Like children," he said and walked off, shaking his head, leaving Henry and me alone to fight our own battle.

Henry's eyes were nearly black in the dim hallway as he glared at me. "You shouldn't have let him do that."

I was fighting back tears when I said, "We were just dancing."

"Now the whole school will see that you're easy."

My heart stopped and my mouth dropped open. I felt like I'd been slapped.

I wanted to tell him that his words were hurtful and untrue but I couldn't bring myself to speak, so I just turned and stomped off toward the exit.

"Elsie. I didn't mean it like that," he called after me, but I was done. He was dead to me.

"I hate you," I said and flipped him off over my shoulder.

———

The ride home from Tapwerks was tense. Henry drove, and even though alcohol usually made me chatty, the night's events had actually stunned me into silence. I found my words again as soon as we were behind the apartment door, and boy, did I intend to use them. "What the hell was that?" I demanded, rounding on him.

Henry just gave me a weary look. "He shouldn't have been kissing on you."

"That's not what happened and you know it."

"Do I? How do I know you didn't actually sleep together and you're just downplaying it?"

My hands itched to slap him on that jealous face of his but I held my fists at my sides. I'd seen enough violence for one night. "You'd better choose your next words carefully, Henry Mason Logan," I said in the most even tone I could muster. "Because I don't appreciate being called a lying whore."

"I didn't call you—"

I fixed him with a glare that could have fried a thousand eggs. I wanted to remind him of that homecoming dance, of his careless words that had almost ended our friendship, but the look on his face told me I didn't have to.

"That's not what I was saying," he said, looking absolutely wretched.

"Then what *are* you saying?" I asked, throwing my hands up in frustration. "I don't know what's going on in that head of yours anymore." Somewhere along the road, I had lost Henry's frequency and hearing nothing but static was starting to drive me insane.

He sat on the arm of the couch and shook his head. "Nothing. I'm not saying anything," he said. "I'm fine. We're fine."

"You are not fine. The Henry I knew never came back from Afghanistan."

I shouldn't have said it. I wanted to take the words back immediately, even before they registered in his brain and hurt spilled out all over his face. He rose to his full height, his face red and jaw clenched but he said nothing. He merely stood there and glared at me.

Fear seeped into my muscles and forced me a step back. He was so angry, so alien to me in that moment that I felt like I was faced with a stranger. "Do you have PTSD?" I breathed.

His head snapped up. "Hell no. Why would you even think that?"

"Then what the fuck is going on?" I asked, completely losing it, no longer caring if the neighbors heard. Henry's anger had infected me, had seeped into my brain and turned everything red. Maybe if I yelled hard enough, Henry would come to his senses. "Are you done with us? Do you want to break up, is that it?"

"No!" He grabbed me by the shoulders, an anguished look on his face. "Why the hell would you even ask that?"

"Then what the hell is your damage?"

He released me and paced, all scowl and coiled muscle, a terrifying vision of a man at a loss. "I don't know, okay? I just . . . I'm just so angry. I'm just fucking furious. I want to kill that motherfucker that killed my best friend," he said, piercing the air repeatedly with a finger. "And I want to put back together that asshole who blew up the gate and killed Jones and mangled up Hanson's leg just so I can tear him apart limb from limb with my bare hands. And I'm mad because you let Dave-fucking-Novak kiss you while I'm off defending the country. And I'm mad at my mom and dad for being such shitty parents that I had to grow up in someone else's house. And I'm fucking pissed off with myself for punching a friend and potentially ruining my career."

He held a fist up to his forehead, holding me in place with his gaze. "And I'm furious with myself for treating you like shit. You deserve so much more, Elsie."

My heart ached for him, for the uncertainty that clouded his features. "I deserve what I want. And I want you."

His eyes searched my face. "Why?" he asked in a broken voice.

Tears rolled down my cheeks as I stared at this roughly drawn replica of the man I once knew. This was not the proud, confident Henry I fell in love with; but what if this insecure man was all that was left?

I walked over to him and wrapped my arms around his body, holding him in place. He bowed his head and whispered his apologies into my hair. "I don't want to lose you too, Elsie."

I squeezed him tighter, my tears soaking into his shirt. "I would go to hell and back for you, Henry. You're not going to lose me." I craned my neck and grasped the sides of his face. "And I want you because you are good and honest. You're brave, smart, funny, and sexy. I'm with you because loving you comes naturally to me, like breathing in air."

He wound his fingers around my hair and fisted it at the nape of my neck. I looked up at him boldly, letting him know that I was not going to flinch at the first sign of trouble. I opened my mouth to speak but he crushed his lips to mine, kissing every thought out of my head.

Suddenly our hands were all over, unbuttoning and tugging and throwing articles of clothing across the room. With his hands under my butt, he lifted me up against the living room wall and plunged into me. I wrapped my legs around his waist and urged him deeper, and he responded by thrusting harder, faster. I could feel him building up, his breathing becoming more labored against my ear, but I couldn't focus, couldn't wrap my mind around our angry sex. A voice in my head whispered that we shouldn't be doing this, yet here we were, panting into each other like dogs in heat.

So I tried to clear my mind and focus on the here and now, but I couldn't stop the image of Henry punching Dave from playing on a loop in my mind. The complete lack of control and regard on Henry's face as he hit one of his closest friends clutched at my heart and refused to let go.

Henry pushed into me one last time as he came, not making a sound, only breathing hard against my neck.

After some time, he loosened his hold and let me down gently. "I'm sorry," he said, doing up his jeans and refusing to meet my eyes. Whatever it was that he was apologizing for, I was never able to find out because he said nothing else and just walked out the front door.

5

PEACE TALKS

Henry was not in my bed when I awoke the next morning. I threw an arm over my eyes, hoping to shield myself from the sunshine peering through the wood blinds but there was no going back to sleep for me. Not with everything that happened last night fresh on my brain.

I crawled out of bed and dug around in my desk drawer until I found his letter. I sat on the computer chair and read it over for the hundredth time, clinging to the idea that I could somehow find a way to break down the wall of rage he'd built and find the old Henry on the other side. I had no clue how to even begin but I was ready to try anything.

Henry came home around noon with an apology sandwich from Subway and my favorite: oatmeal-raisin guilt cookies. Henry and I ate on the floor against the couch in silence, just watching the news. Even after we'd finished our meals we continued sitting there, both unwilling to walk away without discussing last night's events.

"Did you run this morning?" I asked, picking at the carpet between my legs.

"No. I went to see Dave."

I looked up at him in surprise. "And?"

"We talked it over. He told me what happened."

I waited but didn't really expect the apology. Still, it would have been nice if it had come.

"Then I went to see the commander."

"On a Saturday?"

"Yeah, he was at his son's soccer game." He took a big gulp from a water bottle. "I told him about the altercation. He asked me if I needed to see a counselor for PTSD."

I wanted to yell "I told you so!" but didn't think it would help the situation, so I left the words unsaid to float around with the dust motes in the sunshine. "So what now?"

Henry picked at the seam of his jeans. "It's tricky. If I go see a military therapist, it'll go on my record that I have PTSD and my top-secret clearance will get taken away."

"Can you get it back?"

"Eventually. It will take a while, though. So in that time, I won't be able to do my job." He sighed. "And when I don't do my job, my OPR—the officer performance report—will look like shit. And then I'll get passed over during the next promotion board."

"Oh. What are you going to do?"

He looked at me then, his eyes conveying a million emotions. "What do *you* think I should do?"

"Why are you asking me?"

"I can't think of anyone else that this affects more," he said, grasping my hand. "So?"

The naïve girl in me hoped that my love alone was enough to fix whatever was wrong with Henry, but the pragmatic girl knew that sometimes love just wasn't enough. "I want you to let go of that anger that's built up inside, and if it means you have to talk to a therapist, then so be it."

He frowned, doubt coloring his face, but he nodded anyway. "If that's what you want."

I wanted to tell him that I didn't want his career to suffer but hidden in the most shadowy recesses of my brain was a voice whispering that Henry might never have to deploy again if he was diagnosed with PTSD. But what kind of a person would I be if I ruined a career that he'd worked hard for, that brought him great pride? "If you talk to a therapist outside of the military, does your commander have to know?" I asked.

Henry chewed on my words. "No, I don't think he does."

"Then I want you to do that."

He finally looked at me as his lips pulled up into a wry grin. "Dave told me that my one redeeming quality is you."

"Well, he's right," I said. "Count yourself lucky."

Henry leaned over and planted a light kiss on my lips. "I do," he said. "I'm sorry about last night. About everything."

"I forgave you the moment you gave me that cookie," I said, hoping to lighten the mood.

He shook his head. "No, I mean it. I don't want you to ever be afraid of me."

My heart sped up. "I don't want that either."

"And I'm sorry for running out on you like that. I didn't—"

I pressed a finger to his lips. "Stop apologizing," I said. "Just start doing."

"Yes, ma'am," he said with a mischievous glint in his eyes. He grasped the back of my head and pulled me in for an all-consuming kiss, setting me afire and reducing me to ashes.

He pressed me down onto the carpet, supporting his weight on his elbows as he ground his hips into mine. My fingers slipped under the hem of his shirt and found the zipper to his jeans, but he just shook his head and sat up on his knees. He held my wrists away from his pants and brought my hands to the waistband of my shorts. "Take them off," he ordered.

I grinned as I slowly slid out of my shorts, enjoying Henry's take-charge approach. I hated his bossiness any other time, but right now, hearing the confidence in his voice, I felt as if I was seeing a sliver of the old Henry returning. I leaned up on my elbows when he got to his feet.

"Stay right there," he said, taking a step backward. "And you'd better be completely naked when I get back."

I complied, pulling my shirt over my head and undoing my bra, then lying back into the carpet. I could hear him in the kitchen, messing with what sounded like the ice maker. "Did you get thirsty?" I asked when he came back with a cup in his hand.

He chuckled and set the cup down by my leg. "That's one way of putting it," he said, running his palms along the inside of my thighs and spreading my legs apart.

"Am I the only one who will be naked?" I asked as he lay on his stomach, his head directly above my crotch.

"Yes," he said, his breath warm on my skin. He pressed my legs to the floor, laying me completely bare, then flashed a grin before nipping at the inside of my thigh with his teeth, trailing the way to my center. His tongue darted out and swirled around my folds, making me arch my back off the floor to get more of him. He moved at a confident, unhurried pace, making me tingle with anticipation as the pressure began to build.

He pulled away and held my eyes as he sucked one of his long fingers into his mouth and then another, and inserted those same fingers into me. When he dipped his head and began to lick at me again, I closed my eyes and felt every nerve in my body sing. It was almost too much and yet not nearly enough.

His fingers found that sensitive spot inside me and began to rub it in circles, building me to a crescendo, and just as I was approaching the cliff and preparing to leap right off, an intense chill touched my skin and wrenched me back to reality.

"What?" I panted and found him holding an ice crescent above my mound.

"Just relax," he said with a smile and lowered the ice to my skin again, slowly sliding it between my folds.

I closed my eyes and focused on the sensation, the cold was a painful thrill that was almost too much to bear and yet . . .

Henry pulled the ice away and licked the places he had just chilled, his tongue warm and soothing. The temperature contrast just about undid me, but he touched me with the ice again, sliding it lower and lower until it was pushing at my entrance.

I squirmed and he pushed it inside me, invading me with a coldness I couldn't take, but he pulled it away and replaced it with his tongue, and just as I was getting used to the warmth again, he slid the ice inside once more. He alternated like this, the cold and warm, at leisurely intervals until I was fisting the carpet, my muscles coiling, building, rushing toward that cliff's edge again.

Then it was just his tongue as he thumbed my clit in circles and I was lost, tumbling down into the ocean of pain and ecstasy and everything Henry. My legs buckled under his hands, my insides trembled around his tongue, my mouth screamed his name, and I came and came.

Afterward, he crawled up beside me and kissed me, my taste still on his mouth. "God, you are so sexy," he said, brushing hair away from my face.

I moved my hand to give him his turn but he grasped my wrist and brought it up to his face, touching his lips to my palm. "No," he said. "I just want it to be about you right now. Just you."

I was too exhausted to argue so I wrapped his arm around me and curled into his chest, basking in the moment when Henry was both warm and cold, old and new, loving me and only me.

———

On Monday morning, I walked out to the kitchen to find Henry sitting at the dining table still in his pajama pants.

"You're going to be late," I said, leaning against the counter as I looked at my watch.

He took a leisurely sip of his coffee and even though he was smiling, it seemed as if a heavy weight was pulling his features down. "I'm taking some time off."

I found my travel mug already filled with coffee, made up just the way I liked it. "Thank you," I said, giving him a kiss on the forehead, hoping to ease the frown etched between his eyebrows. "How long?"

"I've accumulated eighteen days of leave, so that many."

My heart did a little jig before it remembered that I actually had to work, that his leave did not directly affect me. "What are your plans for the next eighteen days? Hang around and couch-surf?"

"I'm going to California."

I stopped midsip. "Huh?" I asked eloquently.

"Back when I was younger, before you and Jason moved to Monterey, I used to see a psychiatrist, but I stopped during freshman year in high school."

I knew he'd had problems at home, but he never told us he'd needed a psychiatrist. "Because of your parents?"

He closed his eyes and nodded, taking a deep breath. "Anyway, I'm going to go see Dr. Galicia again. I talked to her for a while when you were getting ready. She wants to see me tomorrow."

"Tomorrow?" I asked. "Does that mean you have to leave . . . tonight?"

He nodded and said, "Come with me."

I wanted to say yes, but there was no way I could on such short notice. "I have work."

"That's what I was afraid of." He set his mug down and walked over to where I stood at the counter, wrapping me in his arms. "It's just for eighteen days, less than one month."

I nodded despite the lump in my throat. "Is that enough time?" I tilted my head back to look at him, wishing throwing tantrums was still acceptable behavior. He just got back home and now he was going to leave again. It didn't seem fair.

"I hope so," he said gently, tucking a strand of hair behind my ear. "I'm sorry it's such short notice. I just really need to do this."

"Okay."

"Okay you'll go with me?" he asked with a hopeful lift to his eyebrows.

"Okay you can go," I said. "You've got eighteen days to work through your issues, and then I'm coming for you."

"You're coming to California?"

"No," I said with a laugh. The man was relentless. "It was just a figure of speech."

"But wouldn't it be fun to be back there together? I want you beside me when I tell people that we're finally together."

"Why do I need to be there for that?"

"So they'll believe me." He grinned. "And so that your dad won't beat me to a pulp for boning his daughter."

I laughed at the image of my dad, who was the shorter of the two men, putting up his dukes and challenging Henry to fisticuffs. "Yeah, that *is* worth missing work for."

"So come."

I sighed, my defenses already starting to wear down. "I can't. I'm a responsible adult now."

He huffed. "Okay."

"Okay you give up?"

He released me. "Okay you'd better go to work before I tie you up and throw you into my luggage," he said with a slap to my rear.

"Sounds kinky," I said and shook my ass at him all the way to the front door.

———————

Several hours later, I found myself standing in Will Rogers airport, bidding Henry good-bye once again. I was starting to get the feeling that being with him meant that I would forever be standing on this side, always the one to watch him leave.

"Are you going to see your friends?" I asked after he checked his bags.

He shrugged as he glanced toward the security gate. "Maybe. If time permits."

"How about your ex-girlfriend?" I teased.

He grinned. "Definitely. I'll make sure to see all of them," he said and tickled my side.

"Are you staying with your parents?"

"Yeah. They actually sounded happy to see me."

"Maybe things will be different," I said, squeezing his hand as we walked toward the security gate.

"Maybe."

Once we reached the security line, he turned to me and grasped the sides of my head, pressing his lips to my forehead for a long while. I closed my eyes, inhaling his scent, my body already missing his solid presence.

"You should come out to Cali," he said. "Even just a few days."

"I'll try," I managed to say through the ache in my chest. "I don't have much time off saved up."

He held my face in his hands tenderly as he planted soft kisses on my lips, then on my nose, and finally on my forehead. "It's just eighteen days," he said and I got the distinct feeling that he was saying it more to reassure himself. "I'll be back long before your birthday."

"You'd better," I said. "I'm thinking a costume party to celebrate my birthday."

"Are you going to wear that 'Tomb Raider' costume again?"

"You'll have to wait and see." I kissed him one last time and pushed at his chest. "Get going, buster," I said with false cheer.

He quirked one dark eyebrow and looked down at his watch. "You want me to go already?"

"The sooner you leave, the sooner you'll come back," I said simply, not saying that waiting here with him was torture, that it reminded me too much of that day back in March when we were separated for six months. "So scoot."

He grinned and kissed me one last time before he joined the short security line. It took him all of five minutes to reach the metal detector and another thirty seconds to collect his things and slip back into his boots.

Then he turned one last time and winked before heading off into the terminal. I watched his steady, unassuming gait until he turned the corner and was completely out of view, already making plans of my own, sure that the next time I found myself in an airport, I would not be standing on this side of the gate.

PART THREE

RETREAT

1

REVEILLE

I was calm during the four-hour flight but the moment the plane touched down at the Monterey Airport that drizzly Thursday night, my insides immediately turned to mush.

I'd flown to California many times before, but this time, Henry had no clue I was coming. I had managed to get some time off work to spend the last three of his eighteen days of therapy with him, and was planning to surprise him tonight.

My stomach trembled at the thought of showing up unannounced. A voice niggled at the back of my mind, wondering if Henry would be happy to see me. I didn't even know which version I would face: the one who left for Afghanistan or the one who came back.

As I made my way off the plane, I gave myself a pep talk. It didn't matter which version of Henry greeted me tonight. I loved him regardless.

All of my jitters disappeared when I saw my dad at baggage claim, looking a little rounder around the middle, but still the same man with hazel eyes and light brown hair. He was standing against the wall, his back straight, his arms folded across his chest, looking very much like he was about to start handing out orders.

His rigid demeanor melted the moment he saw me.

"Hi, Dad," I said, greeting him with a hug and kiss on the cheek.

"Sweetheart," he said, gathering me in his arms for a bear hug. "It's good to see you."

I pulled away and looked around. "Where's Mom?"

"She's at home, making sure the entire house is clean and that your room is just as you remembered it," he said with a hint of sarcasm.

I laughed. "You mean you haven't turned it into a workout room or something? Isn't that what you're supposed to do when your kids move out?"

"I've been trying to turn it into a man cave, but she won't let me," he said. "She wants to keep it as is until you have children of your own, then she's planning on turning it into a kid's room."

"That's . . ."

"Crazy?" he asked with a shake of the head. The smile melted off his face and he turned to me with a sort of panicked expression. "She doesn't know something that I don't, right? You're not pregnant, are you?"

"Not that I'm aware of," I said with a snort.

He sighed in relief, wiping imaginary sweat off his forehead. "Okay then. Let's go get your luggage, my sweet girl."

———

My dad was an AWACS pilot in the Air Force and, when he was still a major, he had taken a fifteen-month-long program at the Naval Postgraduate School in Monterey, California. He and Mom had liked the area so much that they'd decided to live there after he separated from the military four years later. They had taken their savings and bought a house in Monterey, not far from the famed 17-Mile Drive. The blue two-story Craftsman house was only five minutes from the beach, but most important, was a mere two houses down from the Logans.

After the ten-minute drive from the airport, I found myself standing in front of the house, fighting against an overwhelming sense of nostalgia and sadness. How could I look at that house and not see Jason and me sitting on the porch steps or playing basketball in the driveway?

Dad must have noticed because he squeezed my shoulder as he walked past with my luggage rolling behind him. "Take your time," he said.

If I stood out there too long, I ran the risk of Henry seeing me, so I sucked it up and went inside.

"Elsie!" my mother called from somewhere within the house. A few minutes later, she rounded the corner from the kitchen with a huge smile on her face. She wrapped me in her embrace and I closed my eyes, just enjoying her Mom scent of lavender and vanilla.

We followed my dad as he placed my luggage in my room. I was perfectly capable of taking it there myself—it was, after all, right off the living room on the first floor—but the golden rule was that guests did absolutely no work. I guess that meant I was a guest now.

"So what are your plans for tonight?" Dad asked, standing in the doorway.

I looked at my watch and realized it was already seven at night even though it was still fairly light out. "I was thinking of dinner with you guys, then catch up with Henry after you go to bed," I said. "What time do you go to bed?"

Dad snorted. "Honey, we're retired. We go to bed in an hour."

Mom laughed, smacking my dad on the arm. "He's kidding. We go to sleep around nine or ten, then we get up early and take a walk at the beach to watch the sunrise."

I sighed, suddenly struck with the wish that my married life with Henry turn out to be just as sweet and romantic as my parents'. I blushed, wondering where the hell the thought had come from.

Dinner was a chatty affair as Mom and Dad asked me about life in Oklahoma, but it was hard to talk without Henry's name being peppered into the conversation. Even harder still was trying to remain nonchalant when speaking his name, as if my tone of voice would reveal our secrets. I could have told them right then, but Henry had wanted to wait until we could get all of our parents in one room before we said anything.

After dinner, we watched some television and then Dad challenged me to a game of Scrabble. I was eager to see Henry but I had sorely missed our epic Scrabble games. It was our special little thing since I was a little girl, when I learned to sharpen my competitive edge. Scrabble with Dad taught me patience, creativity, and the art of losing—or winning—with grace.

It was past midnight by the time we finished. I pulled out a narrow victory with the word *retire* and Dad vowed a rematch the next night.

"I'm not retiring from this conflict," he said as he started toward their bedroom, raising a fist in the air. "I am merely postponing my victory for another night."

"Sure, Dad, whatever will help you sleep at night," I said, putting away the wooden tiles.

"Where are you off to?" Mom asked when she saw me pulling on my boots and grabbing the front door keys.

"I'm just going to say hi to Henry. Don't wait up."

Mom flashed a knowing smile and shuffled upstairs, leaving me to wonder if she had psychic abilities.

————

Even in the dark, I was able to retrace the steps to Henry's house as if I were a teenager again. We had spent a fair amount of time at that place, as the lure of an unsupervised house was just too much for three teens to refuse. We'd played video games, tried cooking different things in the kitchen, looked through his parents' closets. I might have even tried on his mom's shoes once or twice. Allegedly.

My mom, however, put an end to it. She wanted us at our house, where she could keep an eye on us. Now that I'm an adult, I can't say that I blame her.

The side gate to the Logans' backyard gave a little squeak when I pushed it open, but it wasn't as loud as it used to be, thank goodness. I crept to Henry's bedroom window and peered inside. The curtains were drawn but the glass was cracked open. All that stood between me and Henry was a screen and I wasn't about to let that deter me. I pulled a quarter out of my pocket and popped the screen up off the frame and, as quietly as I could, slid open the window farther and hoisted myself up.

For a moment, I sat on the window ledge and watched Henry sleep on the queen-sized bed, his limbs flung out in all directions while a thin blue sheet covered the lower half of his body. My heart thudded in my chest, the very sight of him sending tingles up and down my body.

I pulled off my boots and they landed with a soft *thud* on the wood floor. I walked by a gym bag, a pair of running shoes, and a haphazardly thrown towel on the floor, still damp from a recent shower, before reaching the bed. I stood over him and my eyes traced the contours of his square jaw, landing on the high cupid's bow of his lips.

I was relieved to see that he was sleeping peacefully, no frowns or worry lines on his forehead, and almost regretted carrying out my plan. But I had flown all the way to California to see him, and see him I would.

As quietly as I could manage, I stripped my clothes, then crouched over him. I lifted the corner of the sheet and carefully peeled it away from his body, thrilled down to my panties when I saw that he was completely naked underneath. I paused for a moment to stare at his body, from his expansive chest to his six-pack, to the V indent at his hips, and finally to his muscular thighs. And smack dab in the center of all of that ripped landscape was his impressive penis, already hard, lying on his stomach.

I crawled on the bed, heady with anticipation, and touched my tongue to the soft skin at the base of his erection, running it slowly upward until I reached the head.

He moaned but remained asleep.

I repeated the movement, this time going even slower, licking more of him as I moved up. His hand moved to my head, tangling his fingers in my hair as he continued to groan. My lips covered the head of his penis, then I slowly sucked him in inch by inch, my tongue swirling circles around his shaft. His hips began to roll, pumping into my mouth gently as his breathing quickened.

Then he was pulling me upward, my naked body sliding along his as he kissed me. "Elsie," he whispered against my mouth, his hands running down my neck, over my shoulders. "I've missed you so much." He palmed my butt and gripped it tightly as he positioned himself at my entrance, but instead of sliding in, he paused.

"What is it?" I asked.

He fixed his sleepy eyes on me and flashed a cocky smile. "I want you to beg me."

Even in his half-conscious state, Henry was a bossy guy. I could feel his tip and ached to feel him inside me. Hell, I could beg for one night. "Please, Henry."

"Please what?" he asked, fisting my hair.

I looked him in the eye and said, "Please fuck me. Now."

His teeth flashed in the darkness. He plunged into me to the hilt, pausing for a heartbeat with his eyes closed while I squeezed him.

"Fuuuck," he sighed, his palms caressing my sides. "You feel so good." He craned up and kissed my neck, rasping his teeth against my jaw, then gently biting at my earlobe.

I sat up and ground my hips into him, throwing my head back so that the ends of my hair were brushing his thighs. He held my hips and guided me, his big hands urging me to go faster, harder, but I held steady, focused on moving at my own pace. I'd waited fifteen days to do this; it was going to last more than five minutes for crying out loud.

I grabbed his wrist and guided his hand down to my freshly waxed crotch. His eyes widened when his fingers found my bare skin. "Holy shit," he said and sat up, kissing me with wild abandon.

A second later, he flipped me over so that I was lying on the bed and he was in the dominant position. I groaned when he pulled out, but his mouth was on me a second later, his tongue swirling around my depilated folds with feverish speed. He slipped two fingers inside me as his tongue flicked at my clit and I raced toward the orgasm that I'd been trying to put off.

"Stop," I breathed, pushing his head away. He looked confused, so I quickly added, "I want to come around you."

He didn't need me to ask him twice. He crawled over me, grabbed the sides of my head and kissed me breathless before pushing back into me in one clean stroke. He picked up speed, our skin slapping against each other as he pounded into me with fervor.

I came shuddering around him, his mouth covering mine to keep me from crying out. A few strokes later, he was grunting in my ear, continuing to stroke me until he had completely finished.

He didn't pull out when he fell onto his side, merely gathered me in his arms and twisted me around to face him. I wrapped my leg around his thigh as he brushed the hair off my face and kissed me tenderly.

He sighed in contentment. "Best dream ever," he murmured before he pulled the thick quilt over us and we both fell asleep.

2

BACK IN THE WORLD

I couldn't tell if I was caught in a dream, but it felt real enough when Henry's penis nudged at me from behind. One hand gripped my thigh and opened me up farther so he could slip inside. He rocked gently behind me, one arm under my neck and the other over my waist, as his hands roamed around, kneading and pinching at a leisurely pace. If this was a dream, then I wanted to wake up immediately so that I could make it a reality.

"So, do you think they're together then?" I heard my mother say.

If this was a dream, then it was a seriously sick one.

Henry's movements stopped but he remained completely seated in me.

Henry's mom, Helen, spoke next. "Did Elsie tell you anything?" she asked.

"No. She just said she was popping over here to say hi to Henry."

"Well," Helen said with a chuckle. "She said hi all right."

"Should we tell them we're awake?" Henry whispered in my ear, and that's when I finally realized that this was reality. Our mothers were actually standing over the bed, while Henry and I were lying naked under the covers, his penis still throbbing inside me. I could only hope that the quilt was thick enough to conceal what we'd been doing a few seconds earlier.

I felt my face go up in flames and knew that my blush would be the instant giveaway. The jig was up.

I opened my eyes and peered up at our mothers, who were standing at the doorway, each with a cup of coffee and a bewildered expression. "Morning," I croaked, trying to appear casual even though I was dying inside.

Mom raised an eyebrow at me, then turned to Helen. "We should give them a few minutes to gather their wits, then come out to the living room to explain."

Helen nodded and they closed the door behind them.

As soon as the door latched shut, Henry's arms tightened around me and he began the delicious rocking once again. "I wasn't sure if last night was real," he said, biting my earlobe.

I twisted my head around to smile at him. "I wanted to surprise you."

"You can surprise me like that anytime," he said and kissed my neck.

I sighed, from pleasure and worry. "We can't, Henry. You heard my mo—" My breath hitched in my throat when he thrust in roughly, making my muscles involuntarily clench. "Oh . . ."

Henry reached down between my legs and began to massage my clit in circles. "I just need a few minutes," he said. "Then we can be relaxed when we face the firing squad."

I wanted to disagree, but those crafty fingers and that damn cock had me under a spell, and his gravelly voice whispering naughty things was only pulling me deeper, so I had no other choice but to dive in and enjoy the sensations of Henry.

"Come for me," he rasped against my ear and moved his fingers faster. "I want to feel your pussy convulsing around me."

I twisted around and grabbed the back of his head, bringing his mouth to mine as the orgasm filled and filled and burst with white-hot intensity inside my body.

"Elsie," he groaned and climaxed as well, grasping my hips tight against his as he dug in as far as he could go.

––––––––––

We emerged from Henry's room five minutes later, me dressed in yesterday's clothes and Henry dressed in sweats and a T-shirt, looking very much like two people who'd just had sex. It was bad enough that we were walking out there to face our mothers, but one glance in the dining room showed that the situation was actually worse: Our fathers were also in attendance.

I could feel the weight of everyone's stare as we made our way into the dining room. Henry had offered to walk in first to bear the brunt of the glares, but I'd held his hand and said we needed to do this together. Now I wish I'd taken him up on his offer.

My dad was the first one I dared to look at and I immediately wished I hadn't. His lips were pursed and his thick eyebrows were furrowed. He was disappointed in me; that much was clear.

Henry and I stood at the head of the table, our fingers still entwined. He cleared his throat. "I guess Elsie and I have some news . . ."

"No shit, Sherlock," his dad, Trent, said. The man had always had a colorful vocabulary.

"How long has this been going on?" my mother asked. I met her eyes, feeling like a willful teenager again. Then it struck me that Henry and I were two consenting adults and I had nothing to be ashamed of.

I stood straighter and said, "Right before he left for deployment in March."

"That long?" Helen asked, her eyes flicking back to her son. "And you didn't think to tell us?"

"We weren't ready yet," Henry said.

"When were you going to be ready?"

"Now, I guess," I said. "We wanted to have you all together before we made the announcement."

"Speaking of getting ready . . ." Henry looked down at the watch on his wrist. He turned to me. "I'm sorry, but I have to leave."

"What?" I tugged him down to hiss in his ear, "You're going to leave me to face the inquisition by myself?"

"I have my therapy session in forty minutes."

"Take me with you."

"I'm sorry, I can't." He grinned, looking anything but sorry. "I'll be done in an hour."

My dad stood up then and my heart stopped. Every cell in my body stood at attention in anticipation of his words. He approached us with an expressionless face, stopping in front of Henry.

"Sir," Henry began. "Before you say anything, I just want you to know that I am in love with your daughter. I will treat her with the respect and care she deserves."

I held my breath when my dad lifted his hand. He paused for the longest time, then gave Henry a hearty slap on the shoulder. "I know you will, son," he said with warmth in his eyes. "You're a good man, Henry. Jason was right to ask me to give you a chance."

I felt the shift in Henry's posture, his shoulders sagging a little from relief or sadness or both. "Thank you, sir."

Then Dad turned to me and placed two hands on my shoulders. "I think you picked a good one," he said.

I hugged him. "Thanks, Dad."

"Just please don't get caught naked in his bed again," he said so that only I could hear. "I brought you up to be more of a lady than that."

I nodded as I pulled away. "Yes, Dad."

"How about we all have dinner tonight?" Helen asked, standing up from the table. "I have to meet a client in an hour, but I'll be free for dinner at around five."

My mom nodded. "That sounds like a good idea. These kids are not getting away this easy."

Henry squeezed my hand. "We'll be there."

I met up with Henry at Cannery Row after his therapy session and we had lunch at Louie Linguine's Seafood Shack. We sat at a table by the large windows with an unobstructed view of the dark blue ocean.

"How did the session go?" I asked as we ate. It felt good to be spending time with him again, just the two of us.

He took a bite of his sourdough burger. "Can't tell you," he said with a smile.

"Well, are you making progress?"

He made a noncommittal shrug. "I think so."

I shook my head and ate a spoonful of clam chowder. "You're really not going to tell me?" I asked. "The person who is most affected by all of your issues?"

A shadow of a grin crossed over his face as he shook his head, and I knew, even without his saying, that therapy was working. It didn't look like he'd shaved since he'd arrived in California and his hair was curling a little at the ends from not having it cut for so long, but underneath his scruffy appearance was the light behind his eyes that I was afraid had been extinguished in Afghanistan.

I let out the sigh of relief that I'd been holding for so long.

He raised an eyebrow. "What are you looking at?"

"I'm looking at you, Grizzly Adams."

He rubbed the hair on his cheek. "It's been nice not having to shave," he said. "But I do need a haircut."

I chewed on a piece of the bread bowl as I studied his hair. "I like it. It's a little less military. The whole look is very sexy."

He stared at me for a long time, those intense blue eyes twinkling as they flicked about my face. "You're amazing, you know that?"

"Thanks," I said in surprise. "Where did that come from?"

He leaned back in his chair and shrugged. "I mean, you're here," he said, motioning to me. "You didn't tell me you were coming to California. You just snuck into my bedroom in the middle of the night and had your way with me. If that isn't amazing, then I don't know what is."

I glanced around, hoping nobody was within hearing distance. "That *was* pretty awesome," I said with a wide grin.

"So you managed to get some time off?"

"I just took half of Thursday and all of today off, then I fly back home late Sunday night," I said. "What time is your flight on Sunday?"

"One o'clock, so I have to go to the airport right after my final session with Doc Gal."

"Doc Gal?"

"Her name is Dr. Galicia, but I've called her Doc Gal since I was ten. It kinda stuck, I guess."

"Did she help you when you were younger?" I asked, leaning closer.

"Obviously not if I'm back. But she did help me through some tough times, steered me away from juvie, that's for sure."

My eyes widened, finding it hard to picture Henry as a delinquent. "That bad?"

"I was always getting into fights, stealing, anything that would get me attention from my parents." He grinned then. "Doc Gal told me that my destructive tendencies were just a cry for attention."

"Was she right?"

"On the nose."

I took a big drink of my water before asking, "So how is it now, with your parents?"

He shrugged but his eyes were not so nonchalant. "Getting better, I guess," he said. "It might be too late."

I reached over the table and gripped his hand. "When it's about forgiveness and love, it's never too late."

He suddenly stood up, leaned over the table, and planted a kiss on my lips. He sat back down with a satisfied smile, crossing his arms across his chest.

"What was that for?" I asked, feeling my cheeks heat up, not from embarrassment but from arousal.

"I was just wondering how I got so lucky."

I bit my lower lip and gazed at the man before me, glad that Henry was finally making a recovery. "I was wondering the same thing."

———

We met up with my parents at the Monterey Aquarium. Henry offered to leave to give me some time with them, but my parents just looked at him as if he were crazy.

"Are you kidding?" my mom asked, linking her arm through his as we walked through the members' entrance. "You're coming with us. I am grilling you until the sun sets."

"That's what I was afraid of," Henry said with a smile on his face.

I walked ahead with my dad, giving my mom a chance to talk to Henry.

"You happy?" Dad asked, putting his arm around my shoulders.

"Miserable," I said with a straight face. "Absolutely miserable."

"Yeah, I see that," he said, ruffling my hair. "Henry's a good kid."

I raised an eyebrow and glanced back at the man who towered over Mom. "Kid?"

Dad chuckled. "He might be taller than me, but he'll always be that kid with the braces and the crazy hair," he said. "He almost ate us out of our home."

I laughed. "He wasn't that bad."

"He was so intense at the beginning. I was worried that he was going to be trouble, but Jason asked me to give him a chance," Dad said. "And look how that same kid turned out: captain in the Air Force. A war veteran," he added with pride in his voice.

I wrapped my arm around his side and squeezed. "You were his hero, you know."

Dad smiled ruefully. "I like to think I had a hand at raising that nice young man."

"You did," I said. "More than you know."

"Anyway, let's talk about you," my dad said as we entered my favorite part of the aquarium, the jellyfish exhibit. "Tell me about work."

I talked about work, about the award I'd received for *The Oklahoman* website, about the upcoming promotion boards. "They want to make me a senior art director, which pays more," I said, mesmerized by the tiny jellyfish illuminated pink by the blacklight. "But that means I won't get to do any actual hands-on design."

"Is there a way to do both?"

"I'm going to talk to the execs, present them with the idea of my overseeing projects while also working on projects of my own. And then I'm going to convince them to pay me more money."

"That's my girl."

We entered a large, dark room illuminated only by the bluish glow from the gigantic glass tank. We stood in awe in front of the glass and stared at fish, giant turtles, even sharks that swam by. I turned to my dad but found that Henry had taken his place.

He nudged me. "Hey." His warm hand reached out and took mine.

"How did it go?" I asked, mesmerized by the bluish glow on his face, how his eyes were nearly black in this light.

"Your mom threatened to cut my balls off if I ever hurt you," he said, then his serious façade fell away and he grinned. "She just wanted to talk about how we were getting along. She asked me why it took so long for me to tell you."

"She knew?"

"Apparently, everybody did."

"So, what did you tell her?"

"I told her I was too chicken."

I laughed. "Sounds about right."

———

Afterward, we visited Jason's grave, which was a somber experience until Henry kneeled by the grave and said, "So, hey, man, I hope you don't mind my boning your sister."

"Henry," my dad warned.

My mom snorted and then laughed. I couldn't help it either, and soon her infectious laugh also carried over to my dad and Henry, until all four of us were standing at my brother's grave, with tears of sadness and joy in our eyes.

3

ENEMY CONTACT

Dinner with the parents at P.F. Chang's was not nearly as awkward as the impromptu meeting that morning. The dark ambience of the restaurant lent itself to pleasant, mellow conversation.

At least, until Henry's wayward hand landed on my leg under the table.

I flashed him a warning look but he just gave me that impudent smile that made me want to smack him and kiss him at the same time.

"They can totally tell, you know," I whispered to him, glancing over at my dad, who, thankfully, had no clue what was going on less than three feet away from him.

Henry just winked and pushed his hand higher up my thigh. I finally had to grab him when his fingers inched under my skirt. He just grinned again and ordered his meal.

It was cheesy but we held hands under the table while we waited for our food to arrive. We tried to participate in the conversations around us, but our parents, having realized Henry and I were in a world of our own, just began to ignore us and talk among themselves.

Henry's fingers drew circles around my palm, then he took two fingers and started pulsing them into the web between my thumb and forefinger. He bent close to my ear and said, "This is what my fingers wish they could be doing inside you right now."

I squeezed his fingers, giving him a meaningful look.

He breathed into my ear and said, "It's so hard sitting here next to you, pretending to be the good little boyfriend when all I want to do is throw you on this table and fuck you senseless."

The breath hitched in my throat, my panties instantly moist. "So do it," I taunted.

He bared his teeth. "Oh, you don't know what you're asking."

". . . if only our children could stop flirting and pay attention."

My mom's words snapped me back to reality. "What was that?" I asked.

My mom had an amused smile on her face when she said, "Our food is here."

Henry and I looked down at our plates in surprise. "When did that get here?" he asked, flashing me a grin.

His dad groaned and rolled his eyes. "You guys are fucking gross."

————————

Later, Henry and I attended a party for his friends from high school at the Cannery Row Brewing Company. Kelly and Hass had been a couple since high school, and only now were they getting engaged.

"What have they been doing all this time?" I asked as we walked toward the bar hand in hand.

"I guess they broke up for a while," Henry said, holding the door open for me. "And then decided they were better together than apart."

We stood at the entrance, looking through the crowd for a familiar face. "Maybe they were too young and needed to figure out who they were first."

"Maybe so," Henry said and waved at someone across the room.

I held tight as we waded through the thick Friday night crowd, making our way toward a small group by the back of the bar.

"Logan!" a tall guy with sandy blond hair said, looking very much like the same boy I knew in high school. Hass was softer around the edges, with a little more padding all around, but his warm smile was the same. He clapped Henry on the back and turned to me. "Little Elsie Sherman?" he asked with wide eyes.

I nodded as he gave me a hug. His eyes flicked back toward me, then Henry, then back to me again—which, I would later find out, was the normal reaction from people from our high school—before asking, "You two?"

Henry grinned and threw a possessive arm over my shoulder.

Hass turned around and brought forward Kelly, a girl that I didn't have fond feelings for back in high school. Still, I kept in mind that people changed and sometimes they outgrew meanness and their bitchy tendencies.

"Congratulations," I said, pretending that she and her friends hadn't made the first half of my sophomore year a living hell, that they hadn't been the cause of many tears on my pillow.

Okay, so maybe I wasn't completely over it, but I was trying at least.

Kelly gave me a warm embrace, then said, "It's good to see you, Elsie. I'm sorry for being such a bitch to you in high school."

I pulled away and waved away her apology. "Don't worry about it. That was a million years ago."

"No, really," she said, grasping my hand. "We were really mean. I'm sorry."

I nodded, accepting her apology. What else could I do?

She gave Henry and me that look, then said, "I guess Nina was right to be jealous."

The name made my stomach lurch. Nina Yates, beautiful and

terrifying, who had held the title of Henry's Girlfriend for several months back in his senior year.

Henry squeezed my shoulders. "She's not here, is she?" he asked.

Kelly nodded, looking around. "She's around here somewhere." Hass grabbed her hand and she threw us an apologetic look as she was once again steered toward another introduction.

"Do you want to leave?" Henry asked.

I assessed my outfit and decided that I looked hot enough in my colorblock tube dress and black heels to face off with an arch-nemesis. "No. I'm good."

I led the way to the bar and was stepping up onto the brass railing at the bottom when Henry grabbed me by the waist and whispered against my ear, "You weren't planning on using what you've got, were you?"

"As a matter of fact, I was." I caught the eye of the bartender and called out my order without having to resort to cleavage-baring. I joined Henry on the floor a minute later with our drinks in my hands and a grin on my face. "I think an apology is in order," I said, holding the beer bottle out of his reach.

He wrapped an arm around my waist and pulled me against him, a dark look on his face. "I'm not going to apologize for wanting to keep you all to myself," he said huskily.

I gave him a wicked look. "Then no beer for you."

He pulled me closer as he reached behind me for the beer. I gasped when I felt his erection growing, and he winked.

"Keep going . . ." I said, enjoying the feel of his hard length against me. "A little farther . . ."

"Henry?"

We both turned to see who else but Nina-freaking-Yates standing beside us with her beautiful auburn hair cascading down the sides of her face, looking more gorgeous than I remember.

"Nina," Henry said, getting points for not immediately letting me go. He released me gently, squeezing my side as he did so. "Nice to see you."

Nina fixed her blue eyes on him, completely ignoring me. "Henry." She reached over and kissed him on the cheek.

He stood stock-still until she was done. "Nina, you remember Elsie Sherman?"

Finally, she deigned to look at me. God, did she have to look like she just stepped out of a fashion magazine? Suddenly my dinky little Target dress seemed so inadequate. "Elsie?" she said, pronouncing the last syllable like *sea*. "I didn't even recognize you. You look so adorable."

Adorable, my ass. I was looking pretty damn hot.

"So, how are you?" Henry interjected and kept me from saying something snarky.

"I'm good," Nina said, brushing back a lock of her hair and flashing us the huge rock on her left hand. "I'm married with two kids."

"You're married?" he asked, trying to hide his surprise. "To whom?"

She looked over her shoulder, to a man across the bar in a dark blue suit. "To John Morris. You remember him? You used to play football with him."

I stifled my snort. John, my date to the homecoming dance, who had groped me all over the dance floor right before Henry had pulled him off me in a jealous rage. *That* John. "Congratulations," I said with genuine glee. Really, I was happy for the both of them.

"And how about you two?" she asked, her eyes flicking back and forth. "How long have you been together?"

Henry opened his mouth to answer, but I beat him to the punch. "Since March."

"Oh, I thought you'd been together longer than that."

"Well," Henry said, clearing his throat. "Technically, we've been together for years. It just wasn't official until March."

I raised my eyebrow at him, surprised by his little white lie. Why he felt the need to exaggerate was beyond me.

"You two are married?" Nina asked. Her eyes zeroed in on my bare ring finger and got her answer. "I don't get it?"

"It doesn't really matter," I said. "Henry and I get it."

———

The night went on and I found myself actually enjoying myself. Nina didn't come to speak to us again, and I realized that maybe she wasn't the big beautiful bitch that I remembered her to be. At the very least, she didn't appear to be on some sort of undertaking to win Henry back. I wondered if, maybe, our perception of people is oftentimes tainted by emotion, that the person you hated was really just a girl trying to get through the hell that was high school.

Later, I was in deep conversation with Hass about the upcoming Joomla! Conference when Henry excused himself and headed to the bar. After several minutes of discussing the keynote speakers, I realized that Henry still hadn't returned. My eyes searched for him through the dark room and found him still standing at the bar, involved in a deep conversation with Nina. They stood close together but nothing else about their postures said they wanted any closer. In fact, Nina's back was straight and she was not looking at Henry as they talked.

I felt fear clutch at my heart but I kept it in check. I trusted Henry. He would never in a million years cheat on me.

I just hoped my optimism didn't come back to bite me in the ass.

———

Henry drove home in silence, lost in his own thoughts. I leaned back in the seat and closed my eyes, exhausted from the day's events. The next thing I knew, the car was coming to a stop in front of my parents' driveway.

Henry got out, opened my door, and walked with me all the way to the front door.

"Are you coming inside?" I asked, grabbing a handful of his jacket. "My parents should be asleep by now."

He shook his head with a rueful smile. "I think I should stay on the colonel's good side for now."

I looked up at his face, half hidden in shadows, and asked, "Is something wrong? You've been unusually quiet."

"I just have a lot to think about."

"About Nina?"

He frowned as he wrapped his arms around me. "No. Just about life in general. About where our lives are headed."

"Where *are* we headed?"

He gave me a dubious look. "I think we both know where this is headed."

"Enlighten me."

"We're headed toward a happily ever after," he stated, as if it were the most obvious thing in the world.

A bright little flower bloomed in the middle of my chest. I stood on my tiptoes and kissed him, grasping the back of his head to deepen the kiss. He instantly responded, pulling me closer against him so that I could feel his arousal. His fingers lifted the hem of my dress and dug into my butt cheeks as his hips ground into mine.

"Don't you mean a *happy ending*?" I whispered against his lips, reaching into the waistband of his jeans and massaging him through his boxer briefs.

He gave a little growl in the back of his throat. "I want that too," he said and gave a little groan when I stroked the length of him.

I pulled away with a wicked smile. "Well, good night."

His eyes widened as he tried to catch his breath. "What? But . . ."

I turned away and slid the key into the door when he pressed into me from behind, his arms boxing me in on either side of my head. "So that's it then?" he asked huskily. He rocked his hips into my butt. "You're going to leave me like this?"

I pushed the door open and stepped away from him. "Yes," I said, feeling deliciously cruel. I licked my lips and gave him a slow, sexy look that slid down his body and ended on his bulging crotch. "You have a lot to think about, remember?"

He reached out with one finger and traced my lips, then pinched my nose. "You're a brat."

"And a tease," I reminded him.

He bit his lower lip, giving me a disgruntled look. "You know, we won't have that happy ending if you keep giving me blue balls."

"That's what *he* said," I said with a carefree laugh, heedless of what tomorrow would bring, only happy to learn that Henry was thinking of our future together.

4

ALPHA MIKE FOXTROT

The next day, after Henry's session with Doc Gal, we bought sandwiches and drinks and brought them to a beach in Pacific Grove. Parking was hard to find on a rare cloudless Saturday afternoon, and we ended up walking a long way to get to the beach, but it was worth it. I hadn't been back to this beach since Jason's death; I'd forgotten how beautiful the ocean could be, how the water reached up to meet the sky in the gauzy horizon.

We sat down and ate our lunch on a blanket, our bare toes digging into the sand as we gazed out over the blue ocean.

I leaned back on my elbows and angled my face up to the sun, enjoying its warm touch on my face. "This couldn't be more perfect." When I opened my eyes, I found Henry staring at me with an unreadable expression. "What are you thinking?" I asked.

He blinked a few times. "Have you ever wondered what life would have been like if you'd never moved here?"

The question took me off guard. "Not really." I paused, giving it a little more thought. "Although, I'm guessing I'd now be dating someone else, whoever became my brother's best friend."

"I'm serious."

I laughed. "So am I. I'm a sucker for older men."

He gave a small grin and lay down beside me, folding his arms behind his head. "Do you think Jason would still be alive?"

I frowned, finally taking note of the serious nature of the conversation. "I don't know. Maybe," I said. "Or maybe he would have still deployed and that sniper would have still been on that rooftop."

"If you could turn back time, would you change it? Would you ask your dad to move somewhere else?"

I focused on the cyan sky, wondering what its Pantone color number was, ignoring the pressure behind my eyes. "To save Jason? Yes."

"Even if it means never having met me?"

A lump formed in my throat. I couldn't even begin to answer his question, so I just asked, "Where is all of this coming from?"

He took a deep breath. "Just something Nina mentioned last night—"

"Nina," I said under my breath. But of course.

He turned his head and gave me a look. "Not like that. We were just talking and she just said something that struck a chord with me."

"Let me guess, she asked if you would still be with her if I had never moved to California."

"No," he said. "She just asked, in general, how we would have all turned out if things were different, if some people never entered our lives."

I flipped over onto my stomach and lay on the wide expanse of his chest. I rested my chin on my folded arms. "We'd all be unrecognizable."

He unfolded one arm and began to play with my hair, winding a lock around his finger. "I think I'd be in jail right now instead of a captain in the Air Force. I don't think even Doc Gal could have saved me from that future. If it weren't for your dad and your brother, I'd probably have dropped out of school, maybe become a drug dealer."

Try as I might, I couldn't imagine Henry in that scenario. I shook my head. "No. You're too honorable. I don't think you're giving yourself enough credit."

"What about you? What do you think you'd be like?"

I chewed on my lip. "Hmm. That's a hard one because we could have ended up anywhere. I could have been a cheerleader, or a goth, or maybe a basketball player."

"You think living somewhere else would have made you taller?" he teased.

"Maybe. Growth hormones in the water. Stranger things have happened." I smiled at him, feeling incredibly fortunate that my parents decided to live in Monterey just two houses down from the Logans. Henry, for better or worse, was integral to shaping the person I had become, and I was sure he felt the same way about me. Our pasts were tightly entwined and so too, I was sure, were our futures. "Regardless, I couldn't imagine being anyone else."

He lifted his head and touched his lips to mine but said nothing. There was so much he wasn't saying.

"What's really bothering you, Henry?"

His eyes bore into mine; I almost flinched from the intensity. "I guess what I really want to find out is if you love me because of who I am or because you've had a crush on me forever."

"Both," I said. "I don't understand what you're asking."

"If we just met each other right now—me being an ex-con with honor and you being a really tall goth cheerleader—would you still be attracted to me? Would you still fall in love with meth-addict Henry?"

"Now you're a meth addict?" I asked. "Hmm, maybe not if you have busted teeth."

"Answer the question."

"Maybe. I don't know," I said. I pushed up off him and got to my feet. I looked up at the dark clouds that had crept in on the beautiful day. "What does it matter? We are who we are and we're together. End of story."

If only that were truly the case.

———————

The rain started to fall on our drive home. It started out as tiny drops but by the time we entered our neighborhood, it became an all-out downpour. Henry parked the car in front of my parents' driveway, neither one of us eager to get out and get drenched.

"Typical Monterey," I said, watching the rain pelt the windshield.

"Elsie," Henry began and I knew that he was finally going to tell me what had been bothering him. "I think we need to break up."

His words took a moment to wrap themselves around my brain because they were so alien, so unexpected, that it was like he was speaking another language. I sputtered, I was so taken aback. "Out of all the things I was expecting you to say, *that* was not one of them."

His eyebrows drew together as he looked at me. "I'm sorry it's out of the blue. I just think we need to spend some time apart."

Tear stung my eyes as his words began to sink in. "You said you love me."

His nostrils flared and when he reached out to touch my cheek, his fingers were trembling. "I do."

"Then . . ."

"I just need to figure out who the hell I am, Elsie," he said. "I can't remember a time that you weren't in my life and that scares me a little. I feel like I have no identity without you."

"So you're breaking up with me to go *find yourself*?" I asked incredulously.

"Not just me. I want the same for you. I want you to figure out who you are without me."

Tears were streaming down my face as I spoke. "I don't need to know who I am without you because you're a part of me. Taking you out of the equation is like pulling out one of my femurs and asking me to live a normal life. It's not going to happen."

"I need you to understand where I'm coming from—"

"But I can't understand," I shouted. "I don't understand how you can tell me you're in love with me and ask me to wait for six months, and now that you've come home and we can be together, you're suddenly breaking up with me. And your reason—that you want to find your identity—is flimsy and stupid.

"I thought you were going to tell me you had some horrible illness. And you know, the sad thing is that I wish that was the case, because then that would mean you're not leaving me voluntarily."

He turned away, the muscles in his jaw and neck taut, but said nothing. He just looked out the window.

I waited for him to say something—anything—that would make sense. If he was going to break my heart, I needed a viable reason, something tangible like wanting to be with someone else.

"Oh my God, it's because of Nina, isn't it? Do you want to be with her?"

"No!" he cried, finally looking at me again. "I don't care about Nina."

"And you obviously don't care about me," I said in a broken voice.

"Of course I do—"

I didn't want to hear any more, so I pushed open the car door and stepped out into the rain. I was instantly soaked, but I didn't care. I slammed the door shut and stalked off to the house and went inside, locking the door behind me.

"Sweetheart?"

I spun around and found my mother in the hallway, with an anxious look on her face and a cup of tea in her hands.

"Elsie, are you okay?" she asked.

The gentle worry in her voice undid me so I wrapped my sopping arms around her and let loose a rainstorm of my own.

I sat in the bathtub for the longest time, sobbing into a bottle of merlot. I scoured through memories to find any hints of the breakup, but nothing came to mind. Wasn't it only last night that he was telling me we were headed toward a happily ever after? What had changed since then?

I had so many questions but pride kept me from calling him. I would not break down and beg him to reconsider, no matter how much I wanted that very thing to happen.

Henry had blindsided me back in March when he told me he was in love with me, and he had blindsided me again by telling me he wanted to break up.

At the beginning of the year, I was confident that I knew everything about Henry—his favorite color, his favorite quote, down to which dress shoes he preferred—but something had changed and with each passing month, I realized that I barely knew him at all. Apart from superficial details, did I really know Henry as well as I thought?

And just then, when I was certain I had fallen in love with a complete stranger, was the moment that I finally began to understand him.

I was drunk and nearly numb when I finally got out of the tub and made my way to my bedroom. I had not told my parents about the break up, but my mom, with her uncanny intuition, had guessed and had told my father to give me some space. They had gone out to dinner without me, to a restaurant nearby just in case I decided the loneliness was too much to bear.

I stumbled into bed wearing only a bathrobe, not entirely sure if I wanted company or seclusion.

Seclusion won out. I couldn't tell them what happened, largely in part because I just didn't have the mental faculties at the moment to explain away Henry's actions.

I wondered if this was some phase he was going through, some therapy exercise. The thought offered me a little comfort and I was able to close my puffy eyes and go to sleep.

I awoke some time later when I heard a knock at my window. I rolled off my bed, the room still spinning from the alcohol, and opened the window for Henry.

"Hey," he said with his hands in his pockets. His eyes, I noticed with some satisfaction, were red-ringed. "Can I come in?"

"For what reason?"

"I just . . . I had to see you." He looked at me with his eyebrows drawn together, his eyes pleading.

I gave a nod and stepped aside, holding on to my old desk to steady me. The moment his feet touched the carpet, he strode to me and wrapped me in his arms, clutching at my hair, pressing my face into his chest. I could feel his rapid heartbeat against my cheek, and I realized, even through my drunken haze, that I could never love anyone more. If this was really over, if Henry really wanted out, I would be a ruined mess for anyone else who came after.

He closed his eyes and pressed his lips against my forehead, but what was supposed to be a comforting gesture instead broke my heart into a million pieces.

Henry was here to say good-bye.

I blotted my tears with his gray shirt, memorizing everything: the largeness and solidity of his body, the cool, fresh scent of his deodorant, the *thud-thud* of his heart in his chest. I wanted to flood my every sense with Henry, to lose myself to sensation so that I wouldn't have to think about the fact that he was saying good-bye. So I slid my hands up his muscled back to his head and pulled him down to meet my lips.

I kissed him hard, my tongue slipping against his with hunger and need. He responded with a groan and pushed me against the wall, pinning my body against his. He shoved a knee between my legs and pressed his thigh into my crotch, rocking his erection into my stomach, causing a delicious friction. He stopped kissing me long enough to pull on the back of his shirt, slipping it over his head in one motion.

His hands came between us and grabbed the lapels of my bathrobe, peeling it away from my naked body. He pulled away for a brief moment, his eyes raking over me with that dark look on his face. "God, I'll miss you," he rasped.

I saw red at that moment, balking at his audacity. "You asshole," I said and slapped him across the cheek.

He grunted, his eyes turning feral. "Do it again," he ordered.

So I did, my palm landing flat on his cheek. He grunted again and ground his teeth. When I raised my hand to strike again, he grabbed my wrist and punished me with his mouth, kissing me with an anger and desperation I'd never felt before. His other hand grabbed me by the jaw and forced my head up, then he proceeded to rain kisses on my neck, along my collarbone, nipping with his teeth at every juncture.

The pleasure and fury roiled around inside me like a tempest. I wanted to hurt him back, to give him a taste of what he'd put me through, so I dug my fingers into his back and raked my nails across his skin.

He made a low guttural sound at the back of his throat, then grabbed me by the waist, ripped me away from the wall, and threw me onto the bed. I gaped up at him, trying to catch my breath, as he unzipped his pants, his muscles straining to do battle.

I sat up, ready to resist, when he placed his palm flat over my heart and pushed me back down into the mattress. He grabbed my wrists and pulled them above my head, holding them in place with one hand while the other pushed my legs apart and guided the head of his penis to my entrance.

His eyes bore into mine. "Do you want me inside you, Elsie?" he asked, pushing in just the slightest and retreating.

My breath came out in rapid gusts and my insides squeezed, trying to suck him inside me by sheer will.

"Tell me, yes or no?" he demanded in that gravelly voice.

"Hell yes," I breathed and then he surged inside me, filling and stretching me to my limits.

He groaned long and low as he thrust into me. He grabbed my hips and jerked me closer to the end of the bed to grant him better leverage, then he crouched over and rolled his hips into mine.

I fisted the sheets by my head, on sensation overload. My head was still swimming from the alcohol, magnifying every nerve ending in my body. He was possessing me, every grind of his hips hitting me in twin spots of pleasure inside and out. He looked down at me with intensity, a smirk playing on the edges of his lips as he took charge of my body. He owned me.

He dipped his head and captured my mouth once again, his tongue and cock moving in unison as they plunged into me. Then he pulled out and flipped me onto my stomach. "Get on your knees," he ordered, but before I could even think to refuse, my traitorous body complied. Henry was completely in control now and it was driving me wild with want and defiance. If this was the last time we would have sex, it sure as hell was going to be a memorable one.

I gave a shout when he entered me from behind. He grabbed my waist for leverage as he slammed into me, each thrust harder than the last. I leaned down on my elbows, lifting my butt higher, squeezing him with all that I had, my anger fueled by pleasure. Or maybe it was the other way around.

For a while, the only sound in the room was the slapping of our bare skin, punctuated by his grunts. I kept silent, intent on proving that he couldn't completely dominate me.

I didn't know when it happened, but somewhere along the way, I realized that Henry had taken command of our entire relationship—he'd made me fall in love and taken it all away. But even if I had no jurisdiction of my heart, this—the fucking—was a war zone I could fight in.

He reached between my legs and fingered my clit, trying to get a rise out of me, but even through the pleasure, I bit my lip and made no sound. With his other hand, he grabbed me by the chin and tilted my head back, pressing his lips to my forehead while he continued to pound and massage me. It was almost too much, but I was determined not to give him what he craved.

"Elsie," he ground out. "Come for me."

"I'm not doing anything for you," I said.

He released my head, stilling inside me, finally taking note of the change in me, but the element of surprise only lasted a few seconds. He recovered and dug his fingers into my ass cheeks. He held on tight as he began to pound into me again, hitting me so hard I was lurching forward with every thrust. I braced my arms in front of me, unwilling to give another inch.

Then he wrapped his arms around my waist and fell sideways onto the bed, taking me with him so that we were on our sides, his cock still buried inside me. His hand immediately snaked around to my front, lifting my leg out of the way before claiming my clit. With three fingers, he massaged me, alternating circles and quick flicks all the while pounding into me from behind. His other hand clutched at my chest, pinning my arms in place.

"I'm going to make you come so much, I'll be etched in your mind forever," he said against my ear and, despite myself, the pressure began to build. Still, I was determined; he wasn't going to take this from me too.

I twisted my head around and kissed him. "I'll forget you as soon as you walk out that door," I said against his lips. We both knew it was a lie, but the bullet hit its mark regardless. He released me and pulled out, turning away from me. He made to crawl off the bed but he paused. He looked at me with his eyebrows drawn a moment before he was pushing me onto my back and sliding back inside.

My head was reeling. I didn't know if he was coming or going, hot or cold, but the look on his face as he rocked into me was of pure agony. He rested on his elbows and kissed me soundly, almost reverently, whispering, "Don't forget me," over and over.

The frost wall I'd built around my heart began to thaw, the melted ice leaking out the corner of my eyes. I kissed him back to muffle my sobs. Of course I wouldn't forget him. You could give me a lobotomy and somehow every cell in my DNA would still know Henry's touch.

And then he gave in. I felt his hips jerk and he started to come, his arms clutching me tight against his chest as he continued to thrust into me.

I let go with a moan. I jumped off that cliff after him, my insides convulsing wildly as he throbbed inside me. Even though he was spent, he kept moving, instinctively knowing what I needed. My orgasm went on and on as I clutched at him with everything I had, wringing every sensation out of the moment.

We collapsed together, his weight on me as we caught our breath. After a long moment, he raised himself back onto his elbows, his fingers wiping the tears from my face. "I love you, Elsie," he said, looking into my eyes. "That won't ever change."

"But you might," I said, finishing his thought.

He gave the slightest nod, the corners of his mouth drooping down.

"I get it, Henry." My lips trembled, but I managed to continue. "I understand what you need, but I don't know if I'll still be waiting for you by the time you figure out who you are."

"I'd be a selfish jackass if I asked you to wait for me again," he said. Still, he never said he wasn't either.

He closed his eyes and kissed my forehead, inhaling deeply before pulling away. He gathered his clothes and began to dress. I noticed the scratch marks on his back, pleased that I had drawn blood. My only regret was that it wasn't permanent, that my mark would eventually fade along with everything else we had together.

When he was done, he picked up my bathrobe and handed it to me. He sat on the edge of the bed, resting his arms on his legs, his head cradled in his hands.

"Henry?"

When he looked up, his eyes were red. "I've been in a fucking shootout without batting an eyelash, and I didn't even think twice about running out toward that explosion on base, not knowing if there were other insurgents. But right now I'm scared as hell," he said, his dark eyebrows drawing together. "I'm fucking terrified that I'm making the biggest mistake of my life."

I said nothing because we both already knew what I would say. Instead I reached for his hand and threaded my fingers through his.

"I need to do this," he whispered, his eyes pleading for me to understand.

"So go," I said with a broken voice. "Get the hell out."

He kissed my hand and stood up to leave, but some unknown force made him stop before he reached the window. He turned on a heel and crossed the space between us in three large steps. He grabbed the sides of my face and kissed me with such ache, shattering whatever was left of my heart.

I pushed him away, tears streaming down my face, the pain so fierce I felt like it was ripping my chest down the middle. I wanted to tell him to never change, to come back as the Henry I had fallen in love with, but I had already expended all my words, and tears were all I had left.

"Bye, Elsie," he said, looking me over one last time before being swallowed up by the darkness outside my window.

5

OVER AND OUT

I slept endlessly. Every time I surfaced, I forced my eyes shut and emptied my lungs of air, trying to drown in my dreamless sleep where everything hurt less.

Eventually, though, I had to stop being so dramatic and get up. Life goes on, the world keeps revolving, and all of that, so I rolled out of bed and faced the day, slow as I was. I shuffled to the bathroom to pee but a different urge took over and I crouched over the toilet, vomiting the entire bottle of wine I'd imbibed the night before. Even after my stomach was completely empty, I stuck a finger down my throat and forced myself to throw up, to cleanse my body of everything that was making me hurt.

It didn't work. I only succeeded in getting the full-body shakes from the emptiness. I bent over the sink and gulped down water straight from the faucet, intent on filling that hollow ache inside. Then I climbed into the shower and washed myself, every movement, every swipe of the soapy loofah, symbolic of my need to cleanse myself of the memory of Henry.

I was red and raw by the time I got out of the shower, but the memories remained. How could I possibly wash away someone who's been a part of me since I was twelve years old? I'd have a better chance of forgetting myself.

I dressed and walked out to the kitchen to eat a piece of toast to calm my stomach. I was filling my cup with coffee when I heard voices at the front of the house. One deep, gravelly voice in particular made me want to retch all over again.

"Sir," I heard Henry say as I crept closer, "I just wanted to have a word with you."

I peered around the corner and saw them standing in the foyer, my dad's arms crossed across his chest and Henry standing in front of him with stooped shoulders, holding a paper sack in his hands. Henry was taller by several inches but in that moment, my dad seemed ten feet tall, quite literally the lieutenant colonel berating the captain.

"What did you do to my daughter?" my dad asked in that tone we both knew well, the very one that made us know we were in deep trouble.

"Elsie and I broke up last night," Henry said.

"I gathered that much," my dad said. "Though it seems to me like you did most of the breaking."

Henry looked down at his shoes. "I did, sir."

"You going to tell me why, son?"

"It's for her sake as much as mine," Henry said, glancing around as if searching for words. "We grew up together. We are all that we know. Of course she fell in love with me, because I was always here. I just . . . I want to make sure she wants to be with me for the right reason."

Dad studied him for the longest time, his lips stiff. Finally, he said, "And you think *you* might be with her for the wrong reasons?"

I held my breath, waiting for Henry to deny it, but he didn't. Of course he didn't. "I'm not sure. That's what I'm trying to find out."

Last night I didn't think my heart could break any more, but right then, I felt as if Henry stepped on the shattered pieces and ground them into dust with his heel.

I gathered what wits I had left and walked out from around the corner, trying to maintain a sense of dignity in my black sweat pants and TLC shirt.

Henry started, looking a little panicked at the sight of me.

"Elsie," my dad said, his arms lowering to his sides. "Henry was just leaving."

Henry nodded, then looked down at the sack in his hands. "I just wanted to give you this," he said and held it out.

I looked at the paper bag for the longest time, guessing at its contents. "You brought me a good-bye sandwich?"

He shook the bag. "Just take it. Don't open it until you get on the plane."

I grabbed it and immediately looked inside. "A voice recorder and a few tapes?"

He gave a short nod. "Yeah. Doc Gal taped our sessions so I could go back and listen to them. She thought it might help me."

"So you want me to bring this back to OKC for you?" I asked. "Because you're out of space in your luggage?"

His nose was flaring in irritation when our eyes met. "I want you to listen to them."

"Why would I do that? Is this some form of torture?" I was being insolent, sure, but damn if it didn't make me feel a little bit better.

"You're not making this easier, Elsie," Henry said.

"And tell me, why the hell should I make your life any easier, Henry?" I retorted.

He pinched the bridge of his nose and took a deep breath. "You said before that it's like you don't even know me. Maybe you're right. Maybe you don't. But I'm hoping these tapes will get you started. Will you at least listen to them?"

I shook my head. "I'm not a masochist."

He sighed and reached for the doorknob. "Well, keep them anyway. Just in case."

"When's your flight?" my dad asked him.

"I'm headed to the airport right now." He turned to me, his eyes not quite meeting mine. "I can pick you up tonight when your flight arrives."

I took a deep breath, unable to hold on to my anger. Even when he was being a dick, Henry was still thoughtful. I decided then that I would wipe his entire slate clean. *Considerate*, I mentally wrote with permanent ink. That was one thing I knew about him with all certainty.

"Please don't," I said hoarsely. I didn't even know how I'd get through the night in the same apartment with him.

He nodded. "Okay. Well, I'll see you later," he said and walked out, latching the door soundly behind him.

Saying good-bye to my parents was a sad affair. Any other time, I would have felt only a little tug of regret but today, of all days, I was filled with a sadness that I didn't know how to overcome.

"Can you stay a few more days?" Mom asked on the way to the airport. She sat in the backseat with me for moral support "Just to give you a little while to get over . . . things."

"I can't," I said, wishing I were more impulsive. I was so tempted to quit my job and just stay in Monterey. Living with my parents again wouldn't be so bad. "I have to get back to work."

My mom looked pointedly at the paper sack that was peeking out of my purse. "At least listen to it, hear what he has to say."

"It doesn't matter what he has to say," I said, shaking my head. "The end of the story is still the same."

"This is not the end, sweetie," she said, squeezing my hand. "The boy just wants to find himself first."

"He's not a boy anymore," I said. "He's a man. If he doesn't have his shit together by now, then he never will."

"Elsie," my dad warned, giving me a stern look in the rearview mirror.

I leaned back into the seat and exhaled forcefully. "Great. You are both on his side?"

"There are no sides here," Dad said. "We want you both to be happy."

I looked out the window, feeling utterly defeated.

"Sweetie," my mother said, rubbing my arm. "The only reason we're not coming down hard on him is because we know him. We know he's not trying to hurt you. I had a talk with him this morning after my walk, and he seemed really torn up. But at the end of the day, you're my daughter and I want *you* to be happy. So if you want me to put a hit out on him, just say the word. . . ."

My mouth fell open at my mother's words, then I began to laugh.

"Or we can just get someone to kneecap him," my mom added with a tiny smile.

I leaned over and gave her a hug, feeling a rush of gratitude toward my parents. "I love you guys," I said. "I think I'll be fine."

———

Our parting at the airport was brief by design. I hated protracted good-byes.

"We're here for you, sweetie," my dad said before I entered the short security line. "In case you need us."

I gave them each a hug and went on my way. Once seated in the plane, I pulled the paper sack out of my purse and tipped its contents onto my lap. The voice recorder was an old Sony model, the kind that required mini-cassette tapes. It was so old it still used an analog three-digit counter with a plastic reset button as its timer. I didn't know how something so old could tell me something new about Henry, but hell, I had a four-hour flight ahead of me and had time to spare.

I slipped the first tape labeled "The Henry Sessions #1" into the recorder and put the earphones on.

Henry's deep voice came on the tape, sounding clear and bold. "My name is Henry Mason Logan. My earliest memory is of going to the park when I was two, maybe three years old . . ."

Henry knew me well, knew that I wouldn't be able to resist listening to his side of the story. So I leaned back into my seat and absorbed his words, hoping that, somewhere in the collection of cassette tapes in my lap, lay the secret to finally getting to know him as well.

PART FOUR

THE HENRY SESSIONS

1

My name is Henry Mason Logan.

My earliest memory is of going to the park when I was two, maybe three years old. My nanny, Louise, took me to this tiny park down the street and I played with this kid I'd never met before. He kept referring to Louise as my mom and I never corrected him. I figured she was better than my mom, because at least she took care of me.

My parents were busy career-oriented people. My mom was an up-and-coming lawyer and my dad had his landscaping business. Mom was always working late or dashing off to meet with clients, and Dad, well, when he wasn't working or drinking with his buddies, he was sitting in his man cave and needing his man space.

I was not allowed to enter the man cave unless he was having a football-watching party and he needed me to get them some more chips or beer.

For some reason I always thought men loved having sons because it meant they had someone to teach baseball to or how to build cars. At the very least, they had someone to carry on the family name, but my dad didn't seem to care either way. He didn't do the other things that my classmates' parents did. We never did Little League or Boy Scouts or any of that.

Why? Fuck if I know. He was a shitty parent is what I finally concluded a long time ago. Too selfish to have a kid, that's for sure.

My mom would sometimes show some semblance of affection for me. When she had a spare minute, she'd give me a hug or a kiss on the forehead. You know, easy mom stuff. But what I really wanted her to do was stay home and take care of me, be there when I got off the bus like other kids' moms. I wanted to come home to freshly baked cookies and a glass of milk. I thought that's what moms were supposed to do, not rush off to work every day and come home in time to march me off to bed.

Have I started rebuilding that broken relationship with my parents?

Hell no.

Do I want to?

I don't know if I should even bother. They are who they are and I hate them and love them regardless.

Just . . . sometimes I wish they would at least attempt to apologize, you know? Would it hurt them to say, "Henry, we're sorry we neglected you and allowed you to be raised by a nanny"? I don't know if that's the magic salve that will heal all wounds but it'd be nice to hear them acknowledge it.

They never even called me to say good-bye before I deployed.

————

I was a bit of a wild child when I was younger, as you are well aware. I had my first smoke in fifth grade and tried my first beer in sixth grade. By seventh grade, I'd lost my virginity to this girl—I can't even remember her name anymore—who was just visiting Monterey for the week. I bragged to my friends at school that I'd had a one-night stand but I remember wanting her to fall in love with me.

I'm not sure what that says about me, that I wanted love and acceptance from a girl who wasn't even going to stick around.

Desperate? Stupid? Naïve? All of the above?

The first time I tried pot was at a party at the beginning of sophomore year. I think if I'd been able to get my hands on it, I probably would have done it more. As it was, I wasn't inventive enough to find it and not cool enough to have the right connections to the people who could.

My first fight was with a boy in the playground in second grade. He threw sand in my face so I punched him in the balls. That earned me a trip to the principal's office. Louise was the one to pick me up from the office.

The first time I stole was at this kid's house when he invited me over for dinner. That was my MO back then: I'd befriend someone and go to their house for dinner because the only thing waiting for me at home was another frozen burrito or ramen noodles. So I'd go to my classmates' houses for dinner. One time I was at Tommy Schilling's house and I saw this really cool lighter inside a hutch in their formal dining room. It was this cool brass lighter shaped like an atomic bomb and I just reached into the cabinet and took it.

I was never invited there again. Tommy accused me at school the next week, but they couldn't prove anything, and being that my mom was a lawyer, they didn't really want to pursue it.

I gave the lighter back eventually. It took until the end of sophomore year but I finally gave it back to Tommy and told him that I was sorry.

I knew I was heading down the wrong path but it was like an icy slalom; I could see exactly where I was headed but I couldn't stop. Until the first time I met the Shermans.

Jason first came to school about two months into the school year. I remember him vividly because he was tall even then, with floppy blond hair and an easygoing smile. He walked around the halls with confidence, like he'd been going there since freshman year. Word quickly got around that he was the new kid and by the end of the day, he already had half the female students swooning. One day at school and already he was destined to be the golden boy. For someone who had been trying since junior high to get attention and failing miserably, that was a big boot to the nuts.

I hadn't had my growth spurt yet so I was only about five-six at the time and not much to look at. Jason didn't know about my history, so I thought maybe he was someone I could befriend and he could elevate my standing at school. At the very least, I'd get a warm dinner or two out of his family. So I did my thing and insinuated myself into their dinner plans. Turned out we lived only a few houses apart, so that was a bonus.

Jason seemed like such a nice kid. He didn't even look suspicious when I asked if I could see his house and he automatically just invited me to stay for dinner.

That was the first day I met Elsie.

Who is Elsie? The simplest I could put it is that she's Jason's little sister. The most complicated is that she's the love of my life. I'm going to try to be objective when talking about her, try not to let my feelings for her now color how I remembered her in the past.

Elsie was a cute girl. She was this little thing with light brown curly hair and big hazel eyes. When I walked into the Sherman house, she came running down the stairs with an eager smile, but when she saw me, her expression changed like she'd smelled something bad. I couldn't really blame her. I had braces so I never smiled, and a head of crazy wavy hair that I rarely ever brushed. Turned out that was the thing we'd bond over: our hair.

"Your hair is out of control," I said just to piss her off.

"Yours is worse," she said with attitude. I wanted to tease her more, to see how mad I could really make her, but her mom came out to greet me so I bit my tongue.

"Jason, who's your friend?" she asked, looking me over. But she didn't look at me with distaste like other parents because she hadn't heard anything about me. She just looked at me with curiosity and maybe some amusement.

"Henry Logan," Jason said, clapping me on the back. "Nicest guy in school."

I didn't really agree with that appraisal, but who the hell cared? I could pretend to be the nicest guy in school if it got me free food and some company.

Dinner at their house was like a revelation. Until then, I'd never realized how nice it could really feel to sit at the table with Mom and Dad and talk about your day. The Shermans asked their kids about their day and really listened, but then they asked me about myself and also seemed really interested. It was really sweet and intrusive and made me a little panicked. I think I might have said three words before stuffing my face with mashed potatoes.

I was invited over for dinner twice more that week and I returned, soaking up their normalcy. They were what I'd always wanted in a family but never got.

I don't know if it's healthy to both resent and envy the Shermans, but I will tell you one thing: I never stole a thing from their home. It never even occurred to me.

2

Jason and I became really good friends. At first he hung out with me because I was the only person he knew, and I hung out with him because he was the only one who still would. Eventually though, a real friendship happened.

He was hilarious. He was always telling the nastiest jokes when there were no adults around. He had the largest repertoire of sexual jokes I'd ever heard, and the guy was smart without even trying. The best thing about Jason though was that he was loyal and a true friend. I couldn't tell you how many times other students came up to him and told him stories about my past. Jason just shrugged them off and told them that I was his friend regardless, that I didn't steal from him or beat him up so why should he care?

He was so sure of himself, a trait that he definitely got from his dad, who retired as a lieutenant colonel in the Air Force. Jason was one of the best-looking kids in school and his confidence and that laid-back smile really drove the ladies crazy. He always had to let them down easy. Ugh, it made me sick.

I was the invisible sidekick for the longest time but then I shot up in height and the braces were taken off and all of a sudden girls were looking at me too. Not in the *hey, aren't you the guy who steals things?* kind of way either. I wasn't used to that kind of positive attention, so I took the cue from Jason and played it cool.

Something changed when Elsie turned thirteen. I don't know if it's because she was officially a teen, but all of a sudden I saw her in a different light. I didn't know what to do around her. I'd either clam up or just start saying mean stuff to get a reaction out of her but she was a firecracker and would always dish it back.

I remember one time we were hanging out in their family room downstairs. Jason and I were talking about sex when Elsie came sauntering in, sucking innocently on a lollipop.

I'm sorry if this sounds really crass but for a fifteen-year-old boy, a girl sucking on a lollipop is like visual Viagra. Thank God for throw pillows and the oversized sweatshirt I was wearing.

"What are you talking about?" she asked casually, plopping down on the couch near me.

"About positions," Jason said with a straight face.

"Like football positions?" she asked, all wide-eyed wonder.

Jason shot me a grin. "Something like that."

I played along. "Yeah, like, there's this position called the donkey punch. That guy's responsible for coming up from behind and punching the opposing player in the back of the head."

Elsie frowned. "That doesn't sound right. There's no punching in football."

I continued as if I didn't hear her. "And there's this one play called the doggy style, where one player comes up from behind again and just rams into the other guy."

"That sounds like the donkey punch," Elsie pointed out, looking at me with skepticism.

"No, you don't punch anyone in doggy style," I said, my face nearly exploding from the effort of trying not to laugh.

Jason doubled over, clutching his stomach as he laughed. I let go and laughed along with him.

Elsie stood up and huffed, realizing we were yanking her chain. "You guys are dickheads," she said and stomped off.

"You're not supposed to say that word!" Jason called after her.

She turned around, her hands on her hips. "Yeah? Well you're not supposed to be talking about sex either!"

Jason and I fell back onto the floor in hysterics.

I spent more and more time at Jason's house. I'd come home from school and find my house empty, and it was just so easy to just walk down the street and knock on the Shermans' door. Jason and I would go to the family room and play Nintendo and eat snacks. I swear I owe that family thousands of dollars for the food I ate at their house. His dad kept grumbling that Jason and I were eating them out of their home but I never felt unwelcome. The colonel always made sure I knew he was kidding.

Things at my home were more of the same. Mom stayed at the office until nearly ten, and my dad, well, I had no idea where he was spending his time. All I knew was that he'd come home around nine smelling like alcohol and cigarettes and then lock himself in his man room. I was convinced that my parents were having separate affairs but I never could find proof.

And the sad thing? I didn't even care to find out.

I was so tired of it, of the constant loneliness, so I went over to the Shermans' house and knocked on Jason's window but he didn't answer. The guy's a pretty heavy sleeper. Elsie's window was right beside his so I tried hers, thinking maybe I could go through her room to Jason's and crash on his floor.

Elsie's face appeared in the window, her face sleep-creased, her curly hair tied up into a messy bun. She looked so adorable. She let me in, looking a little bewildered, and asked me if something was wrong.

"Why would anything be wrong?" I asked, instantly on edge.

"Because you're knocking on my window in the middle of the night."

I looked at my watch. "It's only ten thirty, smart-ass."

"But you're in my room at ten o'clock on a school night," she said. "Something is definitely wrong."

I sat on the edge of her bed and sighed, feeling deflated. Jason and I never really talked about our feelings, but Elsie was a girl and girls are pros at that kind of thing. "My parents are still not home," I said.

"That really sucks." She sat down on her bed and leaned against the headboard. I kicked off my shoes and climbed in, settling myself against the footboard. We faced each other in the semidarkness, our faces lit only by the night-light in the corner.

"They always come home late," I said, focusing on the bookshelf above her head. "But I'm so tired of sleeping in an empty house. And when I wake up, they're already gone. It's like I live by myself."

"Sounds like fun to me," she said. "You can do what you want, watch what you want."

"It sounds fun, but it really sucks. I'm not even sixteen yet and I'm already living by myself."

"Are you lonely?" she asked in a small voice.

I pondered my options. Lying was my first instinct but I had already opened up to Elsie, I might as well tell her the truth. If nothing else, it might make me look like a sensitive soul. "Yeah. I really am," I said. I nudged her thigh with my foot. "You and Jason are so lucky. Don't you ever forget that."

Her hazel eyes watched me. "I won't." She slid down onto her pillow. "Henry, can I ask you something?"

"Shoot."

"Is that why you're always here? Are we, like, your adopted family or something?"

"Yeah, something like that." I glanced at her. "Why, do you want me to leave?"

"No," she said. "You can have my family. You and Jason are basically twins anyway. Twin dickheads."

I squeezed her socked foot. "Don't talk like that."

"Why? You and Jason do."

"Because we're disgusting and gross."

"Yeah you are. Your feet smell."

"They do not!" I laughed the comment off. I was at about that age when deodorant and a daily shower had become a necessity.

She scrunched up her nose and giggled. "They really do."

I got up, grabbed my shoes, and headed to the door. "I'll go stink up Jason's room then," I said with a grin before tiptoeing out. "Good night, brat."

3

Elsie started going to Monterey High School when Jason and I were juniors. I don't know if it was his dad's influence or what, but Jason watched over her like a hawk at first. He recruited me to stalk her, to make sure that nobody was messing with her. Elsie was a sweet kid and some of the older students liked picking on the freshmen, so Jason and I had to have words with a few people. We were football players and people actually listened to us like we had real authority.

Elsie, for her part, had her friends and was a genuinely likeable person. Coupled with her good looks—she'd learned how to style her hair a little better by then—she quickly became one of the popular girls at school. I'd see guys trying to talk to her all the time and I'd get this urge to throw my arm around her shoulder to chase them off. I thought at the time that it was just overprotectiveness. Now that I'm older, I can now tell you that those were the first flames of jealousy burning in my chest, but when you're young and have never loved a girl, you don't know those things. Unfortunately, not knowing what the hell I was feeling, I ended up doing some pretty stupid things.

Take, for example, in senior year when this guy took Elsie to the homecoming dance. Elsie was only a sophomore at the time but

John was a senior and a known ladies' man, so Jason and I were already on high alert. John was on the football team too, albeit a second-stringer, so we all chipped in for a limo and rode together. I really pushed for it so Jason and I could keep an eye on the guy and his wandering hands.

Everything was going fine at the dance. I took my girlfriend, Nina, who was smoking hot in her tight green dress, which really looked good with her red hair. We were dancing and Nina was whispering really raunchy things in my ear when I saw John lead Elsie onto the dance floor.

They started off innocently, with her hands around his neck and his around her waist, but there's a lot of truth in John's reputation and he started to get fresh with her. She kept trying to pull his hands away from her ass but he was relentless, until she just gave up and let him touch her all over that dance floor. I'll never forget that blissful look on her face, when she closed her eyes and let him kiss her neck.

It made me so fucking furious.

I pulled away from Nina and ran over to John, grabbing the back of his shirt and throwing him across the room. I turned to Elsie, ready to . . . I don't know. I wanted to yell at her and kiss her and keep her safe from disgusting guys like John.

"What the hell, Logan?" John shouted and pushed me. I pushed him back, waiting for him to hit me. I'd instigated the fight, so if I threw a punch I would get expelled for sure, maybe even get charged for assault.

"You were practically molesting her in front of the whole school!" I yelled at him.

"It's not molesting if she wanted it!" John shouted back.

We were both trying to out-shout each other when Jason got into the mix. Then I realized Elsie was gone. Luckily, someone said they saw her running to the exit, so I took off after her with Jason right behind me.

We caught up with her, and I swear, it took everything I had in me not to just tackle her to the ground and . . . I didn't know. Those damned teenage hormones were firing on all cylinders.

Jason went back to his date right after he realized that Elsie was fine, that we were just acting like children. There, alone in the dark hallway with Elsie, I was filled with so many warring emotions, the main one being protectiveness. I didn't want her with guys like John who didn't respect her, but honestly, I didn't know one guy deserving of her. Me? Hell no. I was just a horny teenage guy too. "You shouldn't have let him do that," I told her.

"We were just dancing." She looked like she was about to cry.

I didn't know what to say to take that look away from her face and ended up saying the first thing that popped into my head. "Now the whole school will see that you're easy." I didn't know why I said it. I meant to say the school would *think* she was easy. "Elsie, I didn't mean it like that," I added quickly.

"I hate you," she said and flipped me off.

"I didn't mean it like that," I said again, but she was already gone. I faced the nearest locker and pounded my head into it repeatedly. Nina found me like that a few minutes later.

"Are you okay?" she asked me.

"I'm great, Nina," I said. "What the hell does it look like?"

"It looks like you got jealous because John was touching Elsie."

I took deep breaths to stave off the headache. "She's like a little sister to me, all right?"

Nina didn't look convinced but she nodded anyway. "Fine. Can we just go back to our homecoming dance?"

I took her by the hand and led her back into the gym, glad for any kind of distraction.

"Well, if you look like a whore and quack like a whore," she said under her breath.

That was the first time I noticed the nasty streak in Nina, but at that point in my life, she was the only female left who could still stand me, so I just asked her to can it.

———

I didn't stop coming over to the Shermans' house but Elsie made sure I felt the chill. She froze me out, refusing to even acknowledge my presence. One night, during dinner, her parents asked flat-out why she was so angry with me.

"Because Henry is a jerkface," she said and kept eating.

The colonel eyed me but said to her, "Can you expound on that?"

Elsie shook her head. Jason spoke up. "It was because at the homecoming dance last week, Elsie's date was touching her inappropriately and Henry put an end to it." Jason yelped. I was pretty sure Elsie kicked him under the table.

Mrs. Sherman shot me a look of gratitude. She loaded my plate with another slice of meatloaf and another heaping of mashed potatoes. "Well, we really appreciate that, Henry."

Elsie sputtered. "What? You're taking his side?"

"Yes. He did the right thing," her dad said, and her face turned even redder. "Who knows what the boy would have done to you if Henry hadn't put a stop to it?"

"It didn't occur to you that maybe I was letting John touch me?"

The colonel's eyes narrowed. "I should hope not."

"Oh my God, you're so sexist!" she shouted and pushed away from the table.

I was pretty miserable by then, my earlier feeling of vindication trumped by how awful Elsie must be feeling. But it was too late. Whatever anger she felt toward me had now been compounded by everyone's support of me. I had inadvertently turned her entire family against her.

"May I be excused?" she said through her teeth, glaring at me through slitted eyes. Then she fled the room.

———————

I stayed away for a while, giving her some time to calm down. By then I knew the way she worked: She had a wicked temper but she just needed to be left alone and she'd eventually calm down. Elsie was someone who forgave her loved ones freely; I just hoped I was still one of them.

After two weeks of refusing to talk to me, I'd finally had enough. I couldn't stand not talking to her so I finally put a real effort into making her forgive me. I'd approach her at school; she'd walk away. I had people give her messages from me; she just threw the notes into the trash. One time, she even pretended to wipe her ass with it before going into the girl's bathroom, presumably to flush it.

Finally, I knocked on her window one night. She pulled open the curtains and just stood there with her arms folded across her chest, refusing to unlock the window.

"I'm sorry," I mouthed through the glass.

She just gave me a sassy look and shrugged, then reached to close the curtains.

I made a choking motion across my throat and pretended to punch myself in the jaw. I fell to the ground then jumped back up and punched myself in the gut.

She tried to hide a grin but I saw it, so I beat myself up some more for a good three minutes. That majestic piece of thespian artistry convinced her to open the window a crack.

"You've got five seconds," she said.

"I'm sorry. I'm a dickhead."

"Yeah you are."

I smiled at her. "I don't think you're easy. I don't even know why I said that. You're the opposite of easy."

She said nothing, just looked me with her big hazel eyes. I swear, sometimes I think she can see into my brain and read my thoughts, and it freaked me the hell out.

"Can we be friends again?" I asked.

"Why? What does it matter if we're friends again?"

"Because you're important to me," I said. It's weird; now that I look back on it, my most honest moments are almost always with her.

That did the trick. She gave me a hug through the window, and I went home, feeling like a weight had been lifted off my chest, replaced by something else, another little anchor of a feeling that I didn't yet know what to call.

P.S. I think it was love.

4

Nina noticed the change in me after Elsie and I started talking again. Nina became even clingier. She was one of the most popular girls in school—and I suppose you could say I was pretty popular as well—so I didn't understand why she was so insecure. She started to ask me if she was prettier than so and so, if she was skinny enough to be a model, if she had what it took to be on the *Real World*. I always said yes because I knew that if I said anything else, she would argue with me until she was blue in the face.

I just wanted some peace in my life; that's why I told her what she wanted to hear.

I took Nina to the Shermans' house one night because Jason's mom, Elodie, wanted to meet her. Dinner was uncomfortable. Elsie was unusually quiet, just pushing her food around on her plate and not even looking at me. Nina, on the other hand, acted as relaxed as if she were eating at her own house. She talked to Elodie and John as if they were peers and even asked if Elodie used low-fat ingredients when making dinner.

The next day at school, I overheard Nina telling her friends that the Shermans' house was a mess, and Elsie's room was decorated like a little girl's. I disputed the fact, but nobody listened to me.

Then Nina and her friends turned their menace on Elsie. I wasn't aware of any of it until I started noticing Elsie's moods when we came home from school. She'd go straight to her room and when she came back out for dinner her eyes were red. Her parents asked her about it but she would just glance at me, then shake her head. Eventually, I figured she must have told them because they stopped asking.

One day, Elodie asked me to help her load the dishwasher. I didn't mind; I offered to help whenever I could. It was the least I could do since they fed me most nights of the week.

"Henry," she said when we were alone in the kitchen. "I think you should be aware of something."

I placed a plate in the dishwasher. "It's about Elsie, isn't it?" I asked. I leaned on the counter and prepared myself for the news. "Is she sick?" My heart clenched at the thought.

She shook her head, smirking at my dramatics. "No, not at all," she said. "It's about your girlfriend."

I froze. "What about her?"

"Elsie told me that Nina and her friends have been bullying her."

"That can't be right," I said. "I've never seen them do anything like that."

"Elsie said they do it when you're not around. They surround her at her locker and say mean things. Last week they trapped her in the toilet stall for fifteen minutes during lunch."

I shook my head, still unwilling to believe that someone I was dating could be so cruel. "That doesn't sound like Nina."

"Apparently, Nina doesn't like that you're friends with Elsie. She wants Elsie to stop talking to you."

I felt sick to my stomach. "I think I've got salmonella," I said, clutching at my middle. "I feel like ralphing."

Elodie laughed. "Henry, I think what you're feeling is guilt." She looked at me for a long time. "Look, I'm not your mother, so I can't tell you who to date. I don't know how much you like this Nina girl, but Elsie is my daughter, and anyone who hurts her is automatically on my shit list."

I nodded, feeling mildly horrified that Jason's mom had used a swear word in front of a minor. That's how I knew she was dead serious.

"So if you could talk to Nina and tell her that I will wring her pretty little neck if she messes with my daughter again, I would appreciate it." I must have looked aghast because she laughed and pinched my cheek. "Now be a good boy and finish loading the dishwasher, please."

———————

I really liked Nina, obviously. I mean, we went out for over six months. She was funny and sexy and we had quite a lot in common. Plus the girl could give head like nobody's business.

I'm sorry, that was crass. But damn.

Anyway, as much as I liked Nina, I just couldn't stand by knowing she was making Elsie's life hell. I don't have siblings but if I had a little sister, I knew I'd be as protective of her as I was of Elsie. So I ended it with Nina, telling her that I'd cheated on her with a girl from another school, throwing in that the girl thought she might be pregnant.

That did the trick. Nina was a lot of things but she was *not* the girl you cheated on.

It was a huge lie but at least it took the heat away from Elsie. If I'd told Nina the real reason why I was breaking up with her, she would have made sure that Elsie's life was a living hell, and I just couldn't take that chance.

Of course, Nina made sure the rest of the school knew I was a cheating bastard, but since I already had a history of delinquency, cheating was just another notch on my proverbial Bad Boy Bedpost. I think, to some girls, it made me an even hotter commodity. Like maybe they wanted their hands on me so they could try to change me.

I noticed Elsie's mood lift immediately. Her smiles reached her eyes and she was laughing again. It made me happy to see her in high spirits and it erased whatever lingering doubts I had about breaking up with Nina. That was the first time I realized that I would do anything to make Elsie happy.

I even almost stayed in Monterey, to attend the local university so that I wouldn't have to be far from her, but the colonel talked some sense into me.

"You know that's not where you ought to be, son," he said to me one night. That was the first time I noticed that he called me *son* and it gutted me and filled me with pride. "You know exactly what your future will be like if you stay here."

He made me believe that I was bigger than Monterey, that I was destined for adventure. "Do you really think I have what it takes to be in the Air Force?"

The colonel didn't even hesitate. "Of course I do!" he boomed. The man had such a mighty presence. "I don't know if you know this about yourself, but you are braver and more honorable than you give yourself credit for. ROTC and then the Air Force will bring that out in you, make you the leader that you were meant to be."

I'd never actually felt like a leader, but I bought his words. He was a military officer, for crying out loud, only two promotions away from general before he'd retired. If the man told me to jump off a cliff because that's the kind of man I was, I probably would have done it. I'd never even thought about my future until he welcomed me into his home.

In many ways, John Sherman was the father I had always wanted so I was going to do my fucking best to make him proud.

I was accepted into the University of Missouri with an ROTC scholarship, the same as Jason. The first day of college, I signed the contract stating I would enter the military after graduating, exhilarated and scared shitless.

My fate was sealed.

5

My senior year of high school came to an end. I was graduating with a surprising 3.8 average and was heading toward a prominent university to study criminal justice. The time came to say good-bye to something I'd loved yet abused all these years: my hair.

It was a month before graduation, but Jason suggested that we go ahead and buzz our hair in anticipation. We went in search of the hair clipper in his dad's stuff but when it came time to use it, we both realized we had no clue.

"How hard could it be?" Jason asked as he held the clipper above my head.

"Don't you need one of these things?" I asked, holding up a plastic guard.

"I don't know."

I panicked and ducked out of the way when the buzzing began. "Oh hell no. There's no way you're using me as a guinea pig."

Elsie swept into the bathroom and promptly took hold of the shears. "Gimme." She picked up a guard and put one on the device. "You were about to shave him bald, dumbass."

I remember feeling an outpouring of gratitude toward her, and as I watched her hold the clippers above my head, I felt relieved.

Somehow I knew I'd be in good hands. Elsie wouldn't do my hair wrong.

She ran her fingers through my hair first, massaging my scalp a little, and thank God I had a beach towel wrapped around me because it gave me an instant boner. Then the buzzing began. I watched her face closely in the mirror as she touched the clippers to my temple so gentle and light, the hair falling away quietly. It didn't even occur to me that my hair was really going to be gone; my entire focus was on Elsie's face, the creamy skin on her cheeks turning a little pink because she knew I was watching her.

When I first met Elsie I thought she was cute in that pinch-cheeks kind of way, but that day, I studied her face in the mirror and realized she had grown into someone truly beautiful. I saw her almost every day so I didn't really notice the subtle changes in her face until then, how her face had thinned a little, making her cheek-bones more prominent.

I could barely breathe during that entire fifteen-minute haircut. My heart was pounding so loud I was sure she could feel it through my scalp. She did this thing where she bit her lip when she was clip-ping around my ears and it drove me absolutely nuts. I wanted so badly to bite down on those lips.

After she was done, she rubbed my scalp again, then faced me in the mirror. She smiled, proud of her handiwork, but her expression softened when our eyes met.

That was when I knew I was a goner. This girl—this young woman—in front of me was going to be my happily ever after, and for a kid heading off to college, that was the scariest feeling in the world.

Whatever terror I was feeling was quickly dashed when I saw the look of sadness on her face. "You okay?" I asked.

She swallowed and nodded. "You just look so different."

I covered my shaved head with my hands. "It's still me under here."

"You're gonna have fun in college," she said and then took off.

"What's her deal?" Jason asked, taking me by surprise. I'd forgotten he was even there.

I only shrugged. My heart was still thudding wildly in my chest, still reminding me that I had made a discovery that doomed me forever. So I used the default guy theory for when a woman was acting a little nuts: "Must be PMS."

6

The weekend before Jason and I left for college, the Shermans threw a huge beach party to celebrate. We dug a huge circular trench in the sand, sculpting seating around the edges, then built a bonfire in the center.

The party was fun, but I was always painfully aware of Elsie, of where she was and what she was doing. When the sun was beginning to set, I noticed that she was missing, so I went looking for her.

I found her by the water's edge, walking alone with a sweater wrapped around her shoulders.

"Hey," I said, approaching her with my hands in my pockets. It was getting cold by then and I had on only a T-shirt.

She looked up at me and smiled. "Hey, I have something for you."

"Oh yeah?" I asked, wondering if I was going to get to kiss her for the first time. Spoiler alert: I don't actually get to kiss her until years later, but at the time, I thought for sure what she was going to give me was a kiss.

"Hold out your hand," she said and placed a damp pebble on it. Damn it.

"A wonky rock?" I asked, turning it over and over.

"It's sort of shaped like a star," she said, touching it with her finger. "I just found it."

I wrapped my palm around it and stuck it in my pocket. "Uh, thanks." I didn't get it, but whatever floated her boat.

She laughed. "I know it's silly, but I wanted to give it to you so you can remember me when you're in college."

"I don't need a rock to remember you," I said. "My head could be filled with rocks and I would still remember you. You could hit me with a huge rock and give me amnesia and I'd still remember you."

She snorted. "Well, if nothing else, you are that rock. You can look at it and know that even though the elements can change your shape, you're still you at the core."

I fisted that rock tighter, a lump growing in my throat. "Okay."

She stepped into my space and wrapped her arms around me. "I'll miss you so much, Henry," she said, and then, as if realizing what she'd done, pulled away. She was blushing.

My chest felt tight at the knowledge that this was the end of our times together. I decided right then that I'd show her how much she meant to me. As if reading my mind, she closed her eyes and angled her face up as I leaned down toward her.

Jason chose that same moment to come ruin the moment. "Guys, we're breaking out the s'mores," he called.

"All right," I said, jumping away from his little sister. "We'll be there in a second."

Jason just shook his head and left.

I looked at Elsie and imagined her life if I kissed her now, then left for college. What I saw was a vision of her pining for me, refusing to date anyone because she was waiting for my return. It was romantic as hell but it gave me a bit of an ache in the pit of my stomach. There it was again, the salmonella poisoning of guilt.

So I decided to make our lives simpler and give her a chance to enjoy the rest of high school. "Elsie, I can't give you what you want."

She was taken aback by my words. "Huh?"

"You want me to kiss you, then you'll want me to be your boyfriend, but that's not going to happen."

"Why not?"

"Because!" I said, throwing my hands up. I searched for a reason that would effectively close the door in her face. "Because you're like a little sister to me."

Her face fell, and my stomach hurt even more. "Oh."

I looked out over the ocean, at the orange sun dipping below the horizon. It was such an appropriate symbol for us right then. "But I really care about you," I whispered, kicking at the sand. I felt like such a jerk.

"Yeah, whatever," she said through pursed lips. "I didn't want anything from you, Henry. I just wanted to give you that rock."

I watched her retreating figure, wishing I hadn't had to be a dick. I wanted to run after her and kiss her silly, but then what would that accomplish? I was leaving. If we got together and then I left for college, it would break her heart.

I never realized until now how I had saved her from that fate once, but it happened years later anyway, when I made her love me, then left for Afghanistan.

7

Being in college was an experience, I'll tell you that. It was crazy and intense. That heady feeling of freedom goes away the moment you get to class and realize you have to actually do work. ROTC involved a class on Tuesday and Leadership Lab on Thursday, where we learned military customs and courtesies, drill and ceremony. There were fifty of us in the program and we all had to wear our blues on Thursdays for Leadership Lab.

I always thought college was a time to let loose and go wild, but ROTC instilled discipline in us early on, made us aware that our actions directly affected our future. Which is not to say that we were perfect angels the rest of the time. Far from it.

———

Jason and I were gone for Elsie's birthday that year, so we decided to send her a birthday package. The Shermans were big on birthdays and holidays so they always did something special. This was the fourth year I was around for Elsie's birthday and I didn't intend on punking out.

In the past I'd given her a box of cordial cherries, which she hated. The year after that, we all went to San Francisco to celebrate her birthday and we went to an arcade on the pier. I remember spending nearly ten dollars trying to win this damn teddy bear that she wanted, but I eventually got it. She still has that bear, sitting on her bookshelf in her room at our apartment. The third year I gave her a bracelet I'd bought from some girly store in the mall.

So that year, Jason and I got a shoebox and filled it with stuff we knew she'd like: Pixy Stix, Nerds candy, and a Sims computer game. We bought her a scarf and a matching beret and sparkly nail polish from the mall. Jason felt awful that he couldn't be there for her—that was the first year he'd be missing her birthday—so he really took the effort to go to those stores to find stuff she'd like.

I still felt terrible about the way I'd treated Elsie before I left, so before Jason taped up the box, I sneaked in a cute little card saying sorry, that I was looking forward to seeing her at Thanksgiving.

The semester flew by. I was so busy with school and ROTC I hardly had time to think about Elsie, which was a blessing actually. I didn't have time to worry about what she was doing, who she was seeing. For the first time in a long time, my mind and my heart felt free.

Then Jason and I drove back to California for Thanksgiving and it all changed again. Elsie was all I could think about on that thirty-three hour drive. It took so long that by the time we got to Monterey, we only had two days to spare before we had to head back to Missouri again.

But in those two days, I drank up the sight and sound of Elsie like a drowning man. Enough to last me until Christmas at the very least.

She was standoffish with me, not quite like a stranger but damn well close. I knew then that I'd hurt her more than I'd intended. I ate Thanksgiving dinner at my parents' house. It was one of the few nights of the entire year that I actually broke bread with them. I was miserable. We had a few relatives over for dinner, most of whom

I don't even care to mention because they never bothered with me the rest of the year so why should I bother with them at all?

I shoveled my turkey down and snuck out of there as soon as we were done. I'm betting nobody even noticed I was gone.

I went over to the Shermans' house and spent time with them, the entire family relaxing on the oversize sectional as they watched the game. John and Elodie grilled us on school, what we'd done, how we were coping with our studies. All the while Elsie sat in the middle, hugging a pillow to her chest and giving me the side eye. She didn't say a word; she just listened to Jason and me talk, and because I knew she was a captive audience, I told my stories with extra oomph and details to entertain her.

She stayed downstairs with us in the family room even after her parents headed off to bed. She laid on the chaise part of the sectional and said nothing, just flipping through the TV channels until Jason took over and turned on the PlayStation.

I wanted so badly for Jason to leave the room, maybe take a shit or something so that I could talk to Elsie, but the opportunity never presented itself. I never got to ask her if she liked our gift, if she read my card and read between the lines.

She never said anything about it, which I guess meant she never did.

8

That December I flew home early for Christmas break to see Elsie. It took some fast-talking but I figured my schedule out so I could leave school two days earlier. It was really important that I got to California before Jason because that was the year I'd finally decided I was going to talk to Elsie.

I'd been away enough from her to know that my feelings were holding firm; they weren't going anywhere. So I needed to talk to her and maybe come up with a solution to my problem.

I was torn between wanting her to reciprocate and wanting her to just tell me to move the fuck on because she didn't see me like that anymore.

When I arrived I immediately went to her house. I was about to knock on the front door when she drove up in her little white car. I must have looked different, because the shock on her face was comical. She ran out of that car and jumped into my arms, nearly knocking me back. My heart just about burst at her overjoyed reaction and I thought, maybe, I had a chance.

Then that douchebag boyfriend of hers walked up and she introduced me as just Jason's best friend—not her friend, not the guy she'd been crushing on since she was twelve, just her brother's best friend—and hammered the nail in the coffin. I had to ask myself what the hell I was doing. I was in college; I should be having the time of my life dating and partying. Instead I was pining for this high school girl who only saw me as her brother's best friend.

I'm a little grateful for what happened because it really gave me the kick in the pants that I needed.

I went back to school and really put myself out there. I went to parties, dated girls, and had the time of my life. Jason and I moved in with another guy in this shabby old house off-campus, and somewhere in the move, Elsie's rock got lost. Actually, I think my roommate Hank might have thrown it in the backyard thinking it was just a silly rock. I was torn up over it for about half a second, then I told myself that it *was* just a silly rock. Whatever meaning Elsie had spoken into it was now long gone, along with everything else.

9

One spring break Jason and I decided to go to Florida and party it up like the rest of the kids our age had been doing for years. We'd heard enough bragging from other guys about their sexual conquests and the amount of alcohol they imbibed. It really made me wonder how it would feel to live my life without worries, so I talked Jason into going. Not that it took much convincing.

We started drinking as soon as we checked into our hotel in Panama City and didn't stop until we got ready to leave. Spring break lived up to expectation in that regard.

We went to all of the beaches. We tried all of the beers. I'm sure I did some damage to my liver that week but I didn't care. I flirted with cute girls wearing little more than triangular pieces of fabric and made out with those who were willing. I had my ass and dick grabbed more times than I could count, and it made me feel like a piece of meat, but what guy doesn't like that?

Jason slept with a girl the first night we were there. They had just met at the bar, and she came to our room and had loud sex on his bed with me sleeping several feet away. I didn't know if she was expecting a threesome but I really wasn't feeling her. Tall blondes are not my thing.

Jason vowed to have a different girl that night after sending the blonde out the door to do the walk of shame. We made a bet on who could get the hotter girl to sleep with him.

Turns out, the girl Jason slept with made a repeat appearance in his bed that night. She ran into us again and apparently Jason wanted seconds. He actually ended up sleeping with only her that weekend. They even kept in touch after spring break, but she went to school in New York, so nothing more happened. I think, though, Jason really fell for that girl.

Me, I picked up a really sexy girl with long brown hair and a deep tan. Man, she was hot. I took her back to the hotel and we fooled around. I was prepared to stop if she didn't want to go all the way but she never said no. Hell, she was begging me to put it in. So I did, and it was exciting and felt good. I hadn't had sex since Nina, so coming into that condom was the best thing that had happened to me since getting into college.

Afterward, as she fell asleep beside me, I felt really strange. I always thought I'd feel like a stud after a one-night stand, but instead I felt like crawling out of my skin. I had just given away a piece of myself to a complete stranger, to someone who would probably just sleep with someone else the next day and I could never get that back. This girl beside me didn't know me, probably didn't even remember my name.

I didn't sleep in my bed that night. I left the room and walked around on the beach just thinking. I was overthinking like usual, I knew that, but I couldn't help it. I kind of internalize things, as you are well aware.

Sometimes I wish I was more like Jason, who was happy-go-lucky and just let the waves of life carry him along. Me, I'm always trying to swim against the tide, always trying to find meaning where there isn't. I wonder sometimes if thinking too much will ruin my life.

God, I hope not.

10

The Shermans, including Elsie, flew out to Missouri for our graduation and commissioning. After Jason and I pinned on second lieutenant, the Shermans took us out for a celebratory dinner.

Jason and I threw a huge party at our house afterward, which thankfully, Jason's parents did not attend. I was already a little embarrassed by the state of our living quarters (we're guys, we're always going to be filthy), and they certainly didn't need to bear witness to our wild parties.

The colonel had reservations about his only daughter attending but Elsie was already a sophomore at UCLA by then so she did pretty much whatever she wanted. Still, the colonel asked Jason and me to look out for her, to make sure no guy took advantage of her. I looked out for her all right, but I can't say that no guy took advantage of her because one did.

Me.

It was a few hours into the party. The music was blaring and the alcohol had been flowing for a while. I had already had several red Solo cups of beer and Elsie, I think, may have already done a keg stand or two. A few of the guys were really gunning for her, and I couldn't really blame them. She was easily the best-looking girl there. Her hair had grown down to her waist and the curls were relaxed, not as corkscrew as in high school. She was wearing these tight jeans that hung low on her hips and this top that kept showing her stomach every time she moved. Of course those guys were interested in her. She was gorgeous.

So it was my duty—and pleasure—to stay by her side all night. We talked like old times. Alcohol goes directly to Elsie's vocal cords; the more she drinks, the more she talks. By that time of the night, she'd had plenty to drink and wanted to have a heart-to-heart.

"I'm so proud of you," she told me as we sat down on the rickety swing on the front porch. "You're a college grad and a second lieutenant in the Air Force."

I shrugged it off. "Thanks. It's not a big deal."

She leaned up and planted a kiss on my cheek. "Not a big deal? Look at what you've achieved."

"Thanks," I said. I took a big gulp of beer. "I'm proud of you too."

"What for?"

"For turning out the way you did."

She turned back to me with a frown. "Huh?"

I laughed, giddy with everything. "You're so grown-up and so hot." Hell, she wasn't the only one affected by the alcohol.

"Well, thanks. Though you should probably be thanking my parents for that, for giving me good genes." She leaned her head back on the swing and closed her eyes, exposing her neck. "I'm so drunk."

"Yeah, you are." My eyes traced her profile, from her lips to her chin, down her neck and finally to the soft swell of her chest. She was definitely grown all right.

The column of her neck was too enticing to resist so I bent down and touched my lips to the point right above her collarbone, just to see what it would feel like.

She jumped back as if I'd electrocuted her. "What are you doing?"

The beer and jungle juice was making me very brave. Hell, I'd made it through college and ROTC, surely I could also tell a girl I liked her. "I was kissing your neck." What? I was chickenshit.

"Why?"

Now or never, Henry. "Because I like you, Elsie. I *really* like you."

She granted me a dreamy smile. "I like you too. You're handsome."

I licked my lips as I stared at her mouth. "Actually, I take that back—"

"What?" she asked. "You can't take something like that ba—"

I leaned over and kissed her. I just pressed my lips to hers, my body on autopilot. For the first second, she was too shocked to respond, but then her mouth opened and invited me in. She sat up with renewed purpose and grabbed my shoulders, pulling me closer.

God, the kiss . . . I don't know how to describe it without sounding cheesy or sentimental. It was just like I'd imagined, all soft and hard at the same time. Her tongue was sweet and sexy at once, and when she bit my lip . . . fuck. It made me hard all over. Even my toes had boners.

I pulled away and I was sure I sounded desperate when I asked, "You want to come to my room?"

"More than anything."

I took her hand and led her through the party, making sure Jason was not around to bear witness. I pulled her into my small, cluttered room and closed the door behind us.

She kissed me again, her arms wrapped around my neck. I devoured her mouth as I gradually lowered her to the bed, pressing her into the mattress as I fought to control my body.

I had to slow down and savor the night. If I wasn't more careful, I'd detonate in five seconds and that was something I didn't want for our first time together. I was doing fine until she wrapped her legs around my waist and moaned against my ear, "Henry, I want you to make love to me."

My hips moved on their own as I ground my dick into her crotch, trying by sheer will to liquefy all the fabric between us. I was this close. All I needed to do was relieve her of her clothes and plunge inside her, but like I said, I needed to slow down.

I pulled away. "Have you done this before?" I asked her as I traced the column of her neck down to her chest and ending at her bellybutton, where I toyed with the hem of her shirt.

"Yes."

I should have been relieved—I mean, having sex with a virgin is not the best, because really, how could you enjoy yourself when you know you're hurting the girl?—but I was mostly angry with myself. "That should have been me."

I didn't know I'd said that aloud until she said, "I wanted it to be you." Her face was all regret and tenderness.

I touched her cheek. "I'm sorry." She closed her eyes and leaned into my palm. That one little move made my heart hurt. "I love you so much," I whispered.

"I love you too, Henry," she said, her eyes remaining closed. "I have since forever."

I was unable to move, afraid that if I did, the spell would be broken and she'd jump up and take those words back. I couldn't have that.

Elsie loved me. Me. Henry Logan. Me. The dickhead who'd made her life miserable.

Me.

I opened my mouth to say something—hell, I didn't know what, I only knew that something needed to be said to cement the moment, but the next thing I knew, she had fallen asleep, her face still cradled in my hand. So I carefully pulled the covers out from under her and tucked her in, my entire body still warm from her words. It didn't matter that we weren't going to make love that night. She loved me and I loved her—we would get to it eventually.

For now, the most important thing had been established. She loved me too.

I pressed a kiss to her forehead and closed the door behind me, making sure to hang a sock on the knob so that people wouldn't come in the room.

The next morning, I woke up and Elodie was in our living room with a trash bag, picking up empty plastic cups. "Good morning, Henry," she said much too loudly.

I sat up from the couch and promptly lay back down again. My brain was pounding the beat of a thousand magnified drums.

"Looks like you boys had a great time," the colonel said, coming from the kitchen with a broom.

"You guys don't have to clean up," I said with an outstretched arm. "Really."

My bedroom door opened and Elsie came shuffling out, looking fresher than she had any right to be. "Morning," she said and kissed her mom on the cheek.

"Did you have fun at the party?" Elodie asked.

Elsie nodded. "Yeah," she said, then her eyes found me. "Thanks for letting me crash on your bed."

The night flashed before my eyes, from the kiss and how close I'd come to making love to her, but mostly to her confession of love. "You're welcome," I said, giving her a meaningful look.

She only shot me a confused look and turned away.

The Shermans took Elsie back to their hotel while Jason and I cleaned up. We all met up for lunch at a Denny's afterward. I was dying to talk to Elsie in private, but we didn't have a chance to be alone. Finally, I pulled her aside as we were all headed to our cars.

"Do you remember what happened last night?" I asked her quickly.

"No," she said, shaking her head. "I can't remember anything past that beer pong game."

My stomach dropped to my feet. "So you don't remember what you said to me last night?"

Her eyebrows drew together as she looked at me. For one moment, I thought she might remember, but she just shook her head. "No. What was it?"

I kicked at the ground as I let her go. "It was nothing. You just said you were proud of me."

She grinned, punching me in the arm. "I am."

Jason and I took them to the airport. I watched her going through the security gate with a glob of disappointment lodged in my belly. I had foolishly thought that that was our time but even though I didn't see it then, I know now it was for the best. I don't know how we would have made it work; she was in L.A. and I was getting sent to Randolph Air Force Base in San Antonio for training, and then after that, who knew.

We were at different points in our lives. Still, it didn't stop me from wanting what I wanted.

11

After graduation, Jason was sent to Lackland Air Force Base for training, which is not that far from Randolph. We were there for nine months and hung out quite a bit.

When training was done we were both sent to Tinker Air Force Base in Oklahoma. That was some seriously freaky shit right there. We said good-bye to each other after college, thinking that our road would fork and I'd go one way and he'd go another. Eventually, we knew we'd see each other again somewhere in the world. The Air Force family is actually quite small, and you'll run into the same people even when you're in backwoods BFE. We never actually thought we'd get stationed at the same place so soon.

We both landed in Oklahoma around the same time and we rented an apartment together on the south side of the city. For a while there, we had it made. We had a really nice apartment, we had our brand-new cars—mine was a convertible Mustang, cherry red, just like I'd always dreamed, and Jason's was a black Camaro—and we had our brand-new jobs. We threw parties every weekend, met friends in each other's squadrons, dated some cute honeys we met in the clubs.

We really lived it up in OKC. I can't say that the life of a bachelor officer sucks. We lived like little kings. Two years in, we pinned on first lieutenant. God, we had it made.

And then Elsie showed up.

Shit, I hate that I'm even saying this, but she really put a damper on our bachelor lifestyle. After graduating she tooled around Monterey for a while before she accepted a web design job in Oklahoma of all places. It felt like high school again, when she'd follow Jason and me around.

It really drove me up the wall because, for one, I can't very well bring dates to my apartment when there's a girl living there, and two, because I still had feelings for her. I mean, there I was ready to let loose and live a little and she was in my space all over again, taking up my thoughts and shit.

She said she only needed a place to stay for a few weeks while she looked for a place of her own, so I at least had that to look forward to. But Jason was a douche and made her sleep on the pull-out couch instead of offering her his bed so every time I came out of my room in the middle of the night, I had to see her lying there, wearing her tiny shorts and a tank top with no bra on. I developed a sudden case of dehydration after that, so I had to go to the kitchen and get a drink of water every night. I was just *so* thirsty.

One night, while I walked past her on the way to the kitchen, she turned to her side and—I swear I tried to look away—her breasts just about fell out of her shirt. She was asleep so she didn't do it on purpose, but the neck of her shirt was really low and when she lay on her side, I could see almost everything. God, I could have stayed there all night just looking at her but I eventually slapped some sense into myself and pulled the sheets over her shoulders. Then I went to my room and jacked off.

The next morning, I went on a hard run and brought back a newspaper. I scoured the classifieds, ready to find a place of my own. I wasn't going to be the bad guy and kick out my best friend's kid sister but there was no way I could live there anymore. My self-control was going to snap sooner or later, and who knows what would happen then.

When I got back from work that day, she had her stuff all packed up by the door.

"Where are you going?" I asked her.

She held up the newspaper with my highlighted ads of available one-bedroom apartments. "I'm going. I can take a hint."

I grabbed the paper out of her hands. "That's not—"

Jason chose that very moment to walk in the door and announce that he was going to deploy. That guy had interrupting down to an art form.

"What?" Elsie asked, her attention completely on her brother. "Where?"

"They're sending me to Afghanistan." Jason looked so proud, so excited. Hell, I was excited for him. This was the first time either one of us had done anything that actually meant something. I mean, we go to work every day, we do our jobs, but for the most part, it's just training. We're just working in preparation for deployments, for war.

That's my job: going to war, and to pretend otherwise is to lie. Our job is to start and end conflicts. Peace means we will be out of a job.

But you know what? Peace is just an idea. There will never be peace on earth, at least, not the kind of kumbaya-harmony people envision. There can be cease-fires and treaties, but we will never know true peace. That's the sad truth of the world.

So Jason getting called from the dugout to play in the big leagues, now *that* was the job we had both been training for.

We went out to celebrate that night and we all got drunk. We took a taxi home and drank some more at the apartment. I relaxed a little around Elsie but before I could tell her that I was the one who was moving out, Jason asked her to stay, to take up residence in his room for the six months that he'd be gone.

Elsie didn't even hesitate. She said yes.

12

I know I haven't said much about Jason lately. I can pepper his name into conversations easily enough but to talk about him, to *really* say something about what kind of guy he was, is hard.

So today, I'm going to try. I've been delaying talking about his death but I've arrived at the point when it can't be put off any longer.

It's so hard to define a friendship, to pinpoint in words what makes you want to spend all of your time with someone. I've thought about it, and I can say some generic things like he's funny or he's loyal, but that's not the entirety of it.

He and I just *clicked*. That's the best way I can describe it. Jason was a good guy down to the core. I would do anything for him, even take a bullet for him, and I know without a doubt that he would have done the same for me.

That's what war buddies become after they've spent time together in the trenches, when you learn to really trust that the person beside you has your back, that even if you're dying on the battlefield your buddy is going to run in and drag your bleeding ass back to safety. It's not something you ask of each other; it's just an understanding. They don't call GIs *brothers in arms* for nothing; except in our case, Jason and I were brothers long before we joined the military.

It was about forty days into his deployment, a few weeks before Thanksgiving, when my commander called me into his office with a grave expression on his face and told me that I'd lost my only brother to a fucking sniper on a rooftop.

I honestly couldn't tell you how I functioned that day. How I didn't get into an accident when driving home was a miracle. All I remember is walking in the apartment and seeing Elsie at the dining table, doing something on her laptop, her life still untouched by the news.

I must have looked like complete shit because she immediately stood and asked, "Are you all right?"

I considered telling her right then and there but I couldn't for a multitude of reasons. First and foremost, my commander had asked that I wait until the Shermans were notified through official channels. Honestly though, I just couldn't find the courage to tell her, to extinguish that light behind her eyes.

If I haven't made it obvious, Elsie loved her brother. They fought a lot but at the end of the day, she adored the hell out of him. She followed him to Oklahoma, for crying out loud. I knew that if she found out about Jason's death she would crumble. I know now that I didn't give her nearly enough credit, that she is far more resilient than I thought, but at the time I just couldn't bear the thought of devastating her life. Everything she knew would change and I wanted to delay that for as long as possible.

As the only brother she had left, I was going to use everything in my power to protect her from pain. That's what Jason would have wanted.

I don't know how I managed to smile through the storm inside me. "I'm just tired," I lied and went straight to my room. I tried to sleep but my brain wouldn't shut off. I paced around the room but I just felt caged. I went to the gym and ran on the treadmill and even that didn't seem enough. The punching bag in the corner caught my eye so I pounded on it until the pain had moved from my chest to my knuckles. I think that was really the only way I was able to get through the next seven days, to hurt my body enough that it superseded the hurt in my heart.

I avoided Elsie as much as I could and just shook my head whenever she asked me if I'd heard from Jason. I told her that work was stressful, a story that she bought until the day her parents called.

For as long as I live I will never forget the look on her face when she was on the phone; her face crumpled and then her eyes landed on me. The hurt on her face made the weight of Jason's death nearly unbearable. It nearly broke me.

I wanted to talk to her right away but she took the cordless into her room and stayed on the phone the rest of the night. The next morning she was gone, leaving only a note on the counter to say she'd flown to California to be with her family, making it abundantly clear that I wasn't part of that.

She was only gone five days but those one hundred and twenty-some odd hours felt like a lifetime. For the first time since I met Jason, I was completely alone. It was . . . unsettling.

I was prepared to grovel and beg when I picked her up at the airport but the moment she emerged from the gate she just fell into my arms and pressed her face into my chest. I couldn't hold it together anymore. I hadn't cried about Jason's death until that moment, when I finally admitted to myself that my best friend was really gone. So I held close the only person I had left, hugged her so tight to me I was sure I was crushing her, but she clutched me closer. I could feel her tears soaking right through my shirt and wetting my skin, and my own were running off my cheeks and onto her hair. We must have looked like long-lost lovers, hugging and sobbing in the middle of the airport, but we didn't care. We were in our own little miserable bubble, two people glued together by our heartache and tears.

It wasn't until a day later when her sadness turned into anger, and she aimed it straight at me. She was so livid that I hadn't told her the day I'd found out. I endured her angry words and accusations quietly, not only because I deserved it, but also because being angry was easier than being miserable. I needed at least one of us to stop being miserable.

Jason's funeral was held a month later. Elsie and I flew to California together this time and we sat in the limo with her family as we followed the funeral procession. Elsie squeezed my hand throughout it all—the draping of the flag on the casket, the firing of the volleys, the bugling. When they folded the flag and presented it to the colonel, I finally broke down. I couldn't play the stoic guy anymore, not when what was left of my best friend was lying in a box a few feet away, and especially not when his sister was falling apart beside me.

There have been very few times in my life when I allowed myself the luxury of being sad, but when they lowered my buddy into the ground that day, I had no control of anything. It was as if a floodgate opened up and I was completely engulfed with grief.

Jason was really gone.

The first night Elsie had a nightmare, I ran into her room and found her flailing around in her bed, screaming Jason's name. Not knowing what else to do, I sat beside her and rubbed her back until she calmed down. She was a trembling mess and she cried in her sleep.

When she woke up, she didn't say anything.

"Having a bad dream?" I asked gently.

She nodded. "I dreamt about Jason walking around in a neighborhood and he stopped to pet this dog. And then . . ." She couldn't choke the rest of the words out.

"Come here," I said, wrapping one arm around her shoulders

and pulling her to my chest. I leaned back into her headboard and held her like that until she fell asleep. It didn't matter that I had a kink in my neck the next day. All that mattered was that I was able to give comfort to Elsie.

The next night I was back there, soothing her again after a nightmare. I could say I was being altruistic but the truth is it was for my sake too. Holding her close gave me a sense of purpose and made me feel a little less alone. She started to sleep on my bed when she had a bad night. Sometimes we'd talk until we fell asleep; sometimes we didn't need to say anything at all. Just being near someone else was enough.

"I'm here," I liked to tell her, to remind her that she wasn't completely alone. "You still have me."

A byproduct of Jason's death was that it cemented my relationship with Elsie and filled in the cracks between us. It was during that year of healing and changes that I finally admitted to myself that my feelings for Elsie were not going to go away; that, in fact, they had intensified due to our new bond. I knew she felt it too but neither of us acknowledged it out loud.

We had just survived the biggest loss of our lives and were finally getting back to a new state of normalcy; we couldn't very well go changing things all over again.

13

Who was it that said that the only thing that is constant is change? Heraclitus? Well, that guy spoke the damn truth.

No matter how much I tried to keep things from changing, life always threw a curveball to remind me that I didn't know jack shit.

Elsie and her boyfriend, Brian, broke up in January. They had only been dating a few weeks before Jason's death, and they were still just at the getting-to-know-you stage. He wasn't staying overnight yet (though I'm pretty fucking sure that asshole got to know Elsie a few times at his own place). Brian seemed like a nice guy, but after we came back from California from Jason's funeral, Brian just kind of freaked out. He didn't know how to give Elsie the comfort that she needed so they broke up.

She didn't date that entire year but it wasn't for lack of invitations. Guys from work asked me if I could fix them up. I just told them that she wasn't ready yet, she was still too vulnerable from her brother's death, which was a little truth-stretching on my part.

Elsie and I spent more time together. I guess, from the outside, it looked as if I had made her my new best friend and she'd made me her new big brother. That wasn't the way of it, at least on my end. Spending time with her felt natural because we had been doing it since we were kids. We went to movies, we ate at restaurants, we planned things around each other's schedule. It was bittersweet, being with her but not really *being* with her, but we were together and for me—at that time—it was enough.

Just when we got comfortable and content, fate pitched a screwball our way. I was told I'd be deploying for six months to Afghanistan.

So how would you do it? How would you tell the person you love that you'll be going to the same place that claimed her brother? Would you tell her right away or would you keep it a secret, like I did? Which one is the braver choice?

For nearly two months I kept that damn secret because it was easier to carry silently than to see the inevitable look of worry on her face. If I could have kept her from the anxiety for even just one day, it would have all been worth it.

Then that night at Tapwerks happened. She was trying to get me to talk by plying me with beer, but boy did that backfire when we got on the dance floor. I don't think she meant to get so close to me, and I certainly didn't mean to shove my boner into her stomach—it just happened. Just like that, I could no longer hide how my body reacted to hers. Who knows what I would have done if she had stayed pressed against me on that dance floor one more second? I would have kissed her—that much was certain—but then what?

I was thanking and cursing every deity for making her pull away.

I had two weeks left before I deployed and I still hadn't told her about Afghanistan. I was getting desperate. I finally decided to just bite the bullet and sit her down the next night. I'd get her favorite flowers, cook her dinner, light some candles, the works. Maybe if I showed her a good time she might not freak out about the deployment.

But then she found out a day too soon and reacted just as I'd feared. She was so angry, so hurt by the fact that I hadn't told her, I was actually a little worried that she was going to punch me. I gave her some time to calm down, and even though it took a while, she eventually saw reason and forgave me.

I knew, when I woke up the next morning to her hands around my dick, that things were never going to be the same. God, that was . . . the most amazing thing to wake up to. Her hands were gentle and firm and insistent and when she woke up and realized what she had done, her skin turned this adorable shade of pink. I wanted to hug her and tell her that it was okay, that I didn't feel violated—in fact, I wanted her to keep going—but I suspected from her reaction that she wasn't ready to hear that yet.

After she literally ran out of my room, I had a few moments with myself. I closed my eyes and pretended Elsie's hand was still in my pants. At the risk of being crude, Doc, I'd have to say it was the best work I'd done in a while.

To my surprise, Elsie kissed me that night, tasting like pizza sauce and pineapples and the sweet promise of release. I could have kissed her all night but then my damn conscience chose that moment to kick in. If I allowed it to continue, I would inevitably hurt her when I left in a little over a week. So even though it was one of the hardest things I'd ever done, I pulled away for her sake. Maybe for mine too because now that I look back on it, I think I was a little afraid that the reality would not live up to the dream.

One thing you don't know about Elsie is that when she puts her mind to something she usually gets her way. I don't know if it's just plain tenacity or if it's a quirk of the universe, but she often gets what she wants and apparently she'd decided that she wanted me.

Not that I'm complaining. Not at all.

She even brought home my favorite ribs to help with the seduction. It was so like her, to think that I would need anything else to be seduced when all I wanted was right in front of me, pushing her cleavage up for my view.

I did everything I could to avoid the inevitable. I counted to five, ten, twenty. I thought about disgusting things like dead skunks, but nothing—nothing—could stop my desire from boiling over.

I stalked over to her and boxed her in with my arms, making sure she couldn't run away. "Do you have any clue what you do to me?" I asked her, hoping she could say something to bring me back to myself. I was lost in arousal. My entire brain was occupied with one thought: to make love to her. My body took over and pushed my erection into her stomach, a promise that I would do everything in my power to make her come over and over.

Still, even as my body kept telling her to yield, my mouth kept asking her to stop. Why? I don't know. Because I was afraid of what would happen if I finally got everything I'd ever wanted? I don't know what scared me more: being with her and ruining the relationship or deploying and ruining our relationship. Every which way my brain analyzed it, the end result was always the ruin of the relationship.

The body won out. I made love to her on that kitchen counter, first with my fingers then with my dick. She felt amazing wrapped around me and when she squeezed me—fuck—there were no words. Imagine the most wonderful feeling in the entire world—say, an orgasm—but prolong that, stretch it out, spread it thin, caress it over and over. It's like that but multiplied by a thousand.

The dream didn't even hold a candle to the reality.

It was frightening how well we fit together, like—and this is going to sound really mushy—coming home. After we came, I was so happy I burst. The feelings I'd kept near my heart lurched out of my throat and exploded out of my mouth. I finally told her that I was madly, stupidly in love with her.

She said that she thought it had just been sex but there was no way that was all it was. There had been too much in our kisses, in the way she gripped me as if she were falling over the edge and intended on taking me with her. I knew she was in love with me; I just needed to wait until she remembered again.

14

Elsie and I spent the next few days wrapped around each other. Every moment we had, we made sure I was inside her, making love to her. She eventually told me that she loved me. I'd always known it and the past few days made it abundantly clear that she was in love with me as well, but to hear those words coming out of her mouth was what I imagine heaven must feel like. To have her completely, body and heart, was like realizing a dream.

Then, like all love stories, we were knocked off cloud nine when my deployment was moved up. I didn't say anything while we were waiting for that bus on base, not because I didn't have anything to say but because if I opened my mouth, I'd probably tear up and lose some macho credibility. There was no way I was going to cry in front of other airmen, but trust me, I wanted to, especially when Elsie broke down. I just held her against my chest and let her cry, taking in deep breaths to keep my emotions in check. It was only for six months, I kept telling myself. Surely we could keep it together for six months.

Elsie was certain I'd end up dead like Jason, which made me more determined to make it out of there alive. I was going to come home and be with her, *really* be with her. We'd been separated enough.

That was the thought that kept me company through the deployment, that kept me from going crazy with uncertainty and worry.

When that fucker blew up the gate on base, I wasn't worried for my safety. I didn't even think when I ran out of my office after the explosion; I was actually fired up. I would finally get to see some action. The aftermath of a VBIED explosion is not as awful as Hollywood would make you believe. I mean, yeah, there's a whole lot of shit that gets blown up but there's no mushroom cloud, no debris raining down from the sky.

It was just a big fucking hole in the ground, a vehicle in flames, and a missing gate.

We found Jones's body a few feet away and not far from the truck was the mangled body of that fucker who brought that bomb on base. As I stared down at his body—he was only a bleeding torso after the explosion—I was overcome with so much anger, but I knew my men were watching, as were others, so I kept it together. What I really wanted to do was get out my M-16 and just shoot the hell out of the asshole, dead as he was. Then I wanted to scour Kabul and the countryside for that fucker who killed Jason, killing anyone who got in my way until I'd avenged my best friend.

I was filled with blood lust. I was a berserker. I was insane with rage.

I bottled all of that up because I couldn't lose my shit, else I get sent home and kicked out of the military.

That anger stayed with me, simmering under the surface until I got home. Only the joy of seeing Elsie again kept me from complete destruction. The only time I felt completely at peace was when I was inside her. For those few precious moments, nothing else mattered, nobody else existed but me and my girl. Until the night I found out that my friend Dave had kissed her. Then all bets were off.

All of the anger that I thought I was successfully handling rose to the surface. I punched that dickhole without even thinking about what it would do to my career. Everything I'd been feeling came to a head and all of this anger poured forth from me and onto Elsie. She didn't deserve to bear the brunt of it but I couldn't stop myself. Things came out of my mouth that I didn't even know had been bothering me.

And that's what brought me here, Doc. The very thought that I could lose Elsie if I didn't figure my shit out. She wanted me to get help, she wanted me to become the old Henry, the one that she knew before I left for Afghanistan.

The thing is, I don't know who that guy is anymore. He was nice and steady, easygoing and cool. He was, in essence, Jason.

I never told Elsie this but after Jason died, I felt lost. I started to get the feeling that I wasn't always composed, I wasn't unshakable, and I have deep-seated insecurities. That guy that Elsie knew all her life—he was a bit of an impostor, just a copycat of her brother. He's not the real me.

15

I did what you asked me to do, Doc. I went through my old stuff. My parents had it boxed up in the attic, but it was all there: the football jerseys, the yearbooks, the Matchbox toys.

I put everything in two piles: one before the Shermans and one after. The *before* pile was pretty sad, just little toy guns and trains and boxes and boxes of Legos. I had a lot of little motorcycle toys, especially this little red Ducati.

I'd always wanted a motorcycle. I mentioned one time at dinner that I was going to buy a Harley as soon as I'd saved up enough money but the colonel told this story about one of his guys in his squadron who had crashed his motorcycle and lost a leg. John had sounded so disapproving and it made me push that idea aside.

The *after* pile was much larger. It was like my life began when the Shermans came into my life.

I talked to my parents last night. I waited up until they both got home, then I called a family meeting. I think they actually sat down in the living room more out of curiosity than anything else. The last time I'd called a family meeting was when I was five or so, when I'd listed out what I wanted for my birthday.

This time I listed out what I wished they'd given me my whole life.

When I was done my mother had tears in her eyes. My dad was looking at the floor between his feet, his hands clasped together.

"I'm sorry, Henry," he said. "I'm a fuckup."

I didn't refute his words because they were true.

"So you've hated us all your life?" Mom asked.

"How could you not have noticed?" I asked. "Oh, maybe because you weren't around to notice."

"I'm sorry," Mom said. "I wish you'd told us sooner."

"Would that have made you take on fewer clients?" I turned to Dad. "Would that have made you spend less time with your friends or in your man cave?"

Mom looked at me with those eyes I'd inherited. "Of course."

"I don't think that's true," I said.

"How—"

"I remember telling you when I was still in elementary school. I asked you to take one day off from work so you could be the class helper. Do you remember what you told me?"

She shook her head.

"You said you didn't have enough time, that you were too busy."

Mom dabbed at her eyes with a tissue.

"I asked you too, Dad, and you said kids were not your thing. That you might end up strangling each and every one of us by the end of the day."

The fact that he wouldn't look me in the eye made me realize one thing about myself: No matter what, I was at least man enough to look the person I'd wronged in the eye. The revelation was a little bit of a relief and it made me feel a little more lenient toward my parents.

"Well, it's all in the past," I said, getting to my feet.

Mom grabbed my hand. She stood up and wrapped her arms around me, hugged me like she didn't know how. "I'm really sorry, Henry. I had no idea," she said. "I just hope someday you won't have to choose between your career and your family. Especially in your line of work, your family will always come second."

I pulled away, not sure how to take her words. "I will never be like you," I said, even though I knew her words held a grain of truth. The military would always come first as long as I was in the service.

"I hope not." She let me go with a sigh. "I'll make you a promise, Henry. If you ever have children, I will be the best grandmother to them. I will always be there for them. You can count on that."

Dad stood up and nodded. "Me too."

"You hate kids," I said to him with too much venom.

"It might change," he said noncommittally.

I just shook my head and left because I had nothing left to say. I had aired my grievances and they had said their piece. There was no building of the bridges; the islands had drifted too far apart. For now, we would just yell at each other across the divide and hope that the message got across.

16

Elsie came to me in a dream last night.

I woke up this morning with her naked body in my arms. Some time in the night, she'd snuck in through my bedroom window and climbed into bed with me. I'll spare you the details, Doc, but damn, it was the best possible way to wake up.

God, I love that girl. She keeps me on my toes. She makes me laugh, makes me crazy, makes me insanely happy. I honestly don't know what I'd do with myself if she weren't in my life. I wouldn't be the man that I am today, that's for sure.

Our mothers found us in bed together. Luckily, we were under the covers but there's no mistaking what she was doing in my bed. The cat was out of the bag. I guess, eventually, they had to know about Elsie and me. I just never imagined that's how they'd find out.

They were all in the dining room when Elsie and I emerged from my bedroom, all looking so amused. I didn't know why I was so nervous since I'm a grown-ass man and Elsie is an adult, but my knees were shaking when the colonel stood up and walked up to us. When he lifted his hand, I swear, I thought he was going to punch me. I would have deserved it. I was boning his daughter after all.

The colonel just gave me an approving slap on the shoulder and said that he knew I would take care of his daughter, that I was a good man.

That just killed me—his complete trust in me. Here I thought he was going to berate me for taking advantage of his daughter but instead he gave me the highest compliment. He still has many contacts in the Air Force; he could have killed my career with one phone call. Instead he gave us his blessing.

His approval brought my relationship with Elsie to a whole other level. It made everything so real. There's nothing left holding us back anymore. The deployment, the anger, her parents' disapproval; they're all gone. It was just the two of us now. And I have to admit, Doc, that that scares me a little because now there's nothing obstructing her view of me. What if the man she sees is not actually the one she wants?

I'm just overthinking this again, aren't I? I should just relax and live in the moment and enjoy the fact that Elsie and I are together, that we're in love, and that we have the whole future ahead of us.

17

Last night, Elsie and I attended an engagement party for my friends from high school. Hass and Kelly had been dating since junior year so everyone assumed they would get married as soon as we graduated, but they broke up some time in college. They didn't talk for years and then ran into each other again at a grocery store just a few months ago. They were engaged not too long after that.

Elsie's theory is that Hass and Kelly just needed some time apart to grow, which makes a lot of sense. We need to know ourselves before we can be with anyone else.

During the party, I had a chance to catch up with Nina. The conversation was nice and mellow. She really seemed like a different person from the girl I knew in high school, more mature and introspective.

"Have you ever wondered what our lives would be like if we didn't grow up with the same people?" she asked as she looked around at all of our friends.

It was such a simple, innocent question but somehow it stuck with me.

Now Nina's and Elsie's words are swimming in my head and making my stomach hurt because I can't help but wonder how I would have turned out if the Shermans had never moved into my street, if I never had Jason's friendship, or the colonel's guidance, or Elodie's mothering.

Or all of Elsie.

It fucking hurts to even think that way but I can't help it now. It's in my head. Did I turn out the way I was supposed to, or did the Shermans somehow mold me into a different person?

In one night, I'm suddenly lost. I have no idea who the hell I am.

And what's worse is that this person, this version of Henry that Elsie fell in love with, might not be the real me. I don't even know who the real me is anymore.

Would I have graduated high school without Jason?

Would I have entered the Air Force without the colonel's guidance?

Would I have just turned to a life of crime, married some girl, and popped out five kids?

What if the only reason Elsie fell in love with me is because I was all she's ever known? If I hadn't been around all the time, would she still even be interested in someone like me or would she be married to some tool like John?

My biggest fear is waking up somewhere down the road and realizing that my love for Elsie is just affectionate and not passionate love. And worse, that she discovers that about me. That would tear me up the most because, knowing her, she would stay with me out of some moral obligation because that's the kind of person she is. She loves until the end.

I couldn't do that to her, to trap her in a lukewarm relationship with a man who had no sense of identity. The guilt would eat me up alive and I'd end up ruining what we have.

I want Elsie to be with the person she loves passionately, someone she *chose* to be with rather than someone fate just imposed on her.

Yes, even if that person is not me.

You asked me before I left yesterday if anything from these sessions has given me any insight and my answer is yes. I've realized that the only thing I've been able to talk about is Elsie. She's the first thing I think of when I wake up and the last thought in my head before I fall asleep. I'm obsessed with her. She is everything.

I love Elsie enough to let her go and grow on her own, to let her find herself without my shadow looming over her. Then, if we are truly meant to be, I will find her and fight like hell to make her love me again.

18

I told Elsie yesterday. She was furious. I feel like, instead of getting rid of my anger and resentment, I've somehow just infected her with it. But Elsie, being the person that she is, tried to understand where I was coming from. She didn't beg me to stay. She let me go.

Did that disappoint me?

Maybe. Maybe I wanted her to fight for me, but that would have just made it harder. Elsie has never tried to hold me back—I love that about her—but I think I might have changed my mind if she'd just asked me to stay. I don't know. I feel like I can't think straight anymore.

I don't know if maybe I'm just intentionally putting another obstacle in the way of my happiness, if I'm just sabotaging this perfect relationship because deep down I think I don't deserve to be happy. Or maybe I'm just making rationalizations for my fucked-up brain.

Whatever it is, I need to figure myself out before I do something stupid. Yes, even more stupid than breaking up with the only person who's ever mattered to me. I need to sort through my shit before

I can even think about being with her again. She deserves that much.

But God, that look on her face when I said good-bye . . .

Doc, I need you to tell me that I did the right thing.

Please.

PART FIVE

ENGAGE

1

CONTINUE MISSION

I walked into my apartment and locked the door, slipping out of my shoes before venturing into the living room. I collapsed onto the tan suede couch, the stack of mail still in my hand. The answering machine still blinked at me from the counter, weighed down by all the messages that had accumulated since August, messages that I hadn't been ready to listen to yet.

Five months had elapsed since my disastrous trip to California, since Henry pulled the rug out from under my feet and made me question everything I'd believed to be true. If there was one thing I would have bet my life on back then, it was that Henry would never intentionally hurt me; but he had, and in the most brutal, unexpected way possible. He loved me, then left me, and the most infuriating thing was that after I listened to his therapy tapes, I kind of understood. His underlying anger stemmed from a case of not knowing who the hell he really was. It wasn't from some deep dark secret from the past; it was just about a man with a serious case of identity crisis.

I understood his issue, which is not to say I liked it or had even come to accept it.

I had come home from Monterey to an empty apartment and a

note from Henry saying he was staying with a friend and would give me the next day to recover alone. I had used that time to enlist the help of every single friend I had so that I could move out of the apartment as quickly as possible. Thankfully, Beth had allowed me to stay with her while I searched for a place of my own, and the situation had improved when she moved into Sam's house after he proposed, leaving me with the apartment. It had all worked so seamlessly that I'd wondered if maybe the universe had finally decided to throw me a bone after screwing me over so much.

There, alone in my apartment, I cried myself to sleep and when I awoke to nightmares, I had nobody but myself for comfort. It was a truly miserable and lonely existence I would never wish upon my worst enemy. Not even on Nina-freaking-Yates.

Still, I liked to think I'd moved on since the breakup. We were in a new year now, and I decided I needed a new attitude. I'd certainly cried enough to last a lifetime. This new Elsie was going to be happy, damn it, and she was not going to hide from the past any longer.

I heaved myself up off the couch and walked over to the answering machine, pressing Play before I could change my mind.

Henry's voice filled the small apartment, instantly suffocating me with memories.

"Elsie, it's Henry. Beth gave me your new number." He sighed. "I wish you'd told me you wanted to live separately. I could have moved out. It wasn't fair that you had to be the one to move all your stuff. Hell, I could have helped you." He groaned. "I'm sorry. I just worried when I got back and you weren't home; I freaked out. I haven't seen you since you came back from Monterey, and I'm really worried. I hope you're doing okay."

I felt the familiar pressure behind my eyes but I was determined not to cry. I'd managed one entire month without tearing up and I wasn't about to break that streak now. I took a deep breath and readied myself for the next message.

"Me again," Henry said. "I just wanted to wish you a happy birthday. I bought you a gift, but I don't know how to get it to you. If it's okay with you, I'd like to come by and drop it off later, around six. Call me back and let me know. My number's still the same." I had come home that day to find he'd taped a blue envelope on my door. Inside were a birthday card simply signed, *Henry*, and a fifty-dollar gift card to Best Buy. He couldn't have been more impersonal if he tried.

There were a few messages from my parents and friends in between before Henry's voice came on again. "I just wanted to let you know that I won't be coming to Monterey for Thanksgiving or Christmas, so you don't have to worry about running into me. Merry Christmas, Elsie."

And finally a weary "Happy New Year."

I took a deep breath. There. That wasn't so bad.

I moved to the fridge and jumped when my cell phone began to ring. With a pounding heart, I picked it up. "Hello?"

The voice on the other line was not Henry. I was disappointed it wasn't Henry, then disappointed again because I was still hoping it would be. I thought I would have stopped hoping he'd call by now. "Elsie," Beth said. "How are you?"

"Hey!" I tried to greet her with enthusiasm. "Sorry I couldn't get to the phone in time the other day."

"No problem," she said. "Things have been busy around here too."

I poured myself a glass of wine as we chatted. It felt good to talk about meaningless things without having to think about the man who broke my heart. Eventually, though, I knew his name was going to come up.

"So, I have news about Henry," Beth said.

I sighed through my nose. "Do I need to know?"

"Well, I think so," Beth said slowly. "He's moving to Korea next week. A one-year remote tour."

I hardened my heart against the hurt. I'd finally started to get the hang of it these last few months. "Oh, that's nice for him."

"You don't have to pretend with me," she said gently.

"It doesn't really matter if he's here in Oklahoma or halfway across the world. Either way, we're not together." Henry concealing his move to Korea was not the worst in the long list of secrets he'd kept from me over the years. I really shouldn't have been hurt by it. "Does it piss me off that he didn't even tell me? Yes, but what's new? That man never tells me anything."

"I just found out through Sam," Beth said. Sam was in the same squadron as Henry and the two were good buddies.

"Yeah, Henry's moved on. That's fine." It really wasn't, but what else could I say?

"I don't think that's true," Beth said. "He's been keeping tabs on you through Sam."

"What would he know about—" I paused, knowing exactly where Sam was getting his information.

"I'm sorry," she said. "You're my friend. I talk about you. Henry just asks if you're doing okay, if you're dating. He asked about the apartment and the neighborhood, making sure it was safe."

I refused to let that little bubble of hope float too high. I pushed it down into my stomach and drowned it with wine. "That jerk," I said through my teeth.

"I think it's kind of sweet," Beth said.

"Well, he didn't break *your* heart," I mumbled. "So when's he PCSing out?"

"The movers have already come. I think he's leaving next week." Neither of us said anything for a long time. Finally Beth said, "We're having a party at our house this Saturday night for his send-off. If you wanted to say good-bye, maybe give him a piece of your mind, then that's where he'll be."

"No thanks," I said much too quickly.

"Well, the party starts at seven and ends when people start puking in the bathtub," Beth said. "Just think about it."

After the call I crumpled onto the couch and turned on the television, refusing to commit another brain cell to thinking about Henry and his impending departure. I decided I wouldn't think about the pained look on his face the last night we spent together, when he'd told me he was scared he was making the biggest mistake of his life. I wouldn't think about his tapes and what he'd revealed in them, that I had consumed him entirely and he'd lost sight of who he was. I would not even think about the fact that, if he came to my door and begged me, I would probably take him back.

No, I thought as I rubbed at my eyes—stinging from exhaustion and not from tears—*I am definitely done thinking about Henry.*

————

I ended up going to Beth and Sam's house on Saturday night because I was a hopeless masochist—but if anybody asked, it was because I'd decided to be an adult and say good-bye properly.

I felt composed when I parked my car in the street and walked up to the one-story house because I'd prepared beforehand by coating my heart with a thick shell to protect from the hurt.

What greeted me when I walked in the door—Henry talking to a pretty blond woman—put a definite crack in my armor. They were standing together in the living room, their heads bowed together as they talked, noticing nobody else in the room. He threw his head back and laughed at something she'd said, then murmured something that made her smile.

My hands turned to fists at my sides. He had no right to be that happy when I was so miserable. The urge to throttle him had never been stronger.

I was about to stalk over there and give him a piece of my mind when Beth touched my arm, making me jump.

"Sorry. I didn't mean to scare you," she said, then saw where I was looking and gasped. "Shit."

I fought to control my breathing, reminding myself that I'd vowed to act like an adult for the night. "I need a drink," I said.

Beth wound her arm through mine and led me to the dining room with the makeshift bar. "He didn't arrive with her, if that helps," she said, handing me a shot glass.

I looked back over my shoulder, seething at the sight of Henry talking so casually, carrying on without a care in the world. "It doesn't make one damn bit of difference. He could still leave with her."

I took a shot of tequila and chased it down with salt and lime. I knew I needed to just turn around and leave, but I couldn't bring myself to move to the door. Henry was like a beam of light and I was a weak little moth, unable to stop looking. Thank goodness there were walls and a table and a whole lot of people between us, otherwise this little moth would be going down in flames.

"I thought that was you," a male voice whispered in my ear, making me freeze. I turned around to find not Henry but Dave Novak. "Haven't seen you in a while," he said with a friendly smile.

I took a sip of my Jack and Coke and smiled. "Yeah, I've just been doing my own thing."

"I heard," he said. "Sorry."

I shrugged. "It's not your fault." He opened his mouth to ask, but I cut him off. "No really, Dave. It wasn't about the kiss."

"Happy to hear that," he said, then his eyes got wide. "I mean, not that you guys broke up but . . ."

"I know what you meant," I said, glad that we were still friends even after Henry punched him because of me.

We stood around for a few minutes, looking around at the other partygoers and searching for something clever to talk about.

"So," he said, taking a large gulp of his beer. "Are you dating anyone?"

"No," I said. "Wait, you're not going to ask me out, are you?"

He barked out a laugh. "Not anymore."

"Sorry. I didn't mean it to come out like that," I said, feeling a tiny smile tugging at the corners of my mouth. "I just didn't want you to get the wrong idea."

"You and Henry . . . ?"

"Hell no. That's been over for a long time," I said much too emphatically. "I'm just not in the dating frame of mind yet."

"Well then we can be friends, right?" He held out his hand and I shook it.

"Friends is good. You can never have too many friends."

Dave motioned to my drink with his head. "You need another drink, *friend*?"

I drained my glass. "Sure do, *amigo*."

I managed to avoid Henry for another half hour. Every time I looked over, he was talking to another person. I was standing in the dining room the entire time hoping he'd notice me and finally come over, but he never did. It was as if I were invisible.

I needed to get out of there, so when Dave asked if I wanted to play pool in the garage, I agreed immediately.

We walked out to the garage where Sam's impressive pool table took up the entire space, and Dave promptly racked up. I chalked a cue stick and broke the rack, sinking two balls in the side pockets. Dave whistled.

"You're a hustler, aren't you?" he asked, standing by with his pool cue.

"I wish." I walked around the table and hit the white ball but barely managed to strike the intended ball. "See? It's all luck."

Dave grinned and took his turn, sinking a ball into the pocket effortlessly. "Did I say you're a hustler?" he asked. "I meant *I'm* a hustler."

The smile dropped away from his face the same moment I felt a solid body looming over me. I didn't have to turn around to know who it was; every cell in my body recognized him.

"Were you ever going to come over and say hi?" Henry asked. He was so close I could feel his breath on my neck.

I stepped away from his intoxicating presence and turned around. "You looked busy with your blonde," I said.

"She's just the sister of one of the guys at the squadron."

I raised an eyebrow. "So you've moved on to another little sister. Nice."

His nostrils flared and he crossed his arms across his chest. "If that's what you think of me, then fine."

"Fine." I turned back around and took my turn, bending over and sticking my ass out, knowing how he reacted to it. I sank a ball and whooped in triumph.

Dave's eyes flicked from me to Henry. "You guys need a moment?" he asked.

I shook my head. "Nope." I walked to the other side of the table, leaving Henry at the same spot to continue glowering. "So I heard you're leaving."

"I'm gonna go take a piss," Dave said and left, leaving me to deal with my ex-boyfriend in the cool privacy of the garage.

"I fly out on Tuesday," Henry said.

"Have fun." I sank the eight ball. Game over.

I saw him coming but I couldn't make my body move. The next thing I knew he was standing beside me with an unreadable look on his face. "Did you get my birthday gift?" he asked.

I snickered. "Yes, thank you. I bought a vibrator with it."

A muscle in his jaw twitched. "I didn't know Best Buy sold those."

"They market it as a back massager." I put the cue stick away and made to leave, ready to end the stupid banter that might have made us laugh back then, back when we still had joy between us.

He followed me and blocked the door with his large frame. "So what are you doing here?" he asked.

"Playing pool."

"I meant . . . Never mind. Did Beth tell you I was leaving?"

I glared at him. "Yes she did. It would have been nicer to hear the news from you."

"I didn't want you to know."

"Oh, is that why you had Beth call me?"

"I asked her not to tell actually," he said. "I didn't want you to come."

His words were sharp and stabbed me right in the gut. "Asshole," I muttered and tried to push my way past him, but he refused to move. "Get out of the way, Henry."

He crossed his arms across his chest. "No."

"Look, you didn't want me to come, so I'm rectifying the situation by leaving." We were so close I could feel the heat emanating from his body; I had to fight to keep from leaning into it.

"Why are you doing this to yourself, Elsie? Why are you still clinging to the past?" he asked, twisting that knife in my gut. "Just get it through your stubborn head that I don't want you anymore."

Despite the immense ache rising up in my chest, I lifted my chin and looked up at him in defiance. "I don't want you either. I was here to tell you good-bye and good riddance." With those final words, I pressed the garage door button, turned on a heel, and stalked out.

2

COUNTERATTACK

I stewed on Henry's words for the next few nights, unable to accept that he no longer wanted me. For five months I'd tried my best to move on, but five minutes in the same room with him and I was back to square one. I reacted to his presence like metal shavings to a giant magnet; wouldn't it make sense that he felt the same?

He made me so furious. I knew without a doubt he still wanted me—physically, at least—and I had every intention of proving it. I would not let him leave the country without a reminder of what he had given up.

Hell, I too could be detached and cold. I could be just like him.

I waited until Monday night before calling Beth and asking if she knew where Henry was staying. She gave me his room number at the Four Points Hotel by the airport before asking why.

"Because I have something to prove," I said, gathering my purse and keys. I wasn't the only one still clinging to the past.

It was nearly ten o'clock when I pounded on his door, and he answered it wearing only his shorts and a bewildered look on his face. "What are you doing here?" he asked with a deep frown.

I didn't ask for an invitation. I just walked past him and entered the room, suddenly glad to find that he was alone. I hadn't thought about what I'd have done if he had had a woman with him. The thought made me stumble mentally, and I had to steady myself and remember my purpose.

"You still want me," I said after he shut the door. "I know you do."

He turned to me, his eyes piercing right into my brain as he stood across the room. "I don't," he said. Anyone else might have been able to believe that statement. Anyone else but me.

I walked over to him, stood on my toes so that we were eye-to-eye and whispered, "Liar."

He pulled away and maneuvered around me. "Please go," he said, motioning to the door. "You're just making this hard on yourself."

I looked down at his shorts pointedly. "It looks like I'm not the only one finding this . . . *hard*."

His nostrils flared as he stalked to the edge of the bed and yanked on a pair of sweat pants. "What do you want from me, Elsie? God, why can't you leave well enough alone?"

"What do I want from you?" I asked, allowing the anger to seep into my voice. "How about some honesty? How about not making me feel like an idiot for missing you?"

It seemed Henry was angry too, though I couldn't fathom why when *I* was the one being lied to. "If I said I missed you, would that make you feel better?"

"It might hurt less than your lies," I said. "You lied to me back in high school and you're lying to me now."

"I'm leaving, Els. I won't be back for a year."

I could barely speak, but I managed to breathe out, "I know."

"I'm trying to stay away. For your sake," he said, but even as he spoke he began to advance toward me. He reached out and gently placed his hands on my arms.

I ignored the tingling on my skin and said, "You're always trying to protect me from the truth. That's not what I want."

"Do you really want the truth, Els?"

"Yes. I want you to admit that you want me too."

He swallowed hard. "Wanting you was never the problem," he said. His gaze was the blue of a stormy ocean and I knew that if I looked too long I'd get caught in the undertow. I closed my eyes, hoping to avoid getting pulled under.

In the next moment, his lips touched mine and ignited something deep in my belly. I moaned and opened my mouth, drowning in the kiss. Henry didn't hold back. He grasped the back of my head and kissed me loudly, groaning into the heart of me.

All of a sudden he jerked back. "We can't do this." He rubbed his head as he paced the room, then sank onto the edge of the bed. "We shouldn't . . ."

I'd anticipated the classic Henry move of toeing in and jumping right back out. I was prepared. "Shouldn't what?" I asked, slipping out of my jacket and letting it fall to the floor.

His head jerked up to watch me, his jaw muscles tightening.

I grasped the hem of my sweater and pulled it over my head, revealing the black lacy bra that he'd loved so much.

"Elsie . . ." he said through his unsteady breathing.

I held his eye as I unzipped my pencil skirt and slid it down my legs. "Tell me to stop," I said, kicking the skirt aside, leaving me in my underwear and heels. My heart was thundering in my chest. I'd never done anything so bold and had never felt sexier. The wonderstruck expression on his face said as much. "I dare you."

His nostrils flared when I sauntered closer. I grasped the sides of his head and forced him to look up at me, forced him to face the woman he'd tried to lie to repeatedly over the years. He should have learned by now that you can act the part convincingly but you can never run away from your own truth.

"Elsie . . ." he said, letting the end of my name thin out.

"Yes, Henry?"

"What are you trying to do?"

I ran my fingernails along his scalp. "Make you admit to the truth."

He palmed my legs and slid his hands around to the back of my thighs, fingering the edge of my lace panties. "You want me to be honest?" he asked, pressing his lips to my trembling stomach. He grasped my butt and slid his fingers inside my panties. "You want me to do exactly what I want and just forget the consequences?"

I nodded, willing his fingers to move closer to my center.

"I don't—Ah, fuck it." He surged to his feet and took me captive with his mouth as his hands cradled my face. I reached behind him and pulled him closer to me, rocking my hips into his.

"Do you believe me now?" he asked, pressing his hard length into my stomach. Before I could answer, he flipped me around so that my back was pressed to his bare chest. His hand snaked up to my neck and forced my head to the side, his mouth devouring mine again. "I will want you always," he rasped, pressing kisses down my neck.

I said nothing as he unsnapped my bra and let it fall to the floor. I'd said all I needed to say and had proved my point: Henry never stopped wanting me. Now my body was on autopilot, simply retracing gestures from the past. I refused to think so that I wouldn't have to feel. Maybe then I could survive this encounter with my heart intact.

He slipped his thumbs into the waist of my panties and slid them over my butt, his rough hands caressing my skin at every juncture. Then he splayed a hand in the middle of my back. "Bend over," he said and pushed me down onto the bed, exposing my privates.

His hands slipped between my legs and he spread me apart as easily as parting curtains. He bent over me and pressed a kiss at the base of my spine. I started when he bit one cheek. He chuckled and bit the other one.

My legs nearly buckled when his tongue slid through my folds.

I gripped the sheets in my hands and smothered my moan into the covers. After all this time, he still knew how to set my body on fire.

His mouth and tongue worked me over, hard and insistent, making me almost come when he issued a rumbling groan that I felt down to my core. Then he was gone, the sudden chill a stark contrast to the warmth of his mouth a second earlier.

I heard the slide of fabric and a moment later the head of his cock pressed at my entrance. "Say it," he rasped against my ear as he slid the tip up and down my slick folds. "Say you want me inside you."

"Just put it in," I very nearly growled.

He gave a startled laugh before pushing in an inch. He withdrew then pushed back in farther, stretching me. He withdrew again and with that third stroke, slid all the way home. "God, you feel so good," he groaned.

A sigh escaped from my lips. To feel him inside me, filling me up again like only he could was a pleasure I never thought I'd feel again.

His fingers dug into my waist as he thrust in and out at a languorous pace. I bucked against him, trying to take control and make him go faster. Anytime now I was going to wake up and realize that I'd just been dreaming; I wanted an orgasm out of the deal at the very least. "Fuck me already," I cried.

He gripped my hips and complied, but it still didn't feel nearly enough. I reached around and grabbed onto his muscular thigh, urging him to go faster, harder.

"So demanding," he said through his teeth and thrust in even deeper, connecting with my core. Then he slapped my ass and made me involuntarily clench. He stilled for a moment then smacked me again, eliciting the same tightening reaction. "Fuck, Elsie," he moaned a moment before he began to pound me again, harder and harder until I was flying, soaring toward the sky. When he reached around and massaged my clit, I shattered into a shower of white-hot sparks, the fireworks going on and on while he worked me from behind.

My convulsing took him over the edge and he crushed his body against mine as he came, his orgasm punctuated by a low, prolonged growl. Afterward we collapsed on the bed and tried to catch our breath.

I felt vindicated but the triumph didn't last long. Even though Henry was inside me, filling me up, the gaping hole in my chest was still present because all of this was just a lie. We were just two people pretending at making love.

Henry didn't linger for very long. After a few minutes, he pulled away from me and went to the bathroom, coming back a few seconds later with a damp towel in his hands. He rolled me over, crouched at the end of the bed and proceeded to gently wipe the inside of my thighs with the warm rag, never once meeting my eyes.

When he was done, he threw the rag aside and crawled over my prone body, still naked and glorious in his masculinity. He stooped over me, his hands on either side of my shoulders as his eyes raked me over.

My heart thundered in my chest at the look on his face, a heady mixture of lust and something else, maybe regret. I crawled backward on the bed, trying to find an escape route but the pillows and the headboard stopped my retreat.

"Do you need more proof that I want you?" he asked.

I nodded despite myself. I think deep down I knew that I would always need proof. He had broken me, made me question everything I ever relied on. Henry had made a cynic of a dreamer.

He sat back on his heels, resting his hands on his thighs, and showed me just how much he wanted me. Again.

I gazed up at the pure beauty of him, from his broad chest and muscular arms down to the six-pack that ended with those sexy hip indentations guys have, and finally to his thick shaft that pointed straight up, ready for round two.

Apparently, I wasn't the only one who'd been silently appraising because he said, "God, you're beautiful." He wrapped one hand around his cock and stroked himself, his dark eyebrows drawing together as his breathing deepened. His eyes roamed over my body, making my skin overheat with warring emotions of desire and discomfort.

I leaned up on my elbows. "What are you doing?"

The corner of his mouth curled up. "Admiring you," he said. He tilted his cock forward, offering it to me. "You want to take over?"

I stifled a smile. "No. I'd rather watch you."

His insolent smile evaporated when he returned to the task at hand, the furrows in his eyebrows deepening as he altered his grip.

My entire body tingled as I watched him, completely and hopelessly turned on. Henry had full command of his masculinity and knew the exact ways to wield it over my body.

"Touch yourself."

His husky words shot straight to my crotch and created a pressure that needed releasing. I swiped my hand along my stomach and then down to my mound, all the while flashing him with what I hoped was a seductive look.

"Yes, right there," he said as my middle finger flicked at my clit. "Put one inside you."

I slipped my finger inside me, pushing it all the way in, then pulling it back out.

His gaze was steady and dark. "Now two."

I slipped another finger in, never once losing eye contact as my other hand reached up to play with my breast, tweaking my nipple over and over.

His breathing became erratic as his hand pumped faster. I too sped up, intent on keeping the pace. He wasn't about to cross that finish line first.

As if sensing my renewed vigor, he stroked faster, the lines on his forehead drawing deeper the more he concentrated.

I felt the pressure building inside me as I watched his face contort, sure that my own was doing the same. Our eyes were locked in a heated exchange. I didn't need words to know what he was thinking. In that moment, as we pleasured ourselves, we were lost together in the thick fog of passion and heartache.

The intimacy was too much for Henry to bear, and he closed his eyes as he started to come.

"Look at me," I said with a raw voice. "Henry, look at me."

When he opened his eyes, they were filled with so much emotion I almost burst into tears. Instead I let go, my insides pulsing around my fingers as the orgasm racked my body. Amidst it all, I felt a strange sense of finality, as if releasing that orgasm somehow released my stranglehold on the memory of us.

"I'm coming," he said, then let out a groan as he climaxed, his seed spilling onto the covers. He never looked away from me, even as he crouched over and caught his breath, or when he reached for the rag and wiped at the puddle he'd made.

When he was done, he collapsed beside me with a sigh. He grasped my wrist and brought my hand up to his lips, but before he could say anything that would make me start to care for him again, I rolled away and climbed off the bed.

"What are you doing?" he asked as I pulled on my underwear.

"Leaving," I said matter-of-fact.

"You're not going to stay?"

"Why?" I turned to him. "You know I don't like long good-byes."

His dark eyebrows drew together.

I swallowed hard, then shook my head. "Henry, we're not . . ."

I wanted to say we weren't the same people as before, but some things didn't need to be said in order to be heard.

"I know, but I thought we could talk." He sat up and scooted to the end of the bed, quietly watching me as I finished getting dressed.

"There's not much left to say, Henry."

He caught my hand as I turned away. "Just . . . stay," he said, his face open and imploring.

"I can't," I said. "There's no point. You're leaving."

He nodded and let me go. I didn't even kiss him good-bye. I just walked to the door with my purse clutched tightly to my side like a life preserver.

"Bye, Henry," I said as I opened the door. "I hope you find yourself in Korea."

3

RETURN TO BASE

Henry was gone again. Story of my life.

The shell I'd created around my heart had not been enough to keep me from feeling something for Henry again. I thought my heart could be detached from my body, but it seemed I was wrong.

And so the process of surviving a breakup began once more.

I had to keep reminding myself to move on. People lost the love of their lives every day, sometimes to things more permanent. I was no different from, no more special than those countless others nursing broken hearts, and wallowing in my grief was not the way I wanted my story told. So I tried to find pleasure in the small things, like the aroma of a fresh bag of coffee beans or the slide of silk on my legs after shaving. I wasn't anywhere near happy yet, but I was nearing content.

When you've resigned yourself to your fate, when you've really decided to move on, time passes in the blink of an eye.

———

I started to date again. One of my coworkers set me up on a blind date with a single friend and I had agreed out of curiosity. The guy was named Seth and he had short blond hair, green eyes, and a dimpled smile. For our first date, he took me to Dave & Buster's, a restaurant and game arcade, and after dinner we took our alcoholic beverages and walked around, playing the games together.

Being with Seth was easy. He gave me plenty of space, laughed a lot, and didn't ask too many personal questions. He liked to play the shootout basketball games and didn't let me win even one, always nudging me at the end and saying, "Good effort."

At the end of the night he walked me to my doorstep and managed to appear both bashful and incredibly sexy as he looked at me, no doubt trying to gauge his chances at a kiss.

It had been ten months since Henry left for Korea; it was about damn time I finally allowed someone else into my heart. So I decided to give him a chance to kiss me.

He touched the side of my face and bent his head, bringing his mouth to mine, gently exploring before I parted my lips and allowed him inside. The kiss was gentle and sweet and held promise, everything that a first kiss ought to be.

Afterward, he ran a hand through his hair and said, "I really like you, Elsie."

I looked at his earnest face and decided that he could very well be the guy to help me get over Henry. "I like you too, Seth," I told him, which was the truth.

He smiled, revealing his dimples. "Do you want to do something tomorrow night?"

"Sure," I said as he began to walk away backward.

"I'll call you later." And he did. He called exactly one hour and fifteen minutes later.

———

Seth became my boyfriend a few weeks after that date. He called me nearly every night and we talked for hours about everything. In the interest of full disclosure, I told him about Henry, and Seth, in turn, told me about his past relationships. Our conversations flowed easily, and he was just so funny. The humor was what drew me to him, how he could make me laugh and forget about the past.

He worked at Dell as a software engineer. The fact that he also worked with computers, albeit in a slightly different manner from me, was one thing we bonded over. I liked to think we were geek kindred spirits.

Still, every time he wrapped me in his arms and kissed me I felt disconnected, as if I were just an observer instead of an active participant. I remained hopeful. I clutched him tighter, kissed him deeper, sure that, given some time, I would finally feel for him what he felt about me.

To celebrate our third month together, Seth took me to Chili's, of all places. It wasn't my first choice for a date but I didn't want to have to talk about Henry on a night when we were celebrating our relationship, so I just shut up and grinned.

"I'm not a cheapskate, promise," he said as he pushed in my chair. He sat down across the table from me and flashed that dimpled grin again. "I just really like their ribs."

My heart ached at the memories brought on by those damn baby-back ribs, but I'd gotten good at ignoring it by then.

I sat across from Seth, stealing little looks over our drinks. He was very handsome tonight in a light blue button-down shirt, the sleeves folded up to his elbows, and gray slacks, his hair slightly tousled. But as attractive as he was, I couldn't help but get the feeling that he would make a wonderful husband for a lucky woman someday.

"Here's to us," he said, lifting his pint glass.

I clinked my iced tea with his beer and smiled.

He set down his drink, his face taking on a serious expression. He leaned across the table and held my hands. "Elsie, there's something I have to tell you," he said. "I've felt this way for a long time now, but I've been too afraid to say it because of . . . you know, your past."

I held my breath, hoping Seth wasn't about to tell me he loved me and ruin everything. I'd be content with our relationship if we never had to confess anything at all.

"Elsie," he began, making my head hurt with the expectant look on his face. "I want us to move in together."

I let out a small breath.

I must have looked shocked because Seth quickly said, "I know it's huge, but I wanted to let you know that I'm ready to take that next step with you."

"Seth," I said, not sure how to respond. My chest ached at the sincerity of his gesture and the hopeful look on his face. "I . . ."

The hope slipped off Seth's face. "You don't want to."

I gently shook my head. "No, it's not that. It's just . . . I'm surprised."

Seth scooted his chair closer to mine and took my hand. "Hey, I know it's a little soon. I just want you to think about it, then when you're ready, you let me know."

A hopeful little glow flickered in my chest but it had been so long since I've felt hope that I almost didn't recognize it until it was too late. "Let me think about it, okay?" I asked, and as I looked at him I wondered for the umpteenth time if Seth was the guy I would grow old with. I didn't love him like I loved Henry, but Seth was wonderful and reliable. We could live together, maybe even get married, and have a perfectly stable and lovely life. For someone who had experienced so much turmoil in the past several years, stable and lovely sounded like heaven.

———————

Of course, just when I was finally getting my affairs in order, fate threw a wrench in the form of a phone call.

"Hello?" I wedged the phone between my ear and shoulder while I opened a bag of microwave popcorn, expecting Seth's voice. He always called after getting home from our dates.

Instead, a gravelly voice from the past said, "Hi Elsie."

It took me a long time to respond, I was so dumbstruck. "Henry?" I set the popcorn on the counter and grasped the phone before I accidentally dropped it into the sink.

"Hey," he said, sounding like he had a smile on his face. "How are you?"

"You're back?"

He chuckled at my shocked tone. "Yes. I got in last night."

"Don't tell me you're back at Tinker," I said. It didn't seem likely; hell, I'd even prayed that he be stationed somewhere across the country so that I wouldn't have to see him again.

"Actually, I wanted to talk to you about that. Can I come over for a bit?"

I was torn, the old Elsie saying *yes please* and the new saying *hell-to-the-no*.

"I just want to talk," he said.

I swallowed the lump in my throat. "Okay."

"Okay I can come over?"

"Sure."

I jumped at the tapping on my door.

"Knock, knock," he said into my ear.

I shut off the phone and went to answer the door armed with indignation. "How dare you assume—" The words stuck in my throat when my eyes landed on Henry, seeming larger than I remembered, looking more beautiful than he had any right to be in his jeans and leather jacket. His dark hair was longer, curling around his ears and he looked like he hadn't shaved in a few days, but he was the same handsome, infuriating guy I'd grown up with.

"Elsie," he said and scooped me into his arms, momentarily lifting me off my feet as he held me tight. He pressed his face into my neck for a long moment, then, as if remembering what we had become, abruptly let me go. "Sorry about that. Old habits," he said, stuffing his hands in his pockets.

I fought to catch my breath. I was always caught off-guard when Hurricane Henry blew into town. "That's okay," I said, the skin on my neck still tingling. I hated the fact that, after all this time, my body still reacted to him in that way.

"You smell different," he said, cocking his head a little.

"I've taken a few showers since you left."

"I don't believe that for a second." He grinned at me, his blue eyes filled with something that looked like joy. "You're using a different fragrance. You used to like that citrusy spray from the body and bath store. Now you smell a little pepperminty."

"Uh, okay," I said, a little taken aback by his observations. "Are you coming in or are we going to discuss my choice in deodorant as well?"

He walked into the living room and headed straight for my large IKEA bookcase filled with books, movies, and little decorative pieces. He paused at a shelf that held several framed photographs. He picked up one in particular and turned to me with a frown. "You cut me out," he said, looking at the photograph of Jason and me holding our skis at the foot of a mountain, with my left shoulder—and everything beyond it—trimmed off.

"Do you blame me?" I asked, walking over and taking the frame from his hands and placing it back onto the shelf. "And stop touching my stuff."

Henry backed away and sat down on the couch. "I come in peace. Honest," he said, holding his palms up.

I took a deep breath and fought to contain my roiling emotions. It was as if I'd spent the last year rebuilding my life on a stable surface and suddenly Henry was back, flipping everything over.

I stood as far away as possible, folding my arms across my chest. "So what did you want to tell me?"

He ignored my question and looked me over with the sexy sliding look that had always given me a case of the tingles. "Did you go somewhere? You look nice."

I gritted my teeth. "I was on a date," I said, hating that he seemed so comfortable while my insides were in upheaval.

He raised an eyebrow. "Oh?"

"Yeah, he took me to Chili's."

A muscle in Henry's jaw twitched but his face gave nothing else away. "Oh?"

"Yeah, he really likes the ribs," I said, enjoying the fact that I was finally disturbing his calm surface.

His lips formed into a thin line and I almost laughed in triumph. "Have you dated him long?" he asked.

"Three months, give or take," I said. "Tonight he asked me to move in with him."

Henry's blue eyes bore into mine as he waited for me to answer his silent question, but I said nothing. I simply enjoyed his discomfort a little while longer. "Well?" he finally said.

I shrugged. "I'm seriously thinking about it."

He rose to his feet but didn't come closer. "I'm out, Els. I've separated from the Air Force," he said hurriedly.

All of the mirth whooshed out of me in one breath. "When?"

"When my tour at Osan ended." He took one step closer. "I'm a free man. I no longer have to deploy. I can live wherever I want."

"Where are you going to go?" I asked, finding it hard to breathe all of a sudden.

His eyes were mesmerizing, holding me in place as he took a step closer. "I don't know yet."

"What about a job?"

"I have some money saved up, so I can spend some time looking. But I think I want to be in law enforcement."

I wasn't surprised to hear his next career choice. "See? You're an honorable guy through and through."

His lips bent into a rueful grin. "I'm glad you still think so." Suddenly, he was in front of me, so close all I had to do was lean forward and I would be touching his chest. "Don't move in with him, Elsie," he said.

My anger came roaring back to life. "You can't tell me what to do," I said, straightening my spine and pulling away from his gravitational pull.

He rested a hand against my neck. "I'm not telling you," he said gently. "I'm asking you."

It took me a moment to find my voice. "It's no longer your place to ask." I took a step away and tried to clear my head. "Do you want a beer?" I asked, turning away and escaping to the kitchen.

He sighed. "Sure."

We sat down at my tiny dining table and I asked questions about what he'd done in Korea to avoid talking about what he was currently doing in Oklahoma. Henry, for his part, didn't bring up my moving in with Seth again. Instead he leaned his elbows on the table and talked animatedly about his adventures in Asia as easily as if he were talking to an old friend.

I hoped, as I sat across the table, that the round slab of wood was enough distance to keep me from falling again but the erratic thudding in my chest indicated otherwise. The tree had been old judging from the growth rings on the table's lacquered surface, but its age was nothing compared to my long history with the man sitting across it, a history that was far too ingrained in my identity to ignore.

The conversation came to a natural end around three in the morning. I yawned and stood up, collecting the empty bottles of beer on the table.

"Shit, it's late," Henry said, stretching his arms above his head. "I'd better get going."

"Where are you staying?"

"At a buddy's place in Norman. His couch smells like ass but it beats the floor."

A small part of me wanted to offer him the pullout couch, but I knew that doing so would make me a fool. "Well, it was nice to catch up with you," I said instead and walked him to the door.

He gave me a tentative little hug at the threshold. "You too."

I closed my eyes and relished the feel of his strong arms around me, catching glimpses of my yesterlife on the back of my eyelids.

"You shouldn't be with him," Henry said as he pulled away.

I blinked up at him, momentarily addled. "Who?"

"Your boyfriend."

"Why not?"

"Because you don't love him."

I folded my arms across my chest. Just like that, Henry was back to being a dickhead. "How the hell do you know that?"

One side of his mouth quirked up. "Many things have changed about you, Elsie, but one thing is still the same and that is you still wear your emotions on your face. If you loved him, you wouldn't blush whenever I touch you." He pressed a cool finger to my warm cheek, proving his point. God, I hated it when he was right.

"Well who I love is not really your business," I said, swatting his hand away and stepping back into the safety of my apartment. "Good night." I moved to close the door when his hand slapped its surface.

"Go on a date with me," he said.

Despite my racing heart, I tried to play it cool. "I have a boy-friend, remember? We were *just* talking about him."

He scratched the back of his head. "I know," he said, searching for words. "I just . . . I miss you."

Before, my heart would have soared at his confession; now it just cautiously leapt around a little, afraid to take flight. "I appreciate your honesty but—"

"One date," he said, holding up his finger. "If, after that date, you decide that you don't want me back, then I'll go away. I'll move to another state."

I shook my head. "I don't think a date is a good idea."

"Give me one chance. It doesn't have to be a date. It can just be hanging out with an old friend," he said, grasping my hand. "I know I can make you happier than that guy."

True, but he could also devastate me to a greater degree.

"Please."

It was that one word coming from the bossiest man I knew that finally caused me to reconsider. "Okay," I said. "We can hang out once."

A wide smile lit up his face, reminding me of the boy I knew so long ago. "Tomorrow?" he asked and pressed a quick kiss to my cheek when I nodded. Then with a wink he walked off into the night. A few seconds later, I heard a loud rumble that sounded sus-piciously like a motorcycle, the sound rolling off into the distance.

4

PEACE TALKS

Henry showed up at my door the next afternoon wearing a pair of black sweat pants and a long-sleeved Under Armour shirt, a backpack slung over one shoulder.

I looked down at my own outfit of skinny jeans, a loose cashmere sweater, and heels and wondered where we'd gotten our wires crossed. "I thought we were going to the art museum?" I asked as I stepped aside and let him inside the apartment.

He grinned and kissed my cheek, smelling like fresh sweat. "Sorry, the showers were down at the gym. Can I use yours?"

I tried not to stare at the muscles encased in the tight shirt as I nodded. "The door to the left."

"I'll just be a few minutes," he said, flashing me a grin before rushing off.

I tried to occupy myself with a food show on television but my mind kept wandering off to the naked guy in my shower, the water dripping down his olive skin in rivulets as he rubbed his body down with soap. . . .

I chastised myself. I had a boyfriend and his name was Seth and he was wonderful and funny. Henry was just taking a shower, like billions of people had done before him. The fact that he was naked in my bathroom at this very moment meant nothing.

Nothing, absolutely nothing.

But then Henry came out, dripping wet and completely naked except for the balled-up shirt that he was holding against his crotch. I was pretty sure a little nuclear bomb went off in my nether regions at the sight of him. "Where are your towels?" he asked with a raised eyebrow.

Careful to shield my thoughts, I stood up from the couch and walked past him to the linen closet. "Didn't you bring one?" I asked, shoving a towel in his chest. I averted my eyes as I walked past him again, though I caught a whiff of his fresh, cool scent.

"Thanks. I never bring one because they usually have them at the gym," he said. He turned and walked back into the bathroom, deliberately giving me an unobstructed view of his firm ass and muscular thighs.

"Henry, put some clothes on!" I cried as I turned away, his chuckles echoing in the bathroom as he shut the door.

———————

Ten minutes later we were finally on our way. He was wearing dark jeans, black shoes, and a purple button-down shirt peeking from a gray sweater, and he had shaved. I was little sad to see the stubble go, but clean-shaven Henry was painfully gorgeous in his own right.

It didn't really matter, I told myself, because I had a boyfriend. What Henry looked like was not the point. He was just a friend and we were just hanging out.

Still, he looked really handsome as he drove the pre-owned Volvo S80 he had recently purchased to the Oklahoma City Museum of Art downtown. I couldn't help but sneak glances at him, as guilty as it made me feel.

We paid for our tickets separately because I insisted that it would be too much like a date if he paid for mine. He put up a fight, but I was determined to keep it platonic and got my way in the end. It was a quirk of the universe, sure, but it was also because when I really wanted something, I never gave up.

We were walking around the Dale Chihuly glass exhibit when I finally asked, "Why here?" We approached a wall of swirly glass sculptures of different shapes and colors that looked like a collection of frozen underwater creatures.

"This is the most platonic place I could think of," he said, glancing at me before turning his attention back to the art. "I figured we both hadn't been here before, so there would be no memories attached to the place to make you uncomfortable."

We walked through a narrow hallway with a low ceiling filled with the glass sculptures that cast a colorful glow all around. "Memories don't make *you* uncomfortable?"

We walked to the middle of the deserted hallway and stopped. He looked up at the hundreds of glass sculptures. "No," he said, taking my hand. "Our memories give me peace. They give me a sense of identity."

I looked at the kaleidoscope of colors on his face. "Have you found yourself, Henry?" I asked softly, afraid of the answer.

His eyes found mine and he nodded.

I felt relief, sure, but also an overwhelming sense of doubt. "How do you know?"

"Because I feel it," he said, bringing my palm up to his chest. "I've discovered many things about myself, things I never would have known if we were still together."

"Like what?"

"Like the fact that I love *Firefly*."

I cracked up. "You already did before."

"I know," he said with a grin. "But I was never sure if it was because you and Jason loved it or if that was my real, honest-to-God opinion."

I squeezed his hand. "Henry, I never meant to take over your life," I said. "All I wanted was to be in it."

He shook his head, his eyebrows drawn together. "It wasn't your fault, Elsie. I'm the messed-up idiot who thinks too much, who made a mess of everything." He turned to face me, making my stomach flutter. "I know this guy. All his life he loved this girl who was perfect in every way but just when he finally convinced her to be his and they're deliriously happy, he went and messed everything up."

I swallowed down the sob that was ready to erupt. I blinked away the tears that were already starting to form. I chased away the hope that was threatening to explode all over my heart.

"But the thing that this guy finally realized is that, after he made peace with himself, he was still lost without his girl. Like living without one of his femurs, he was incomplete without her," he said, repeating my words back in Monterey.

I pulled away and walked out of that damn romantic hallway, afraid of his words and of what they did to the coating around my heart.

"Elsie?"

"I don't know how to believe you," I said. My legs moved at a fast clip, too afraid to stop moving in case they started to buckle.

"Elsie, stop," he said, grabbing hold of my wrist, but I twisted away and kept on walking toward the exit. This nondate, as far as I was concerned, was over.

———

"Did you listen to my tapes?" Henry asked as he drove me home.

I looked out the passenger window and said, "Yes."

"Well?"

"Well what?" I asked, finally looking at him. "What do you want me to say?"

"That you forgive me."

I raised my eyebrows. "Oh, was *that* your apology?" I asked. "You should have just made me a mix tape."

He sighed as he pulled into my apartment complex. "I get it, you're not going to make this easy."

"Ha." As if he had ever made anything for me easy. I jumped out of the car before he had a chance to open my door, then strode to my apartment.

Henry was hot on my heels, still in my space.

"So I gave you one chance. Now will you go away?" I asked, struggling to get the key into the hole.

"Is that what you really want?" he asked.

I looked away, unable to bear looking at the pain on his face. "That's what's best for me right now."

"Okay."

"Okay?" I cried, feeling my control start to dissolve. "I thought you said you were going to fight like hell to get me back?"

"I'm picking my battles," he said. "I have the rest of my life to win you back."

I didn't know if I wanted him to keep trying but one thing was certain at that moment: I still loved him, changed as he was. I hated him, sure, but the love I'd always felt for him was still present.

If only I could make that feeling go away.

Henry started to walk away but spun on a heel and came right back. "But before I go, will you come to Dallas with me next weekend?"

His question took me aback. "What's in Dallas?"

"There's someone there I want you to meet."

"It's not a girlfriend, is it?" I asked, the very idea filling me with dread and copious amounts of rage.

He let out a strangled laugh. "That would be such a dickhead move."

"I wouldn't put it past you. Since you are one." I felt like a five-year-old but sometimes saying exactly what goes through your head is therapeutic.

He gave a nod. "True. But no, this is not a girlfriend. Or a fian-cée, or a wife."

"Then who?"

"Just come with me and see."

The idea of a road trip with Henry seemed risky. Three hours with nothing to do but talk was going to be hazardous to my health. "I don't think that's a good idea."

"What if I said we could stop at Braum's on the way there and on the way back?"

"Tempting me with ice cream?" I asked. "That's low."

He reached out and took my hand. "You'll love it, I promise."

I gazed at his face, at how much had changed in the past year. He was still recognizable, but I saw the tiny changes in him, knew that he was in a happier place in his life. Despite my reserve, I still felt the need to get to know this new Henry, if only to satisfy my curi-osity.

I sighed. "Fine, I'll go."

He smiled. "Wear warm clothes," he said before giving a short wave and leaving.

———

Seth called that night, wondering how my Sunday had been. I hadn't told him about Henry being in town, had only said that a friend and I were hanging out, which technically was not a lie. But I knew that little white lies had a way of accumulating until they became an avalanche of untruths, so I told him about Henry to avoid getting buried.

Seth was silent for a long time after I was done with my confession. Finally, he said, "So he's backing off after Saturday?"

"That's what he said," I said with a pit of remorse in my stomach. Seth was a good guy and didn't deserve to have a girlfriend who was still in love with someone else. "I'm sorry, Seth. I didn't mean to lie about it."

He cleared his throat. "Do you think he'll actually leave?"

"I hope so."

"Do you? Really?" he asked. "I'm not blind or deaf, Elsie. I know what's going on here. I can already tell something's different about you."

"I just need some time to absorb things."

"You're not going to move in with me, are you?" he asked quietly.

I sighed. I had already known the answer, even before Henry came whirling back into my life. Seth, as nice as he was, just wasn't the guy for me. I knew it all along; I just refused to admit it. "I don't think so, no."

"Are we breaking up?"

My eyes watered at the thought. "Do you want to?"

"No, of course not. I know I haven't told you this, but I love you," he said, breaking my heart. I hadn't known about the depth of his feelings for me. "So no, I don't want to break up, but we have to because you don't feel the same way about me."

"I really wish I did," I said. "I want to be with you."

Seth sighed, seeing right through me and my half-hearted attempt at our relationship. "No you don't. You want to be with Henry."

He was right, so we broke up.

5

ASSIGNED MISSION

Henry rang the doorbell at exactly nine o'clock on Saturday morning, wearing nearly identical jeans-and-leather-jacket attire. "You ready?" he asked, standing outside with his hands in his pockets.

"Will this work?" I asked holding my arms out to show my jeans, tall boots, and a purple turtleneck sweater.

He grinned as his eyes took me in. "Almost," he said but didn't elaborate. He held out his hand. "Come on, let's get going."

"I knew it," I said as he led me to a Harley motorcycle. It was red, black, and chrome, and larger than life. Hazardous to my health indeed.

"It's a Softail Deluxe. I bought it the day I arrived." On its seat were two helmets and a black leather jacket. He lifted the jacket and walked around behind me. "Try it on."

I slipped my arms into the buttery soft leather and turned around to face him. "Fits perfectly," I said. "Your ex-girlfriend's?"

"In a manner of speaking," he said. "Yours." He zipped it up slowly, his knuckles lightly grazing my breasts as they glided up, then popped the snaps at the collar.

I didn't know if it was the jacket or Henry's proximity, but I suddenly felt warm all over. "I can't keep this."

"Yeah you can," he said, zipping up his own jacket. "Think of it as a belated birthday and Christmas present."

I played with the jacket's ruffled bottom, which lent a flirty, feminine touch to what was otherwise an androgynous jacket. "Thank you. It's exactly what I would have bought."

He flashed me a grin. "I know," he said then held out the smaller of the two helmets.

"You know this is going to ruin my hair, right?" I asked, gingerly pulling the helmet over my head. So much for having nice hair today.

"It'll be worth it," he said before flipping down my visor. He climbed on the bike and flashed me a grin, all muscle, metal, and pure confidence. He had never looked sexier. I might have gasped inside the privacy of my helmet. "Climb on," he said and popped his helmet on.

I'd never been on a motorcycle before so I didn't know how to even approach the metal beast. I came at it slowly, a little wary of what it could do to me.

He laughed. "You can use the peg to step over."

"Okay." I settled in behind him and wrapped my arms around his waist, feeling solid muscle even under all that leather. "We're going all the way to Dallas on this?"

He nodded. "It's a nice day; I think we can make it there in two hours tops." He squeezed my arm. "If you need to stop, just pat me on the chest twice."

"How the hell am I going to hold on for two whole hours?" I asked. Already my muscles were aching from clutching at him.

He turned around to face me. "You don't have to hold so tight. Once we get going, you can lean back a little and relax," he said. "Don't worry. I would never let anything happen to you," he added and flipped his visor down. A few seconds later, the bike roared to life.

I nodded. We were off.

The ride was smoother than I anticipated. After realizing that we weren't going to crash every time we leaned into a corner, I finally relaxed and loosened my hold. I was most grateful for the backrest, which stopped me from flying off the back every time he accelerated.

The ride afforded us absolutely no time or means to talk, which came as a bit of a relief. I really didn't know how to tell him about Seth without making it sound like the breakup was because of him, even if it really was. Henry already had an overabundance of confidence; he didn't need one more thing to inflate his ego. For now, I was going to play this card close to my chest.

At about an hour in, we took a break in Gainesville, Texas, to use the restroom and stretch our muscles for a few minutes.

"So why did you get out of the military?" I asked as I rolled my neck. "You never did say."

Henry ran a hand through his hair. "They didn't kick me out, if that's what you're wondering."

"Then what?"

"Living in Korea made me realize a few things about myself, about my life. I went back and forth a lot, not sure if I really wanted out."

"What made you finally do it?"

He gaze was steady. "You," he said and promptly put his helmet on.

"What? What do you mean?" I asked but he pretended not to hear. "You can't just say something like that—"

The bike rumbled to life, effectively cutting off all conversation.

Thoroughly miffed, I climbed on behind him and smacked him upside the helmet. I couldn't be sure, but I thought I felt him chuckling as we pulled out of the parking lot.

It was nearly eleven thirty by the time we exited the interstate and rode into a suburban neighborhood filled with brick houses. We came to a stop in front of a beautiful two-story house with white columns flanking the red door. We climbed off the bike and removed our helmets, and I tried to salvage my hair by twisting it up into a bun.

"What did you mean back there?" I asked as I followed him up the concrete walkway.

He looked over his shoulder with a faux frown. "I don't know what you mean," he said and rang the doorbell.

"You know exactly what I mean," I grumbled. I meant to say more but a tall woman answered the door. She was tanned, her blond hair pulled off to the side in a messy-chic ponytail and she had the most beautiful blue eyes I had ever seen.

My heart fell at the sight of her, whoever she was.

"Henry?" she asked with an excited smile. He held his hand out but she waved it away and threw her arms around him instead. "I'm so happy to finally meet you."

Henry pulled away. "I think we've actually met before. In Florida?"

Her eyes grew wide. "You're right. I'm sorry, that was a while ago," she said. "Anyway, come in. I'm so rude."

We walked inside and were greeted with a cinnamon-apple scent. The house was beautiful, with comfortable furniture and an old country cottage feel. My eyes flew to the collection of bird figurines on the mantle over the fireplace. There must have been several dozen of them in different shapes and materials.

"Oh, I know, it's kinda corny," the woman said when she noticed me looking. "Birds are kind of like my emblem."

I nodded, suddenly deciding that I liked her, whoever she was. She was too sunny to hate, even if she and Henry were involved.

Henry's hand pressed into the small of my back. "This is Elsie."

"I'm Julie," the woman said, giving me a firm handshake. "It's so nice to finally meet you. Jason told me so much about you."

My skin tingled and I felt hot and cold at the same time. "Jason?" I breathed. I prayed that Julie was about to tell me that Jason had been alive all along, just living two hours south of me.

I felt Henry's hand squeeze mine. I looked down at our entwined fingers, not knowing when that had even taken place. "She and Jason were dating when he was killed," he said.

"You were?" I asked, my eyes flying back to her pretty face. "I didn't know he was even seeing anyone."

"We'd been on and off since college," Julie said. She motioned for us to sit down and she followed suit. "I lived in New York until five years ago when I moved here to Dallas for work. Come to find out, Jason lived only a few hours away. We started seeing each other a few months before he was deployed." She bowed her head, losing the sunny smile on her face. Her big blue eyes were filling with tears when she suddenly exhaled and stood up. "I'm really sorry for your family's loss."

"His death was your loss too," I said and in that instant, as our eyes locked, I somehow got the feeling that she and I would be friends. I didn't know how I knew it, only that I felt a kinship with her through our shared love of Jason.

She blinked and shook off the cloak of sadness. "Anyway, would you guys like a drink? Or maybe some apple pie?"

"I'm starving," Henry said. He stood up and patted his stomach. "Would you like some help?"

"Sure, thanks," she said and they walked off, leaving me alone in the living room.

I stood up to look at the birds again, my eyes landing on a little glass eagle with its wing outstretched as if about to take flight. It was different from the other birds, which were all cutesy and pretty, and I wondered if maybe Jason had given it to her.

I was reaching out to touch the tip of its glass wing when a little voice said behind me, "Who are you?"

I turned around to find a little boy of about four standing by the coffee table. He had a round face, floppy blond hair, and a familiar smile. "Hi there," I said. "My name is Elsie."

He marched straight to me with his hand outstretched. "My name is Will," he said and shook my hand like a little man.

I stifled my smile. "Nice to meet you, Will. Is Julie your mom?"

He nodded. "But I don't have a dad," he said solemnly. "My mom says my dad died in *Apganistand*."

My heart dropped to my feet and blood rushed to my head. "What . . . What's your dad's name?"

"Jason, like my middle name," the little boy said proudly. "I'm William Jason Keaton."

"Will."

Both of our heads whipped around at the sound of his mother's voice, and my eyes instantly connected with Henry's. He glanced at Will, then back at me, giving me a little nod and a smile.

"I guess you've met Will," Julie said, setting a tray down at the table. She touched the little boy's blond hair, which was the same color as Jason's. "Will, this is Henry Logan. He was your dad's very best friend."

Tears filled my eyes and I turned away to hide my crumpling face.

"Nice to meet you, Henry," I heard Will say.

"I'm very happy to meet you, Will," Henry said, his voice closer now. He touched my shoulder. "This is your aunt Elsie."

I took a few seconds to collect myself before turning back around to face my nephew.

Jason had a son.

"Hi," I said with a wavery voice. Julie handed me a tissue and I looked up at her with gratitude and newfound respect. "Did Jason know?" I whispered.

Julie nodded and took a tissue for herself, dabbing at the corners of her eyes. "I told him the same day he . . ." She pursed her lips, unable to continue.

"I received an email when I was at Osan," Henry said, trying for a little levity. "Julie said she'd been looking for me, that she really wanted me to meet her son. I told her about you, Els."

"Are you sure?" Even as I asked the question, I already knew the answer. With that easygoing smile and that open face, the little boy was the spitting image of my brother.

"There was nobody else," Julie said, sitting on the couch and gathering Will into her arms. "Jason and I were even talking about getting married."

I turned to Henry. "Do my parents know?"

"Not yet," he said. "I thought that maybe you'd want to tell them."

I was overcome with emotion as I looked at Henry, wondering how I had managed to be without him for so long. I thought that maybe, like that tape recorder, I had simply put my life on pause while I waited for his return.

I turned back to Julie and the amazing being in her arms. "Can I hug you?" I asked Will. He gave a shy little nod and came over.

I wrapped him in my arms, his little body so small yet overflowing with life. He hugged me back, squeezing my neck like only a child could. When he pulled away, he tugged at one of my wayward curls, just like his dad used to do and my heart burst with bittersweet love.

I tickled his sides and reveled in the utter abandon and joy of his laugh, taking a little bit of it for my own. Jason may have died out there in Afghanistan but a small part of him survived here in Dallas where he lived on in his child.

"You doing okay?" Henry asked as he walked me back to my apartment after our ride home.

"I'm more than okay," I said, reaching for my keys. I shook my head, still reeling from the day's events. "I'm an aunt."

"Yeah, you are."

I beamed up at him. "Thank you for taking me. That was the most amazing surprise."

"I'm glad you liked it," he said, sticking his hands in his pockets.

I opened the door, stepped inside, and waited. "Are you coming in?"

He shrugged. "I didn't know if you wanted me to."

I nodded and led the way in. I got him a beer and myself a bottle of water and we sat at the dining table once again. "So a Volvo and a Harley," I said. "How very bipolar of you."

"I bought the Harley the day I got back, and the Volvo, well, I figured I needed something sensible to counterbalance my metal death trap."

"I like them both."

"Even the motorcycle?" he asked hopefully.

"Especially the motorcycle," I said.

He said nothing, just looked at me with joy in his eyes.

"So tell me, New Henry," I said, pointing my bottle at him. "What else is different about you?" I took a swig of water, waiting for his answer.

"Well, I've started to paint."

I sputtered water all over the table. "Really? I didn't know you were artistic."

He laughed. "As a matter of fact, I used to draw a little back in high school. Then I took an abstract painting class in Korea because I was bored, and I guess I've kept up with it."

"Can I see one of your pieces?"

"No way," he said. "Well, maybe one day. They're nothing special."

I smiled, suspecting that anything Henry did was the opposite of *nothing special*. "So, what you said back in Gainesville," I started, knowing he had nowhere to run. I was sure; I'd locked the front door. "That you got out of the service because of me. What did you mean?"

His nostrils flared. "It doesn't matter. I shouldn't have said anything."

"Why wouldn't it matter? It has to do with me."

"Because you're involved with someone," he said. "It wouldn't do you any good if I told you that I got out because I wanted to make you my first priority, that I didn't want to be separated from you any longer. What would it serve if I told you that I'm still in love with you and I would follow you wherever you went?"

I was grinning by the time he was done. "You're right," I said. "It wouldn't serve anything."

"That's what I thought," he said, playing with the label on the beer bottle.

"Except that Seth and I broke up."

His head snapped up. "What?"

"You heard me."

With a dark frown, he shifted in his seat and reached into his pants pocket. A second later, he placed an object onto the table with a loud thunk, his hand hiding it from view.

"What do you have there?" I asked nervously.

He lifted his hand and revealed a pebble in the shape of a wonky star.

"I thought you'd lost it," I said, picking it up and turning it in my hands, remembering the day I'd found it. I had been sitting on the sand, just thinking about Henry when I felt something poking the back of my thigh. I'd picked up the rock and thought it a fitting symbol as both the boy and the rock were pains in my ass.

"I thought I had, but I was cleaning out my closet before PCSing out of Korea and found it in an old running shoe." He gazed at me for a long time. "Do you remember what you told me that day at the beach?"

"That you were the same at the core."

"Well that, but you also gave it to me so I could remember you." He gently plucked the rock from my fingers. "The day I saw that rock again, I *remembered* you. I found it again at the exact time that I needed to. Finding this rock again was a sign from the universe that I had to make my way back to you before it was too late."

He placed the rock on the table between us. "This morning I knew I was already too late but I put that damn rock in my pocket anyway. I was going to give it to you as a parting gift when you finally told me to hit the road, so that every time you looked at it, you would remember me." He looked down at the rock and then up at me. "Tell me I get to keep this rock, Elsie," he breathed.

I couldn't look away; our eyes were welded together. I wanted so much to believe him and his pretty words. "How do I know you won't just leave me again and go on another self-finding walkabout?"

He shook his head. "I won't. Give me a chance to prove it."

"I already gave you a chance and you blew it."

"Then give me another, please," he said firmly. He stood from his seat and crouched down in front of me. "Just give me . . . three dates to make it up to you and erase every doubt in your mind. And at the end of those three dates, if you still don't believe that I'm here to stay, then I will give you back the rock."

"This is an old deal, Henry," I said with a raised eyebrow. "One that you lost."

"I'm making you a better deal," he said, resting his palms on my legs. "I'm betting everything."

"I want the motorcycle if you lose," I said with a grin.

"You can have the Volvo too if you'd like. And anything else you want."

"Okay."

"Okay?" he asked with eyes wide. "You'll give me three dates and I can take you anywhere, do anything?"

"Within reason."

"Anything?" he asked with a saucy smile and a wagging eyebrow.

I snickered. "To a point."

"Can I give you a *point*?"

I smacked him on the arm and laughed, feeling a renewed sense of optimism. The self-preserving part of me was shouting to take cover, but the other part—the one who'd run back out to the fray without armor—wanted nothing more than to give Henry his chance. Everybody, including the man who had completely devastated my heart, deserved a second chance, right?

Despite the tears I'd shed the past year and a half and the vows I'd made to myself that I would never get hurt again, deep down I was still the same hopeful, naïve girl. I still wanted my happily ever after with Henry, damn it. If that made me stupid, then so be it.

"So, New Henry," I began with a thundering heart, "your assignment is to make me fall in love with you in three dates or less. You think you can handle that?"

"I will do more than handle it," he said with that ornery look I'd known so well. He gave my legs a squeeze as he stood up and headed toward the door. "And Elsie?"

"Yeah?"

"Challenge accepted."

PART SIX

CAPTURE

1

FIRST DATE

I woke up with a smile. For the first time in a long time, the ache that had taken residence in my chest was absent; instead I was filled with optimism and a healthy sense of curiosity. I had given Henry Logan three dates to make me trust him again and the possibilities left me prickling with excitement. Our first date was not scheduled until this coming Saturday, so I had to suffer through the entire week imagining what kind of things he could come up with.

Really, the weekend could not get here fast enough. The love of my life had returned and was actively trying to win me back. If that didn't make me wish for Saturday to arrive sooner, then I don't know what would.

I jumped out of bed, eager to get the day started. After I showered and dressed for work, I found a text message from Henry on my phone.

Can't stop thinking about you.

Those five simple words stayed with me throughout the day, keeping that candle inside me flickering with a happy little glow.

The flame was extinguished after lunch, when I received a call on my cell phone from an out-of-state number.

"Hello?" the female voice said. "May I please speak to Elsie Sherman?"

"This is she," I said, holding the phone against my shoulder as I continued to work on a web project.

"Hi, Elsie, this is Rebecca Holt from Shake Design in Denver."

I was so stunned I dropped the phone. I'd completely forgotten about the resumes I'd sent out in the middle of last year when I was desperate to get out of Oklahoma. It hadn't mattered where I was going as long as it was out of this state, away from all of the memories. Rebecca was the only one who had called me back. The phone conversation had gone well and even though they weren't currently hiring, she said she'd keep my resume on file.

I hadn't thought about that phone call until now, when leaving Oklahoma was the furthest thing from my mind.

I forced myself to breathe again and retrieved the phone. "Hi, Rebecca. Sorry about that."

"No problem," she said. "I was calling about a position for an art director-slash-senior designer. It's a hybrid position, created for our last designer but he has since moved on."

I couldn't believe my ears. It was exactly the job I'd been trying to convince my boss to create for me but hadn't been able to due to the flagging economy.

Rebecca described the job and its responsibilities and said, "We received your resume last year and were really impressed. Now that a position has opened up, we would like to offer it to you."

I spoke in a low voice so as not to be overheard. "And the salary?" Screw tact, I needed facts. There was too much at stake to beat around the bush.

Rebecca threw out a figure that made my ears burn. It was, needless to say, substantial. Almost double what I was currently making.

"Thank you, Miss Holt," I said, with my heart pounding wildly in my chest. "Would I be able to give an answer in a few days?"

"Of course," Rebecca said. "But I'll need an answer by Friday at the latest."

"Thank you. When would I have to start if I accepted?"

"In three weeks."

My heart dropped to my feet. Five days to decide to leave the love of my life for a dream job; it didn't seem nearly enough time.

"Okay. Thank you so much, Rebecca." I ended the phone call and stared at the computer screen for a long while, feeling like the normally unhurried pace of my life suddenly made the jump to light speed.

I had never been gladder for radio silence from Henry than I was today. He didn't text or call until I arrived home from work and was in the middle of cooking dinner.

"Hey, what are you making?" he asked when he heard the clanging of the wok on the stove.

I put him on speaker as I began to chop the vegetables with a nearly manic intensity. I almost felt sorry for the poor carrots and peppers. "Beef stir fry," I said. The wok hissed when I threw in the vegetables.

"Mmm. I can smell it all the way from here."

"What are you having?" I asked, distracted by dinner and life.

He snorted. "Ramen noodles."

"Oh, I'm sorry to hear that." I picked out a carrot and absentmindedly munched on it while the rest of the food cooked, my mind in a faraway place.

"Please invite me over."

I finally took note of the longing in his voice. His tapes came to mind then and what he'd said about coming home night after night to an empty house with nothing to eat but ramen noodles or frozen burritos. My heart hurt at the thought, unable to stomach the idea that he was reliving his lonely childhood. "Okay, come over."

"Really?" he asked in surprise. "This won't count as a date, right?"

I sighed impatiently. "Just get over here," I said. "You've got fifteen minutes."

"I'm out the door right now!" he said and I heard the door slamming before he hung up the phone.

Even though the drive from the house he was renting usually took at least seventeen minutes, I heard the rumble of his motorcycle no more than ten minutes later.

"You shouldn't speed on that thing," I said as soon as I opened the door and let him in.

He ignored my words; instead he wrapped his arms around my back and held me against his body. He let out a long sigh. "Man, I've been dying to do this all day," he said against my hair.

I allowed myself one moment to enjoy his warmth, closing my eyes and breathing in his unique scent, before I pulled away and made my way back to the kitchen. "I hope I made enough," I said, turning my back to him as I prepared two bowls of food.

"Anything you can offer me is enough," he said, making me wonder if that was indeed the truth.

We sat on the living room floor, leaning against my couch out of habit, with bowls of stir-fry and rice in our laps. I usually made enough food for at least two meals and thankfully had enough to feed even a sizable hungry man, and boy, was Henry hungry. He finished his dinner in record time.

He placed his bowl on the floor and leaned his head back into the couch, quietly gazing at me. He looked so content in that moment that I decided I couldn't tell him about the job yet, so I just smiled and tried to bask in this little slice of heaven.

"How was your day?" he asked with a lazy grin. He reached out and held my hand, tracing circles on my palm with his thumb.

"Fine," I said. "How about you?"

"Well, I heard back from the OKC Police Department today," he said, his face becoming animated. "My application was approved. I go in tomorrow for the physical and written test."

"So you're really doing it."

"Yep, I'm really doing it." He grinned, looking so excited at the prospect of becoming a police officer. Of course, a new career in law enforcement along with the rental house agreement he'd just signed meant that he was tied to Oklahoma now. It wouldn't be impossible for him to break those ties but the real question was: Did I even want him to?

Instead of facing the tough question, I opted for the easy way out. "You know, I don't think that uniform is going to be anywhere near as sexy as your BDUs, but I guess it'll have to do," I said.

He quirked one dark eyebrow. "I still have some BDUs somewhere. I'll wear mine if you wear your Tomb Raider costume."

I chuckled. "You're still fantasizing about that?"

"What? It was amazing." He lifted my hand and kissed it. "You're amazing." The expression on his face softened and I suddenly knew exactly where this was headed. One kiss from Henry Logan had the capacity to send me careening straight into an often-visited town called Trouble.

I extricated my hand from his grasp and gathered our bowls. "You're washing the dishes," I said, handing him the stack.

He studied my face for a moment before he rose to his feet and headed to the kitchen.

Thirty minutes later he had washed, dried, and put away all of the bowls, utensils, and the wok. He looked around but found nothing else to aid in his obvious procrastination. "I guess I'm done," he said, wiping his hands dry and hanging the towel.

I stood from the dining table, where I'd been pretending to work on my laptop but had really been watching him from the corner of my eye. Judging from the way he'd grinned to himself the entire time, I had a feeling he probably knew.

"I guess it's time for me to go," he said, hedging for a rebuttal.

"I guess so."

At the front door, he turned and bent down to press a warm kiss on my forehead. "Thank you for letting me invite myself to dinner."

"It's tradition." I grinned. "It wouldn't seem right if you didn't invite yourself to dinner with a Sherman."

A shadow of a smile crossed his mouth. "You listened to all of the tapes?"

"Yes." So maybe I'd even listened to them more than twice, but he didn't need to know that I had clung to his words like buoys to keep me from sinking into the depths of hopelessness. Just knowing that he had loved me at all had gotten me through the night on more than one occasion.

"You don't remember that night at my college graduation party?" he asked, his eyes flitting across my face.

"I wish I did," I replied, shaking my head. I would give anything to remember the first time Henry had told me he loved me.

He drew me to him. "Me too."

"Do you want the tapes back? I have them in my bedroom," I said, trying to twist out of his arms but he wouldn't let go.

"No, you hold on to them. You're the keeper of my secrets."

I stilled at his words. I held my breath, then let it all out, letting go the opportunity to tell him about another secret.

As he walked out, I called out, "Hey, Henry?"

He turned on a heel. "Yeah?"

"We may need to speed up the three-dates thing."

"Why?"

I tried a nonchalant shrug. "I just can't wait that long."

"Then when?"

"Tomorrow night?"

He thought for a moment, then said, "Okay."

"Looking forward to it."

"Hey, Elsie?" he called as he walked away, his voice echoing in the hallway.

"Yeah?"

"I love you."

Henry returned to my apartment the next day, after I came home from work.

"You do remember we had a date, right?" I asked, looking pointedly at his long-sleeved Under Armour shirt and black workout pants. For a wild moment, I wondered if he was taking me to the gym but quickly dismissed the thought. It wouldn't top the list of the worst dates ever, but I was pretty sure it'd be in the top ten.

He folded his arms across his wide chest. "Go get some sweats on. I'm taking you to Krav Maga."

"What Maga?" I asked. "That sounds painful."

He walked past me, right into my bedroom. "Krav Maga. It's an Israeli fighting style."

I stopped at the door and watched him going through my closet. He came out holding a pair of running capri pants, a moisture-wicking shirt, and my running shoes. "You're taking me to the gym for our first date?" I asked with a sinking feeling. I had just gotten home from a long day at work; the last thing I wanted to do was exercise.

He handed me my clothes. "I'm sorry if it's an awful idea for a date, but you didn't give me much time to prepare. And since class is usually on Tuesday night, I thought I'd take you to see something I'd been working on."

"You're really going to take me to watch you beat up on other people?"

"No," he said with a grin. "You get to do some beating up of your own."

With a resigned sigh, I walked into my room to get changed. Henry moved to the doorway and just leaned against the jamb with his arms crossed over his chest. "A-hem, I'd like to change," I said.

"Go on. I'll wait," he said.

"I'll Krav Maga all over your butt if you don't get out," I muttered, pushing him out of the room and locking the door. "I might just start beating up people right here."

He chuckled on the other side of the door as I undressed. "I've seen you naked before, remember?" he asked. "I've seen your breasts fit snugly in the palm of my hands. I've seen that ass of yours turn red when I spank it."

My face burned at his words. I caught a glimpse of myself in the full-length mirror and turned around to look at my butt, curious what shade of red he was talking about.

"And I've seen your inner thighs, when I run my tongue along the smooth skin all the way up to . . ." His words thinned out. He cleared his throat.

I pressed my head against the door, aching to hear more. But he said nothing. "Henry?" I asked.

"Get dressed, Elsie," he said with a strained voice. "Or I'm going to break this door down and we'll never make it to class."

———

We made it to class on time. The drive over had been tension-filled, and I might have caught Henry adjusting his pants a few times but he didn't breathe another word about naked body parts. He seemed to understand that I needed my space and he actually tried to respect my boundaries. *Tried* being the operative word as the man still took advantage of his uncanny ability to turn me on.

Henry had notified his instructor earlier that he would be bringing a guest along and they accommodated me by explaining the principles of the fighting style, then performed some basic maneuvers, moving at half speed for my sake. I practiced some elbow and knee strikes with Henry but I called it quits after a while, feeling guilty that I was keeping him from real training.

I sat on the sidelines, content to watch Henry and the others doing their thing. My eyes were fixed on him as he worked with a partner on punching combos, amazed at his fluidity and speed. He looked in his element as he punched and elbowed the hand pads, all the while bouncing on his toes. As they changed sides, he looked over to me and flashed a wide grin that I automatically returned.

After the class he took me back to his place, which was a one-story redbrick house with two bedrooms and a one-car garage. He parked the car in the driveway and entered the house through the garage, past the Harley, a lawnmower, and a small collection of tools.

"So thanks for taking me to a stinky gym for the first of three very important dates," I teased as he led me inside. "There, amongst all of those sweaty, grunting men and women, I fell madly in love with you."

He laughed in surprise. I grinned like a fool beside him, infected with his good mood. "I thought you might like to see what I've been working on the past year. And like I said, you kind of ruined my first-date plans."

"What were they?"

"Now you'll never know," he said.

I puffed out my lower lip in a mock pout. "Aw, come on."

"That's the first and last time that's going to work on me," he said, flicking my lower lip as he grinned. "I was going to take you to a romantic dinner at the new Devon Tower, then maybe a horse-carriage ride through Bricktown. Or maybe a boat ride along the canal."

I wasn't successful in suppressing a snort.

"What?"

"Sorry, sorry," I said quickly. "It's just . . . too much."

"Good thing I went with the sweaty, grunting plan then," he said and disappeared down the hall, leaving me to stand in the living room by myself.

I looked around, noting that the interior had clearly not been updated since the eighties with its dark brown carpet and wood paneling. Henry had not decorated yet; picture frames were still leaning against the walls and boxes were still stacked, unopened.

I ventured down the hallway and peered into his bedroom, which looked very much the same as before, down to the same blue covers. I would have thought the new Henry would have at least bought new sheets to match his new life.

I was about to look into the second bedroom, hoping to see his paintings, when the bathroom door opened and he came out, rubbing his head with a towel.

"Did you just take a shower?" I asked, taking note of his fresh clothes. "While you had a guest waiting?"

He gave an impatient little sigh and beckoned me over. "Just get over here."

I walked over, pretending I hadn't just been caught snooping, and looked inside the bathroom. The lights were off, but the room was filled with the soft flickering of candles that ran along the sides of the filled bathtub. "Oh," was all I could say.

"Is this *too much*?" he asked.

"No." I walked inside, shaking my head. I turned around, nearly running into him. "But I don't have a change of clothes."

"You can borrow some of mine," he said and motioned to a pile of folded clothes on the counter. "And before you start assuming, no, I won't be joining you. This is just for you. I'll be cooking dinner while you take a bath," he said. He gave me a kiss on the cheek, smelling so fresh. "Enjoy."

Okay, I had to admit that the bubble bath was a smooth move. I sighed when I slid into the warm water, not realizing until that moment that my body had been tense all afternoon. The truth was, even though I'd agreed to this challenge, I was still very much afraid. Every time Henry was near, I felt tight with worry that each moment we spent together would be the last, always looking out for signs that he was going to leave me again.

Then again wasn't that the goal? The challenge was a chance for him to prove that he was trustworthy, that I could believe in him again. He was trying, at least. I had to give him points for that.

I closed my eyes, leaned back and tried to clear my head, but I could hear Henry moving around in the kitchen, clanging pots and various things around, putting him front and center in my thoughts.

True to his word, Henry left me alone during my bath, but several minutes later the noises in the kitchen stopped and I found I could no longer sit still. I jumped out of the tub and dressed in his clothes—a tan shirt and a pair of gray sweat pants—and practically ran out of the bathroom.

Henry, thankfully, was still in the house. He hadn't run away.

I sat at the dining table just off the kitchen, watching him drain pasta noodles as I silently berated myself for being so silly. Of course he was still here. Did I really believe he was going to just ditch me in his own house?

Did I?

"That was quick," he said, scooping the spaghetti into bowls. He placed them onto the table with a flourish and said, "*Voila!* Spaghetti a la Henry."

I made a big production of sniffing the food. "Mmm. What is the secret ingredient, Chef?"

He winked. "Love."

I snickered. "And cheese. Plenty of it."

With a grin he sat down beside me and we began to eat, the atmosphere in the tiny dining room reminding me of much simpler times, back when a quiet attraction was the only thing between us.

We watched some television after dinner, but inevitably he had to take me back home.

"You can keep the clothes," he said at my doorstep, giving me that sexy sliding look.

"Oh no, you're not going to tell me I look good in your clothes, are you?" I asked. "You know, that clichéd thing that guys do?"

"No. I was going to say keep them until you wash them" he said. He pinched my cheek. "But you really do look cute in my clothes."

I laughed and gave him a light jab in the stomach.

He grasped my wrist, then brought my hand up to his lips. He wrapped an arm around my waist and pulled me close. "Well, I'd better get going," he said, sounding like he wanted to do anything but.

I wanted to invite him inside—at least, a part of me did—but it was too soon to let him jump with both feet into my life again, so I just stood on my tiptoes and pressed my forehead to his mouth. "Good night, Henry. Thank you for the strange date."

I felt his lips forming a smile against my skin. "Are you in love with me yet?"

"Not yet."

He didn't look too bothered when he drew away. "I still have two more dates to win you over," he said, wriggling two fingers at me.

"Good luck to you, Mr. Logan," I said, giving him a very formal handshake.

He gave me a quick peck on the lips before pulling away. "Good night, Miss Sherman. I love you."

2

SECOND DATE

The next morning I received an email from Rebecca detailing the new job description along with a link to the company's website. I sat at my desk with a heavy ball of worry in my stomach, looking through photographs of the large, creative office space complete with a Zen garden and a rock-climbing wall. Shake Design was one of Denver's most promising companies and boasted several large national clients, and according to their website, also treated their employees well. The benefits package that Rebecca had attached was proof enough.

Shake Design was offering me a huge opportunity—a job that would allow me to direct while still getting my hands dirty with design. To top it off, I'd always wanted to live in Colorado. It was, in a nutshell, the offer of a lifetime and only a fool would refuse.

But then again, when it came to matters of the heart, I haven't always done the smart thing.

Henry was waiting for me in the parking lot when I got off work that Wednesday afternoon. He was seated casually on his motorcycle, his helmet in his lap, looking like an ultra-sexy magazine ad for Harley-Davidson.

His face lit up when he saw me approach. "Hi."

I placed my purse inside one of the saddlebags and settled in behind him, feeling heat emanating through his jacket. I squirmed when I slid closer, my crotch pressing against his ass.

"Stop that," he said. "Or I will take you on this bike right here, right now."

"Empty promises," I teased, suddenly unable to keep from thinking about having sex on his motorcycle. I didn't even know if it was possible, but boy, did it sound erotic as hell.

He turned and flashed me a wicked smile. "This is no empty promise, Els," he said, his voice taking on a gritty quality that indicated he was really turned on. "The past few days have been torture. Just say the word and I'm all yours."

I gulped, seriously contemplating saying yes just to see what he'd do. "You're right, we'd better get going," I said and popped the helmet over my flushed face instead.

Henry took me to a coffee shop on the north side, near the Oklahoma City University campus.

"The Red Cup?" I asked as we got off the bike. I didn't want to judge, but was he taking me to an artsy-fartsy coffee shop for our second date?

"Yep." He grabbed my hand and led me through the parking lot toward the converted house, painted a bright green. On top of the roof was a giant red cup with a silver spoon. It was quirky and cute, sure, but didn't really indicate *grand gesture*.

Inside the place was a riot of color with black-and-white-checked floors, brightly painted walls, and art everywhere. After we ordered our food, Henry led me to the back—to what I assumed was the old living room—and we sat down in a yellow pleather booth that curved around a corner.

"So, interesting place," I said, studying the eclectic collection of art and people. There were students, paintings, bohemians, prints, hipsters, and suits. "Why here? This place is not exactly romantic."

He leaned back into the booth, his head nearly hitting the canvas painting on the wall above him. "You didn't want romance, remember? It was *too much*?"

I glanced around. "Yeah, but . . ."

He raised both eyebrows. "Yes?"

"I want a little bit of romance," I said, holding two fingers close together.

He shook his head. "I can't win with you, can I?"

I grinned. "Is it too much to ask that you read my mind?"

"I'm sorry. Next time I will use my ESP and take you to Starbucks instead." He smiled widely, his features relaxed.

I studied his face for a long while, then said, "You seem happy." It was true; he seemed so at ease with the world, no longer that brooding guy who didn't know himself. This new Henry was grounded and relaxed, different but still the same boy I'd fallen in love with many years ago. It felt strange, like I was cheating on the old Henry with the new.

"I am." He stretched his arms on the back of the booth and gathered me into his side. "Deliriously," he said in a sigh.

I leaned my head on his shoulder, wishing I could say the same and completely mean it.

We sat in comfortable silence for a long while, his hand rubbing my shoulder as he occasionally kissed the top of my head. It was cozy, even if beneath my skin ran an undercurrent of tension and worry. We finally separated when the waitress brought our food, and we ate in silence all the while casting glances at each other.

I was keenly aware of the little things: the faint scent of Henry's cologne, the hint of orange in my salad vinaigrette, the love song playing softly in the background. It was as if all of my senses were heightened, and even though it was nearly overwhelming, I wanted more.

Then I saw it.

I was studying Henry's wavy hair—noting how different it made him look from the buzz cut—when I noticed that the signature on the canvas behind his head said *H. Logan*. I twisted around in my seat to get a better look at the large painting, which was an abstract in browns, tans and blues.

"It's about time you noticed," Henry said with a chuckle, wiping his mouth with a napkin and twisting around.

"You did this?" I asked him, still staring at the painting, trying to make sense of the shapes and swirls.

"You like it?"

"Yes," I said. "What is it?"

"I'll give you a hint: It's a semi-abstract. It's titled *She Is Love*."

Then it all came together, the oval that came to a point at the bottom, the brownish green orbs for the eyes, and the long curly hair. "It's me?"

He nodded. "Beautiful, don't you think?"

"Yeah, it really is," I said, unable to believe that Henry could create something so wonderful. Being a designer, I liked to consider myself aesthetically selective; I had seen many illustrations and paintings, had even created a few of my own. Perhaps I was being a little subjective, since I was the inspiration for the piece, but Henry's painting was definitely gallery-quality.

"I wasn't talking about the painting," he said, his eyes fixed on my face, making the air in the entire place too thick to breathe. He was going to kiss me and, as much as I wanted to taste him, I couldn't risk getting attached again. Not when I was considering leaving.

I blinked and cleared my throat. "So you learned to paint in Korea?"

He leaned away, trying to hide his disappointment. "Yeah. I took a class on base, taught by this old skinny guy who always smelled like whiskey," he said. "Davis was critical, which really helped me improve. He told me over and over to loosen up, to stand back to get a better perspective."

"And that worked?"

His eyes were on my face, the heat of his gaze warming my cheeks. "It helped with my painting. And I'm hoping it'll help with other things in my life."

I turned my attention back to my food, picking at a piece of lettuce. "So what else did you do in Korea?"

"I worked a lot. Also tried a lot of classes."

"Did you date?" The question slipped out of my mouth before I could catch it. I hadn't meant to bring it up right then.

He hesitated before saying, "I did. I dated two women before I gave up." He paused, taking my hand. "But neither relationship lasted more than a few dates."

My eyes flicked up to his face. "Why not?"

"*You* know why."

My heart throbbed in my chest, begging me not to ask the next inevitable question. I swallowed hard. "Did you sleep with them?"

His eyes were all intensity as he looked at me. "I thought about it, but no." He paused for a long, tense moment before asking, "How about you? Did you and Seth—?"

I hadn't expected his answer. I had steeled myself for a yes, and was now instead faced with a confession that did not match my own. "Yeah, we did."

His nostrils flared as he stared down at the table. "Fuck," he said under his breath, crumpling the napkin in his hand.

It felt like an apology was in order but upon further reflection, between the two of us, I was the one definitely owed.

"I'm sorry, Elsie," he said, his eyes meeting mine. "I'm a grade-A dickhead. I'm the one who fucked everything up and now I'm jealous as hell that someone else, someone *not me*, got to sleep with you."

"You *should* be sorry," I blurted, taking even myself by surprise. "You ruined everything we had." I could feel the energy crackling around us. This was the first time we were really hashing it out, the first time I was voicing my opinion that, yes, he screwed up. Finally saying those words felt good in a small way and terrible in an even bigger way. "You took what we had and threw it away because you felt confused," I said, gathering steam. "Well guess what, Henry? We all get confused about ourselves but we don't go hurting those we love just so we can get some clarity."

"I'm sorry, Elsie. I was a selfish bastard." He grasped my hand on the table. I tried to let go, but he held tight. "I'm so, so sorry."

I shook my head and tried to keep my lips from trembling. "It might be too late, Henry. I really don't know how you can prove to me that you're sticking around for good, that I can trust you again."

"I don't know how either," he whispered. It was the first time since he'd come back from Korea that I'd seen his confidence falter. He looked genuinely fearful, a feeling that then spilled over onto me. "I have no clue how to gain your trust back."

I looked away, trying to collect my thoughts and steady my breathing. I didn't realize until that moment how angry I still was, how unwilling I was to forgive him. He had made the past few years of my life miserable; I'd have to be a saint to forgive and forget so easily.

"Elsie?" Henry asked tentatively, giving my hand a squeeze.

I looked down at our hands, then up at him. "I received a job offer in Denver," I said with more bravado than I felt. "And I'm going to take it."

The breath whooshed out of him in one word: "What?"

"A big design company in Denver offered me a job. I'd be crazy to turn it down."

"I didn't know you were looking," he said, his eyebrows drawing together.

"I was, several months ago, before you came back. Even before I met Seth."

The frown deepened. "When did you find out?"

"Monday."

His face turned red and the veins in his forehead swelled. "So these dates are all for nothing? I've been racking my brain trying to figure out how to make you love and trust me again, but you're leaving anyway?"

I jerked my hand away. "You're not seriously angry that I'm leaving, are you? Because at last count, you've left me a grand total of four times. This is our history, Henry: I trust you, then you leave. Well guess the fuck what, you're not the one who gets to leave this time." I slid out of the booth, gathered my purse and jacket, and stalked out. God, it felt so gratifying to finally be the one to do that.

My jubilation was short-lived, however, when I got outside and remembered that I'd come here with Henry. I stood over by the Harley and gave the back tire a kick, imagining it was his crotch I was inflicting pain upon. The guy had some nerve.

Henry came bursting out of The Red Cup a minute later. The worry on his face eased when he saw me standing in the parking lot. "Elsie," he said, stopping a few feet from me. He didn't say anything for a long time; he just stared at me with deep lines creasing his forehead.

"Just say it, Henry! Demand that I stay in Oklahoma for you, because that's what you do. You demand and take. And me, I give." I choked on the words. "But I'm done giving."

"Then tell me what you want me to do and I'll do it," he said with a desperate tint to his voice.

"I don't know what I want you to do," I said. "I only know what I *need* to do."

―――――――

That night I lay in bed, staring at the ceiling for a long time, just thinking about my life—where I had been and where I was headed.

There was no question in my mind that I loved Henry, but was it worth more than my love for myself? I had given him so much, had followed him and waited for him, and still it hadn't been enough.

He had come back for me, and even though I wanted nothing more than to finally get to our happily ever after, a little voice in my heart kept insisting that I needed to do right by me first. My job here had become stagnant, the promotion I'd been hoping for dissolving when the company fell on hard times. The job in Denver was going to be a leap in my career. Now more than ever I needed to put my own future first even if it meant leaving my past behind.

If Henry really loved me like he claimed, he would do the right thing and set me free. I had let him go once, to go find himself; he needed to do the same for me now.

So it was with an aching heart that I turned on my laptop, composed a new email, and told Rebecca Holt of Shake Design that I was going to take the job.

3

THE LAST DATE

I didn't hear from Henry for the next few days, which was just as well. I didn't need him around trying to change my mind, clouding what had become my clear path. On Friday I put in my official letter of resignation at work and had an emotional talk with my boss about my career. She told me that she would have done anything to keep me, but that she unfortunately had no raise or promotion to offer. It was tough to say good-bye to the place I'd called home for the last several years, but deep in my gut I knew it was time to move on.

When I came home from work that night, Henry was waiting for me in the apartment parking lot. He got out of his car when I emerged from my own and he approached me tentatively.

"Hey," he said with his hands in his pockets.

I gathered my purse and coat, not meeting his eye. "Hi."

"How are you?"

"Exhausted," I replied, heading toward my apartment. "You?"

"Pretty shitty." He followed me inside, both of us too tired to deal with manners. He stood in the living room with his hands in his pockets, looking like he wanted to say something but not knowing if he should.

"What?" I asked, a little irritated.

"I passed the written exam and physical. Next week I have the initial interview."

"Oh. Congratulations," I said, busying myself by decluttering the kitchen counters. "I handed in my letter of resignation."

He sighed, his shoulders visibly sagging. "So you're still leaving."

I couldn't look at him because I knew what I'd see on his face was going to make me cry, and the last thing I needed to do right now was lose my composure. "Yes. I have to start in three weeks."

"When do you move?"

"Next Friday."

"I'll help you."

I looked up in surprise. "You want to help me move?"

He rubbed a palm across his forehead. "What else can I do, Els? You're leaving and there's nothing I can do to stop you. So I'm going to spend every last minute with you, even if it means helping you leave me."

"Henry, you know this isn't about you, right?"

"Yeah," he said softly. "I've been thinking and thinking and even though I hate it, I know you have to do this. I left you once, it's only fair that you do the same."

"It's not about being fair or about getting even. It's about pursuing a dream, even if—"

He nodded. "Even if it doesn't include me."

"I have to do this," I said, a tear slipping past my defenses. I quickly wiped it away. "Otherwise, I'll always wonder *what if*."

"I understand, Elsie," he said in a broken voice. We were quiet for a long time, just staring at each other, until he said, "Can I hug you now?"

With trembling lips, I walked over to where he stood and fit myself into his arms. He kissed my forehead in that tender way I loved so much. "I love you, Els."

I wasn't able to return the sentiment, not because I didn't feel it but because saying it meant I'd forgiven him.

"I'm really sorry for what I did to you, Elsie," he said. "For leaving you and making you doubt yourself. For hurting you and making you doubt me."

I nodded against his chest, feeling a lump in my throat.

"I'm never going to hurt you again. I'm back for good."

"I want to believe you."

He held me at arm's length, looking into my eyes. "I'm sticking around, Elsie. I'm going to be by your side until you tell me to go. I don't know how else to prove to you that I'm here for good except by just *being here* day after day," he said. "Please try to believe me."

"I want to believe you," I repeated. "That's all I can do right now."

He pulled away and headed toward the door.

My heart leapt into my throat, that undercurrent of worry turning into a full-on tidal wave. "Where are you going?" I asked in a panic.

He spun on his heel. "I'll be right back," he said quickly. "I just have to get something out of the car."

I forced myself to nod and calm the hell down.

To my relief, Henry came back less than a minute later with a large canvas in his hand. "I wanted to give you this," he said, turning the painting around. "For your new place."

I thought it might have been the painting from the Red Cup, but this was different. The style and colors were the same but there were two stylized faces on the canvas, one oval and one square. The faces overlapped, meeting at the lips.

"I can't decide on a title. Either *H and E*, or *The Kiss*," he said with an embarrassed shrug. I reached out to touch it but he said, "Watch out, it might still be a little wet. I just finished painting it less than an hour ago."

"Thank you," I said, trying to make sense of my emotions. I kept trying to suppress that warm ache in my chest, telling my heart that I couldn't afford to fall back in love with Henry again, not right now. As I looked at the canvas, I reminded myself that the painting was a good-bye present.

I had almost convinced myself to stop wanting the impossible, when he said, "On second thought, I think I have a new title."

"What's that?" I asked.

His blue eyes were bright, illuminating the one thing that had always been true about us. "It's called *I Will Love You Always*."

———————

I ordered Chinese food and Henry stayed for dinner. I figured it was the least I could do since he had just given me a meaningful gift. His undying love in exchange for a box of steamed rice and General Tso's chicken; it was almost a fair trade.

After dinner, we sat on the couch and watched *Top Gear*. Several minutes into the show, Henry's arm came around my shoulders and nestled me close.

I don't think either one of us meant for the kiss to happen. I looked up to ask a question the same time he was bending down to whisper in my ear and our faces bumped into each other.

"Sorry." He swallowed as his eyes flicked down to my lips.

"It's okay."

We were quiet for a charged moment, then he leaned down and whispered huskily, "I'm dying over here, Elsie. I don't know what to do with myself."

"What do you want to do?"

"This." He leaned down and touched his lips to mine, gently at first, then becoming bolder. I kissed him back, feeling a moan rise up from my throat. In that moment I was ready to forgo everything else—yes, even that fantastic job—and just stay in Henry's arms forever. We could paint and make love and while the days away, entangled in each other. We could be happy.

I pulled away, wrenching myself from the daydream before I was too lost. "You should go home, Henry," I said, covering his mouth with my hand. He raised his eyebrows and tried to speak but I held his mouth shut. "Yes, I'm sure."

———————

Our third date began early the next day when Henry came knocking at my door at nine o'clock with a bouquet of flowers in his hands.

"What's this?" I asked, still drowsy from sleep. I had only just managed to rinse my mouth and twist my hair into a bun before I'd answered the door.

He handed me the bouquet of flowers, which, upon closer inspection, consisted of paper rolled and folded to look like roses. Some flowers were plain red, while others were made from pages of a book.

"My buddy's wife makes them, so I ordered some for you," he said, sticking his hands in his pants pockets.

"They're beautiful." I looked closer, trying to figure out what book the pages came from when I saw the name Mr. Rochester. The story of Jane Eyre seemed strangely appropriate; the inexperienced woman refusing to accept anything less than what she deserved from the only love of her life.

"I remember you said a long time ago, after Brian brought you flowers on your first date, that they were a waste of money because they died anyway," Henry said. He touched a finger to one paper rose. "These will last forever."

"Thank you," I said, surprised that he remembered a throwaway comment I'd made many years ago.

I caught him checking out my shorts and tank-top attire as he walked inside the apartment, but he tried to play it off with a shrug. "I'm going to go change before your eyes fall out of your head," I said.

"Please don't. I have a soft spot for that tank top," he said. "Or rather, a hard spot."

"It's too early for sexual innuendo," I groaned.

He laughed. "Okay," he said, holding his hands up in defeat. "No innuendo at least until after breakfast."

I set the flowers down on the counter and went to the fridge to get some eggs.

"Where's your coffee?" he asked, and retrieved it when I pointed the bag out. He filled the coffeepot and started a brew. He found the bread on top of the microwave and placed two slices in the toaster while I cooked omelets, then placed them on plates. It was all too easy to fall into our old pattern.

"What do you have planned for the all-important third date?" I asked, sipping my coffee as we sat across the table from each other.

"I was going to leave that up to you," he said. He took a moment to finish chewing his toast. "Today, we are doing anything you want to do."

"That sounds like lazy planning to me."

He grinned. "The past two dates were about me. I didn't mean to be selfish about it; all I wanted to do was show you a little bit more about myself. But today is about you."

"Whatever I want to do?" I asked with a raised eyebrow.

"Even if you just wanted to have sex all day," he said, nodding gravely. "I would make that sacrifice."

I laughed and rolled my eyes. "You wish."

The laughter slid off his face. "I do," he said.

I felt my face heating up. Was it hot in here? "I'm going to go take a shower," I said, pushing away from the table. "And no, that's not an invitation for you to join me."

"Well, damn, I'll do the dishes then," he said with a grin and gathered the empty plates.

––––––––––

For our third and final date, I chose to go down to Dallas to see Julie and Will a day early. I had already planned on driving down there on Sunday because my parents were flying in to meet their grandson, but I wanted to get to know Julie a little better before my parents met her.

The three-hour drive in my Prius afforded Henry and me some time to talk nonsense and just shoot the breeze, but even though our conversation consisted of mostly jokes and innuendo, the air inside the car was stuffy with words that were not being said.

We arrived at Julie's house around two in the afternoon. Will seemed a little shy at first, which was not surprising since we just met the week before, but he warmed up when Henry handed him a rubber-band gun we'd bought at the Cracker Barrel restaurant on the way down.

"Cool!" Will said as Henry demonstrated the toy, shooting me in the butt while I talked with Julie.

Julie shook her head with a tiny smile on her lips. "You're a bad influence, Henry."

"Jason would have done the same," he said with an impish shrug. He turned to Will and asked, "So your mom doesn't buy you toy weapons?"

"What are weapons?" Will asked.

"Guns, bows and arrows, rocket-propelled grenades."

"No," Will said with a puppy-dog look. "She only gets me Legos and video games."

I looked at Julie's frown, suddenly understanding where she was coming from. Jason had been killed by a gun; of course she wouldn't want to introduce those same things to her son.

Henry must have sensed the change in Julie because he said, "Okay, no grenades. How about a Super Soaker then?"

Julie nodded, flashing him an appreciative smile. "Super Soaker's fine. Even a Nerf gun is okay," she said with a resigned sigh. "But I draw the line at flamethrowers."

———————

We all went to a fun little place called JumpStreet, per Will's request, which was an indoor play area made up of trampolines. One half of the room was taken up by long swathes of trampolines made to look like bouncy racing lanes. The other half was set up in different sections, with a dodge-ball court, a few slides, and an area for smaller children to play in.

I'd thought that Henry would sit it out and just watch from the sidelines, but he seemed more excited than Will. Julie and I opted out of the bouncing, not because we didn't want to play, but mostly because I wanted to know more about the woman who had known a side of my brother I'd never seen.

We sat at the tables by the waiting area, watching through the Plexiglass wall as Henry and Will jumped. Will grabbed on to Henry's hand as they stepped onto the trampolines, still a little wary of the unsteady ground beneath his feet. Henry led him to the trampoline lane closest to us and they waved at us before taking exploratory jumps.

"Will's never been on a trampoline before," Julie said. "Can you tell?"

"How's that possible?"

She shrugged. "I don't know. I'm such a helicopter mom. I'm so scared something will happen to him."

I looked back at my nephew and was happy to see that he had let go of Henry's hand and had already begun bouncing on his own.

"I guess I'm going to have to just let him be his own person, find his own way. Kind of like what you did with Henry."

"Yeah," I agreed mindlessly, watching Henry. Then her words sank in. I turned my attention back to her. "Um, what?"

She gave a sheepish little grin. "I'm sorry. That was the worst transition in the history of mankind," she said. "I just wanted to bring up the subject of your relationship with Henry. He and I exchanged several emails while he was stationed in Korea, so we were able to talk about things."

"About Will?"

"Mostly about Jason and Will. But I noticed that your name always came up in his emails, so I just flat out asked him what happened between you two. He was surprisingly open about it and told me about therapy and what he'd done to you."

"Did he sound torn up?" I asked. I imagined Henry crying into his ramen noodles and stifled a grin.

"No. He sounded . . . determined. He said he was going to get you back." Julie waited for a reply. When she didn't get one, she asked, "Well? Did he?"

"Not quite. He's still trying to make it up to me." I explained to her the challenge and the added problem of my impending move.

Julie's face fell at the news. "I'm really happy for you but I was hoping Will could get to know his aunt."

"I've got it all worked out," I assured her. "Direct tickets from Denver to Dallas are cheap, about a hundred bucks round-trip. I plan on visiting every month if you'll let me."

"Of course," she said, her sunny smile returning. "Come as often as you want!"

I smiled at her, wishing she could have been my sister-in-law. "Did you love Jason?" I asked, which took her by surprise.

She blinked a few times. "Yeah. With everything I had."

"How did you two meet?"

Julie's eyes were misty but she gave a rueful smile. "You're going to think I'm a complete whore, but I met him at a spring break party and we slept together," she said, then added, "but he was the only guy I slept with that whole time."

The puzzle piece clicked together. "Henry said something about you. That Jason really liked you but you lived too far away from each other."

"We had an on-again-off-again love affair, you could say."

"I wonder why he never told us."

Julie looked pensive. "I've wondered that too. My guess is that he just wanted to make sure we were on-again permanently before he broke the news." She looked down at her bare left hand. "It was during the deployment that he brought up the subject of marriage."

I grasped her hand, the one with the phantom engagement ring, and squeezed. "Why didn't you try to contact us sooner? Didn't you have the apartment phone number?"

"I did, but I knew Jason wasn't due to come home for a few more months so when I didn't hear from him for two weeks, it didn't even occur to me to call his apartment. I just started scouring the news for his name, looking for something I hoped to God I'd never find. The day I saw the story about the airman killed by a sniper in Kabul, I became seriously depressed. My roommate even called my mom, who came down to try and talk some sense into me, not knowing I was pregnant with a dead man's baby."

She pulled a tissue out of her purse and dabbed at her eyes, keeping her mascara from running.

"I'm sorry. We don't have to talk about this if you don't want to," I said. My own tear ducts were threatening to let loose as it was.

"I want you to know what happened," she said. "Anyway, I stayed with my mom for a while and tried to pick my life back up. When my coworker Kyle—who had been in love with me for forever—asked me out I said yes and we began to date, pregnant as I was. The day Will was born, Kyle came to visit us in the hospital with a teddy bear for Will and a ring for me. You have to understand, I was vulnerable and was full of excess hormones so I said yes. I just didn't want Will to grow up without a dad.

"Kyle and I got married and we lived in Denton and life was nice for a while. He even wanted to adopt Will, but I always put it off because, in my heart, it didn't feel right. Maybe that was the first indication that our marriage wasn't going to last." Julie stared off into space for a few seconds before collecting her thoughts. "Anyway, by the time I left him and it occurred to me to look for you, you and Henry had both moved out. I'm sorry it took me this long to find you."

I squeezed her hand again. "Don't be sorry. I'm so grateful you contacted us." I glanced back over to Will, who was jumping circles around a laughing Henry. "I feel like I have a piece of my brother back."

"Are your parents going to hate me after they hear that story?" she asked.

"No way," I said with a shake of the head. "How can they hate you when you've given them a grandson?"

We turned when we heard crying and saw Henry approaching with a sobbing Will in his arms.

"He scraped his knee," Henry said with his eyebrows drawn. He set Will down on a chair and crouched in front of him. "You okay, buddy?"

Julie pulled an antibacterial wipe from her purse and handed it to Henry, who proceeded to clean the raw knee gently.

"Ow, it hurts!" Will said and jerked his leg away.

"Now, Will," Henry said firmly. The little boy took immediate note of the change in Henry's tone and sat up. "I know it hurts a little bit but I need to wipe it down to make sure it's clean. Do you think you can sit still for me?"

Will's lower lip trembled but he nodded. He winced when Henry touched the wipe to his knee again but didn't cry out.

After he was done, Henry said, "Good job, Will. You are one tough little man."

Will sat a little straighter. "Thanks, Henry."

Julie nudged me and whispered, "He'd make a great dad."

I nodded. I couldn't have agreed more.

———

Julie insisted that we stay at her house that night, setting us up in a charming guest room with a queen-sized bed.

As soon as Henry saw it, he looked at me and said, "I can sleep on the floor."

I agreed to the arrangement, but at the end of the day, when it came time to turn off the lights, I found I couldn't sleep. I felt a dull ache in my stomach as I lay in that soft bed, thinking about Denver and what my new life would be like. By the time I decided that things would be so much simpler without Henry, the pain had moved up to my chest, radiating around one stubborn muscle. "Are you comfortable down there?" I asked him in the dark.

He didn't answer for so long, I thought he'd already fallen asleep. Then he said, "Not really."

Before I could decide against it, I said, "Do you want to sleep up here?"

His head popped up above the mattress. "You sure?"

I patted the bed. "Come on, let's bunk."

He climbed under the quilt beside me, careful to keep his distance, and folded his arms behind his head. "Remember when this used to feel so natural?"

"Yeah," I said wistfully. I turned to my side and laid a hand on his chest, threading my fingers through the dark hair covering his pecs. "I can't believe how much we've changed since then."

He wrapped a hand around mine and pressed it closer to his heart. "But some things are still the same."

"Are they?"

"The way I feel about you will never change," he said in that husky tone.

But I knew that had changed too. How could it not when the person himself was no longer the same? "I'm not sure that's true," I said.

He blew out a breath. "Are you going to question everything I say?"

His anger took me by surprise, rendering me speechless.

"I'm trying here, Elsie. I'm trying so hard to be the good guy, to show you that you mean everything to me," he said with an edge to his voice. "But this won't work if you never give me the benefit of the doubt."

"Well, do you blame me?" I asked.

He was quiet for a long time. Finally, he said, "I don't. But I wish you would stop doubting me." He turned over, giving me his back. "Good night."

I heard the frustration in his words but his anger only fueled my own. "You put the doubt there," I said, flipping to my side and taking a large portion of the blanket with me.

His gruff voice reached out in the darkness. "I love you."

I sighed, wishing that, just once, the exasperating man would let me stay angry.

———

The next morning, when the sun was beginning to peek through the blinds, I woke up to find Henry's body pressed into my back. I realized cuddling was not all he wanted when his hand slid under my shirt and palmed one of my breasts. He moaned into my ear and pulled me closer, gently rocking his erection into my backside.

Even though we were on unsteady ground right now, I was only human and needed to release the tension that had started building up since Henry's reemergence into my life. Unable to resist, I squeezed my butt against his hard length and felt his cock jump each time.

His hand left my breast and slid down my stomach to the waistband of my pajama pants. The breath hitched in my throat when his fingers crept under my panties and began to draw lazy circles on my clit. His other hand grasped a breast, his thumb playing with my nipple.

"Elsie," he groaned and bit on my earlobe before kissing along my neck. He pushed one long finger inside me, then two. "I want to be inside you like this," he said, his hips matching the pumping of his hand. He let out a soft hiss when my vaginal walls squeezed at his fingers, bending them so that they were grazing that sensitive spot as they slipped in and out. "Yes, squeeze me like that."

Fairly soon I was panting, my entire body coiling tighter and tighter. Henry was everywhere, invading all of my senses, inside and out and all around. I twisted my head around and kissed him, sighing when he pivoted his hand slightly so that his thumb was rubbing against my clit as he screwed me with his fingers.

"Come for me," he breathed against my ear and I flew apart into a thousand euphoric pieces. I buried my face in the pillow, biting down on it as I tried to come as quietly as possible.

His fingers kept up the assault as he wrung out every inch of that orgasm until I was a trembling, moaning mess. When the tremors inside me had subsided, he pulled his hands away. I twisted around to face him just in time to see Henry bring his fingers up to his mouth, sucking on each one with a grin.

I grabbed the back of his head and kissed him, tasting myself on his tongue.

"God, Elsie," he groaned into my mouth. He grabbed my hair and tilted my head back to lick at my neck. "I want you. I want to be inside you and drill you until the only thing you remember is my name."

His words did strange things to me, making me tingle with anticipation all over again. I reached down between us and asked throatily, "Do you want to fuck me, Henry?"

"Hell yes." His entire body went rigid when my palm made contact with his cock. I squeezed the tip once, twice, but just when I started to stroke, the bedroom door squeaked open and a little voice said, "Excuse me."

Henry pressed his face into the pillow and stifled a groan. He took a few deep breaths, then lifted his head to look across the room. "Yeah, buddy?" he asked with a tight voice.

"Do you want to play Xbox?" Will asked, standing at the foot of the bed. "Mom got me a new game and it can have two players."

Henry shot me a longing look; I squeezed his cock in return. He closed his eyes, his eyebrows furrowing as I squeezed him again, then turned back to Will. "Okay," he said, surreptitiously extricating my hand from his pants and sitting up. "I just need to take a long, cold shower okay?"

Will's face lit up. "Awesome! I'll go set it up!" he cried and ran out of the room.

I grinned up at Henry as he got out of bed to gather his clothes and toiletries, his lips taut and his pants bulging. "Good morning," I said with a languid smile, stretching my hands above my head.

"For you," he grumbled and leaned down to give me a kiss. He gazed at me longingly a few seconds longer, then, with an exaggerated sigh, stalked off to the guest bathroom.

4

ARRIVALS AND DEPARTURES

Julie was nervous as hell at the airport as we waited for my parents to deplane. The original plan was to have Henry pick them up but Julie decided that it would be less stressful to meet in neutral territory first. My guess was that she was worried they would judge the life she'd provided Will before they had a chance to judge her character. I assured her again that they would like her no matter what, but that didn't stop her from tapping her foot anxiously as we waited.

I was first to greet my parents when they came out of the security gate, giving them each a warm hug. With our elbows linked, I led them toward the nervous group. "Mom, Dad, this is Will," I said, motioning for the little boy to come forward.

My mom dropped her bags and crouched down. She already had tears in her eyes by the time Will made his way over.

The kid held out his hand all businesslike. "Hi. My name is William Jason Keaton."

Mom laughed as she shook his hand. "Well hello, sweetheart, my name is Elodie Sherman. I'm your grandma."

"Are you my dad's mom?" Will asked.

"Yes, yes I am." She gave him a watery smile. "Can I give you a hug?"

Will gave a small nod and was immediately encircled in my mother's embrace. "Oh my goodness," she kept saying over and over. "My little grandson."

I looked up at Dad, and he too was a little misty around the eyes. "He's the spitting image of Jason," he murmured. He swallowed down the oncoming grief and took a step toward Julie with his hand outstretched. "You must be Julie," he said. "It's nice to finally meet you."

"Same to you, Mr. Sherman," Julie said with a tentative smile.

"Please call me John."

Mom stood up but instead of shaking hands, she hugged the surprised Julie instead. "Thank you," Mom said. "Thank you for giving birth to this little wonder and for letting us be a part of his life."

Julie shook her head. "I'm sorry I didn't do it sooner."

Mom looked down at the miniature version of her son. "Well there's lost time to make up for. That just means we're going to have to spoil him extra rotten."

Julie laughed. "As long as you don't get him a flamethrower, we'll be fine." When my mom cast her a confused look, Julie added, "Henry's been giving Will toy weapons."

All eyes swiveled around to Henry, who had been standing quietly at the edge of the crowd with his hands in his pockets. He met my parents' eyes and I swear there was dread on that handsome scruffy face.

On the way back, I rode in the car with Julie and Will as my parents insisted on riding with Henry. When we arrived at the house, Henry emerged from the car looking more than a little shell-shocked, his face pale. I hadn't told him that my parents already knew about his return from Korea and his objective to win me back. I guess I could have given him a heads-up, but where was the fun in that?

Dad pulled me aside as we made our way toward the house. "We talked some sense into that boy," he said, his lips twitching. "Gave him a good talking-to."

I glanced behind us at Henry, who was bringing in the luggage. "What did you tell him?"

"The gist of the talk was that if he really loved you, he would let you go and fulfill your dream."

"And?"

"He said that's what he was trying to do," Dad said. "Is that the truth?"

I nodded. "Yeah, he's trying to be supportive."

"Good," Dad said. "I'd hate to think Henry would do something so selfish as to keep you from your dream job."

"He's trying," I said. "Did you tell him anything else?"

Dad had mischief in his eyes when he said, "I said if he ever hurt you like that again, I would castrate him."

We spent the rest of the day at Julie's house, catching up on the lost years. My mom commented on how much she loved Julie's decorating style and was especially drawn to the collection of birds. Julie showed her the glass eagle that I had guessed correctly was a gift from Jason.

"He knew how much I loved birds," Julie said softly. "Every time we said good-bye, he liked to tell me to *fly on home, little bird*."

Mom took great care in placing the fragile figurine back onto the mantel. "You should come to Monterey soon. We can show you where he grew up."

Julie nodded. "I'd like that."

After Will showed off his room and his impressive Lego collection, he set up the Xbox and the men started a game of "Lego Star Wars." Mom, Julie, and I—content to play out gender stereotypes for one afternoon—went to the kitchen to start making an early dinner.

"I'm glad you're giving Henry a second chance," Mom said as she cut vegetables for the salad.

"You are?" I asked, tearing apart the lettuce leaves. "I thought you wanted to put a hit out on him."

Julie coughed out a surprised laugh as she headed toward the pantry.

Mom grinned. "I know, but the boy seems genuinely contrite," she said. "Still, I hope you're making him grovel."

"He's suffering, that's for sure," I replied, thinking back to that morning.

Julie joined us at the counter with some fixings for the chicken. "You're not mad at him?" she asked my mom.

Mom shrugged. "I am but I'm not. I just think that his actions were not as selfish as they first seemed," she said. She turned to me. "Before your dad retired, I met a lot of the airmen under his command. I noticed that when they returned from their deployment they felt alienated from the world, like they no longer fit in. And worse, their friends and family didn't—or just couldn't—understand them and what they were going through. It's a pretty common problem for soldiers coming home from war and each person deals with it differently."

I stared at her as I absorbed her words.

"Henry could have handled it better, but also had the added pressure of losing his best friend." She touched my arm. "Of course the boy came unhinged. Did he act rashly? Yes. Was it understandable under the circumstances? Probably so. It took me a while to finally see that."

Her words squeezed at my insides. "Why didn't you tell me before? It could have saved me so much heartache."

"I didn't want you to get your hopes up, sweetheart," she said.

"But you told me in the car in Monterey, on the way to the airport, that the story wasn't over yet."

"It's not," she said, giving me a tender look. "I just didn't want you to hold your breath while you waited for that next page to turn."

———————

Henry and I made our way back to Oklahoma at around six o'clock that night. Mom and Dad wanted to stay another day in Texas but I had to get back home to finish my last week of work and start the dreaded packing process.

"About last night," I said somewhere between Ardmore and Pauls Valley. "I really don't mean to question everything you say."

"If you never believe anything else I ever say, just please trust that the way I feel about you never changed," he said, his voice tender and deep. "Do you remember what I said on the tape, about the day you cut my hair in high school?"

"That you were sure I was going to be your happily ever after," I said, remembering how he'd said the same thing the night he'd broken up with me.

"I'm still sure," he said. "That one fact has been the only constant in my life."

My eyes were fixed firmly on the road, my knuckles white as I gripped the steering wheel.

"Believe me," he said. "Believe *in* me."

I nodded, choosing to lift the wall around my heart and let that little confession slip under. "I do."

He reached over and tenderly cradled my cheek in the palm of his hand. I leaned into his hand, relishing the strength and vulnerability of Henry.

A little over an hour later, Henry and I arrived back at my apartment and said our good-byes at the parking lot.

"So about this morning," he said, gathering me into his arms. "Does this mean . . ."

I looked up at him as I contemplated his question. "Maybe," I said with a tiny smile.

"Right now?"

I bit my lip. "I'm not sure. When the time's right, we'll know."

"I can live with that." He gripped my hair and crushed me closer, kissing me with the passion that had accumulated since this morning. His tongue swept into my mouth, his other hand grasping my ass and pressing me into his erection.

I wanted to stay there forever, our mouths locked in an exchange of breath. My mom's words echoed in my head, weakening the walls around my heart, shedding new light on Henry and his actions.

We pulled away when someone walked by and cleared their throat. Henry was breathing heavily when he said, "I have to go take another cold shower."

I bit my lip, trying to catch my own breath. "Me too," I mouthed.

"How about now? Is now the right time?" he asked.

I shook my head. As much as I wanted Henry, there was still a part of me that was holding back, that still hadn't completely forgiven him.

"Worth a try," he said. He retrieved the car keys from his jacket and slung his backpack onto his shoulder. "I'll see you tomorrow after work?"

I nodded and grabbed the lapels of his jacket, pulling him down for one last, lingering kiss. "Good night, Henry," I said against his lips.

"Night, Els," he said as he walked away with a smile on his face. "I love you."

It wasn't until after he had driven away that I whispered, "I love you too."

———

The week went by in a blur. Henry came over every night but we did more talking or horsing around than packing. Henry had a story for nearly everything, reminiscing about each object before packing it in the box. Those he hadn't seen, he asked about. Needless to say, what would have taken a day lasted an entire week. I had a feeling that had been Henry's plan all along.

The relocation package from Shake Design allowed for a moving company, but I opted to keep the money for an apartment deposit instead and move everything to Colorado myself. Mostly it was just a thinly veiled excuse to have Henry come with me. He had agreed to drive the truck while I followed in my Prius, and I'd purchased a walkie-talkie so we could talk nonstop during the drive.

On Thursday, I picked up the moving truck and invited friends over for a moving party. They brought beer, pizza, paper plates, and their muscles. Everyone helped load boxes and furniture into the truck and afterward, we all went back inside the empty apartment and said our good-byes. Beth and Sam were the last to leave, lingering long after the others left.

"I'm going to miss you, girl," Beth said, giving me a warm embrace. "Come back and visit, okay?"

"Of course."

"Maybe we can get stationed in Colorado next," she said and shot her fiancé a questioning look.

"It's possible," Sam said, giving me a quick hug. "Peterson Air Force Base is on my dream sheet."

Beth turned to Henry. "You too, Henry. Good luck over there."

He frowned. "I'm just driving her up there, then coming right back. I'm not staying."

Beth smiled like a Cheshire cat, making me wonder if she knew something I didn't. "Oh, my mistake," she said.

Whatever it was she knew, Henry was not in on it. We just shot each other confused looks as Beth and Sam left.

I stayed at Henry's house that night, slept in the same bed nestled in his arms. He didn't try anything sexual, didn't even want to talk before we fell asleep. He simply kissed me, told me he loved me, and fell right to sleep.

———————

The next morning he was gone when I awoke. After I showered and dressed, I found him at the kitchen counter with breakfast already made. "I didn't want to wake you," he said, not meeting my eyes as he sipped his coffee. He turned his attention back to the newspaper, to whatever article he was so engrossed in.

Swallowing down my disappointment, I sat with him and ate quietly, stealing glances at his face. He looked weary, with dark circles under his eyes, but he forced a tight smile when he caught me looking.

"Did you sleep okay?" I asked, trying to get his attention.

"Wonderful," he said, keeping his eyes on the newspaper.

I set down my coffee mug. "We don't have to say good-bye yet, Henry. We still have the long drive together."

He finally looked up from that damned newspaper. "I'm not saying good-bye yet."

"Then why does it feel like you are?" I felt the pressure of tears behind my eyes and took deep breaths to keep from breaking apart.

His blue eyes bore into mine. "My heart is breaking here, Elsie," he said softly. "I'm doing everything I can to keep from begging you to stay."

I looked down at my plate, hiding the tears that were threatening to slip out.

"Helping you pack and letting you go is the hardest thing I've ever done. I mean it when I said I wanted you to fulfill your dream." He motioned to himself. "This, what I'm doing, is just my way of internalizing everything so you won't have more sadness to bear."

But the weight was already too much for my tired heart to carry on my own, so I got to my feet and stumbled to Henry. I threw my arms around him and buried my face in his neck, letting loose the tears that I'd been suppressing the past week. "I love you, Henry."

His arms were like bands of steel as they came around me, holding me tight.

"You won the challenge," I said. "You won me over."

He grasped the sides of my face and looked at me with red-ringed eyes and damp cheeks. "Thank you," he said, kissing my lips over and over. "For trusting me again."

———————

I followed the moving truck out of my neighborhood and onto the interstate with my heart lodged firmly in my throat. I silently said my good-byes as we passed by landmarks, taking in the sights for the last time. I had experienced so much heartbreak while living here, yet Oklahoma was the place I had grown the most and become my own person. This place would always have a special place in my heart.

On the way out of the state, somewhere along I-35, Henry's voice suddenly crackled over the walkie-talkie. "There's a rest stop coming up. Pull over," he said in an urgent tone.

"Why? Is something wrong with the truck?"

"Quick, just pull over! It's an emergency."

I followed him into the rest area with a pounding heart and parked my car beside the truck. My heart jumped in my throat when the truck door flew open and he jumped out, rushing toward me. I scrambled with the seat belt and got out, wondering what the hell fate was throwing our way now.

"What's wrong?" I cried a second before he grabbed the sides of my head and kissed me so thoroughly it literally took the breath from my lungs. He pressed me against the car, his hard body trapping me in place as the kiss went on and on.

I didn't know how long that kiss lasted before he finally pulled away. "Nothing" he said, biting his lower lip as he smiled. "I just needed to do that," he added before striding back to the truck.

That wasn't an isolated kissing emergency.

According to Google Maps, the drive up to Denver was supposed to take nine hours and thirty-five minutes but we stopped at nearly every rest stop to make out, adding an extra two hours to the trip. Still, it was well worth it. It reminded me of the beginning of our relationship, when we couldn't get enough of each other even if our time together had an expiration date.

We arrived at the Holiday Inn hotel in Denver at close to ten o'clock that night. We were so exhausted from the day that we just fell into bed, skipping dinner altogether. I meant to seduce him, to finally make love to him again like I'd been fantasizing the entire day, but the moment my head hit the pillow, I was out.

I awoke the next morning to my cell phone ringing and buzzing on the nightstand. "Hello?" I croaked.

"Miss Sherman?" said a male voice. "It's Ian Lang, the manager at Heritage Creek Apartments. I believe we had an appointment at nine o'clock?"

I sat up with a start, noting that the clock on the nightstand read nine fifteen. "Oh my God, I'm so sorry!" I cried, rolling out of bed. "We overslept."

"No problem, Miss Sherman," he said. "If you can make it here by ten, I can still fit you in."

"I'll be there in fifteen minutes." I threw my phone into my purse and slipped into my jeans that had lain crumpled on the floor. I rummaged through my luggage and pulled out the first shirt I found, which was blue and had a faded Captain America shield on it, and pulled it over my head. I finished dressing before I realized that I was forgetting something, or rather, someone.

I looked over my shoulder at Henry who was still softly snoring, and made the decision to leave him be. The poor guy needed the sleep, and besides, what apartment I ultimately chose was not his business. So I left, not bothering to leave a note.

The apartment complex was in Glendale and was modern and bright. Even though it was slightly overpriced, the amenities included a pool, a hot tub, and a fitness center. What sold me though was its close proximity to work and the park across the street with a running path.

So it was with a pounding heart that I signed on that dotted line, taking one step closer to my shiny new life.

When I made it back to the hotel, Henry was already showered and dressed, drinking coffee and watching something on television. "Hey," he said a little stiffly. "How did it go?"

"It went. I signed."

He frowned at me. "I thought we were going together."

"I'm sorry. I didn't want to wake you," I said. "Besides, you didn't really need to be there. It wasn't a big deal."

He nodded, his jaw muscles working, but he said nothing.

It was bothering him, being left out of my decision process, but we both knew he had no say. This was my life we were talking about. "Are you angry that I didn't bring you?"

He gave a nonchalant shrug that was anything but. "I just thought I was going to look at it with you. So I could give you my take on the place, on the neighborhood, the state of the apartment."

"I'm perfectly capable of doing all of that myself. I have done it before."

His face was stony as he turned back to the television.

I hugged myself, painfully aware of the chill that had descended upon the room. "I don't know how to explain this without hurting your feelings, so I'll just say it: You weren't needed in the decision process."

He turned back to me, and instead of icy blue eyes, I was instead faced with a dismal look. "I know," he said. "It kills me that you don't need me in your life."

"We've lived years without each other. We can do it again." And even as I said those words, I recognized them to be completely true.

He shook his head vehemently, a lock of dark hair falling over his forehead. "Those years without you, that wasn't living. I was barely surviving," he said. "I just want to experience as much of your new life as I can before I have to go back to Oklahoma and go back to just surviving again."

I walked over to him and held out my hand. He took it and squeezed. "Well, let's go then," I said, pulling him to his feet. "Let's go see my new place. You can experience unpacking with me."

5

RETURNING HOME

Unloading my stuff was not nearly as tough as I'd feared, since my furniture was lightweight and I had chosen an apartment on the ground floor. Only the large bookcase and bedroom dresser gave us trouble, but with the help of a hand truck we were able to maneuver them inside the apartment with only a few scratches and dings. It was strenuous work but we worked well as a team, knowing instinctively when the other needed a hand. We placed the furniture in their permanent placed, set up the bed, and stacked boxes against the wall.

"And the pièce de résistance," I said, hammering the nail into the wall and hanging Henry's painting above the mantel. "Is it crooked?"

Henry cocked his head and smiled. "It's perfect."

I climbed off the ladder and stood beside him, holding his hand as we admired his work. "Don't stop painting. You have something wonderful here."

He gazed down at me. "I do have something wonderful right here," he said, bringing my hand up to his chest and holding it against his heart. He yawned. "I'm beat. Let's take a nap," he said, leading me to the couch and pulling me down.

I lay in front of him, burying my face in his neck, molding myself into the hollow spaces of his muscular frame. With a sigh, I closed my eyes and focused on the thudding of his heart, and soon the steady beat lulled me to sleep.

I woke up a little while later with my legs and feet cold. I tried to wriggle out of Henry's arms, but they tightened around me. "Stay," he murmured into my hair.

If only he knew how close I was to asking him the very same thing. "I need to take a shower," I said instead.

"Mmm, good idea," he said, letting me go and stretching out, his hands and feet hanging over the arms of the couch. "I could use a good soaping down."

I chuckled as I stood up and found the box labeled *bath stuff*, grabbing everything we'd need for a shower. I was loose-limbed and relaxed from our nap until I entered the bathroom. Finding Henry in there, taking up more than his fair share of the space, gave me a sudden case of the butterflies. It had been over a year since we'd had sex; what if it wasn't as good? Or worse, what if it was mind-changingly fantastic?

Able to read the hesitation on my face, Henry said, "We don't have to do anything." He took off his shirt, revealing his muscular torso. "I just thought we could shower together to conserve water."

I had to laugh to hide the fact that my fingers were shaking. I set the towels on the counter and made a big production of putting the toiletries in the bathtub. Henry was beginning to unzip his jeans when I cried out, "Oh, we don't have the shower curtain up!"

He grinned, reached behind the door and produced a rod with the rings and curtains already in place. "Taken care of," he said, stretching the tension rod to fit above the tub.

I watched him twisting the rod, the muscles in his back jumping with each movement, until I could no longer help myself. I leaned forward and touched my lips to the center of his back.

He froze. I felt a shiver travel across his skin. He went back to the task at hand, twisting the rod with more urgency. I ran my nails down his back to get another reaction. "Oh, you are asking for it," he growled through his teeth.

My anxiety melted into playfulness; I pulled down his jeans and pinched his ass through his boxer briefs.

"Why is this rod so hard to put in place?" he muttered.

I reached around and ran my hand along the hard length of him. "Yes, the rod certainly *is* hard; as for putting it in place . . ."

He moved faster and faster, then with a final cry of triumph, twisted around to face me. "Get over here, you brat," he said, catching me around the waist. He bent his head and tickled my neck with his stubble, his fingers dancing along my sensitive sides relentlessly. I threw my head back and laughed, half-heartedly trying to wriggle out of his grasp.

The laughter died in my throat when I felt the wet heat of his tongue on my neck, as it slowly traced a line up to my jaw, to my lips. Then he kissed me and all of the nervous energy dissolved, to be replaced by something else, something so palpable it was almost tinting the air around us.

I pulled away, holding his eye as I undressed, my confidence fueled by the dark look on his face. When I stood before him completely naked, he ran a finger from my collarbone down to my chest and around one breast before pinching the nipple. He looked at me with a question on his face.

I grasped his wrist, brought his finger up to my lips and sucked it deep into my mouth as I nodded. "It's the right time," I said.

"You sure?" Even as he asked, he was slipping his boxer shorts down his thighs.

I nodded again as my eyes followed the trail of hair on his stomach down to his crotch, where his cock was standing at attention. Was it possible he had grown larger over the years?

I bent down to take him in my mouth, but he stopped me. "No, I want you to have the first one," he said and lifted me onto the laminate counter. He pulled my thighs apart, throwing my legs over his shoulders, and was dipping his head down when I grabbed his hair. "Stop," I said. "I haven't taken a shower since yesterday."

He actually laughed, the infuriating man. "Okay," he said and reached behind me for the faucet. He came back with a handful of water and swiped it all over my mound and through my folds. He repeated the process, this time rubbing me a little slower, a little more deliberately. "Are you satisfied?" he asked, his thumb playing with my clit.

"Almost," I said and leaned back on my hands, opening myself up for him.

He gripped my thighs and, with our eyes locked, slowly made his way down. He touched the tip of his tongue to my clit a few times, and just when I was about to cry out in frustration, he dove in and worked me in earnest. His tongue was at once rough and gentle, thick and thin, swirling and lapping. There was no finesse or tact in his movements; he was like an eager contestant at a pie-eating contest.

I watched him, finding the visual of his tongue dipping into me even more of a turn-on. Then his mouth covered my mound. He looked up at me with a raised eyebrow as he continued the assault.

The pressure built and built until I threw my head back and came with force, my insides quaking around his tongue as he continued to devour me.

A moment later his tongue was gone, replaced by the head of his cock. He crouched over, planting his hands on both sides of my hips as he asked inches from my face, "You want me inside you?"

I flicked my tongue out, tracing the cupid's bow of his upper lip. "What do you think?" I reached around him and dug my fingers into his ass cheeks, pulling him toward me, inside me. To be filled by him after all this time was excruciatingly exquisite, my insides stretching slowly to accommodate all of him.

I remembered his words on the tape, when he'd said being inside me was like coming home. At that moment, I knew exactly what he meant.

He held still, lodged completely inside me, as his eyes locked on to mine. "Els," he breathed when I squeezed his cock. "Do it again." I don't know how he held still, but he didn't move a muscle when my vaginal walls squeezed him over and over. Only the expression of euphoric torture on his face revealed his inner struggle.

Then he started to move a bit at a time until he was pulling almost all the way out and thrusting back in. His hands grabbed my hips as he continued the assault, our eyes locked the entire time.

Just as I was building another charge, Henry pulled out. I gave him a disgruntled look when it became clear that he wasn't coming right back.

"Time for a shower." His chest was heaving as he helped me down from the counter.

"Why are we stopping?" I asked as we stepped into the bathtub. He twisted around and turned on the water. The spray hit his back, shielding me from the initial temperature change. "I want to make this last," he said, running his fingers along my lower lip.

I bit him. "You're just trying to torture me."

He raised an eyebrow. "Hey, you've already come once, remember?"

I licked my lower lip. "I want more." I spun us around so that the water was hitting my back and reached for the body wash. I poured some into my hand and rubbed it onto the wide expanse of his chest, soaping his dark hair. My hands ventured down, rubbing along the deep ridges of his six-pack.

"Mmm." He held my wrist and guided my hand lower. "You may need to concentrate on this area. I'm really, really dirty down here."

I held his thick cock in my hand and used the body wash to stroke him from the base to the tip and back down again. He groaned as the water washed away the soap and created more friction.

"My turn," he said and soaped me up, spending extra time on each of my breasts, massaging them tenderly. He lifted my leg so that my foot rested on the side of the tub and got on his knees to wash between my legs, running his fingers to the crease of my ass, the tip of his finger pausing at my anus, then sliding back to the front. When the soap had all washed off, he dipped his head and licked the inside of my thigh, from the knee all the way to my crotch, where he nipped at the trembling skin.

Then he stood up, towering over me, and swiveled me around so that my back was to the cool wall. He held my wrists above my head with one hand while the other lifted my thigh. He bent at the knees and thrust his cock into me at the same time his tongue invaded my mouth, pinning me in place with his entire body. His shaft rubbed my clit as it slid in and out, creating the most delicious sensation, then he freed my wrists and hooked both hands under my knees, lifting me up and bearing all of my weight as he rocked into me.

"You feel so fucking good," he said between his teeth.

My lips traveled all over his face, kissing the cleft on his chin and along the stubble of his square jaw. He was everything and everywhere and I loved him and cradled him like we had no tomorrow.

When I felt his muscles tightening, I squeezed harder and sped up my own impending orgasm. He was breathing hard, continuing to plunge into me even as he started to come. "I love you so damn much, Elsie," he rasped and I climaxed with his words, my insides trembling as intensely as the emotions roiling through me.

I laid my cheek against the wet skin of his shoulder, overcome with love for the man. He was my beginning, my middle, and my inevitable end.

Henry and I made love on my bed once more before we fell asleep out of sheer exhaustion. My body was worn out but it was my heart that bore the most fatigue. I was glad that sleep stole me away because I was sure I'd have stayed awake the entire night, trying to second-guess my decision to move.

That night I dreamt of Jason, but unlike my previous dreams, in it he was still alive. He and I were kids, sitting on our porch in Monterey as we waited for the school bus. I couldn't hear what we were talking about, all I saw were our mouths moving. Then we stopped and turned to watch an adult Henry approaching. He sat beside us on the steps and joined the conversation in his deep, gravelly voice.

The bus came and stopped in front of us with a loud hiss, and both Jason and Henry climbed aboard. I remained sitting on that porch and watched as the bus doors swished shut and pulled away from my lonely step and me.

In the morning I woke to soft kisses traveling across my shoulder. When I opened my eyes, I found Henry clamping his mouth around my breast and laving it with his tongue. "Morning," he said against my skin with a sexy grin, his hair messy from sleep.

"Morning." I arched my back and stretched as he continued his adoration of my body, moving his attention to the other breast. He slipped his arms under my back, kissing along my neck as he pulled me up to sitting position.

I wrapped my arms around his shoulders and ran my fingernails on the back of his head, moaning as he nipped his teeth along my jaw.

We didn't talk about the fact that he was leaving today to drive the truck back to Oklahoma. We didn't talk about what the future held for us. We only held each other tight as he slipped into me and we made love for the last time.

I began to move, rising and falling onto him, but it wasn't nearly enough; I needed all of Henry. I bobbed faster, squeezed harder, my fingers digging into his shoulders as I pushed my leg muscles—and in turn, my heart—past the burning point.

Henry's hot palms caressed my back, then slid down to grip my ass. "Slow down, Els," he whispered. "We've got time."

"No we don't," I said, continuing the rapid pace. All too soon, my legs gave out and I collapsed onto him in frustration. I buried my face in his neck and cried, unable to stave off the sadness any longer. My tears rolled off my cheek and onto his back as I clung to him, held him so close I imagined us melding together; maybe then neither of us could ever leave the other.

His eyes were red when he pulled away. He held my neck in his hands and rubbed my cheeks with his thumbs as the grief creased his face. "This isn't over," he said, his nose flaring. "Nothing will keep me from you." He kissed me tenderly as he started driving his hips up, carrying me when I was too paralyzed from grief to move.

"I love you, Henry," I said over and over against his mouth.

I came first, my entire body trembling as I kissed him desperately. Then he too was climaxing, holding me down onto him like he never intended to let go.

The time came to say good-bye too soon. We tried to put it off with an elaborate breakfast (which, of course, necessitated hunting through boxes while I went to the store for groceries), but after our second cups of coffee, we knew we couldn't put it off any longer.

It was raining when we walked out the front door and down the concrete pathway toward the parking lot. I was glued to him, tucked into his side as we huddled under my sad little umbrella, limp and battered from years of use.

"Drive safe. Call me when you get home," I said to fill the silence. "Thank you for helping me move."

He kissed the top of my head. "You're welcome."

We reached the truck and stood there for a long moment, both unwilling to let go. Eventually, we pulled apart and faced each other.

"So . . ." he said, anxiously fidgeting with the keys in his jeans pocket.

I plucked up the courage to ask *the* question. I didn't know what to expect but I needed to hear his answer anyway. "Henry, why haven't you asked to move with me?"

His lips formed a thin line as he gazed at me. "Because what I want might confuse what you want. You need to make decisions that are in your best interest."

"I appreciate that," I said, not at all surprised to hear the logical, diplomatic answer. Still, I couldn't help but shiver from the disappointment chilling my skin.

"Before I go, I have to give you something," he said, his hand still in his pocket.

My heart skipped a beat. "What is it?"

He held out his hand, his fingers closed around the object. "Something that belongs to you." He unfurled his fingers to reveal not a diamond ring but a different kind of rock altogether, one that was in the shape of a wonky star.

I felt like I'd been punched in the gut. I didn't know until then just how much I wanted Henry to stay, how much I wanted to marry him and grow old together. "I don't want it," I said but he insisted, pressing it into my fingers until I finally held on.

"This is just temporary, Els," he said, bringing my fist up to his cheek. "When you're ready, you let me know."

I nodded and reached up to kiss him, committing to memory every taste, every feeling, creating memories to hold close in the coming weeks. There was no fight left in that kiss, only grim acceptance.

His jaw muscles were jumping when he pulled away, his blue

eyes taking me in. He kissed my forehead one last time. "Don't forget me," Henry said and got into the truck.

With a breaking heart, I watched him back out of the space and drive out of the parking lot and out of my life. The world closed in around me, suffocating me until I was gasping for breath.

I faced the apartments and closed the umbrella, allowing the rain to pelt my face to keep my tears company. I looked down at that stupid rock in my hand, blaming it for everything that was wrong in my life. I formed a fist around it, wanting nothing more than to hurl it into the bushes, but I knew I would just run right over and drop to my knees to search for it. There are just some things in life that are not worth losing.

I couldn't hear anything beyond the rain and the pounding of my heart, so when I heard my name being called, I thought I had just dreamed it up.

Then I heard it again. "Elsie!"

I spun around in time to see Henry jump out of the truck and run toward me. He nearly bowled me over when we collided, but he caught me, steadied me.

"I couldn't do it," he cried, grasping my head and kissing me desperately. "I turned that corner and couldn't make myself leave. I would have to be the biggest moron on the planet to leave you again.

"I love you, Elsie. I want you to be happy and live your dream, but I can't pretend that I don't want to be by your side throughout all of that. I want to be part of your life always," he said, raining kisses on my face and stopping at my forehead.

I reveled in the warmth of his lips and in the power of second chances. "I want that too. I want you here with me."

"Do you?" he asked. "Are you sure?"

"More than anything," I said with a happy sob.

He reached into his pocket again. "I don't want to live another day without you, Els," he said, grasping my left hand. "I've made some huge mistakes but I know, I *know*, that if I drive away right now without asking you this question, I will regret it for the rest of my life."

He got down on his knee, on the wet ground and all, the ring poised at the end of my finger. "I know I broke your trust in me, but if you let me, I will spend the rest of my life trying to make it up to you. Just . . . marry me?"

I fell to my knees in front of him and slipped that ring all the way down my finger. "Okay," I said through a smile that was breaking my face wide open. "I'll marry you, Henry."

He let out a relieved laugh and pulled me to him, lifting me off my feet as he stood up. I wrapped my arms around his neck and simply gazed at him as he carried me down the stone pathway.

My vision of Henry may have been blurry from the tears and the rain, but what I felt for him was crystal clear. The years apart—the hurt and the anger—all of that washed away until only the two of us remained.

6

THE HAPPY EVER AFTER

"You ready?" Henry asked, coming around behind me and resting his chin on my head.

"Hold on, one more thing," I said, finishing with the image touch-up and saving the JPEG. As I emailed the file to the junior designer on my team, I glanced down at my ring again, at the princess-cut diamond on a simple platinum band that encircled my finger. "Tell me again about this ring," I said, a little embarrassed to say that four months had passed and I was still mesmerized by it and what it symbolized.

"You've already heard that story."

"I'd like to hear it again," I said, leaning back in the computer chair to look up at my fiancé.

He gave an impatient sigh but told the story anyway. "After you issued the three-date challenge, I went to BC Clark the next day and bought it. The woman who helped me asked about you so she could help me find the right ring."

"And what did you tell her about me?"

He spun the office chair around and bent down, his hands on the armrests as he faced me. "That you're a brat," he said, pinching my nose. "And that you wear simple and classic jewelry."

"What else?" I urged with a smile. I'd heard the story several times before, but didn't think I'd ever tire of hearing it.

"I told her about the challenge, that you'd given me something nearly impossible to accomplish. She told me that this ring, this expensive bauble, was sure to make you forgive me and I shook my head and told her that I wasn't trying to buy your forgiveness or your love. I was getting the ring as an alternative to that other rock."

He looked into my eyes and gave a rueful smile. "The day I was getting ready to leave you in Denver, I had both of those in my pockets and I kept touching them, wondering which one to give you. I wanted to give you the ring but I thought giving you the rock was the right thing to do," he said. "Good thing I don't always do the right thing."

I touched my lips to his and kissed him tenderly. Four months had passed since that rain-soaked proposal, four months since Henry gave me the ring and delayed going home by a day. He had stayed in Oklahoma for a few more weeks to give me some space to think clearly, to get situated with work and my new life. As it turned out, taking that job was one of the best decisions of my career. I was able to live in both design worlds as an art director and a senior designer. Some days I could even work from home.

Henry got his affairs in order back in Oklahoma before moving to Colorado for good. He had given up the deposit on the house he was renting, sold most of his stuff, and had cancelled his application to the Oklahoma PD, starting the entire process over in Denver.

For now, we lived in my apartment and it was almost like old times, except I no longer had a room to escape to whenever things got too stifling. Luckily, I'd only signed a six-month lease so we would be able to find a larger place fairly soon.

Have I completely forgiven Henry? I like to think so, but some of that anxiety lingers on, the worry that he might up and leave at any time still niggling at me at random times. But true to his word, he was here day by day, building a life with me.

"You ready?" Henry asked, standing beside our luggage at the front door.

I turned off my computer and nodded. I grabbed my leather jacket and purse and we loaded the bags in the Volvo.

The flight to California took seven hours. We had a connection in Phoenix, so it was evening by the time we arrived in Monterey. We thought my dad was the one who would pick us up; instead Henry's mom, Helen, was waiting for us past the gate, an excited smile all over her face.

She hugged me first, then gave her son a proud little smile before pulling him down in her embrace. Henry's lips were set in a thin line the entire time but I spied something there in his eyes, a spark that looked a lot like optimism.

At my insistence, Helen parked the car in her driveway so that Henry and I could just walk over to my parents' house. The moon was bright in the night sky, illuminating the streets with a soft bluish light. I hoped wildly that the next few days would be just as clear and mild.

"What are you thinking?" Henry asked as we walked up to the house.

"That it doesn't rain on Sunday," I replied.

We stood at the front door and just gazed at each other. "I can't believe it's really happening," Henry said, breaking the silence.

"Not too late to back out," I joked weakly.

He touched my cheek. "There's no way I'm backing out. You're stuck with me forever." He rolled the luggage out of the way and stood closer. "I was just having a hard time believing that in two days, I'll be your husband and you'll be my wife. If anything, I'm a little worried that it won't happen because I want it so badly."

"It'll happen," I said, touching his cheek.

He was dipping his head to kiss me when the front door suddenly burst open and Will came out, interrupting the moment.

"Hey, Grandma, they're here!" he called back over his shoulder. He grabbed my hand and tugged. "Come on, guys."

Henry shook his head as he gathered the bags, a tiny smile playing along his lips. "That kid has interruption down to an art form," he muttered. "Exactly like his dad."

———————

Julie slept in the guest room at my parents' house that night while Will had the distinct pleasure of sleeping in Jason's old room. My mom had taken great care to put out Jason's old toys and photos, showing each one to a rapt Will. I don't know if he gets it right now—that he is sleeping in the very same bed that his dad used to or that he's playing with the same toys—but my hope is that one day, he will come to know his father in some small way through Jason's old things. Maybe then Will won't grow up feeling like he never knew his dad at all.

———————

The day before the wedding was insanely crazy. Everyone was out running errands, tying up loose ends. Julie, Mom, and I were in a mad dash to finish the decorations, putting together the floral centerpieces and filling seashells with wax to use as candles on the table. Meanwhile Dad and Henry worked in the garage to finish building the archway that was to be our backdrop during the ceremony. Henry's parents were busy with work, as usual, but they both came home early enough to help out with whatever they could.

The rehearsal dinner consisted of just the two families sharing some salad and lasagna at the Logans' house. It was cozy and warm, full of laughter and nervous energy. Every now and then my eyes flitted across the table to find Henry watching me and we'd share a secret little smile.

"To Elsie," Dad said near the end of dinner, giving me a warm look. "You will always be my little girl."

We raised our glasses for the toast.

"And to Henry," he continued. "Who's been trying to infiltrate my family for years and, it looks like, will finally succeed."

We all laughed as we toasted, our stomachs full and our hearts overflowing.

––––––––––

Finally, the big day arrived and the entire household was thrown into chaos. Mom rushed around trying to get everyone ready, very nearly freaking out until Julie calmed her and said she'd help with the decorations.

"What about Will?" Mom asked, her hair only half styled.

"I'm all ready!" Will announced, standing there in his little tan suit, complete with a blue tie.

"You look so handsome," I said, the sight of him bringing tears to my eyes, making me wish for the millionth time that Jason was here to join in the celebrations. I took deep breaths to collect myself, to keep the tears from ruining my makeup.

The cake was delivered to our house, three-tiered and entirely white with swirly detailing at the bottom of each layer. The topper was the iconic LOVE logo in blue, with the O taken out and the wonky rock glued in its place. It was perfect.

I had only one glimpse of it before it was taken, along with the rest of the decorations, to where both fathers were setting up on the beach.

My dress was a sleeveless mermaid-style gown with a beaded belt and three layers of organza ruffles past the knee, and my curly hair was swept off to the side with a crystal hairpin. When I was finished dressing, I stood in front of the mirror, completely taken aback by the person staring back. She was absolutely glowing.

Mom had tears in her eyes as she stood behind me. I always knew she would cry at my wedding but I was not at all prepared to see her breaking down so soon. "You're beautiful, sweetheart," she said, pushing a lock of hair off my shoulder. She hugged me from behind and we looked at each other in the mirror, basking in the bittersweet moment. "One story ends and another one begins."

I grasped her wrists and pulled her arms tighter around me. "I love you, Mom. Thanks for believing in Henry even when I didn't."

Dad was back from the beach when I emerged from my room. He looked at me with a healthy dose of shock on his face and maybe a hint of sadness. "My little Elsie," he said, gathering me into his arms for a crushing embrace. "You grew up too fast."

We all drove to Carmel Beach together and I waited in the car while the guests were seated. My stomach was literally trembling with nerves as I sat in that car and wondered how everything came together. As if reading my mind, Julie messaged me a picture of the beach—of the chairs, the gauze-draped archway, and the handsome groom arriving with his groomsmen.

Seeing that tiny picture made it all the more real. This was really happening. I was really getting married.

Before I could freak out, Henry sent me a message that brought me back on point: *Where are you?*

I smiled, imagining him standing by the priest while he texted. *Waiting in the car. Where are you?*

I'm here, Elsie. I'm waiting for you.

Then it was time to walk down those sandy steps to the beach, where wooden folding chairs had been set up in two sections and the aisle delineated with gauze and light-colored flowers. At the end was the archway and underneath it stood the priest with the Bible in his hands. The picture had given me an idea of what to expect, but the real thing still managed to take my breath away.

"Ready, sweetie?" Dad whispered, holding out his elbow.

I lifted the bouquet of paper roses higher, tucking my *something borrowed*—Jason's Purple Heart medal—safely inside, then linked my arm with my father's. "Are you?" I teased.

Even though he was smiling, Dad's eyes were bright with unshed tears. "Never."

The violinist began to play a slow, hopeful tune and we began the march. Julie and Beth walked ahead in their navy blue dresses, and soon strains of the wedding march filled the air. Dad and I walked unhurriedly as I looked around at everyone's face, trying to smile at each and every one of our family and friends. All too soon, we reached the end of the aisle and I finally allowed myself to look up at Henry.

His blue eyes bore down on me, the expression on his face nearly unreadable, but somewhere in that chaos of emotions I saw the one I was searching for: certainty. I let out the breath I'd been holding for months, finally surfacing from the depths of insecurity.

My dad kissed my cheek before he handed me off to Henry with a handshake. Dad clapped Henry on the shoulder and said, "Take care of her, son."

Henry performed a perfect salute and said, "Yes, sir."

And then it was just us: Henry and me together under the clear blue sky. The waves behind us played a soothing symphony as the priest began the ceremony, welcoming everyone to the joining of our hearts.

I couldn't tear my eyes away from Henry, from his handsome face, the khaki suit, and blue tie that matched his eyes. His hair was brushed away from his face with a few loose locks waving in the ocean breeze.

"You look beautiful," he mouthed at me.

I smiled up at him, too overwhelmed with emotions to move. I only clutched at his hand tighter, hoping to never wake from this dream.

When it came time for the rings, Henry crouched down next to his tiny best man. "You got the rings, buddy?"

Will nodded and reached into his pants pocket. He leaned in to Henry and said, "I wanted you to marry my mom."

I fought to contain my laughter but Henry only shrugged. "I'm marrying your aunt, so that means I'll be your real uncle."

"I wanted you to be my dad."

"Uncles are better than dads, though," he said so that only Will and I could hear. "Dads have to enforce the rules. Uncles, on the other hand, can be cool and buy you lots of toys and spoil you like crazy."

Will's face lit up. "You're right! That's better!"

Henry stood up with the rings in his hands, allowing me a glimpse of the downcast expression on his face before it was replaced with a smile.

"Jason's here," I whispered to him as he took my left hand. "He's here with us."

And then came time to say our vows, before God and our witnesses.

Henry was first to go. He took a deep breath before starting. "I, Henry Logan, take you Elsie to be my wife, my equal, my best friend. I promise to love and cherish you, to be there for you whenever you need me. I promise to respect you, to remain faithful, to keep you safe, but most of all, I promise to love you with everything I am even after I spend my last day on earth.

"Els, I haven't always done the right thing, but I promise to you that I will strive to become the man you deserve. I loved you then, I love you now, and I will love you always."

I wiped away a tear as I held his hand, the wedding band poised over his finger. It took me a minute to collect myself, to keep from bursting into delirious tears, but I finally managed. "I, Elsie Sherman, take you Henry to be my husband," I began softly. "I promise to love you unconditionally, to support you in your dreams, to honor and respect you for as long as we both shall live."

The priest opened his mouth to continue when I gave him a little shake of the head. A soft titter went through the crowd.

I turned back to my groom. "Henry, I love you. Those three words have a deeply embedded history. They come with a whole lifetime of laughter and tears. So when I say them, I hope you feel the weight of my words because they bear everything I hope. They bear everything that I am."

Henry didn't wait for the priest to say the official words. He just grasped the sides of my face and kissed me in front of our friends and family, in front of the endless ocean, and anyone who might have been watching from above.

And we were married.

The reception was a simple affair. We set up two whitewashed wooden tables and placed the seashell candles and bouquets of flowers along their center. The place settings were a pretty mixture of mismatched plates and silverware with a tiny starfish attached to each white napkin.

When the sun set, the candles were lit and our little party glowed on into the night. Dad and I danced on the sand while Henry danced with his mother.

There were a few mishaps—wax spilled out of the seashells and onto the table, napkins flew off in the breeze and sand got into everything—but we didn't care. None of it mattered.

After dinner Henry and I shared our first dance as husband and wife under the stars. Hass played an acoustic version of "I Won't Let You Go" by James Morrison on his guitar as Henry pulled me by the waist and gathered me close, pressing a kiss to the top of my head. I leaned my head against my husband's chest, breathing in his cool scent, sure that any second now, I was going to fly apart from all of the joy and love inside me. Only Henry's strong arms kept me in place and held me steady.

"I'm here, Els," he said against my ear as we swayed, holding my palm against his heart. "I'll never let you go."

Turn the page for a special short story
about Henry and Elsie's honeymoon

R & R

Available in print in this edition only!

"This place is, uh, interesting," Henry said the moment we walked into the room, pursing his lips at the overenthusiastic beach-cottage décor. The walls were covered in whitewashed bead board and the furniture was all white rattan, even the headboard. Seashells, real and plastic, were scattered on nearly every surface.

He set the bags down on the worn wood floor and entered the only other door in the room, painted a faded blue. "Well, at least we have our own bathroom."

"No dorm-room sharing with other guests then," I called, drawing aside the frilly white curtain and looking at our view of the quiet street and the abandoned little shack across the road with a large For Sale sign in its broken window. I grinned to myself. This place certainly had its charms.

"This place is *not* like they said on the website," Henry said, emerging from the bathroom, shaking his head.

"I think it's kind of cute."

Henry raised an eyebrow. "Cute?"

I jabbed a thumb out the window. "Yeah, in the way that the hobo at the corner is cute."

"There is not . . ." He walked to the window and looked out. He let out an exasperated gust of air. "Of all the bed-and-breakfasts in Key West, I chose the most ghetto one."

I hugged him from behind, pressing my cheeks against his back. "It's fine, Henry," I said. "As long as we're together."

He grasped my linked hands and held them up to his lips. "This is not how I pictured our honeymoon, Els. I wanted to give you something classy and nice."

"This is perfect," I insisted. We hadn't been able to afford the trip to Prague that we'd envisioned, so we had opted for something a little closer to home. Key West, with its warm waters and lively atmosphere, seemed like a wonderful alternative.

Henry turned in my arms and took my face in his hands. "You sure?" he asked, his dark eyebrows drawn together. "We can get a room at the Waldorf Astoria."

I shook my head. "We can't afford that." Both of our savings accounts had been depleted after the wedding and putting a down payment on a house in Cherry Creek, Colorado; it was a minor miracle that we'd managed to go on a honeymoon at all. I wasn't about to start nitpicking minor details because, at the end of the day, I was with Henry, we were healthy, and we were in love. Everything else was just icing on the cake.

"How about the Best Western then?" he asked with a teasing grin.

I squeezed him. "This bed-and-breakfast is perfect. Really."

He kissed my forehead, inhaling deeply. "I just want to give you so much more."

I pulled away and walked over to the bed with the simple white covers and lay down, leaning back on my elbows. "Give it to me then," I said in the most seductive voice I could muster.

Henry reached behind his neck and tugged his shirt off in one swift movement, advancing toward me even as he worked on the fly of his shorts. My eyes raked over his firm and angular form, the perfect complement to my soft, smooth body.

With a dark look on his face, he swooped down and captured my lips, kissing me with the same passion we'd had since the beginning. He slipped his hands under my back and held me close to his naked chest, his erection digging into my crotch. One hand slid along my thigh and under the hem of my skirt where his fingers found my panties. He tugged them down with slow deliberation and threw them across the room.

He crawled over me, undressing me while we kissed, our lips only breaking apart long enough to slide my tank top over my head.

"Starfish," I said against his lips, shifting my backside.

He pulled away with a wicked grin. "You want me to play with your starfish?" he asked, his fingers massaging my ass.

I burst out laughing. "No, I meant there's a starfish digging into my back," I said, shifting again and dislodging the large red starfish that had lain on the pillow moments earlier. I held it up to him, still racked with laughter.

He chuckled with me, grabbing the starfish and throwing it across the bed. He fell sideways onto the bed, a smile still splitting his face, and pulled me close.

I gazed at the beautiful man in my arms, having to remind myself that he was now my husband. When he grasped my hip and slipped into me, I realized that no other man could ever complete me like Henry could. Nobody else had even come close. I held on to the back of his head and pressed my forehead to his, our eyes burning into each other as we said with our bodies what our words could not.

We made love on that simple bed that afternoon, bathed in the warm sunlight, completely absorbed in each other. The outside world could fall apart around us and it wouldn't have made a difference.

We were together.

———

After taking a nap on the surprisingly comfortable bed, we headed out for a night on the town. We walked down to Duval Street and took in the sights and sounds. The street was lined with restaurants and souvenir stores, all of which appeared to be overflowing with customers.

"I didn't realize how busy this place would be," I said, feeling a trickle of unease at the sheer number of people walking around us. Everywhere I turned there were people in shorts and dresses, most in various stages of inebriation.

Henry squeezed my hand, walking ahead of me to part the way like he'd always done. He must have sensed that I was starting to feel claustrophobic because he abruptly pulled me into a store alcove, a pocket of calm away from the crowds. "Better?"

I nodded, my heartbeat slowing. "What's going on? Is there a parade or something?"

"I think I saw a flyer about a brewfest."

"Figures," I said, laughing softly. "We schedule our honeymoon during drunkfest."

"Brewfest," he corrected.

"Same thing." I looked at him as he craned his neck around, no doubt in search of the location of the festivities. "You want to go, don't you?" I asked, a smile tugging at the corners of my mouth.

His eyes flicked back down to me, gauging my reaction. "Only if you want to go."

His answer came as no surprise. Henry was never one to turn down a cold one. "Come on then, let's find this brewfest," I said, tugging on his hand.

"Are you sure?" He pulled me close, holding my body against his. "We can skip it if you'd rather do something else."

"No, really. I'd like to try a few beers myself."

He hugged me tight, lifting me off my feet a few inches. "Best wife ever," he said into my hair.

"Damn straight," I said, laughing.

A little bit of wandering later, we finally figured out that the brewfest had adjourned from the beach to a place called the Porch. After asking around, we finally found the place a few blocks from Duval Street. The Porch was actually a house that had been converted to a bar. Patrons could either sit at the bar inside or take their drinks outside and sit on rattan furniture on the porch. We did the latter, preferring to steer clear of the rowdy crowds.

We took our frosty glass mugs and sat in a white loveseat at the end of the porch. Henry automatically lifted his arm and I snuggled into his side; we sighed at the same time. "I love you," he said.

I looked up to return the sentiment when I realized that he was looking pointedly at the beer in his hand.

"I love you so much," he said before taking a sip. He glanced at me and grinned.

I smacked him in the stomach. "I love you too, my pear cider," I said, taking a large swig of my drink. Henry chose the same moment to touch his cold mug to my cheek, taking me by surprise. I gulped, tipping the mug too much and getting foam all over my upper lip and nose.

He laughed, deep and untroubled, then stared at me with a warm look in his eyes. He cupped my cheek in his palm and bent his head down, but instead of kissing me, his tongue darted out and lapped at the foam on my lip. A second later, he kissed the end of my nose. "Woodchuck is a good taste on you. But if you tasted like beer, you'd be the perfect woman."

I pulled away and raised an eyebrow. "If you tasted like chocolate, I'd suck on you all day long."

His eyes widened. "Well what are we waiting for?" he asked, taking a large swig of his drink. "Let's get out of here and go melt some chocolate."

I laughed. "Fondue for dinner then?"

"I'm not above dipping my dick into scalding chocolate if it means you'll suck on it all day long."

"Your Gristle Whistle, you mean?" I asked with a grin.

He threw his head back and laughed. "My purple-helmeted airman," he said.

"Your Vlad the Impaler." I shook my head and giggled, realizing that other people had heard us and not caring.

Henry was suddenly close, his breath on my ear. "God, I love you so much," he said, and in the next moment, his lips were on mine and the rest of Key West dissolved.

Twenty minutes later, we were back in our room with a bar of chocolate in hand. We hadn't found a fondue set or even chocolate syrup, but hoped that melting chocolate with our own body heat would be just as sexy.

Henry lay in bed completely naked with his arms folded under his head as we watched for the rectangle piece of chocolate to melt on his erect penis.

"Anytime now," I said, on my knees between his legs as I held his shaft steady.

He sighed. "We've been waiting for ten minutes. My bushwhacker is very impatient to whack some bushes."

"Give it a few more minutes," I said, leaning down to study the chocolate. "It looks like it's starting to soften."

"The chocolate or me?"

My tongue darted out and licked the tender skin at the base of his penis. "Better?"

"Mmm," he said, closing his eyes. "Maybe you need to do a bit more of that to melt the chocolate."

I took a deep breath, inhaling his masculine scent. "Ah, fuck it," I said and bared my teeth. I only saw a glimpse of Henry's wide eyes before my open mouth descended on his cock and I bit the piece of chocolate. I let it melt in my mouth for several moments before I took his cock into my mouth and coated his skin with the chocolate. I pulled away and studied my handiwork. "Yum."

"You are a genius," he said between breaths. He sat up and kissed me, the milk-chocolate flavor intermingling between our tongues.

I pulled away and focused on my chocolate treat, wrapping my lips around the tip and, with a vacuum-tight seal, sucked my way down. His fingers laced through my hair and he held on, neither speeding me up nor slowing me down.

"God, Els," he groaned, his hips coming up off the bed when I cupped his balls. I stopped when I heard his breathing change, when his taut muscles signaled that he was starting to crest that hill. His eyes flew open. "What is it? Do you need more chocolate?" he asked, his hand scrambling for the chocolate bar.

I wiped at the corners of my mouth. "My turn."

He tried to catch his breath and nodded. "You're a genius, yes, but an evil one." With a deft motion, he flipped me over so that he was on top and put two pieces of chocolate in his mouth and chewed on them. He moved to my crotch but I stopped him.

"Not there," I said. When he frowned, I added, "Just trust me."

He nodded and moved up my torso, stopping at my breast. He covered one mound with his mouth and I felt his gooey tongue sliding along my skin, making circles until he reached my nipple. He took the tip between his teeth and smiled up at me a second before he bit down gently. He lapped up the sweetness and moved to the other breast, laving it with the same loving attention.

Struck with an idea, I slid out from under him and stood. Hey, we'd already played with food. Might as well try this too.

"Where do you think you're going?" he asked, taking hold of my wrist.

"Just wait," I said, digging into my luggage, then running to the bathroom to change. "Did you know this place used to be a bordello?" I called out.

"Yeah, I read that somewhere on the website."

Several long minutes later, I came back out and struck a pose in the doorway. Henry's jaw dropped as his eyes raked over me, making me feel every bit as sexy as I felt.

I sauntered over to him in my fire-engine-red corset and matching lace panties, a crop with a feather in my hands. He visibly swallowed when I straddled him, running the feather down his torso.

"Elsie, you're so sexy," he said, his fingers digging into my ass cheeks.

"I'm not Elsie tonight," I said, leaning over so that my breasts were nearly falling out of the tight bodice. "Just call me Madam."

"You planned this, huh?" he asked with a grin. "I approve . . . Madam."

"Anything to please my one-and-only customer," I said, raking my nails along his sides.

He folded his hands behind his head. "Then go ahead and please me."

I leaned down and grabbed his wrists, taking the opportunity to run my tongue along the pronounced cupid's bow of his upper lip. "Keep your hands up here," I ordered in a husky voice. "The one rule in this bordello is that you must not touch me with your hands."

He lifted his hips, his erection nudging me in the most delicious way. One dark eyebrow rose in question.

"Yes, you may touch me with that." I sat up and whipped his nipple tentatively with the leather side of the crop.

He made an inarticulate noise like *ungh* before I whipped the other nipple. The muscles along his jaw were jumping but he kept his hands by his head. "I didn't know you liked this kind of stuff."

"I like anything that involves teasing you." I ran the feather end of the crop along the length of his erection.

"Teasing?" he said in a pained voice. "More like tormenting me."

With a smile, I sat back on my heels and gave little gentle lashes on his penis, making it jump each time. Six, seven, eight times, each time hitting a different area, finishing with one final whip at the tip.

His chest was heaving and the muscles in his arms were straining. "I want to try that whip out on you," he gritted out.

"No touching me, remember?" I asked and stood up on the bed. I slid my palms along my waist, my fingers hooking into my panties and pulling them down as my hands continued sliding down my thighs. Completely bent over, I stepped out of my panties and flashed him a seductive smile, knowing my breasts were in his full view. I walked my fingers from my feet to his legs, up his muscled thighs and to the twitching muscle in between. My nails raked at his velvety skin, teasing him.

"That's it," he said and bolted upright, capturing me in his arms. In the next instant, I was on my back and Henry was crouched over me, his face dark and triumphant.

"You're breaking the bordello rules," I said breathlessly, completely aroused by his show of dominance.

"Fuck the rules," he said and grabbed my thighs, pulling them apart with no amount of gentleness. Then he was surging inside me, taking me like a man deprived. He pushed my legs upward, resting them on his shoulders as he thrust into me over and over. He leaned forward, the strain on my legs a delicious mixture of pain and pleasure, and nudged at me even deeper. He caressed his cheek against the inside of my leg and then bit at my skin.

I came instantly, my legs trembling above me even as he licked at the tender spot on my calf. He continued the assault, taking me over and over before he grabbed both my ankles and plunged one last time, his face contorted into ecstasy.

———

Later that night, after the chocolate and costume had all been put away, we lay together completely sated.

"You were wonderful, Madam," he said, kissing my head. "I think I might have to hire you full-time."

"Works for me," I said, snuggling into his side, feeling the hair on his chest tickling my cheek.

"Els?"

"Mmm?"

"Do you like that stuff?" he asked in a soft, raspy voice. "Play-acting like that?"

I opened my eyes and lifted my head. "Like bondage?"

"Not just that," he said quickly. "I mean, just trying other stuff."

I bit my lower lip and considered his question. I looked down at the man, his face open and hopeful, and I knew I would do anything and everything with him. "I'll try it all with you."

He grinned like an excited little schoolboy. His expression changed a moment later as his eyes took on a meaningful glint. "You sure? I can think of a lot of kinky things to do to you."

"Kinky, huh?" I asked, my heart beating wildly at the thought of things to come. "Bring it on."

———

The next day we woke to the smell of cinnamon rolls. We dressed and wandered downstairs until we came upon the dining room. Jan, the B and B owner, was setting up food at the sideboard while guests sat at the dining table. My mouth instantly watered at the sight and smell of it all.

"Good morning," Jan called and motioned to the table. "Find yourself a seat."

The dining table was already full, with only one seat left open. With everyone still eating, I guessed one of us would have to stand to eat.

Henry walked over to the empty seat and promptly sat down. I was about to grumble about chivalry when he patted his thigh. "I have the best seat in the house for you," he said with a grin.

I sat on his leg, slightly concerned about propriety. Sitting at the table with us were two women in their twenties as well as an older couple, a man and a woman with gray hair and age-lined faces.

"You two on your honeymoon?" one of the girls asked, eyeing our wedding rings.

Henry wrapped an arm around my waist. "Yes. Is it that obvious?"

Jan set two coffee cups in front of us and filled them. I reached for the cream and sugar and fixed our coffees.

The girl, who had long dark hair and a beautifully exotic face, nodded. "Yes. You two have the look."

"What look?" I asked, taking a tentative sip.

"The *just fell in love* look," the other girl said.

The older lady shook her head. "I think they look more like they just had some wild sex," she said with a faint smile. "Of the sweet, sticky kind."

I nearly spit out my coffee. Henry let out a low, deep chuckle. "That obvious, huh?" he asked.

"Our room is right next to yours," the older woman said, causing my face to flame instantly. I didn't realize that Henry and I had been so loud.

The older gentleman touched her arm. "Lori, stop. Can't you see you're embarrassing the young lady?"

"I'm sorry if we were a little loud," I said.

The woman named Lori shook her head. "No, there is nothing to be embarrassed about. You're on your honeymoon. Be as loud as you want."

"So tell us your story," one of the girls said. "How did you two meet?"

"Well, her brother was my best friend, so we pretty much grew up together," Henry began, his palm warm and comforting on my back. "We were just roommates until Elsie here changed everything."

"It wasn't my fault," I said in indignation. "At least, not entirely."

So we told our story, beginning with the night at Tapwerks when we'd danced and the flames of lust had devoured us both. Breakfast was long over by the time we'd finished. The younger girls had excused themselves and gone on their way to meet with friends, but the older couple, Lori and Stan, stayed until the very end of the story.

"You're lucky, young man," Lori said, wagging a bony finger at Henry. "If I were her, I would have moved in with Seth and told you to take a hike."

I felt Henry's muscles turn to stone beneath me at the woman's words, but he said nothing. He just sat there silently while Lori gave him a tongue-lashing, telling him things that he'd no doubt thought of already.

Finally, I couldn't take it anymore. I mean, this was my husband we were talking about. "Trust me, Lori, he *knows*, and has been trying to make up for it ever since," I said, squeezing Henry's leg under the table.

Her face softened. "I'm glad to hear it."

"On paper Seth seems like the logical choice, but I didn't love him," I said, leaning into Henry's chest. "I love this guy here, the one who makes mistakes and admits to them. The one who's loved me since I was a little brat."

Stan gazed at us, silent and strong, reminding me of someone else I knew. "Indeed," he said. "If you had done the logical thing, you wouldn't be here right now on your honeymoon."

Lori smiled with some mischief in her eyes. "I just wanted to make sure your husband knew how lucky he is."

"I'm very much aware of it," Henry said, his breath so close to my ear it was almost a private moment. "I'm the luckiest guy in the world."

———————

After breakfast we walked a few blocks to the scooter rental store. We had enough money for two scooters but decided one was much more romantic. Henry was suffering from the misconception that I would be passenger, which didn't pan out for him when I insisted on taking the proverbial wheel.

It was a tiny yellow two-seater scooter and I'm sure he felt like a giant on it, but he didn't complain. He just climbed on behind me and grasped my waist.

"You ready?" I asked and twisted the throttle. The bike jumped forward, throwing us backward in our seat. Henry's feet immediately found the ground and he steadied us as I pressed on the brakes.

"Please don't kill us," he said, laughing.

I turned around and flashed him a smile. "Chicken?"

"With you at the wheel? Yes."

I tested the sensitivity of the throttle and, after a few test runs in the parking lot, we were finally off.

I took us around Key West in a nonsensical fashion, driving by Ernest Hemingway's home, then taking in the open-air aquarium. It was wonderful, being in control of where and when we were going. Whether it was imagined or not, I felt a surge of power, as if I was finally in charge of my destiny. Henry had given up control of our relationship and was allowing me to take the lead. It was exhilarating and scary, but most of all it was liberating.

It was around four thirty by the time we found ourselves at the southernmost point of the island, at the famous red, black, and yellow concrete buoy. We got off the scooter to take pictures like the rest of the tourists. I was exhilarated that Henry and I were here together, at the southernmost point of the continental United States during the northernmost point in our lives.

After a dinner of delicious Cuban food we took a walk on the beach and watched the sun set. As the sun went from orange to purple, Henry pulled me to a stop by the water's edge and gathered me into his side. "There is nothing more beautiful than the way the ocean refuses to stop kissing the shoreline no matter how many times it's sent away," he murmured.

His words sent tingles down my spine. "That's beautiful."

He squeezed my shoulder. "It's a quote from Sarah Kay, a spoken-word poet. I just thought it fit the moment." He turned and faced me, his face rendered in shadows by the waning light. "You're the shoreline and I'm the ocean, and I will never stop coming back to you." He led me deeper into the water, the waves now lapping nearly up to my knees.

He faced me, cupping my cheeks in his hands. "Every time I look at you, I can't help but want to tell you how much I love you," he said, then grinned. "Corny, isn't it?"

I dug my toes into the sand to keep from swaying. His words, coupled with the tender look on his face, made my heart clench in my chest with a feeling so powerful it rendered me speechless. I simply nodded and tried my best not to cry.

He looked away to the horizon where the sea was kissing the last remnants of the sun and took a deep, cleansing breath. "Life is good."

I was about to issue a heartfelt agreement when I felt a sting on my leg that began at one point and quickly spread around my calf. "What the hell?" I asked, jumping backward. "Ow."

Henry scooped me up into his arms and carried me back onto the dry sand where he set me down and crouched by my leg. "Jellyfish," he said with deeply furrowed eyebrows. He picked me up again and started toward the water.

"What are you doing?" I screeched.

"We need to wash the venom off," he said, looking at the water closely for any signs of jellyfish before dropping me in, ankle-deep. He reached for his wallet and pulled out a credit card, then began to scrape at the tentacles that were still on my leg.

I winced, hissing between my teeth to keep from crying out loud. I didn't know what hurt more: the stinging tentacles or the plastic grating along my tender skin. Either way, that shit hurt.

"Sorry," he said, scraping gently but insistently. "We gotta get all of it off." When he was satisfied, he scooped up some seawater and poured it over my leg where several angry lines were already puffing out. He repeated the process a few times and asked, "Does that feel a little better?"

"Surprisingly, yes," I said. I thought the salt in the water was going to make it sting worse, but it had the opposite effect.

"Let's go to the drugstore." Henry tried to pick me back up but I wriggled out of his grasp.

"I can walk," I said, wincing with each step.

He rolled his eyes, bent down, and threw me over his shoulder. "Just because you can doesn't mean you should," he said, walking back toward the street.

"I'm fine," I protested, noting a few people glancing our way. "I'm not completely useless."

He set me down by the scooter. "Listen," he said, rubbing my arms. "I promised in front of God and everyone that I would take care of you, so just let me, okay?"

"Okay, fine," I said, then reached into my pocket and handed him the key. "Here. You drive."

We stopped at the drugstore, where Henry asked the pharmacist for jellyfish sting treatments, then proceeded to buy everything that was suggested.

My leg was stinging and itching something fierce by the time we got back to our room, but we were armed with a bunch of stuff that included a bottle of vinegar, some hydrocortisone cream, and even a can of shaving cream should the vinegar not work. Henry emptied the plastic bag on the bed and scrutinized the loot with his hands on his hips. "Which should we try first?"

"Vinegar," I said and got up to get a washcloth.

Henry grabbed me by the waist and set me back down on the bed. "Let me," he said and went to the bathroom with the bottle of vinegar. He came back a few moments later with a damp, smelly washcloth in his hands and a towel over his shoulder. He laid the towel underneath my leg and placed the washcloth over the puffy red welts on my leg. "Okay, so thirty minutes of this," he said, sitting down beside me. "How does it feel?"

"It's nice and cool," I said, leaning back on my elbows. "It still stings pretty bad."

"You want an Advil?"

I shook my head. "The pain's still bearable," I said. "It just sucks that it ruined our moment. It's not everyday you recite poetry to me."

Henry grinned. "It'll happen again. Maybe."

"Now?" I asked with a hopeful look.

He stared at me for a long time. Finally, he said, "Nothing. I got nothing."

"Why Henry, is this your first case of performance anxiety?" I teased.

A wicked grin split his face. "I don't get performance anxiety," he said and crouched over me. He took my face in his hands and kissed me insistently. "It's just that you smell like a jar of pickled onions."

"Aw, you know just the right words to make a girl's panties melt." My hands stole under his shirt and played along the taut muscles of his stomach.

"How does your leg feel?" he asked in that raspy, turned-on voice.

"Still hurts. I think you need to kiss it better."

"Oh, I'll kiss it better. I'll kiss it all better," he said, running his palms under my skirt, up and down my thighs. His lips captured my mouth again, but as turned on as I was, the stinging on my leg wrenched me out of the moment. Henry must have sensed that I wasn't in the mood because he pulled away and peeked at my leg under the washcloth. He patted the cloth back into place and fell back onto the bed beside me.

"Hey, Henry," I said, holding his blue gaze captive. I licked at my lips, my mouth suddenly dry at the thought of bringing up a subject that I'd wondered about for months.

"Hey, Elsie," he echoed with a tug on the side of his mouth.

"Remember when you said at the museum that our memories gave you a sense of identity?" I asked.

He twisted to the side and propped his head on his hand. "Yeah?"

"But in the tapes, you said that you'd lost sight of who you were because I consumed you?" I said. "What did you mean?"

"It's both," he said with all sincerity. "They're two sides of the same coin. That thing that confused me, that made me feel lost, turned out to be my salvation in my darkest hour. Everything changes. That changed."

I swallowed. "What if it changes again and you leave me?"

"That will never happen. You're my wife now."

I turned away. "That's sweet," I said with a voice as sour as the liquid on my leg. "Staying with me because some piece of paper said so."

He held up my left hand and fingered the rings there. "Please stop trying to pick a fight," he said, kissing my knuckles. "I'm not staying because a piece of paper or some priest said so. You know that."

"You'll change again, Henry. We both will."

"Els, leaving you was the hardest thing I've ever done, but it helped me come to terms with myself."

"What if *I* need to leave and find myself?"

"Then I'd let you."

I recoiled. "You'd let me go?"

"If that's what you needed."

"And if I don't come back?"

"Then I'll come and get you," he said simply, lacing a hand around the back of my head. "You're stuck with me forever, remember?"

"We're back to staying together because we're legally bound."

"I see our marriage as a give-and-take, a pliable, moldable thing that will transform over time. A house, children, grandchildren; all of that will inevitably change us. But the thing that you can count on is that I will be there for you, because I made a vow." He kissed my forehead. "And I wholeheartedly intend to keep it."

His blue eyes bore into mine, wordlessly asking me to believe. "I'm never leaving you again, Elsie," he said. "And if need be, I will reassure you every single day of our lives. If that's what it takes to convince you."

I nodded, taking a deep breath. "I'm sorry," I said, shaking off the nerves that seemed to sneak up on me at random times. "This is not appropriate honeymoon conversation."

He swallowed, his Adam's apple bobbing up. "I hope one day you'll finally, completely forgive me."

I didn't say anything. I just looked into his face and hoped the same thing for myself. For as happy as we were right now, our old issues were still lingering under the shiny surface of our new life together, and sooner or later the sheen was going to wear off and the issues would show up once again.

Henry got up then and went to the bathroom to rinse off the washcloth. "Another thirty minutes of vinegar?" he called.

I looked at the red welts and weighed the pain against the smell. "No. I think it's ready for the hydrocortisone."

He came back out with a non-smelly washcloth and wiped my leg before applying a healthy dose of the cream. "Do you feel better?" he asked, moving all of our drugstore purchases off the bed and onto the bedside table.

"It's getting there," I said with a meaningful look. "Thank you for taking care of me."

He resumed his place on the bed beside me. "Anything for you."

That last night of our honeymoon was the only time we didn't make love. We were happy enough to simply snuggle, bare skin touching, and talk. Henry tended to my leg a few more times before he finally gave me some peace about the damned sting. It was only later, when his breathing against my hair had deepened, that I finally understood his motives.

My forgiveness wasn't the only thing Henry was waiting for, because the man still hadn't completely forgiven himself.

———

Our honeymoon came to an end the next day. We woke up early to return the scooter, Henry riding it to the dealership while I followed in the rental car.

Then began our three-hour drive back to Miami to board the plane that would take us back to reality. Back to the fixer-upper we had just put a down payment on, back to my job at Shake Design, and back to the police academy where Henry would take the twenty-seven-week course to become a cop.

The sun was only just beginning to rise when we traversed the bridge over the body of water between Stock Island and Boca Chica Key. I gazed out over the horizon, at the brilliant yellows and oranges staining the sky, finding it an appropriate symbol for the dawn of our new life.

Henry reached over and grasped my hand. "What are you thinking?"

"I was just thinking about our new chapter together, wondering what's in store for us."

"It will be perfect," he said with a confident nod of the head. "We'll be that boring old couple with the drama-free life."

I smiled up at him, hoping he was right. "I'll learn to knit and you can smoke a pipe while reading the newspaper every evening."

He caught my teasing tone and tickled my sides. "Exactly. It'll be smooth sailing from here on out."

We really should have known better than to tempt the fates.

Turn the page for a preview of June Gray's
next Disarm novel

ARREST

Coming soon from Berkley Books

PROLOGUE

I ran my hands through soft waves of dark hair, the ends of which curled around my fingers. I looked up and into the blue eyes of the shirtless man staring at me through the wall mirror. "Are you sure it needs to be buzzed completely off?" I asked, disappointed that I'd once again have to cut off the very thing that had brought us together.

"Yes. Academy standards."

Call me sentimental but I loved Henry's hair, which was a deep brown and had grown long over the past year. For the past several years I'd seen him with it cropped short, and it was only after he separated from the military that I was able to watch it grow again. Inch by inch, it felt as if the old Henry came back with each wavy strand, not only in appearance but also in attitude. The spark of mischief came back into his eyes, his smiles seemed wider, his laughter deeper.

I loved this unruly dark mess because it represented him as a teenage boy. It was a constant reminder that we had loved each other for nearly forever.

And now I had to cut it off. Again.

"Els?" Henry said, craning his head around to look up at me. "It's just hair."

"It's *not* just hair," I said, running my fingers through his dark locks again. "Once you start the police academy, then that's it. You'll never be able to wear it long again."

"I can when I retire."

"By then you'll be old and wrinkly and you won't look sexy with it anymore," I said, only half teasing.

He spun around in the computer chair and grabbed me around the waist. "You think I'm sexy?" he asked with a cocky grin.

"Always." I held his face in my hands, finding it hard to imagine his olive skin lined with age. It occurred to me then that I had the rest of my life to find out what he'd look like, and the thought filled me with joy.

"Okay, old man," I said, spinning him back around and reaching for the clippers. "Let's get this show on the road."

I took the first swipe in the center of his head, going all the way to the back. I grinned at him through the mirror, pausing long enough to chuckle at his odd appearance, and then went back to the task with more care.

As his dark hair fell quietly away, I thought of Henry's words in his therapy tapes, when he'd talked about the first time I cut his hair back in high school.

That was when I knew I was a goner. This girl in front of me was going to be my happily ever after.

I bet when he made that realization, he never would have thought he would somehow find himself in nearly the exact same place many years later, with our happily ever after no longer a whispered wish but a reality.

"You're so beautiful," Henry said in a soft, raspy voice, drawing me away from my thoughts.

I looked up and studied my reflection in the mirror, looking at my curly brown hair, hazel eyes, light skin that Henry had once likened to milk. I'd always considered myself somewhat average in the looks department, but nobody else made me feel gorgeous with just one look. Nobody but Henry.

I met his eyes through the mirror, and for one brief moment, I saw that kid again, the one who wore braces, who stole trinkets from people's houses, who went home night after night to an empty house. Who could have guessed that kid would grow up to be this noble, honest, caring man?

"I think you're good to go." I rubbed his bristly head, brushing hair off his bare shoulders.

Quick as lightning, his hand shot out and captured one of mine. He brought my palm to his lips, pressing a soft kiss against my skin. Then he stood up and turned to face me, standing so close, my breath was ruffling the hair on his chest. "This is what I should have done back then," he said and kissed me like we were just two kids in love, without a clue what the future held. "This time last year, I was in Korea, thinking I'd lost you for good. And now I'm here, with you, building a life together," he said. "I could ask for nothing more."

"I'd say we got pretty lucky."

He shook his head with a tender smile. "Luck has nothing to do with it," he said. "We're just two willful people who moved mountains to be together."

1

Several months later . . .

"Honey, I'm home." I unloaded my purse and laptop bag on the floor as soon as I shut the front door. When I heard nothing, I kicked off my shoes and carried them through the living room and to the kitchen. Still no sign of Henry. "Hello?"

"I'm up here."

I eyed the cold pasta salad on the counter wistfully, my stomach reminding me that it was past eight o'clock and I hadn't eaten dinner yet. I grabbed a fork and took a few mouthfuls, chewing quickly before heading upstairs.

I found Henry in our master bathroom, folding a box and stuffing it into the small trash can. "Hey," he said planting a kiss on my lips. He pulled away, licking his lips. "You taste like Italian dressing."

I looked around the bathroom, trying to figure out what he had changed now. Since closing on the house in August, we had been slowly trying to update the outdated interior. But with Henry's long days at the police academy and my hectic hours at work, we hadn't been able to do much at all. We were nearing Thanksgiving and all we'd accomplished was replacing the dingy carpet, painting the trim white, and changing the color of the walls.

Too tired to keep playing sleuth, I finally asked, "Okay, what did you do?"

"Here, let me show you." He pulled his T-shirt over his head then reached out and started to undo the pearl buttons on my teal shirt.

God, even with a nearly bald head, Henry's stark beauty never failed to strike me. Even at the end of a long day, when I was so tired I could barely stand, the very nearness of him sent ripples of arousal across my skin. "How do you do that?"

"Do what?" he asked, reaching behind me and undoing my bra.

"Wake up at six in the morning and still manage to be so perfect by the end of the day?"

He cupped my breasts in his large hands, flicking at each nipple. "I skipped the gym and took a nap."

Well, that answered that. I bet I'd look gorgeous too if I'd had some beauty sleep.

"Then I went to Home Depot and got something for you." His eyes glittered as he pulled the gray shower curtain aside and motioned to the new chrome fixture with two showerheads, one of which was on a handle. "You've been complaining about the old one for the longest time."

I stepped into the tub and turned on the water, nearly squealing with delight when the water came shooting out strong and straight. Henry stepped in behind me and reached for the handheld fixture. He twisted the control valve and then held the pulsating stream of water against my shoulders. "Oh, that feels good," I said, bowing my head and closing my eyes. He kneaded my other shoulder and I about melted.

"So how was your day?" he asked, continuing the water massage.

"Not great," I said. "My computer froze, so I restarted and then I got the spinning ball of doom. I had to work on the old iMac for the rest of the day, which is an exercise in frustration."

"I hope you didn't lose any work."

"No. Thankfully everything's saved on the servers. It was just a little stressful since we're still working on that Go Big campaign." Go Big Sports was Shake Design's largest client to date, so a lot of resources and manpower were being utilized to make sure the company was happy. We were in the middle of a complete brand overhaul as well as a new web store design. The entire project was already a daunting and exhausting task, but as head of the team, I was under extra pressure to perform. The death of a computer was not a huge deal in the grand scheme of things, but it was added strain on an already-stressful day.

Henry pressed a soft kiss on my neck, pulling me away from thoughts of work. "Hey, come back. No more thinking about work for the rest of the night," he murmured.

"Easier said than done," I said and was about to launch into the next day's long to-do list when water was suddenly pelting me on my stomach, due south.

"Open up," he said, nudging my legs apart with his foot. He brought a palm to my back and bent me over, exposing my backside while I planted my hands on the wall. "I'm going to make you forget about everything for the next half hour."

"Half hour? We'll run out of hot water long before—oh!"

He had changed the spray to a stronger, more concentrated stream and was aiming it directly onto my clit.

"I love this showerhead," I said between moans.

"Me too." The water disappeared and was replaced by the different sensation of his tongue licking between my folds.

I peeked between my legs and saw him palming his erection as he lapped at me, sending an energizing jolt of desire through me. "I want you."

He stood up and loomed over me. "You want me where?" he asked, pumping his length along the crevice of my ass.

I reached around and wrapped my fingers around him, guiding him to my entrance. "I want to feel you in here, filling me up."

"Do you want it slow or rough?"

I sat back, allowing the head of his cock to penetrate my cleft. "Rough. Hard."

He gripped me around the chest and with one swift thrust was inside me, stretching me, filling me. "Like this?" he rasped against my ear, sliding out and driving home again, causing me to lurch forward with its force.

"Fuck, yes."

He obliged, kissing along my neck and nipping my skin with his teeth as he continued the assault. He kept murmuring sweet and nasty things as he pummeled me, the noisy slapping of skin intermingling with the sound of running water.

I closed my eyes and surrendered, content to give Henry full control of my pleasure. The man did not steer me wrong; he knew all the right ways to touch me so that I was racing toward that orgasm, my muscles coiling, grasping for tighter hold. When he held the strong stream of water against my clit once again, I broke apart. "Hell yes," I hissed as my inner walls convulsed around his shaft.

"Here," he ordered, pressing the showerhead into my hand. With both hands free, he gripped my hips and drove into me faster.

I flicked the water setting to a softer stream and pointed it between my legs and directly onto his balls. He made a pained noise, but when I pulled it away, he growled, "Keep it there. Keep it there. Don't stop. Fuuuuck..." His hips bucked wildly as he climaxed, thrusting into me one last time.

I could feel his heartbeat thudding on my back as he gasped against my ear. It took him several long seconds but when he recovered, he pulled out and reached for the shampoo bottle.

My scalp tingled as his fingers massaged the shampoo through my hair, turning all the bones in my body to jelly. I leaned my head into his firm but gentle touch and sighed with pleasure.

Then he soaped up the loofah and washed my entire body, spending a long time washing between my legs. I noticed his mind was no longer on cleansing when his fingers probed me, sliding inside and finding that sensitive nub.

"I can't... I have no energy to come again."

"I'm just making sure you're completely clean," he said, his fingers rubbing and kneading. He brought his mouth down to mine and kissed me, his tongue bringing me back to life.

I squeezed at his fingers, feeling the warmth spread throughout me, and unbelievably, I started to come again. I leaned against the tile wall when my legs buckled as Henry's hand worked its magic.

When the last of my orgasm had subsided, he turned off the water and reached for a towel and handed it to me.

"I don't think I have any energy left for work," I said, wondering how I was even going to manage drying my hair, let alone do anything else.

"That's the point. You go to work early, get home late, and then do more work until nearly midnight." He swept me off my feet and carried me to the bed. "Tonight, you deserve some rest."

"I'm still wet," I laughed, trying to sit up.

He held me down by the shoulders, a laugh playing in his eyes. "Then we shall have to dry you off, won't we?" he said and swept his tongue along the length of my stomach, lapping at the water droplets.

I grabbed the back of his head, too worn out to do anything but moan. "You're going to give me death by orgasm."

He looked up and grinned. "Can't think of a better way to go."

———————

"Sherman." The deep voice of my boss, Conor McDermott, echoed over the block of cubicles as he stood outside his office with his hands on his waist. "My office, now."

Kari, a senior designer on my team, peered over the wall. "What did you do?"

"I have no clue." I saved my file, straightened my blouse, and prepared myself for what was to come.

Conor was leaning against his desk when I entered his glass-walled office. "Sit down, please."

I perched on the curvy chair made out of one thin piece of wood, uncomfortably close to where Conor stood. The Irishman was in his mid-thirties, with dark auburn hair and an intense icy blue stare that was currently fixed on my face.

"My last name is Logan now," I said, trying to diffuse the tension. It was no secret that Conor was a ladies man, with a natural charisma that made him seem flirty without trying. Being the owner of Shake Design, he wore expensive suits, but he also rarely shaved, so that he was a mixture of crispness and scruff, professionalism and impudence. It was no wonder women fell at his feet.

"I'm sorry, I forget," he said with a slight Irish brogue. He crossed one foot over the other and regarded me for another few uncomfortable seconds.

I tried to meet his gaze but felt a little strange doing so, as if simply finding another man attractive was an act of adultery.

"Are you happy here?" he asked, a question that took several seconds to sink in.

"Yes, very." I raised an eyebrow. "Why?"

"I've been keeping an eye you. You've been working really long hours, showing a lot of dedication to Go Big. I just wanted to make sure that you're happy." He gave me a roguish grin. "Basically, I want to make sure no other companies try to steal you away."

I returned his smile. "I'm happy to hear that."

"So what can I do to make your life easier?"

"Make the Go Big execs agree on everything from here on out?"

He chuckled. "I suspect nothing short of a miracle can do that."

"Can I have one more designer on the team then?" I asked.

He let out a long breath through his nose. "I was afraid you'd say that. I can't do that, however, as all of our designers are busy with other projects, but I will look into hiring a freelancer."

I shrugged. "How about an icee machine for the break room then?" I joked.

"That I can probably arrange," he said with a deep laugh.

"How about giving us all the entire Thanksgiving week off?"

"Now you're just pushing your luck."

I shrugged. "Worth a try."

Still smiling, he stood up and motioned to the door. "Well, if there's anything else you need—within reason—then my door is always open."

"Thank you, I will keep that in mind," I said, walking past him and catching a whiff of his expensive cologne.

"Elsie," he said with a smile, one that held no hidden intent, only genuine joy. "I'm glad you're on my team."

"Me too," I said quickly and walked out. When I got back to my desk, my phone immediately rang.

"Psst," Kari said into the other line. I stood up and shook my head as she held the phone against her ear and a hand over her mouth. "What did sex-on-a-stick want?"

I snickered. "Nothing. Just making sure I was content here."

"So he didn't bend you over his desk and spank you for not getting those mock-ups done to perfection?"

I sat back down, stifling a surprised laugh. Kari and I had spent many hours together in the past several months and had become really good friends. One thing I really loved about her was her unabashed love for erotic romance novels, and the one about a troubled billionaire, in particular. "You are a sexual harassment lawsuit waiting to happen," I whispered. "Conor is *not* Christian Grey."

"But he could be," Kari giggled. "You never know what he's like behind office doors."

"He's got glass walls."

"So he's an exhibitionist too."

"You're crazy."

"You love it."

"You're projecting your fantasies onto a mere mortal."

"Give me one night with him and I'll turn him into a god."

"You're nuts." I wished her luck with her plans of seduction and hung up, still laughing to myself even after I went back to work.

———

That night, Henry was already starting dinner when I walked in the house.

I kicked off my shoes and washed my hands at the sink before standing on my toes to give him a kiss. I pulled away, noticing the redness around his eyes. "What happened?" I asked as I started to chop the bell peppers by the chopping board.

"We were pepper-sprayed at school today," he said, pouring oil into the wok. "We stood there one by one and got sprayed in the face. It was . . . not fun."

I looked down at the ingredients on the counter. "So you didn't get enough peppers? You wanted to eat it for dinner too?"

He shrugged. "Next week we get tasered."

"Where? In the balls?"

He coughed. "Let's hope not. Ugh, that sounds like the worst pain known to man."

"Then we can have rocky mountain oysters that night," I teased, jabbing him in the side.

"You're sick," he said, pulling me in for a noogie and making a mess of my hair.

"Stay away from the hair," I said and held up a sliver of pepper. "I'll spray you again if you're not careful."

He held his hands up in defeat. "I surrender."

The good mood continued on into dinner as we talked about our days while eating chicken stir fry. I knew it wouldn't always be like this, that once he became a LEO—law enforcement officer— our times together would be unpredictable, at best. So I held onto the moment, completely immersing myself in the simple joy of being with the love of my life, and tried to avoid thinking about the future.

———————

Henry and I didn't go back to California for Thanksgiving. Instead, we spent a fair amount of the day in bed, snuggling while watching the Macy's Thanksgiving parade on television. There was something romantic about spending our first holidays as newlyweds alone together, starting our own traditions in our new home.

"How long until we eat?" Henry asked with his arm around me.

I stretched my limbs, straightening my toes and fingers. "The turkey's not even done thawing yet. And we haven't cooked anything else."

"But. I'm. So. Hungry," he said, grabbing his stomach for effect.

I laughed at his theatrics and pinched at his side, unable to find an ounce of fat anywhere. "Poor baby, starving on Thanksgiving."

"It wouldn't be the first time," he said. "Remember that Thanksgiving when we went skiing and Jason forgot to make restaurant reservations?"

I nodded, feeling a sudden rush of emotion at the mention of my brother and that time long ago before death and heartache had touched our lives. Jason, Henry, and I had all gone to Vail, Colorado, to spend the holiday weekend skiing. Without dinner reservations, we had ended up going to the grocery store and buying bread and sliced turkey, eating the sandwiches in our hotel room instead.

"How could I forget? Jason poured jarred gravy on his sandwich, thinking it would taste good. It was nasty but he ended up eating that sandwich anyway," I said, laughing as the memory of my brother filled me with warmth.

"I tried it. It wasn't so bad," Henry said. "Though it would have been better if we'd had a microwave to warm it up in."

"Yeah, no. It was gross."

"That was a fun vacation," he said, his voice taking on a wistful tone.

"Yeah it was." I sighed. "I miss him."

He cleared his throat and turned his attention back to the television, grunting out a soft, "Yeah." But despite his nonchalant attitude, I knew Henry still missed his best friend. He and my older brother Jason had grown up together; they had gone through ROTC, college, and even the Air Force together. Jason was a part of Henry as much as he was a part of me, and even now, nearly six years after Jason's death, his memory was like a phantom limb, a daily reminder of the person we loved and lost.

Sharing the death of a brother—whether by blood or by choice—bound Henry and me together, made certain that we were always linked by that common loss.

Determined not to keep dwelling on the past, I slid out of bed and pulled on some yoga pants and a T-shirt and twisted my hair up into a bun. "Come on, let's get cooking."

He was pulling on a pair of gray Air Force sweat pants when the phone rang. He read the name on the caller ID before answering. "Hello?"

I raised my eyebrows at him, trying to decipher by Henry's voice if the caller was my mom, or maybe Julie, the woman my brother had intended to marry.

"Bergen!" Henry called, his voice taking on that brash tone he used with his male friends. "What the hell are you up to, man?"

Satisfied the call wasn't for me, I went downstairs to start preparing the food. Several minutes later, Henry followed. "That was my old buddy, Bergen. We were stationed together in Korea," he said, standing by the counter and snapping the green beans with his fingers.

I slipped my hand inside the turkey, reaching around for the elusive giblet packet. "Where the hell is it?" I mumbled, grimacing at the cold, clammy things I was touching.

"Is it wrong that I find your turkey fisting incredibly hot?"

"You should see what I can do with a duck," I grumbled, my fingers making contact with something plastic.

"Please tell me it rhymes with cluck."

I came up with the plastic package and threw it into the sink. "What's Bergen up to today?" I asked, placing the small turkey inside the pan and rubbing two entire packets of French onion soup mix all over it, a trick I'd learned from my mom.

"He's driving through Denver on the way to Colorado Springs. Do we have enough food for another person?"

"Oh definitely," I said, helping him with the green beans once the turkey was in the oven. "You want to invite him over for dinner?"

He grinned sheepishly. "Already did," he said and crunched on a green bean.

––––––––––

A few hours later, while I was still getting ready, the doorbell rang. I could hear Henry greeting his friend downstairs, their deep, masculine voices echoing throughout the house.

I hurriedly dressed then applied my makeup. I looked at myself in the mirror, trying to decide what to do with my hair, but laziness won out, so I just pinned it up and left a few tendrils down. "Good enough," I said and went to meet our guest.

Bergen, a tall man with beautiful chocolate skin, a shaved head, and a bright smile stood up when I entered the room. "You must be the lovely Mrs. Logan," he said, holding out a hand. "Henry has been talking about you for years."

I smiled and returned the handshake. "And you must be the mysterious Mr. Bergen."

"Major Jackson Bergen, ma'am." He waited until I sat down before following suit.

"I'm glad you could make it, but if you call me ma'am again, you're not getting any pie."

"Yes, sir," he said with a tiny salute, the skin around his eyes crinkling as he smiled.

"At ease." I grabbed Henry's beer from the coffee table and took a sip.

"Hey now," Henry said, and touched his cold fingers to my neck in retaliation.

"Whipped," Bergen coughed into his hand.

Henry laughed, leaning back into the couch and resting his arm across my shoulder. "I guess I am."

Bergen smiled. "That's good to hear, man."

_____

We ate our Thanksgiving meal at around three p.m., passing dishes around the table wordlessly as we heaped food on our plates. Years of cooking with my mom had conditioned me to prepare more food than was necessary, so we thankfully had enough to share with a large man with an equally large appetite.

"So, Bergen," I said after we'd been eating for several minutes. "What was Henry like at Osan?"

The two men exchanged a quick look that sent my spidey senses tingling. "He was a mess when he first got there," Bergen said nonchalantly. "He was one depressing peckerhead, always talking about the meaning of life and finding yourself."

"Ah, I wasn't so bad," Henry said, washing his food down with beer. "So anyway, what are you doing in Colorado Springs?"

Bergen took the hint and moved on, talking about his new job at NORAD. I sat back and listened, chewing thoughtfully and watching Henry's face as they exchanged stories. Something about the way he talked—carefully, with every word thought out—gave me the feeling that he was being extra cautious about what was being said.

There was something the man wasn't telling me and I, being who I am, intended on finding out.

_____

After dinner, Bergen and Henry cleaned up while I was banished to the living room for some R and R. I turned on the television and burrowed under a blanket on the couch, in a pleasant state of drowsiness.

My eyes were starting to get heavy when I remembered something. With great effort, I pushed up off the couch to remind Henry to put the pie in the oven but the sound of their hushed conversation froze me from around the corner.

"She doesn't know about what happened at Osan," Henry said in low voice, almost inaudible under the sound of running water.

"You never told her?"

"No. It's not exactly something you want to tell your wife, you know?"

I walked around the corner, deciding that getting the answer from the horse's mouth was better than eavesdropping. "What is this big secret?" I stood in front of the two men, who were behind the sink with identical looks of *busted* written all over their faces.

Bergen took a deep breath and said, "I need to use the restroom," and left the room, not bothering to slow down and ask where the restroom was.

I crossed my arms across my chest, staring down my husband even as he towered over me.

"It's not a big deal." He scratched his forehead.

"Then why are you keeping it from me?"

His jaw tightened and eyes turned wary, reminding me of that same stranger who came back from a six-month deployment to Afghanistan. "I'm not keeping it from you to hurt you, okay?" he said, his voice taking on a frustrated edge. "It has nothing to do with you."

"Really, Henry?" I asked. I glanced down the hall to make sure our guest was still out of earshot. "This is how it's going to be again?"

He ran a palm across his scalp, a nervous habit that persisted even without his long hair. "There are some things that I can't tell you, Els."

"Is it classified?"

He blinked a few times then said, "No."

"Then why can't you tell me?"

"Because it's personal."

"I'm your wife. I think I can handle personal."

"There are some things that need to be kept secret between us."

"Why? What's the purpose of that?" I asked. "I tell you everything."

"Am I supposed to believe that you've told me every little thing about you, every shameful detail of your past?"

"Yes, for the most part." I shook my head. "Anyway, this isn't about me. This is about you keeping secrets again."

He dodged around the counter and came toward me with an exasperated look. "Els, can we please just drop it for now and enjoy the rest of the day?" he asked, rubbing my arms.

"Why can't you just tell me? Whatever it is, it can't be worse than what my imagination can cook up."

His eyebrows drew together as his eyes roamed over my face. "Yes, it can," he said and left it at that.

Bergen stayed until late into the night. He and Henry pounded beer after beer while they caught up, and by the time midnight rolled around, it was clear he wasn't going to be driving anywhere. I offered Bergen the guest bed and he accepted readily, if a little ungracefully, kicking off his shoes before stumbling face-first into the pillows.

Henry was usually a chatty and affectionate drunk, but he sensed my foreboding mood and didn't try anything in bed. I turned away from him, the ball of frustration growing in my belly. How many times had he kept secrets from me only to have it blow up in his face? You'd think he'd have learned his lesson by now.

I stared at the digital numbers on the clock, seething. When I could no longer keep it in, I sat up and shook his shoulder. "Wake up," I hissed.

He stirred and immediately took in his surroundings. "What? What is it?"

Trying to take advantage of his drunk state, I said, "Tell me what happened in Korea."

He rolled onto his back with a sigh and covered his eyes with one arm. "Elsie," he groaned. He was quiet for so long, I thought he'd fallen asleep again, but he finally gave a deep sigh and said, "I was cornered in an alley and assaulted by a group of men."

"What? Why?"

He shrugged. "Money. Maybe because I looked like a big, dumb American."

"Were you badly hurt?"

"Bad enough to be hospitalized," he said.

"Where? How?" I couldn't find words beyond those breathless questions. How had I not known that Henry had been so badly hurt? Wouldn't I have felt it in some way?

"I don't want to talk about it anymore, Elsie," he said. "Please. I told you what happened, don't make me relive the entire night again."

I couldn't sleep that night, imagining Henry being attacked and unable to defend himself. When my alarm rang at six, I decided that it was just as well, because my sleep would no doubt have been riddled with ugly, violent images anyway.